THE HOUR OF THE FOX

ALSO BY FRANCIS JARMAN

THE GARDENS OF THE WEST SERIES

The Eagle's Wing

THE LEMNOS SERIES

The Gate of Lemnos
The Call of Lemnos
The Curse of Lemnos

OTHER WORKS

A Star Fell
Culture and Identity
Encountering the Other
Girls Will Be Girls
Intercultural Communication in Action
Invictus: A Play
Lip Service
White Skin, Dark Skin, Power, Dream

THE HOUR OF THE FOX

THE GARDENS OF THE WEST, PART TWO

Francis Jarman

WILDSIDE PRESS

The author's website for the series, including maps,
competitions, and a full list of characters, can be found at:
www.thegardensofthewest.com

Published by Wildside Press LLC.
www.wildsidepress.com

I

MARA ON THE RUN, WITH A LARGE HORSE AND A SMALL BOY

✠ *The Great Provincial Road, and the forest.*

First they rode north, alongside but at a safe distance from the road. Mara knew this—it was the way they had come. But it was only taking them back to Fanum Fortunae. And why should they go back there, to that house of death, where Castor had been murdered and where she and Phrygillus had both been slaves?

Soon they reached the place where the main road joined the road that they hadn't taken, and they found themselves inside the fork. Mara steered the horse right, across the second road and then onto the open fields beyond. Now they were traveling not north- but eastwards. She remembered what Manasa had told her about these lands. If they continued they would soon reach the forest, and beyond that was the Great Plain.

Only when they reached the Plain would she feel free.

They couldn't ride fast in the dark. With their double weight, the horse was more likely to stumble on rough ground. She had carried little Phrygillus behind her, moaning and whimpering and clinging on tight, but she was worried that he might slip off and pull her with him. She stopped the horse and put the boy in front of her, where she could talk to him and comfort him better.

Going at a slower pace, the horse seemed to have no problem with the double load. Phrygillus was a different matter. She tried shifting him to different positions: sitting astride the horse, or held in front of her like a bundle, or clinging on desperately behind her. Phrygillus and horses were not meant for each other. He was like a great big baby who wouldn't shut up.

If this was what children were like, she thought, why did women ever have them? She was tempted to let him slip off the horse's back and stay there, the little beast, while she rode on.

She might even have done it—if she hadn't sworn a solemn oath to Castor that she would look after his "treasure". So, like it or not, the wretched little boy was going to have to be *alaphé* with her, or She with the Talons would come one moonless night to claim the oathbreaker's heart.

She looked forward to seeing her father, and her family and all her friends. She had so many stories to tell them. None of *them* had seen so much of the world of the Citizens, not all of which was bad. She laughed to herself: she would be "ironical" with them, and see what happened! None of the Horse People would appreciate irony. They spoke honestly, whether to friend or enemy, and they laughed directly without tricks or cunning meanings. How puzzled they would be!

Would any of them understand? The wise women would. Her father might too, after she had explained it to him, and her grandfather certainly would, because he was a man of great wisdom. But none of them would approve. The ways of the Citizens were peculiar, and what good did they ever lead to?

Her cousins would be unable to grasp it. They were simply too stupid. She had always known that, though.

And Hengilo, her admirer? No, he wouldn't understand it either. What was it that she had once liked about him? He was good-looking, that was true, and he was honorable. He would be loyal as a husband, and support her well. But could she be his woman, and live with him, obeying him without question and having his children? Could she be *only* that, and nothing more?

Now that she knew that there were other kinds of men, she realized that she would be endlessly bored with Hengilo. He was a puddle that would barely make her toes wet. There were other men, men with depths that would draw you in, deep, dark pools in which you could drown—or truly find yourself. Castor, with his knowledge, and kindness, and his irony of course! Or Victor, with his twinkling eyes: Victor who was so beautiful and charming, and yet so deadly.

No-one among the Horse People was like that. They were simple, and straightforward. You could read their thoughts. There were no hidden meanings. The only person who was a little different was Hengilo's older brother, Gisso, who was already a warrior. Sometimes she had caught him looking at her with his head tilted, as though he wanted to say something unusual but couldn't find the words. And when he did speak, what came out were only the traditional words that you would expect a young warrior, one who was respected in the counsels of her father, to say.

Gisso. What was it that he had said to her the last time they had spoken together?

And then it came to her, like the sudden crack of a twig under her feet, as abrupt as a thunderclap, or like the loud, sharp "snap!" as you broke a dry branch for kindling.

Gisso!

The horrible thoughts burst out one after the other. It was *Gisso* who had betrayed her. The voice had seemed familiar. She had tried to match it with her memories of the young men of her clan, and she had failed. She had barely considered the warriors, though. And why should she? Each of them had sworn a sacred oath to her father, an oath in the secret name of the God Who Cannot Be Named. Such oaths were guarded by… No no, Mara had already thought of Her once too often, better not to think of Her again, lest all that thinking might cause Her to wake in the darkness.

Anyway, no-one ever broke such an oath. You simply didn't.

But Gisso had done.

More thoughts came. Gisso had no children, but he had a wife, a good, hardworking woman. Mara knew her well. Why had he then betrayed his chieftain's daughter, the chieftain whom he had sworn to honor and to protect? He couldn't make her his woman by force—yes, such things were not unknown, even among the Horse People—because he already had a wife, and Mara was not some slave or captive.

Mara felt her skin going cold, and it was not from the coldness of the night.

That was the reason—it was *because* he could never make her his own. His intention had been a different one. He had wanted to hurt her, to take his pleasure from her body, in the ways that men did, and then to sell her on to the slavers for a few coins.

He hadn't done it for the money. Orcus the smelly man had said that the traitor didn't care about money, and that they hadn't given him much anyway. What he had really wanted was to… She shuddered. No, she couldn't bring herself to repeat the words for such a horror.

When she told her father, Gisso's life would be over! Every single man of the Speaking Bird clan, from the chieftain to the youngest boy who had barely learnt to ride, would be given a whip or a stick with which to strike him. He would be kept apart, and fed on scraps. After his wounds had healed, he would be dragged behind a horse—he was forbidden ever to ride one again—to the next assembly of the Council of the Horse People, where her grandfather Haimo, in the name of his son's clan, would ask for the oath-breaker's life.

When this was granted, as it surely would be, what was left of Gisso would be sent to Esbus in the cruelest possible way. Such was the tradition. Only the punishments laid down by the ancient laws of the Horse

People for horse-thieves were crueler.

Mara had never seen such things done, because no-one ever broke such an oath. It was unthinkable. And no-one had ever stolen horses from the Horse People either, except slaves, or strangers.

Gisso's shame would become a legend!

But it wouldn't happen. How could she prove it? Who would ever believe her? She could swear a sacred oath, yet so could he. And he had already shown (to her) that he was shameless, that he had no respect for oaths. It was her word against his, and he was a warrior.

What was she? She was an unmarried girl, whose name was never used. They would call her "Corvo's girl" or "Haimo's son's girl" until one day she became "Hengilo's woman". Or they would call her "the crazy one".

She was known by everyone throughout the clan and beyond to be wild and spoilt. Now she was seeking to destroy the life of a warrior whose voice she may or may not have heard, out on the Great Plain, distorted by the sighing of the wind, and planted in her thoughts by girlish daydreams…

Would even her father believe her?

It was bound to be like that, but what other choice did she have than to tell the truth?

Taken up by her thoughts, she must have neglected to hold on to Phrygillus, and now the "treasure" did indeed slide off the horse's back and land with a thud and a loud yelp on the ground.

He refused to get back up onto the horse.

"It's a devil horse! That's why it's called Demon! I hate it!" And then more plaintively: "My bottom hurts."

Mara thought: this is why the Horse People don't give their horses names! What nonsense that was! Calling a horse Demon didn't make it one. The horse was not to blame. There were no bad horses, only bad riders. (And, she thought ruefully, riders who forgot to pay attention to what they were doing.)

She slipped down and took Phrygillus by the hand.

"There is the forest. Let's walk to the trees and find somewhere to rest for the night. We can't stay out here in the open. It's not safe. *He* might be following us."

The mention of Victor made the boy stop whimpering. He looked at Mara.

"*He* killed Castor," he said in a small, choked voice. "Who is going to look after me now?"

"*I'm* going to look after you now"—she could hardly believe she was saying it—"but you must help me. We're almost there. Walk carefully. We won't go far. The trees will protect us tonight. I'll hold you tight, and tell you a story."

"He killed Castor…"

No, she thought, it wasn't Victor who had killed Castor, it was Lelia. And she had cut the throat of one of the soldiers too, and had boasted of it. Perhaps in his terror the boy hadn't heard her clearly? Let him think that it was Victor. That it had been Lelia, Lelia who had cuddled him, and petted him, and fed him sweets—*that* would be far more frightening, when the dark thoughts came between the little boy and his sleep.

But why had they done it? Why did Castor have to die? Why did they try to kill *her*? And what had Phrygillus done to harm them?

Once inside the forest, they couldn't go far in the dark without risking the horse on the uneven ground and in the tangled brush between the trees. She stumbled over a thick tree-root and almost lost hold of the horse. Phrygillus began to complain again, in a low whine. He didn't like the forest. He was cold. His bottom was still hurting. He was frightened.

Mara was exhausted. She needed to sleep. Food, water, all that would have to wait until the daylight came.

They were now deep enough into the forest to be safe. The Citizens hated the forest, Manasa had said, and they wouldn't go into it at night; or even in the daytime, except in large hunting parties. Was Victor a Citizen? She wasn't really so sure. But Victor had no proper horse, and he wouldn't want to ride a mule, or the dray-horse. He was much too proud for that! And even if he picked up their trail alongside the road, he wouldn't be able to track them in the darkness.

Mara found a little hollow formed by a circle of small trees. It was filled with fallen leaves and soft undergrowth, and it would offer them both shelter and a place to sleep. She tied the horse to a thick branch, then untied the riding-cloth and, with the last of her strength, rubbed the horse down with it.

"Sorry, horse, this is all I can do for you tonight. I know, I know, it's not what you're used to. I'll spoil you tomorrow. I promise."

She was so tired that she could barely stand. The ground looked inviting.

Phrygillus was already fast asleep. She slept too.

Their sleeping-place had been well chosen. Cuddled up together for the night, with leaves scooped over them, Mara and Phrygillus were not as cold as Mara had feared they would be. They had been very, very tired.

When they woke, Phrygillus started up almost at once about how hungry he was. Food, she realized, could be a problem. The horse had already located a clump of grasses close to where she had tethered it, and was grazing with great concentration. They would find water in the forest, too, for all of them. But what could she and Phrygillus *eat*? On the Plain, there were at least grasses that they could chew to hold hunger at bay, though Phrygillus, spoilt and cosseted as he had been for his whole short life, would doubtless protest. Here in the forest, though, she had no idea which fruits or berries you could eat, and which ones would screw you up in agony.

Her grandmother had always said, "The bright-colored ones are dangerous" and "If you cook it, almost anything is safe to eat". Mara wondered whether her grandmother had ever been in such a forest, and how many of the fruits and berries she would have recognized. Cooking was certainly a good idea—if they only had some way to start a fire. Mara had been taught how to make a fire with dried grass, sharp flints and a piece of iron rock or a knife. Where could she obtain the stones that they needed? Perhaps if they found a stream with gravel banks, or a rocky outcrop?

They should press on. Phrygillus insisted that he didn't want to ride the horse—the soft insides of his thighs were raw—so they would walk. That would be safer anyway. They shouldn't risk anything happening to the horse—the horse would be vital once they left the forest.

Food! Phrygillus demanded food. Why couldn't they kill some animals, and eat them? Such as a nice rabbit or two? They could cook them with herbs, in a tasty stew. The forest was full of green, herby stuff!

Mara hadn't seen any rabbits in the forest (there were plenty of them out on the Plain, she told him). She had seen some ugly, crow-like birds, and she had heard scampering sounds in the night that might have been rats or mice.

"We could dig for worms, if you like, and eat them raw?"

That shut him up for a while.

Even though they wouldn't be riding, she tied on the horse's riding-cloth carefully, so that it wouldn't slip off and get lost. They would need it later. While she was doing that she felt something hard inside the folded edge of the cloth. Something that she had missed when she was rubbing the horse down.

She ran her fingers over it. Was it a stick? Despite more protests from Phrygillus she made them wait while she untied the riding-cloth to examine it properly. It had a sort of pocket, secured with tiny hooks. She opened it, and took out…a knife.

Now that was a good surprise—the day had started well! They could use the knife for cutting up fruit (if they were successful in finding any, and decided to risk eating it) or for meat, if they could work out a way to kill something (and preferably cook it, too). Best of all, it might be useful for starting the fire.

It was a peculiar object, unlike any knife that Mara had ever seen before. It was curved and delicate, of very fine, light metal, and with curvy decoration on it, or maybe it wasn't decoration but writing in an unfamiliar script. *All* scripts were unfamiliar to Mara, except the basic letters of the Citizens' Tongue, which her father had taught her. The Horse People had little use for writing, other than the charms and curses that the wise women scratched out in magic shapes.

The knife was too small to be used as a serious weapon. If someone attacked them, and she brandished the knife, the attacker would merely laugh.

She searched the rest of the edge of the riding-cloth in the hope of finding another pocket, perhaps this time with gold coins, or striking-flints; there was nothing, however.

Leading the horse, they walked through the forest until, in the distance through the trees, they saw the lake. Mara didn't want to go too close, but following the edge of the lake would eventually bring them out of the forest and onto the Plain. That would be much cleverer than trying to follow the sun, which was often hard to see and hidden by thick gray clouds.

They crossed several small streams that fed into the lake, and saw plenty of stones of different shapes and sizes. Mara wasn't actually sure which ones might be useful and which ones not, so they gathered an assortment and packed the stones into an improvised sack that Mara constructed by folding together the corners of the riding-cloth.

Phrygillus was put in charge of the stones—it was time for him to take some responsibility—while Mara led the "demon".

They had yet to see anything that resembled fruit. While they were examining the hard, knobbly berries on a low bush, they heard a loud rustling in the undergrowth nearby.

"There!" Phrygillus whispered excitedly, but she had already spotted what was causing the noise. It was a family of large, flat-footed birds, a mother bird and half-a-dozen of her young. They were stupid birds that didn't look as though they would be able to run or fly very fast.

She held Phrygillus back from chasing them.

"Listen to me, and I'll tell you what we're going to do."

The boys of the Horse People, before they began learning how to use weapons, were trained in speed and agility. She would watch her cousins practicing in the evening what they had been taught during the day, and she would join in when they allowed her to—which they didn't always do, because she was usually better at the games and exercises than they were. If they said no, she would go off in a sulk and practice on her own.

One of the exercises was to throw a round stone at a target, with as much speed and accuracy as possible. They were told by their teacher, the oldest and wisest of the warriors, "You should learn to master a simple object like a stone before you have a sharp weapon placed in your hand."

The trick was to pick the right-shaped stone, and to give it a slight spin. That became especially important when you advanced from throwing the stones at a sitting target to throwing them at moving objects, in this case the scavenging birds and rodents that constantly lurked around the edges of the camp. (Only a fool would throw stones at the camp dogs, who were useful for guarding the camp at night and who would bite you if you provoked them, once they had seen that you weren't a big warrior with a sword.)

The game was good practice, because it was quite hard to hit a crow or a rat. These had long become used to being stoned by malevolent little boys, and they were adept at scampering or fluttering out of the way! Mara, however, discovered that she was better than most at braining them.

These birds looked encouragingly slow and lazy, and maybe they'd never had stones thrown at them by nasty children?

It was worth a try.

They would have to track the birds at a distance, she said, and it might take hours if (as she expected) their first attempts were unsuccessful and the birds scattered in panic. But the birds were a family, and so after scattering they would eventually find each other again, allowing another attempt to be made.

One of them, she said, must keep further back, holding the horse. Mara wasn't sure whether Phrygillus would be up to that, or whether the horse would be happy either, but he would have to do it because she was going to be the huntress.

She only needed to hit and stun one of the birds; she could then finish it off with the little knife. Afterwards they would get a fire going with the remaining stones, pluck and prepare the bird, and have a feast!

If that sounded too good to be true, it was because it was.

The first obstacle was that Mara, for all her years of practicing, and her confidence in her own skill, couldn't manage to hit anything. Well, nothing that they could eat.

She had picked out a promising stone and sent it spinning in the direction of the mother bird—why not go for the biggest target, with the most meat on it?—only to see the stone rebound with a dull "thunk!" off a nearby tree-trunk.

The birds scattered, of course, and it was some time before they reassembled and she could try her hand again.

Her second attempt was no more successful, and the same with her third.

In this manner they wasted half the daylight without obtaining anything they could eat.

Now Phrygillus demanded the right to try. "Girls are useless," he told her, "Everyone knows that. Let me have a go."

She didn't see the point, and told him to be quiet, but he kept on nagging her, and in the end she let him pick out a stone just to shut him up.

He hurled it with much small boy enthusiasm and no obvious sign of skill straight into the middle of the birds and, to Mara's amazement (and annoyance), felled one of the chicks. Beginner's luck?

"See? I told you! You should have let me go first. Now let's eat it."

The bird was already dead. Holding the pitiful little object in her hands, she realized that there was hardly any meat on it. Fruit would have been a better idea.

But Phrygillus wanted cooked meat, and cooked meat they were therefore going to have, even if there wouldn't be very much of it.

The next obstacle was that they couldn't start a fire. She had seen it done often enough, yet no matter how hard she tried, she couldn't get the stones and the knife to produce the necessary sparks. And when Phrygillus insisted on trying, with another sneer along the lines of "Girls are useless", this time he had no more luck than she did.

If she plucked the bird, and cut off the meat for him, would he eat it raw?

No, he certainly wouldn't! He wasn't a barbarian like her! And she had no appetite for raw meat either.

Now he started crying. Mara wanted to cry as well, but what good would that do them?

She told him to guard the horse, and said him that she would make another attempt to find some fruit. It was late summer—there must be some stupid fruit somewhere.

He needn't be frightened. The horse would protect him (it wasn't called Demon for nothing), she knew their position, and she wouldn't go far. She would be back long before it got dark.

And she was; and not empty-handed. She proudly showed him half-a-dozen tiny apples (though were they apples, or something else?), a spray of gleaming white berries that she didn't completely trust, and a handful of juicy black fruits that she knew were safe, because, after scratching her hands to reach them, she had already eaten every second one that she had picked. These were therefore only for him, and if he liked them they could go back the following day and pick some more.

That was their supper. Phrygillus ate everything; Mara only a couple of the apples, because the black berries were for him and she wasn't sure about the white ones. They drank water from the nearest stream, in which there were some wild onions growing. Mara warned him not to eat too many of them.

Afterwards, still hungry, they made themselves as warm as they could with heaps of leaves and curled up for their second night in the forest. Mara was now grateful that they had been given warm clothes for the journey from Fanum Fortunae. Phrygillus was terrified of the dark, and so she told him more stories and even sang him a song. That made him laugh.

"You can't sing at all, can you?"

They probably hadn't been sleeping for long when she was woken by his crying. He felt ill, he said, and his tummy hurt. She hoped that it was only the wild onions, and not the white berries! Although the forest was chilly, his head and cheeks were burning with fever. Mara was concerned for him, yet she was also frightened that his wailing might attract wild animals. It would have been better if they had lit a fire.

He began seeing things.

"Look at the eyes!"

And he pointed frantically out into the darkness. Mara couldn't see anything.

"The eyes! Red eyes!"

Had wild beasts tracked them? She couldn't see, hear or smell anything. Her father had told her about bears, and she had seen wolves out on the Plain, but wolves were only dangerous in snow weather, if at all.

She had no idea what to do if it was a bear.

But there was nothing there: Phrygillus was dreaming in his fever. The gods sent visions to confuse you, or to give you glimpses of the spirit world where your ancestors lived. What he was seeing was not real.

Even so, she held on tightly to the little knife.

Exhausted, Mara slipped away into sleep, before he woke her once again. He was sobbing and shaking.

"The eyes!"

The horse was whinnying anxiously. Had he sensed wolves closing in on them? Mara raised herself on one elbow and looked around her. Now she, too, saw the eyes: red eyes, disembodied, dancing in the darkness.

Were they both feverish?

The eyes came closer, and she saw that there were small shapes. They were surrounded, encircled, though not by wolves. They were surrounded by *children*.

II

FLORIANUS HAS AN UNCOMFORTABLE TIME AT THE PALACE

✠ *The Imperial Palace, in the City.*

Stripped of his chain of office as High Chamberlain, and jostled from all sides by those who had once lived in fear of him, Florianus tried not to look like what he now was: a frightened, flabby little eunuch surrounded by his enemies. He scurried down corridors, seeking the shelter of his office, but it was not to be. White-cloaked Imperial Guardsmen grabbed hold of him, and he was frogmarched down into the cellars beneath the Golden Rooms.

On the way, a Palace servant slapped his face, a slave-girl threw dirt (or worse) at him, and a footman spat at him, viciously, though with less accuracy than the slave-girl had managed. He was pointed out, and laughed at. He had expected all of this. Were there so many who held grudges against him? Probably not—they were just powerless riffraff enjoying the novelty of being able to slap or spit at a High Chamberlain. There would be far worse to come, from those who *did* hold grudges against him.

In the cellars, as he knew only too well, there were storerooms and holding cells. There were also torture chambers.

The cells were on several levels: first, comparatively spacious rooms containing straw mattresses, wall-brackets for torches, and even a table and chair perhaps (if only for the use of the interrogator); below them were small, cramped cells that were barely large enough for a man to stretch or move about in; finally, there were dark, deep pits into which prisoners were thrown through an opening in the floor. Food and flasks of water might or might not be lowered to them, or thrown in occasionally, but those who went into the pits were seldom known to come out again.

Please, not that! Florianus had no wish to rot slowly in the darkness. Better an appointment with the executioner.

To his relief, he was bundled into one of the larger cells, and left to his own devices.

What comfort, if any, could he take from his situation? He wasn't dead, and so someone must have a reason for keeping him alive. And he was proud that he hadn't shat himself yet, even though he was genuinely terrified. At first he thought he was alone, until a rat scurried past his feet and buried itself in the mattress. Florianus wanted to sleep; he didn't want to wake up, though, and find a rat gnawing at his toes. Fear and tiredness struggled for mastery, until he finally collapsed onto the straw. They hadn't left him a torch, but some light shone in from the corridor outside through a grille in the door.

He may have slept for as little as a few hours, or for as long as a day and a night—there was no way to tell the passing of time. No food had been provided, only water in a jug.

Florianus was woken by the door clanging open. A second prisoner was brought in; he was to have company other than the rat!

It was the eminent Senator Gaius Cornelius Rufus, joint leader (with Gnaeus Julius Placidus) of the Red faction in the Senate, now looking less than eminent, with torn clothes, both eyes blackened and dried blood caked across his face.

Florianus instinctively vacated the straw mattress for his distinguished cell-mate.

Rufus groaned and sighed. Florianus had had dealings with the Senator in the past, mostly backroom meetings to discuss the wording of a legal motion or some complicated voting strategy—not many dealings, because Rufus's Reds seldom had cause to vote with the Imperial Whites. Behind the scenes, he had experienced Gaius Cornelius Rufus as being exactly what he was held to be by many in the City: a decent man with strong religious convictions and moral integrity who happened to be politically associated with monsters: the Placidi.

Who had maltreated him so brutally? The Senator told him how Quintus Naevius's thugs had recognized him at the Palace gate and manhandled him, with savage delight and increasing violence, before a Guards officer arrived to take him into custody.

The hunt was on for all Red Senators, he said, but to his knowledge he was the only one who had been seized. Gaius Placidus had left the City days before, heading north (why that? Florianus couldn't help thinking), while Gnaeus was predictably on his way down to the family stronghold in the south. Others had been less fortunate. A few of Rufus's colleagues had been murdered by the mob—he had seen their heads impaled on the Palace railings. He had been "proscribed", though, the officer had said, and he would be detained at his Imperial Majesty's pleasure.

He was terrified for his family, especially his wife and his daughter Cornelia. They were wholly innocent, but would that save them?

His niece Fannia was doomed. She was known to be intimate with young Sextus Placidus, and anyone with *that* name, whoever they were, even a harmless poet like Sextus, was now as good as dead.

All this information, recounted by the Senator between sobs of self-pity, was stored away in the eunuch's mind for possible use. Florianus was powerless now, but he was far from helpless, so long as there were people who could be worked on and manipulated—for which he needed information.

Now that there was a Senator in the cell, food was brought, a lead platter of bread and cheese that was placed in front of Cornelius Rufus. Nothing was given to Florianus. After the warder had left, the Senator offered to share the food with him. A man of generosity!

Despite his hunger, Florianus was uanable to concentrate his attention on the food. Why was he being kept alive? There must be a reason.

He was about to find out.

Once again the cell-door clanged open, and a Guardsman towered over him.

"You, bastard eunuch, you come."

Like most of the Imperial Guardsmen, he was a hairy northern barbarian, and to judge from his horrible accent one of the so-called Free People. His command of the Citizens' Tongue was rudimentary, but Florianus understood what was wanted of him and followed him out of the cell. As he stepped through the doorway, another burly figure scooped him up from behind and flung him over his shoulder. To his outrage, Florianus was carried out of the cellars like a sack of grain.

Maybe sensing his indignation, the Guardsmen laughed.

"You fucked, little eunuch. You fucked real bad."

Despite the awkward position he was in, Florianus could see that they were entering the Golden Rooms. He was brought to a large office that was occasionally used as an informal audience chamber. The room was crowded. So many people wanted to watch his humiliation!

The Guardsman placed him carefully on his feet in front of a low couch. There was no dramatic show of throwing him to the ground—that was something at least.

Maximillus was seated on a portable throne, flanked by Guardsmen. The Emperor was wearing a dazzling robe of cloth of gold, and clutching a small lapdog with enormous ears, an import from some realm in the distant east. He was tormenting the dog by pulling at his ears. The dog was frightened, or wasn't being fed properly, because it had left a noticeable smear of feces on the Imperial robe. Maximillus seemed not to be aware of this.

The couch was empty. It had been put in the center of the room, and beside it stood Julian, now wearing what had once been Florianus's chain of office. He was bursting with self-satisfaction, his chest puffed out like that of a horny pigeon so as to better emphasize the chain.

Quintus Naevius stood just inside the door, at a safe distance from the Emperor.

By the wall was a lighted brazier.

Oh no! Torture? Branding? But Florianus couldn't see any branding-irons.

Though unable to reach the Imperial robe, or the red leather shoes that only Emperors were allowed to wear, Florianus immediately did the full obeisance.

"Majesty—."

"Shut up, you little prick," came the voice of Quintus Naevius from behind him. "Slaves don't speak in the Presence."

Maximillus giggled.

Slaves? What did that mean? Florianus wasn't a slave. He had been freed many years ago by the Emperor's father of blessed memory. Were they going to make him a slave again? And brand him? Could they do that, even by Imperial Prerogative? They could, though not so quickly: there were legal procedures to be followed, even in such cases. Or maybe there weren't—lawless wild beasts like Quintus Naevius now ruled the world. No, that couldn't be, Quintus's father Marcus Naevius was a man who was known to respect the law, and the General still commanded the armies of the West.

The Emperor stood up, and peered down at Florianus. He was hugely amused at the sight of his former High Chamberlain reduced to a bedraggled heap of misery.

"Poor Florianus. Poor, poor little Florianus. You're not High Chamberlain any more. No more bossing people about, no more telling even *me* what to do! You didn't do your job properly, and so Julian now wears your chain of office. See?"

At his signal, Julian took a step forward, and held out the chain with his hand.

"And it makes a difference," he said, looking down at Florianus with contempt, "when the High Chamberlain is a *man*, you little faggot. Don't you agree?"

Florianus was shocked that Julian had dared to speak in the Presence without an invitation from the Emperor, but Maximillus seemed not to care.

"It is our Imperial pleasure," he said, "to care for our servants, and we have therefore assigned you some new duties."

Florianus's throat was horribly dry. "As your Majesty pleases," he croaked.

He crouched down as low as he could. Was the storm passing?

"You will serve the new High Chamberlain, as he once served you."

"Your Majesty is too kind."

This time Maximillus laughed nastily.

"But in one respect you will serve him in a way that he couldn't serve you. I wish to see the reversal of your roles...*enacted*. There should be no doubt in anyone's mind about who the master is, and who the slave."

Quintus Naevius: "Strip off your clothes, eunuch, and get on the couch."

No, surely not? But Florianus did as he was told, and crouched on the couch on all fours, naked. He sensed Julian coming up behind him.

The Emperor sniggered.

"Isn't this fun? Come on, man, go to it! Show us what you can do!"

Julian laughed too, and Florianus shuddered as the new High Chamberlain entered him with force.

"Hold still, slave!" he bellowed.

It hurt, though nothing like as much as everyone else in the room must have imagined.

Florianus had been penetrated many, many times, both before and after the cutting. He had been a very pretty boy, and an even prettier eunuch, and one master in particular had never left him in peace. Yet even he had lost interest eventually, and had sold him. He had been brought west, and purchased for the Palace, where there was a need for eunuchs. His new master, the Emperor's father Maximus the Younger, had never demanded of him anything like this, and he had allowed him to assume increasingly important duties in the Imperial service.

Florianus had become used to being taken, and he had occasionally instructed one of his own slaves, a kindly old footman named Minnermus, to use him gently in that same way. He liked the man, and it was the nearest that he could ever come to feeling trust and physical affection. He could never marry, or live in a relationship, and if he did, he would have to be the "wife", but he could at least play at being loved by someone.

It hurt, as Julian grunted and thrust into him repeatedly. His smell was overpowering, and Florianus could picture the man's glowing red face and goggling eyes.

He knew what he had to do.

Julian had no interest in those of his own sex. With women he was like a goat, but he had never taken advantage of pretty male slaves or servants, or asked some desperate petitioner to bring him her beautiful son.

What was happening now was not about erotic gratification. Florianus was no longer an object to be lusted after by anyone. No, this was about doing the Emperor's bidding, and about power and revenge.

Then why not let Julian have that passing satisfaction? It could be brought to a conclusion more quickly if Florianus yelped and squealed and begged for mercy. That was what Julian really wanted from him.

Florianus put on as much as a show as he dared, and the new High Chamberlain spent himself quickly and pulled back with a sigh of contentment. Florianus threw himself forward on the couch, whimpering theatrically and groaning as if his new master had broken him in two.

The Emperor laughed with delight.

"That was such fun, wasn't it? From now on, keeping your master satisfied will be the first of your duties, eunuch!"

With his face pressing into the couch, Florianus could see nothing. He heard the laughter, not only the Emperor's but also that of Quintus Naevius and maybe the Guardsmen. Yet he had the feeling that someone else had just entered the room.

Behind him, Julian was still breathing heavily. Surely he didn't want to do it all over again? Though if the Emperor commanded him to… Then the laughter stopped, and Florianus heard another voice. This time, it was a voice of imperious command.

"No, your Majesty. With all due respect: no."

He lifted his head and squinted to look, though he knew whom the voice belonged to: Marcus Naevius, leader of the Blues in the Senate. Through his son's gangs he was master of the streets of the City, and soon he would become the grandfather-in-law of the Emperor.

Maximillus was no longer amused.

"No? *No?* Remember who you are speaking to, Senator!"

"Your Majesty, I am speaking to my Emperor, I am aware of that, but to an Emperor whose authority unfortunately doesn't extend much beyond this room." The Senator's voice was calm. "An Emperor who may still be in great danger. Your Guards control this corner of the Palace—and not much more than that. My son's men have the rest of the Palace in their power, and most of the City, and half a league in every direction beyond the walls. Am I right, Quintus?"

"You are right, father. And tomorrow it will be more than a league, have no fear!"

"But we are not alone in the world, your Majesty, and not everyone is your friend."

"I know that, Senator."

Maximillus spoke in a different tone of voice now, one that Florianus recognized: the voice of a sulky, spoilt brat being disciplined.

"The troops of Ogilo—there, I have named the wretched man, necessity forces me to!—control the north, and they are all that stands between us and the Blood-Drinkers. Have you ever met a Blood-Drinker, your Majesty?"

"What a stupid question!"

"Good. Pray that you never do. Then there are the Placidi—"

Quintus shouted, "Or what's left of them!"

"Gnaeus Placidus is raising an army of Sybarite heretics even as we speak. His brother Gaius has disappeared, and could be undertaking something even more sinister to our disadvantage. He is after all a wizard, many would say a necromancer."

"Sol protect us!" someone shouted, and there were appeals to the Blessed Slave.

"Who knows what unspeakable evil he may be conjuring up to harm your Majesty. The world beyond the Palace walls is a dangerous place—or does your Majesty disagree? Have I forgotten some vast, secret army of faithful supporters, willing to give their lives in your service? Do you distrust my loyalty? You are about to honor me by marrying my granddaughter."

Maximillus squirmed petulantly, and threw the dog off his lap. He pouted at the Senator. Everyone knew that the Emperor didn't like being lectured to.

"No, Senator, of course I don't distrust your loyalty. How could I? You are my greatest hope. *You* should be Imperial Guardian, and not Ogilo! I hate him! And let your son be City Prefect!"

"Ah, you are so kind. And all that can perhaps be arranged, your Majesty, in good time. But first, please ask yourself: surrounded as we are by enemies and false friends, what do we have with which to defend the person of our Emperor and the integrity of our faith? At present, not much I fear. Our resources are limited, and we should employ them carefully. The eunuch is such a resource. Miserable creature that he is, he can still be of great use to us. He should not be wasted as a mere toy for the amusement of a Palace servant." He turned to Julian. "Chamberlain?"

"My Lord?"

"Earn his Majesty's gratitude, and you can look forward to many further rewards. But for the present, leave us please: you must have other duties to attend to?" To the commander of the Guardsmen: "Take the eunuch away, and clean him up—he is unsightly. Give him food and drink, whatever he desires, and then bring him back to us."

"My Lord."

"Quintus: you will fetch the Senators, all those that we agreed upon. Make sure that Marcus Vulpeculus is among them. We must try our best to keep ahead of events, and there is no-one in the City who has a sharper mind than Senator Vulpeculus. We have an important task for him—just as we have one for the eunuch."

Every instinct of survival told Florianus that the most desperate time of danger had passed, and that he had been saved. And at the back of his mind, an idea was even beginning to shape itself as to how he could take fitting revenge on Julian.

III

MANASA TRAVELS NORTH ON HER MASTER'S BUSINESS

✠ *Fanum Fortunae to Cascantum.*

Decimus arranged for her to travel to Cascantum with a military chandler, who was transporting supplies to the fortress. A female slave traveling alone was slightly unusual, but Thomasius had provided her with a parchment authorizing her to do so. Instead of pretending to be her master, as he had first intended, Decimus informed the chandler who Thomasius was, and emphasized that the Sub-officer enjoyed the special favor of Lord Commander Rhaetius.

The chandler made his living from the Citizen Army, and a very good living it was, too: he was perfectly happy to cooperate.

Then Decimus set off down the Great Provincial Road in the other direction, in search of Mara.

Manasa's journey was more leisurely. She rode in the back of the chandler's bumpy old cart, which was probably less comfortable than the wagon that would be organized to transport Thomasius on the same route a few days or a week later. There was a thick, tent-like covering to protect the goods, which would also protect Manasa from the elements. Summer was coming to an end, and the days were getting cooler.

The covering tended to insulate the inside of the cart from the sounds of life outside, and what with that and with the constant thudding and shuddering that the cart made Manasa found that she could barely hear the dull chatter of the chandler and his driver, who were both perched on the driver's box in front of her. Which was such a blessing! She squeezed herself in between two of the large wooden crates, making herself a nest out of bundles of rope and sacking, in the hope that she wouldn't be thrown against the sides of the jolting cart too often.

It would only be for one day. The convoy that they were in, slow as the carts and wagons might normally be, nevertheless had to reach the safety of Cascantum before dark. How could that not involve jolting?

Everyone was nervous. This northernmost stretch of the Great Provincial Road was ominously empty. At one place the wagons stopped and the merchants and their drivers climbed down. They peered worriedly at what seemed to be smears and tracks of dried blood alongside the road.

The chandler had hired two hefty thugs to protect his person and his wares. Some of the other travelers had also obtained the services of armed escorts or bodyguards. (Those who hadn't would be obliged to carry their own weapons, and to look to their own safety.) Men like these—who were honest former soldiers if you were lucky, and murderous, cut-throat ex-convicts if you weren't—could be seen at the main gate or in the market square of any city, strutting about to impress the girls, pissing in the gutter, annoying passers-by, and waiting to be hired. They might put the fear of all the gods into run-of-the-mill robbers or highwaymen; how much use they would be if the convoy encountered a marauding band of Blood-Drinkers was more questionable.

A woman traveling alone was a soft target for any man with evil intentions, as Manasa knew. A slave-girl was even more vulnerable. The chandler had seen her authorization and he had too much respect for the military to make her life difficult. The two thugs were a different matter…

When they halted for a short lunch break, one of them jumped up onto the back of the cart and told Manasa what he wanted of her. At once. Or else.

What a nuisance! Manasa was hungry, and had just begun to investigate the little parcel of provisions kindly provided by the innkeeper at Fanum Fortunae. There was a tiny savory tart that looked most promising. She had experienced her share of bullying, groping and abuse from unattractive men—this was the daily fate of slave-girls, from the northern wastes to the shores of the Southern Ocean—but on this occasion she was not inclined to accept it.

She was small, and the man was too big for her to fight off, even if he had merely been a "respectable" Citizen and not a vicious bully, well-schooled in violence. She showed him the authorization, and he simply laughed at her. Oh yeah? So what? He couldn't read, he said with a leer (she definitely believed him), and, much as he would enjoy it, they didn't have time for her to explain to him what the squiggles on the parchment meant. He wanted it *now*, from *her*, *quick and juicy*, before the convoy moved off again and he'd have to get back up on his stupid mule.

If she was nice to him, he'd make sure that his friend didn't come and pester her. His friend had a tendency to damage the goods, if she understood what he meant?

With a sigh, Manasa opened up her clothes and let him play around with her tits. They were beautiful, she knew that: firm, medium-sized, with large nipples. No man had ever failed to like them, and he gave them his undivided, purring attention. What fools men were! This one was no exception, and he was in for a little surprise.

Before he could advance to the next, even more exciting stage of his seduction, she pushed his hands away.

"No, now it's my turn. Fair's fair, show me what *you've* got to offer!"

He chortled happily and unveiled it to her.

"That's just what I was hoping you'd say. Take a look at *this*, sweetheart!"

The object was standing to attention and obviously ready to move into action. The brief moment in which the man glanced down admiringly at his pride and glory proved to be his undoing. With clucking noises of feigned approval, Manasa seized the treasure with her left hand and bent forward, her mouth promisingly wide open. The man leant back in satisfaction, expecting her lips to caress and then swallow his scepter.

He was to be disappointed. Instead of sending him to the ultimate seventh heaven of male bliss (as only Sybarite girls knew how to, it was widely believed), Manasa pulled out from under the sacking the small, sharp knife that Thomasius had given her ("Don't hesitate to use it") and pricked him sharply with it.

She did this, moreover, in a certain place where he had been anticipating pleasure rather than pain.

"Shut up! And don't you dare move, or my hand may slip!" She looked him in the eye. "Listen, *friend*. I am the valuable property of Company-commander Thomasius" (there was no harm in giving her master a temporary promotion), "the well-known slayer of Blood-Drinkers, who eats boys like you for breakfast and spits out the pieces. *Are* you listening?"

The man yelped, "Yes!" She was, after all, holding the knife against the softest place in his body, with the point pressing into the flesh. He was already bleeding slightly.

"Oh dear, I think I've cut you. Oh, that's nasty, I can feel blood seeping out! Keep very, very still, and listen, or the knife will go in deeper. My master serves Lord Commander Rhaetius, and I have a message for him. If I don't report to him in Cascantum, he will come searching for me. You've heard of the Lord Commander, haven't you? He's a man with no sense of humor. If anything happens to me, he'll find out, and he'll cut your balls off." And to make her point, she gave the last-mentioned a vicious twist. "Sorry about that! At least you've still got them. Now if you behave, I won't say a word about you. You've had your fun, and our time is up. Go back to your mule, and do your job. There might be Blood-Drinkers out there."

She kept the knife in her hand for the remainder of the journey, in case he should come back, perhaps this time with his friend. It made her feel better, though there was no sense in it. Maybe they would rape her. If they were determined to, she could hardly hold them off. But what she had said about the Lord Commander (and about Thomasius) might have impressed the man.

Or maybe the chandler just kept him busy.

Either way, he stayed on his mule.

They reached Cascantum as night was falling. It was noticeably colder, with a chilly wind gusting through the enormous conglomeration of shacks and hovels that clustered at the foot of the fortress. Manasa was not at all impressed: she had already seen several great cities in her life; this, by comparison, was a dirty, ugly place.

The two thugs were paid off in Maximians, and slipped away to find themselves a tavern or a cheap brothel. The cart drove on. Maybe the chandler didn't want them to see him making his trade in the fortress; or they considered that helping to unload a cart was not what they had been hired for.

At the gate they were very nearly refused entry. It was now dark, and the gates of the fortress had been closed for the night. But these were badly-needed military supplies that the chandler was bringing. There was nothing for it: it had to be done. With much heaving, creaking and the sound of loud complaints, the gate was re-opened and the cart was allowed to enter.

Once inside, they were surrounded by Citizen soldiers. A Sub-officer spoke briefly to the chandler, and then the soldiers (with more cursing) began unloading the cart. The supplies had been expected.

Keeping one eye on what the soldiers were doing, the chandler spoke to Manasa for the first time since they had left Fanum Fortunae.

"Well, whatever-your-name-is, we got you here safely, didn't we? Tell your master how well you were treated, and if he ever needs help again I'm his man."

She kept her eyes demurely lowered.

"I shall tell him, Master."

The chandler looked her up and down.

"You're a pretty thing. Tonight we'll all have to stay in the fortress— they won't open that gate again before the morning. I expect they'll give me a room in the guest-house. It'll be a cold night. If you need some-where to sleep…?"

"Thank you, Lord, but I must now look for my master's fellow of-ficer, to bring him my master's news."

The chandler was disappointed.

"Yes, of course, your master's business must come first, I understand that. Maybe tomorrow, if you don't have quarters here in the fortress? Ask for me down in the town, at the sign of the Fighting Cocks. I can promise you a clean bed, good food, drink, and generous company!"

He clinked his little purse of Maximians, as though to underline the offer.

Generous company indeed! Tipping her a couple of debased silver coins so as to avoid having to spend his money on a local woman…what a cheapskate! He'd had the whole journey from Fanum Fortunae to chat her up, and he hadn't even bothered to try, so why this sudden interest? Perhaps it had crossed his mind that a Sub-officer's trusted slave-girl would likely be a whole lot cleaner than any Cascantum whore that he could afford?

She thanked him politely for his kind and indeed most generous offer. (There was certainly no way that she would accept it.)

The Sub-officer had spotted her, too, so with her most charming smile she introduced herself as Sub-officer Thomasius's personal property and showed him the travel authorization, which included instructions for her to seek out her master's friend and colleague Sub-officer Grassica. Her master was on his way to Cascantum, she said, and he would be deeply grateful for any assistance that the noble lord could give her in the matter.

"Thomasius, eh? And Grassica. Those boys are Seventh Division. They're round behind the next gate. I'll send one of my men with you. I'd love to take you in hand myself" (no doubt he would!) "but I can't leave all this stuff here, can I now?"

"Thank you, Master."

He called one of his men over. Manasa noticed with approval that he had chosen an older man, one who wouldn't be much use anyway in unloading the military supplies. These weren't Sueni layabouts like the troopers she had met in Fanum. As a Sybarite, she had no great love for the Citizen Army, but with Blood-Drinkers lurking on the horizon it was comforting to know that in the fortress they would be defended by well-disciplined soldiers, intelligently led.

"He'll take you to Sub-officer Grassica's quarters. You can bed down there till your master arrives. Oh, and a word of warning," he added with a smile. "Don't come on to Tricky Grassica—his lady friend might not like it…"

Tricky? As she was escorted towards the officers' quarters of the Seventh Division, she asked herself what Sub-officer Grassica might have done to earn *that* nickname? Did Thomasius have a nickname too?

If not, she'd soon find one for him!

The friendly Sub-officer at the gate had been decidedly handsome, and clearly well-aware of her charms. There was no reason not to make a friend who might be useful. He was certainly better-looking than Thomasius was. Was "Tricky" Grassica equally good-looking? Was that why his lady friend, whoever she was, was jealous?

The woman who came to the door to greet them was an attractive but blowzy northerner—a Sueni, Manasa guessed—who towered over the soldier too. Gemma (that was her name) left no-one in any doubt as to who was in command in that particular corner of the fortress. She sent the soldier away with a small copper coin, and not a word of thanks.

Manasa introduced herself, recounting how she had met her master in Fanum.

"You belong to Thomasius? He won you at *dice*? Well, he couldn't have bought you, could he? Not on what a Sub-officer earns. I like Thomasius—he's a steadying influence on my man Grassica, so you be good to him! And I bet I know who taught him the dice tricks!"

Manasa saw where the nickname came from.

Gemma had decided that she liked Manasa long before Sub-officer Grassica returned to his quarters, and she was as forthright and direct to his face, showing little or no respect, as she had been in discussing her "man" with Manasa. The Sub-officer was small and ferrety, with quick movements and a friendly manner. He gave no indication, though, that his eyes would be roving in Manasa's direction. Either he preferred northern girls, or Gemma had him completely under her muscular thumb.

Manasa was no great respecter of persons, either, but slaves had to be careful until they knew it was safe to speak their mind. (It hadn't taken her long to get that far with Thomasius.)

Gemma made her sit with them and share their food. Grassica seemed to have no objection. She would show Manasa her master's quarters the next morning, and give her a brush and some cloths for cleaning them— the soldier that Thomasius paid to carry out those duties was as good as useless. That night she should sleep in their kitchen, though, and Gemma would bring her water for washing. It wouldn't be safe for her to go to the bath-house on her own at night, and the water there would be cold anyway. In the morning there was an hour when the bath-house was reserved for women only, and then she could go with Gemma and her sister Gemmella.

As Manasa tucked herself up for the night in the blankets that Gemma had given her, she felt safe. The fortress was solidly built, and full of soldiers who knew what they were doing. It was warm, it was well-provisioned—to judge from the supper that they had shared—and it was protected from the northern wind and gusts of rain now swirling about outside. Let the Blood-Drinkers come, and crash against the walls of Cascantum like the waves of the Sybarite Sea that Manasa remembered from her childhood!

Tomorrow she had a task to fulfill, if Sub-officer Grassica could arrange a meeting: to bring news of Mara and Decimus to the Lord Commander. She would have to tell him about the Sybarite killer, and about Lelia, too, a thought which made her deeply uneasy.

And she had seen things that it was unwise to see.

Sleep came slowly.

The next morning, the two sisters took her to the bath-house as they had promised.

Sybarites were very clean in their personal habits, unlike many of the northerners and most of the barbarians that she'd encountered in her life. That list now included Gemma and her sister Gemmella. Sueni women couldn't help being slovenly, and as for the swampie men—well, the less said about them, the better.

Hard as she might try, she couldn't quite banish the memory of Urtho, the Sueni cavalryman who had briefly been her master. He was such a typical specimen! He had stunk out of every recess of his massive body, he had simply laughed when she pointed out how filthy the bedclothes were, and both before and after his cursory "love-making" he had treated her to a concert of malodorous belches and farts. He had snored like a deep-sea monster, and her main concern during that long night had been for her own survival: to avoid being pushed out of the bed, or being crushed and injured by his bulk whenever he turned in his sleep.

"Dream People", they called themselves? "Nightmare People" would be more like it.

The two Sueni women were friendly enough, and they were far from stupid. When Manasa got to meet Staff Officer Petronius, Gemmella's handsome employer and "protector", she quickly deduced who was in command in *that* relationship.

Gemmella was smaller and far prettier than her sister, with a fine-featured, child-like face and trim body. After bathing, she would pass as a beauty by anyone's standards. But both women were unattractively hairy. They hadn't even bothered to trim the body hair between their legs to a shape that some men—the unsophisticated ones at least—might conceivably find appealing. The girls had no excuse for that, since they had regular access to all the amenities of a bath-house.

In comparison, for Manasa visits to the bath-house had always been a rare luxury.

During the time when she had been a slave among the Horse People, she had only had the river for bathing—and slaves were not allowed to use it until after the horses had been seen to. That was because a man was judged by the quality and appearance of his horses, and not by whether his slaves smelt sweet!

As for the years when she had been a slave within the Empire, her successive masters had not been the kind of men who had a proper bath-house at home, and she hadn't accompanied them to the public baths—not that it was actually forbidden, but because of the whores who lurked in the corners and side-rooms of those establishments. These fearsome women would kick up a huge fuss, and become spiteful and aggressive, whenever they saw, looming into view, what they thought was an intrusion into their territory, and a threat to their livelihood.

"Get out, you bitch!" they'd shriek. "We don't want any part-timers here! We're professionals, and this is our patch! Ply your trade somewhere else!"

Hair would be pulled, faces would be scratched, and a great deal of noise made. If the girl's owner tried to intervene, *his* hair and face would risk getting the same treatment.

The other bathers would laugh—at first—but soon the screeching and shouting would begin to get on everyone's nerves. Then there would be complaints to the management about the "unseemly disturbance"; the management would send the whores packing for one or two days (but not for longer than that, because they were getting a cut of the whores' earnings); the man would be told that he should stay away from the bath-house for a while; and the slave-girl would get a hefty beating from her angry, humiliated master immediately they reached home.

It was so convenient to have slaves: whatever happened to you, you could always give them the blame and take out your anger on them!

But Manasa herself had never been in this situation, because her masters had known very well that men found her so attractive that the whores would go for her like demons from Esbus the moment they saw her.

Nor had she ever accompanied any of her mistresses to the bath-house either. None of them had liked her (which was because her masters too obviously did) and they had never wanted to have her at the baths with them. A slave-girl's normal duties were to pamper, soothe and massage her mistress, not make her tetchy; and if a slave attracted the attention of male bathers by her charms, causing them to overlook those of her mistress, that would make her mistress very tetchy indeed.

So how had Manasa regularly managed to find her way to the public baths?

There were days, a few times in the year, that were unpopular with certain groups of paying customers.

For example, the adherents of the old religion were strictly forbidden to bathe for a week before the Feast of the Horned One. Men who broke that injunction would be punished with impotence for a whole year until the next feast day came around, while women would suffer itches and rashes where they least wanted them, and vile-smelling discharges!

That was only once a year, but for followers of the Slave there were frequent occasions when they would be expected to avoid the bath-house. Particularly pious cult members associated personal uncleanliness with spirituality. (You would catch a whiff of these holy men long before they came into view.) For them, bathing was "an immersion in sin", "an ungodly wallowing in fleshliness", and "an invitation to lustful temptation". At the numerous high points of the Slave cult's religious calendar, these disgusting saints would whip up other, normally less fanatical, believers into a short-lived frenzy of self-castigation, exaggerated wailing, and ostentatious personal neglect.

Among the religions, it seemed to Manasa that only the worship of Sol required regular washing and bathing when- and wherever possible (which for soldiers was not always an option). Thomasius, she had noticed, smelt quite acceptable—for a northerner—and tried to keep himself clean.

It therefore made commercial sense for the owners of the baths to sometimes close them to the public temporarily. During these periods, they would be hired out for the ablutions of slaves from households in which there was no bath-house—or where there was only one bathing facility, which the master and mistress preferred not to share with their maids and footmen.

Male and female slaves attended at different times, and under strict supervision. There was a good reason for that separation. The male (or female) slaves from one's own household might be boring, all too familiar, and wholly lacking in charm, but could the same be said of a good-looking stranger from another household? That way lay danger, and many masters were very concerned that there should be no untoward, unplanned pregnancies, especially among those female slaves who were being used for breeding (with carefully selected studs).

Manasa, a natural leader among the women, was often put in charge of such groups of female bathers. Luxuriating in the water with Gemma and Gemmella, she was reminded of the fun that they had had back then.

For example, teasing the grouchy old bath attendant (why were bath attendants always old and bad-tempered?), who resented having to work for women (especially when they were slaves or barbarians), but at the same time enjoyed ogling them.

Gemmella was as shameless as any of the slave-girls that Manasa had supervised. She would deliberately stand on the steps where the water was shallow, her legs slightly apart to give the man a better view.

"Oh, Gemma," she would sigh, "I am so *sore* from the shafting he gave me last night! Look how red it is!"

And the bath attendant would turn away, muttering to himself.

Then there was the endless talking about men. Men were the biggest problem that women had in their lives, but also (irritatingly) the main reason for living. Manasa was taken aback by how candidly and disrespectfully the Sueni women talked about their respective boyfriends. Had they no loyalty?

Manasa had always been used by men, and she had never had a boyfriend of her own free choice. As far as she was concerned, talking scornfully about your master was fair enough. Why should you respect a man who mounted you whenever it suited *him*, and usually without a single friendly word? Or offered you to his gross drinking companions at the end of a drunken party, or to some neighbor he owed money to, or to the fat old lawyer that he wanted to ingratiate himself with?

If it was someone that you liked, though, and who liked you in return? She had no doubt in her mind that Gemma and Grassica were fond of each other, and that Gemmella and Petronius would stay together. So why did the women have to mock their boyfriends so cruelly?

She found herself thinking about Thomasius. She was under no obligation not to make fun of him, but why should she? He had treated her with more decency than any other master she had had. And he was a nicer person, too.

Don't be stupid! she told herself. Why should he be any different? He'll rape you the first opportunity he has. Except that it won't be rape, because it's his right as your master, In any case, once he has made his intentions clear you'll spread your legs for him the way you always do.

Gemma had been as good as her word, taking Manasa round one corner and then another to where Sub-officer Thomasius had his living quarters. She gave her some cleaning tools and materials for cleaning, and left her to it.

"Can you find your own way back?"

Manasa was confident that she could, and when Gemma had gone she realized that the cleaning wouldn't take her long. Thomasius's quarters were even more modest than Grassica's, They amounted to a handful of badly-lit, box-like rooms that were scarcely bigger than cupboards. One of them was a tiny kitchen, but (unlike Grassica's) it didn't look as though it had been used very often for preparing food.

Gemma had been right when she said that the soldier didn't do his job well. The surfaces were dirty or dusty—or both. Why did he bother to pay the man?

Well, that was a way in which he could save some of his money. *She* was there now, and she would take charge.

Before getting down to the cleaning, she allowed herself time to explore. This was his territory. What could it tell her about him?

His few belongings, mostly clothing, were all sorted and tidied away where you would want to find them. The soldier wouldn't have done it—that could only have been Thomasius. And his military gear and weapons were beautifully clean and well-maintained. That too could only have been him.

She looked for any sign of a woman—items of female clothing, simple jewelry, anything that he had kept to remind him of a former girlfriend—but found nothing.

Some of his clothes had been repaired, but crudely, and obviously not by a woman.

For better or worse, Thomasius was now part of her life, so best to find out as much as she could about him! Yet nothing that she discovered in his quarters gave her cause to change the view that she had already formed of him.

She finished her cleaning and dusting, and went back to join Gemma.

Visiting the bath-house became their morning routine. There was not much else for her to do, as neither Grassica nor Petronius had been able to see the Lord Commander, let alone arrange for Manasa to meet him.

One morning Petronius joined them in the bath-house. That was strictly forbidden: the morning hour was reserved for women only. But who was going to quarrel with a Staff Officer?

Gemmella flirted with him, coyly playing peek-a-boo, splashing him naughtily with water and then wading away from him, inviting him to come and catch her. How sweet—they were in love!

Petronius was almost impossibly handsome, though Manasa did observe that (as was so often the case) the gods had endowed liberally with one hand whilst withholding an important gift with the other. The Staff Officer's man-part was of exceptionally modest proportions.

She hoped that the bath attendant wouldn't notice that. He himself probably had a thing like a donkey's.

Petronius told them that Lord Commander Rhaetius was beyond the fortress walls, with a large part of both the divisions that were stationed in Cascantum, as well as most of the auxiliary cavalry. For reasons of security he wasn't permitted to say more than that—though he now did, pompously, and at some length.

In the past this excursion by the troops would have been no more than a maneuver exercise, with the additional purpose of reconnoitering to ascertain movements of friendly or hostile barbarians.

"Friendly barbarians" were the Sueni, naturally, many of whom had friends or family members serving with the Citizen Army, or the Horse People, who hadn't, but who had been allowed to cross the Great River and settle within the Empire. They were "under the eagle's wing", as the Lord Commander liked to put it.

The "hostile barbarians" were the Blood-Drinkers, obviously. And maybe the Free People, too—you could never be sure with them.

While Petronius was holding forth, Gemmella gazed at him in adoration. It might be exaggerated, but to the Staff Officer (who didn't strike Manasa as being the most perceptive sort) it would have been very convincing! And there did seem to be a genuine affection between them.

He apologized that he had been unable to pay much attention to the ladies.

Ladies? Manasa had to laugh. She could vividly imagine the old bath attendant (and much of the rest of the male population of Cascantum) more likely describing them as "swampie trollops"!

And (acknowledging Manasa with a nod) he politely expressed his regret that he had not found any time to talk to Sub-officer Thomasius's slave-girl.

"What was your name again, girl?"

"Manasa, Master."

In the absence of both Lord Commanders, he, Petronius, had had to shoulder a heavy burden of responsibility for the remainder of the garrison. Such onerous, such time-consuming duties! And in a sensitive position of *leadership*, he added.

"He is a good man, your master," he told Manasa with a look of intent seriousness. "One of our very best Sub-officers. With the potential to reach even greater heights!"

Or so the Lord Commander had confided in him.

(Manasa noted for future reference that whatever was confided in the Staff Officer soon afterwards became public knowledge.)

She nodded submissively, to show her gratitude for his kindness. He did her master such honor, she whispered.

The two Sueni "ladies" clucked at Petronius appreciatively. He was their hero. Come what may, be it Blood-Drinkers or any other loathsome threat from the distant north, all of them would be safe in Cascantum while the noble Staff Officer Petronius was in command!

Gemmella offered to give the hero her "special massage", to help lessen the aches and pains of stress that he must be feeling, and her sister signaled to Manasa that they ought now to leave and allow the couple to be alone.

The two women returned to Grassica's quarters. Manasa wondered when Thomasius would arrive. She wouldn't be wholly displeased to see him.

IV

THOMASIUS FOLLOWS
THE CALL OF DUTY

✠ *Fanum Fortunae.*

Thomasius had been thoroughly miserable in Fanum Fortunae. He had had sword-wounds before, though never in such an awkward place. His fellow Sub-officers would laugh at him when they heard about it. And he didn't like lying around uselessly in his room at the Eagle Inn— lying, because sitting was not a comfortable option.

Not that the room itself was uncomfortable, even if the bed was somewhat narrow. Apart from breakfast, the food was the usual over-priced muck that they sold at inns, but he persuaded one of the maids to fetch him grilled meat and vegetables from a street vendor; also the local sausages seasoned with marjoram that he so liked.

As maids at inns were expected to do, she offered him certain other services. If he so wished, she would be ever so gentle, seeing what terrible injuries the master had. Might she touch the horrible wound on his….? She would soon kiss it better!

She had a magic amulet, which would help his wound to heal if she placed it there and recited a spell.

She was not offended when he said no, the pain was simply too great.

Even so, he couldn't help thinking that the doctor had exaggerated the seriousness of his wounds in order to keep him there longer. The man had seen the bag of heavy silver pieces that Lord Commander Rhaetius had given him for his expenses, and his eyes had opened up to the size of Sub-officer retirement medals. It was just as well that he hadn't seen the gold as well, or he would have immobilized Thomasius for months.

The sooner he could set off for Cascantum, the better. This wasn't a holiday.

He was also worried about what might have happened to Manasa, on the road, or at the fortress. After the way she had stood over him and held off the Sybarite assassin, he would almost trust her to fight off a Blood-

Drinker—well, a very young, inexperienced one, perhaps, with his hands tied behind his back—but would she be able to fight off all those lecherous colleagues of his at Cascantum? That would be more demanding!

Was he getting jealous? He'd never owned a slave before, and he wasn't too sure what the rules were, but one of them must be that you didn't fall for them.

It was going to be very difficult with Manasa—that much was already apparent.

Day after day of grumpy boredom passed. Left alone with his thoughts, none of which were constructive, and with his aches and pains, which he noticed all the more because he had nothing to distract himself with, Thomasius decided that it was time to leave. There were excellent army doctors at Cascantum who could take out the stitches, and who wouldn't charge him a single debased Maximian for doing it.

When he spoke to the innkeeper about his intention to leave, the man grinned obsequiously, displaying the horrific ruins of what were once teeth. Although he was deeply disappointed, he said, not to be able to continue serving the master at his modest hostelry, he would be sincerely honored to be of assistance to the Sub-officer in making travel arrangements for him.

For a small fee, he could reserve a place for him in a luxurious merchant's carriage. Delicious refreshments for the journey would be provided. A bodyguard (or better, two?) could be hired. A young girl to nurse him tenderly, if he so wished…

Thomasius declined the bodyguards, and the young girl. The bag of silvers to be returned to the Lord Commander was going to be quite light enough as it was. He would leave the following morning.

Just as the day was ending, Decimus arrived. He tut-tutted when he learned that Thomasius intended to return to Cascantum prematurely. Though he wasn't able to dissuade him, he couldn't resist needling him a bit.

"Is it wise for my Lord to be traveling before his honorable wounds have healed?"

"Honorable wounds? Sol's bollocks, the fewer people who know about my bum, the better!"

Decimus adopted the pose of a pompous orator and raised an admonitory finger.

"How would Terebinthian put it? Let's see! Whenever in the course of our duty we face our enemies," he intoned sententiously, "is it for *us* to say where their cruel sword-cuts will land? Sol the Radiant has determined the warp and weft of our lives. (Or the Blessed Slave, of whichever persuasion you happen to prefer.) But for all eternity we will carry those scars with pride, and we will show them to our children, and later to our grandchildren—"

He couldn't keep it up, and they both laughed.

"Not *that* scar, Decimus! Definitely not that one!"

Comfortably or otherwise, the Sub-officer would be traveling alone, because Decimus would be riding south again. He had met a courier on the road, a man in the General's service whom he had known for years, and he had learned from him that the General was on his way to Maidunum, to meet with a deputation of Senators.

"There has been turbulence in the City. But the man wouldn't tell me more than that. My duty now is to my master the General, not to the Lord Commander. I have to report to him quickly. Perhaps he'll have another task for me."

"And Mara?"

Mara was no longer important. The trail had gone cold. Decimus told Thomasius what he had discovered.

He had crossed the bridge over the river from the north, the one that fed into the Amethyst Sea. Where the road forked, he had chosen the right-hand branch, which was the Great Provincial Road that led (after many leagues) to the City. At inns and villages along the way they had told him about the little party that had passed through: two soldiers and three slaves, including a horsey-girl and some pervert's bum-boy.

His search for them had ended near a ruined watchtower, where terrible events must have occurred. Decimus found an abandoned wagon, a dray-horse, and three bodies. One of the bodies was that of a dead slave, with brutal sword-wounds. The other corpses were those of the two soldiers; their throats had been cut.

But no horsey-girl, and no bum-boy.

Thomasius was impressed.

"So poor, sweet little Mara killed them all, and rode off back to her clan, taking the boy with her! Or maybe he just ran off into the forest. Clever girl! Even those horsey women know how to fight. But why didn't she kill the slave-boy as well, while she was about it?"

No, Decimus, told him, Mara hadn't killed any of them. Two Sybarites had passed through the village near the watchtower, a man and a woman, riding southwards on a huge black stallion; the next day they were riding back north—on mules! And they had asked bad-tempered questions in the village about a girl and a boy on a horse. But the villagers couldn't help: they hadn't seen them.

"Aha, so Mara now has the horse, and *they've* got the mules that the soldiers were riding."

The villagers had helped Decimus, however, by giving him a detailed description of the two southerners. Sybarites weren't popular in the north, unless they were well-behaved slaves, the kind that were seen and not heard.

It had taken a while, however, to extract all the information that he needed, and it had been an exhausting business. Just imagine being a country magistrate and having to listen to the driveling complaints of villagers all day! Decimus imitated their slow-witted rural manner of speech.

"And a right handsome young man he was, even if he wasn't from these parts. (But tell 'im about the clothes!) Shut up, I'm coming to that! Well, he was dressed all in black. Expensive stuff it was. Don't see much of that in the village, I'm telling you. (Because decent folks like us can't afford it, that's why!) An arrogant guy, that he was and no mistake. Yer don't see strangers like him much round here. (And a right good thing too.) He had a wicked-looking sword, he did, for slicing bits off yer, and nasty eyes. (May the Horned One take him!) Now if I had my way with all those southerners... I reckon we should've finished 'em off in the last war! Stuck it to 'em good and proper! Was there anything else? I dunno. (Go on, tell 'im about the tattoo!) What tattoo? (You know, the one on his arm!) Well, yes, he had a tattoo on his arm. A sort of starfish, like—"

"My Sybarite friend with the curved sword," Thomasius said, with a grim smile. "Whom I'd so much love to meet again. And the other one, the woman?"

"From the way she was dressed, a slave-girl. Attractive, but with old scarring on her face, caused by burns." And he added, before Thomasius could say anything, "Yes, the Lord Governor's kitchen-maid, the one accused of murdering Castor. So perhaps she did it after all, whatever Manasa thinks."

The arrogant southerner had asked the villagers for horses, offering them gold coins and the two mules in exchange, but the villagers had none. They would have loved his gold, who wouldn't, but what would villagers be doing with fast horses? And having seen the wicked-looking sword, none of the yokels was likely to try and relieve him of his money by force.

"If they're on mules they're hardly going to catch a horsey-girl on a stallion, are they? Even if she's got the boy with her—he won't weigh much. But shouldn't you come to Cascantum with me, to report all this to the Lord Commander?"

No, Decimus said, there was no urgency. Not even because of the other information that he had: from the detailed description that the villagers had eventually given him, he now knew the identity of the Sybarite assassin.

"I met him once, when he was staying as a guest of the Lord Governor here in Fanum. Damn it, if I had only seen the tattoo! But he was wearing a long-sleeved robe. His name is Victor—if that's his real name—and he's a trader in luxury goods. Slaves as well, but only the most expensive kind. Not girls like Mara. You can tell all that to the Lord Commander. You don't need me to help you. And you can tell him that Mara is most probably on her way back home."

Thomasius was puzzled. And slightly piqued.

"Why isn't that information urgent? We know now that Sybarite killers and slavers are on the loose in the north! Kidnaping, and murdering, and upsetting the tribes. And all that about the Cause, and the Sleepless Ones. You even have a name: Victor. I'd venture a guess that they're all in the pay of the Placidus brothers! They're the ones who control the south, aren't they?"

Decimus shrugged.

"Maybe. Who knows? Until we catch them, we won't know who their paymasters are, or who they're in league with."

Thomasius had the distinct feeling that the freedman knew much more than that, but didn't want to share it with him; he didn't press him further.

"Anyway, I just hope that you track this Victor down, and chop him into tiny bits! A pity that there won't be anything left for me, though. Aren't you going to look for Mara, too?"

"No, not unless our paths happen to cross. She's not of interest now. She's just a runaway slave, like the boy."

Thomasius couldn't understand that. Didn't they have a responsibility for finding Mara and returning her safely to her father?

"You know, strictly speaking, she isn't a runaway slave at all," he added, "because she was taken illegally. She's been badly wronged, and someone should put that right."

Decimus gave him a strange look, as if Thomasius had just put his finger into a wound. Then he slipped back into ironic mode.

"I stand astonished, my Lord: who would have expected a Citizen Sub-officer to be so soft-hearted? The backbone of the armies that conquered the world! But you're quite right—it's advisable that we do everything that we can to keep the Horse People on our side."

"No, I don't mean it like that! Well, I do, I suppose." Thomasius realized that he was confused, and that his feelings had run ahead of his thoughts. "Of course, it's political too. But I've seen her father. The man's lost his child." He paused. "Can't you imagine what he's going through now? Or what the girl has suffered?"

Decimus, who had been pacing up and down the room, stopped and sat down on the bed beside Thomasius.

"No, not really."

"Oh!"

"You think I'm heartless, don't you? Come on, be honest! That's what they always say about freedmen, isn't it? That we're cold-blooded."

"I didn't say that."

"And while we're about it: they say that we make cruel slave-masters, because when you're a slave your heart dies, and you can never get it back. Or, because we want to make someone else pay for what we suffered, even if it's the innocent."

"That isn't what I meant, Decimus."

"I'm not trying to offend you. Look—you've killed, haven't you? In battle, certainly."

"Yes. And I've executed men too. Even a crucifixion once. That was hard. Messy. Not a good way to die."

"Well, I don't know how many times I've killed, and I stopped counting long ago. I don't find it difficult. Afterwards, if I think about it at all, I ask myself what one person's pain should matter, when you're trying to protect a whole empire."

He told Thomasius what he had seen on the road to Cascantum: what Blood-Drinkers had done to a prisoner. How the man had been staked out, mutilated, and disemboweled.

"The Blood-Drinkers are cruel," Thomasius said.

"*They* wouldn't say so. For them, it was nothing special: it's what Blood-Drinkers do to their prisoners. Those are their ways. And when they have the time, they do even worse than that. All it did was make me more careful for the rest of the journey. It didn't touch my feelings."

Thomasius regretted that he'd spoken.

"I'm sorry, I was just rambling. You know, I've been lying here for days, twiddling my thumbs, with only what I had in my head for company. You get to think about strange things."

"What kind of things?"

He had had a lot of thoughts about Manasa, but that wasn't a topic he wanted to discuss.

"For example, Mara, her father…they're people, too. That's something I wasn't really aware of before, but I know that now. When they hurt, they hurt just like us. And so do the Sueni—even if they don't wash all too often." He laughed. "I'm not sure about the Blood-Drinkers, though!" He looked at Decimus. "So…friends?" Decimus smiled back—and thumped Thomasius playfully on the shoulder. "Ow!"

"Oops, wrong shoulder! But it's healing now, isn't it? Sorry about that." Decimus felt the bed-clothes. "Hmm. Nice and soft, very inviting.

It's all clean, isn't it? And there aren't too many cockroaches? I wonder whether they've got a room for me, too, for one night."

"They might have a room. But if you're thinking of entertaining a girl, I can't comment on how clean the maids are at this establishment."

Decimus laughed.

"I have it on good authority that the girls at the Stork are the best. However, tonight I need to sleep. It's a long ride down to Maidunum."

They didn't see each other the next morning, even though they both got up and left Fanum very early.

V

FLORIANUS FINDS A NEW HOME

✠ *The Imperial Palace, in the City.*

Florianus indeed felt much better after a wash and a change of clothes. The Guardsmen had taken him to their guardroom at the entrance to the Golden Rooms, a place he had never been to as High Chamberlain. It was just as filthy as he had expected it would be—a typical stinking barbarian hole.

They gave him bread, wine, and some moldy-tasting cold roast chicken, and there was a washroom, with a cracked stone basin, in which they allowed him to clean himself without disturbance. He felt no shame: this had been done to him by others, for no good reason, and he was in no way to blame for it. The Guardsmen may have laughed while he was being humiliated by Julian, and they were brutal men, but they knew what was just and what was unjust. They would have no respect for Julian, and they would see the new High Chamberlain as the loathsome creature that he was.

Finding clean clothes that fitted him was tricky—the Guardsmen themselves were all twice his size at least. Finally one of them brought Florianus a spare footman's uniform, which was still too big for him but not ridiculously so.

He was taken back to the audience chamber. The throne had been removed, as had the hated couch. A crowded meeting was already underway, and nobody paid much attention to him as the Guardsmen trundled him in and deposited him on a stool in the corner.

Florianus glanced around the room. The Emperor was not present and it was Senator Marcus Naevius who was seated at the front, with his son Quintus next to him. Facing them were twelve or fifteen Senators, Blues and Whites, all of whom Florianus recognized. He saw Lentulus, the city Prefect, and Anthemius Capito, whose pathetic daughter had taken part in the bride-show. Two Senators were of particular interest, because the eunuch could see that Naevius was fixing his attention on them.

Gaius Ambibulus Necro was a leading White. He was a well-known authority on political procedure and rituals, a boring, narrow-minded man with a high opinion of himself. Although he was vain about his looks, he had a cleft lip and couldn't close his mouth easily, so that he tended to dribble slightly when he wasn't speaking (and dribbled anyway when he did). Florianus had had plenty of dealings with him when the voting in the Senate needed to be coordinated, and Necro had always made the eunuch feel unworthy. But wasn't the arrogant Senator an "incomplete man" too?

The other man was more interesting, and also far more dangerous. The hawk-nosed Marcus Vulpeculus was a Senator of the Blues, the party of Naevius. A clever lawyer, he had amassed a fortune by offering his services to slum landlords; then he became one himself, investing his money in moldering tenement blocks. He had a well-earned reputation for ruthlessness, and was not a man that you crossed.

Naevius was speaking to him, but now broke off and addressed Florianus.

"What you hear in this room, eunuch, you keep to yourself. Do you understand? After your performance at the bride-show, you know that you have nothing to hope for from our friend Ogilo. And the Emperor would like to give you as a plaything to his new favorite. So you have nowhere else to go. Can I depend upon your loyalty? Are you our man?"

Quintus sniggered. "Hardly a *man*, father!"

"Be that as it may, you are ours now. Is that right?"

If it had been the Emperor, Florianus would have thrown himself theatrically at his feet; instead, he looked the Senator in the eye, and Naevius gave him a look back that, while it was not quite respect, had something in it of approval.

"I am yours, my Lord. Yours entirely."

"Good. Senator Vulpeculus you know. He will be leaving tomorrow for the north to meet the General, and will confirm what I have already told the man by fire-beacon. Ogilo will retain his position as Master of Horse and Foot—unfortunately we have no army to take that away from him—but he must surrender to me the title of Imperial Guardian. That is entirely appropriate, as my granddaughter is soon to become Empress, and from the legal point of view it is wholly acceptable." He turned to Vulpeculus. "Am I right, Senator?"

"The obvious alternative would be a Guardianship entrusted to your son, the father of the Empress, and *that* would be even more difficult for the barbarian to swallow."

Marcus Vulpeculus had a stentorian lawyer's voice, which made such pronouncements sound as though they were engraved in legal tablets of stone and could never be challenged.

"Indeed, Senator. It will be hard enough for him to swallow *me* in that role." There was laughter. "But to sweeten it for him, both his powers and mine will be under the jurisdiction of the Imperial Council. After many years in abeyance, the Council will now be reconstituted, its members being, as protocol requires, the High Priest of Sol, the City Prefect"—he nodded in the direction of Lentulus—"the Master of Horse and Foot naturally, equally naturally the Imperial Guardian, and a prominent representative of each of the factions." He smiled. "Not of the Reds, of course."

"Where *are* the Reds, father? I do believe that I saw some of their heads spiked up on the Palace railings!"

Quintus seemed to find that a joke.

A Guards officer spoke up: "We have Senator Cornelius Rufus in the cells, my Lord."

"And let him stay there. I bear the man no personal grudge. He might be useful later for a prisoner exchange—for some reason, the Placidi value him highly. If not, he can rot quietly in his cell. At the next meeting of the Senate, the Red faction will be formally disbanded. Though not many of its members will, I think, be honoring the session with their presence!"

The last remark caused general amusement. Vulpeculus held out a parchment.

"I have here a full list of the Senators of the Red faction. They have been proscribed as traitors, their lives and property are forfeit, and all male members of their families are to be put to death if apprehended, allowing for exceptions in individual cases, as with Cornelius Rufus."

"Proscribed only as traitors?" another Senator asked. "And not as heretics, too?"

Vulpeculus swiveled round to stare at him.

"Only as traitors. Let us be pragmatic, dear colleague! The day will come when we shall deal with the heretics as they deserve. In the meantime, we have to forge an alliance of Blues, Whites and Greens." He continued, in a more unctuous tone: "That alliance will contain those of us who are followers of the Blessed Slave of the *true* persuasion, the so-called 'Lesser Worship' that is, in reality, the greater. It will also contain adherents of the state religion of the West, whose patron, may I remind you, is his Imperial Majesty, the Chief Servant of Sol, and whose followers include many in the ranks of the Senate and even more in the ranks of the army. It will furthermore contain, in the Province, and among the Greens, those who still worship the old gods—"

"Disgusting!"

"Filthy pagans!"

Florianus couldn't see who was shouting.

It was Naevius who responded to the interruptions.

"No, no, gentlemen. My colleague is right: this is an alliance of need, not of love. Without the Greens, we have no army. Ogilo must therefore be allowed, must be *empowered*, to hold the Blood-Drinkers in check."

"What do you mean: we have no army? We have troops on all the frontiers! And in Sybaris!"

With great patience, Naevius explained how far away those frontier divisions were, and how uncertain the political loyalties of their Lord Commanders. Moreover, that those units of the Citizen Army that were stationed in the south were seen there as an army of occupation, were surrounded by a hostile population, and were safe only in their barracks. As long as they held out in their fortresses, embattled but steadfast, Gnaeus Placidus would be unable to march northwards against the City—but that was all that could be asked of them.

"When the threat from the Blood-Drinkers has passed, *that* will be the right time to use Ogilo's troops against the Placidi. Until then, we must keep him sweet. By all means let him think that the Imperial Council is only there to clip *my* wings" (there were shouts of "No, never!") "while he himself, in the bosom of his loyal army, is untouchable."

Several Senators now came forward to offer Naevius their own promises of undying loyalty. Looking around, Florianus saw only Blues and (to his disgust) Whites, but no Green Senators.

Slaves entered carrying trays of delicacies: roasted quails, eels in vinegar, salted eggs and fermented fish-entrails. Wine and fruit-juices were served. It was obviously intended that the meeting should continue, and since the Senators were not being permitted to go home to their suppers, refreshments had to be provided.

The air in the room was very bad. There are too many fat, lazy slugs here, Florianus thought to himself, too many pampered old couch-farters. But these were now his friends; this would now be his political home. He didn't see what his own role was meant to be, or understand yet why he was being allowed to attend such a politically sensitive meeting. He would be loyal, though, he told himself, in return for their protection.

That was the secret of survival, a secret that he had learnt very early in his life. And as Naevius had reminded him: he had nowhere else to go.

The Senator re-started the meeting. They must press on. Other duties called, and his son was needed beyond the Palace gates in urgent matters of public order.

He recapitulated that Senator Vulpeculus would leave the next day for the north. He would meet the General at Maidunum, the northernmost town in the Province and so the closest to Fanum Fortunae. This would enable Lord Governor Faustus Atticus to be present at the meeting, too.

"One of us," he said. "A reliable man."

But a second journey also had to be undertaken. A delegation must travel to Neopolis, to inform Emperor Theodore of the impending marriage of his Imperial cousin and invite him to the wedding.

Vulpeculus: "His Eastern Majesty won't come, but he naurally has to be invited."

Anthemius Capito asked whether there would be enough time for such a journey before the festivities took place.

"Yes," Naevius said, with a sigh, "because the marriage will not be solemnized for many months. Their Holinesses the High Priest of Sol and the High Priestess of Luna must first be satisfied with all the arrangements. My granddaughter is not of the same faith as his Majesty, and she is not prepared to convert—"

Quintus laughed. "That's my daughter: she knows what she wants, and she gets it!"

"Yes, Quintus, she is a very strong-willed young woman. Which is admirable. But it does make the marriage procedures more complicated."

"So what? If he's so horny, he can bed her as soon as they're betrothed. That's right, isn't it, Necro? You're the big expert, I'm told. Not in fucking, of course."

Ambibulus Necro ignored Quintus, but confirmed to Naevius, with a humorless nod, that this information was correct. The marriage could be consummated directly after the betrothal, if the young couple so wished. Naevius responded with a frosty smile.

"Thank you, Senator. It is clear that there will be time enough for this delegation to travel to Neopolis and back. An important delegation, a mission from the throne of the West to the throne of the East, needs to have an important figure at its head: *you*, Senator!"

A look of utter panic flashed across Necro's face.

"But I've never been to Neopolis! It's so far away, and I don't know anyone there!"

Yes, Florianus thought, but you're expendable, and it's a fool's errand anyway.

Naevius made a gesture of brushing aside his objections.

"It has to be a White, someone to represent the Emperor, and not a Blue linked to the hated Lesser Worship and the abominable House of Naevius. You, dear colleague, are simply the most distinguished White Senator"—Florianus heard a distinct, sharp intaking of breath by several of the other Senators present—"the most distinguished White Senator *that I can spare*" (with which that breath was released). "You are also a master of procedures, formalities and rituals, and therefore ideally qualified for the task. As for your being unfamiliar with the East, I shall give you a traveling companion who is only too familiar with the court of Neopolis: the eunuch Florianus!"

That came like lightning out of a blue sky.

Suddenly Florianus had no wind left in his body, and his head spun. He barely heard the chortling and the bemused comments, or the protestations from Senator Necro.

"No, that's ridiculous!"

"I assure you that it isn't, Senator. It's not ridiculous at all. The eunuch once served Quintilianus Asper, who is now Master of Horse and Foot and, as we all know, the most powerful man in the Eastern Empire. Our Ogilo, so to speak, though of somewhat better breeding. And Master Florianus speaks the Eto fluently."

The Eto was the common tongue of the Eastern Empire; it had few similarities with the Citizens' Tongue.

"As do I!"

Florianus doubted that very much—Necro's knowledge of the Eto could only have come from the study of Eastern legal texts.

"Assuredly, Senator, assuredly. But he will be able to give you full support. Are these not sufficient reasons for including our little friend in the delegation?"

Necro was still indignant.

"A eunuch! A grotesque half-man!"

That really was too much. What a bastard! At the first opportunity, Florianus decided, he would slip a little something into Necro's food, a powder to cause him dizzy spells, or a condiment that would make him foul himself uncontrollably.

"You will both have your duties to fulfill. While you, Senator, are discussing essential details of courtly and matrimonial etiquette"—Naevius made little effort to mask the contempt in his voice—"the eunuch will be looking for answers to other, less pressing questions. Such as: are our Eastern cousins paying the Blood-Drinkers to ravage our borders? Are they supporting the Placidi? Where is Issachar of Maritima, and what role is he playing in our troubles?"

With a start Florianus realized that he was being offered, despite the fiasco of the bride-show, a second chance to bestride the great stage of public affairs, and to change the course of history. What eunuch had ever been granted such an opportunity *twice*? But did he have the nerve for it?

"My Lord, you honor me."

"No, no, just do your job, eunuch. When you return, we'll find you something more commensurate with your abilities than your present, er, position here at the Palace, under Julian" (unpleasant laughter). "Why not, for example, a position of responsibility at the City Prefecture? He could run your secretariat for you, Lentulus!"

That would be a huge opportunity for Florianus. The City Prefect was old and incompetent, and whoever ran his secretariat would be able to wield power throughout the city.

Necro was still protesting vehemently.

"You are sending me off to the East with just a eunuch and a bagful of diplomatic gifts?"

"Oh no, Senator, you will have a grandiose entourage. And I was even considering sending two other Senators with you, to represent the Blues and the Greens. It's all a question of balancing the factions in outward appearance."

Necro nodded sagely.

"If I might make so bold as to put forward the names of one or two eminently suitable colleagues—"

Naevius cut in, before the names of which Blue and Green Senators met with Necro's approval could be revealed.

"That was what I was considering. But then I had a visit today from Senator Lucius Atticus."

"The Green? Well, yes, but do you really think…?"

Lucius Atticus was undoubtedly not one of the names that had been on the tip of Necro's tongue.

"Lucius Pomponius Atticus: he's an important man. He is currently the sole leader of the Green faction, since Terebinthian is sulking and won't talk to anyone."

Quintus cleared his throat loudly.

"Flabby-guts will talk to *me*, father. Just give the word, and I'll have him here yelping loudly enough to wake the dead. But what did that scumbag Lucius Atticus want? And are you really thinking of sending *him*?"

"He came on behalf of his nephew, the wastrel who calls himself Aulus Atticus. He wants his nephew to pursue a Senatorial career after all, and asked me whether there might be a junior magistracy available for him, or some other public service duty. Actually, I think he is frightened that the boy's intimacy with Sextus Placidus could place him in danger. He's not on any of your lists, is he, Quintus?"

Quintus grunted unpleasantly.

"He *might* be."

"Oh dear, we can't have that! Don't forget that his father is also a respected Senator—and a Lord Governor, and a Blue. We can't let anything happen to the lad just because of the dubious company that he keeps. Or because his uncle is a nuisance. I told Lucius Atticus that I would consider his request, and then the happy idea came to me: let us send the boy to Neopolis! To keep him out of harm's way."

"You mean: to keep the little shit out of *my* way, father."

Naevius ignored his son's remark.

"Young Atticus will accompany you, Necro, and in doing so represent *both* the other factions, his father's and his uncle's. It'll cost us much less than sending two fully-fledged Senators. An elegant solution, don't you agree? What's that old Sybarite saying? To skewer two Citizens with one spear-thrust? Such a charming image. Of course, the brat doesn't know of his good fortune yet."

VI

AULUS HAS VISITORS, SOME MORE WELCOME THAN OTHERS

The house of Senator Lucius Pomponius Atticus, in the City.

When the first visitors came, Aulus had not exactly "retired for the night" because, although darkness had fallen, it was not really night-time yet, and he was in any case much more of an owl than a lark. But ever since the day of the bride-show he had been depressed, and frightened. He knew that his friends were being hunted, and his comfortable world had been turned upside down.

The City had always been a violent place. Now the violence had stretched out its claws beyond the slums and the tenements. It had reached into the wealthier quarters of the capital, where the richest Citizens had their villas and spacious town-houses and where (until now) they had enjoyed relaxed lives of leisure and security.

Wealth was no longer a protection. It hadn't saved the merchant Labienus, a Sybarite business partner of the Placidi, whose vulgar palace had spread across the lower part of the hill where the smaller, more sedate mansion of Lucius Pomponius Atticus also stood. The mob had torched the buildings, after dragging the miserable Labienus out onto the street.

Aulus had heard the screaming, high-pitched above the baying of the mob. Did it come from the fleshy Labienus, or from one of his unfortunate slaves?

"Can't we help him, uncle? You're a Senator."

Lucius Atticus had turned away, so that Aulus didn't see his face.

"No. Anyone from Sybaris is a target now. We must try to keep our Sybarite slaves inside the house. I can't help Labienus—he was proscribed."

"How can you be so sure, uncle? He's just a merchant. He isn't a Senator."

"I know that he's on the list, Aulus, because I put my name to it, for the Greens."

"*You* signed the proscription list?"

"Yes, I signed it. One of us had to. It should have been Terebinthian, but he made himself unavailable. Very convenient for him, too. I suppose he's shaping what the history books of the future will write about him. And what will they write about me?" Still keeping his face averted, he added, in a whisper that Aulus could barely hear: "Just let it be, Faustus, I'm not proud of myself."

He had used Aulus's real name, Faustus. Davus the secretary took the young master's arm and led him away from his uncle.

"Please try to understand him, sir. He's very ashamed, but he had to do it. And better to *sign* the list than be on it! He did it to keep all of us safe."

Davus would always take his uncle's side. The freedman had total faith in his former master. Aulus wished that he had someone like that in his life, someone who would trust him and look up to him. What had he done to deserve it, though?

A few hours later Beltran the footman came to wake him, cursing as he stumbled over a pile of Aulus's clothes. The young master had thrown them on the floor just inside the door of his sleeping cubicle. Beltran was the most recent in a line of house-slaves delegated to look after the chaotic young man after Decimus, his personal servant, had been freed. It was the least coveted job in the orderly household of Lucius Atticus.

"Wake up, master! Wake up!"

Aulus was only half-asleep. He struggled into a sitting position. Beltran was already holding out his clothes, offering to help him dress.

There was no lamp lit yet in his cubicle, but light came in from outside.

"Let *me* help him, Beltran!"

Aulus tried to focus his eyes. Oh no, it was Sinica! What was she doing there? Why her of all people? He tried to wave her away. Or was he simply imagining it? Was he still asleep, and this was a nightmare?

But now he heard the sounds from the street. The mob had come.

"Master, please, you must go the door, before they break it down."

"Where is the Senator?"

The master had been called to a meeting at the Palace, Beltran said, and had not yet returned.

"Oh. And Davus?"

Davus would know how to deal with this, even though he was only a freedman.

Davus had accompanied his master.

Esbus! Demons from the Pit of Damnation! If only Decimus were there… He *always* knew what to do.

Why me? Aulus thought. Why can't they leave me in peace? This was Labienus all over again. Horrific pictures flashed through his mind. More than anything else he wanted to hide under the sleeping couch until they all went away. Or until someone came who knew what to do.

"*Please*, master, there is only you." Beltran's eyes were boring into him. "If you don't speak to them, they will burn the house down."

"Why should they listen to me?"

"Because your father is a Blue. They will respect that."

Naturally! His father—the bosom friend of Naevius! Whether by wisdom or by chance, Beltran had chosen the only words capable of giving Aulus a touch of courage. Perhaps he could do it after all? His father's name would surely protect him! He waved Beltran away, dressed himself and stumbled through the house to confront his fate.

Servo the gatekeeper stood, trembling with indignation, beside the great wooden door that let out onto the street. With one hand he gripped his spear, with the other he restrained his old mastiff. Despite being nearly toothless, the dog was growling impressively. Servo had opened a tiny picket window in the door, and must have exchanged words and perhaps abuse with the crowd gathered outside.

"Open the door, Servo!"

Aulus could hardly believe he was saying that. If Fannia could only see him now: Aulus the hero! He didn't turn round, but he knew that the house-slaves would be assembled behind him, watching everything he did. He was their last hope. If the house was stormed by the mob, none of them would be spared. There would be rape and murder as well as looting, before the house went up in flames.

Servo hesitated, until Beltran whispered something to him. Then, putting down his spear and entrusting the mastiff to Beltran, he did as the young master had told him. With a great creaking and groaning the massive door swung open, and Aulus stepped out onto the street.

Illuminated by the flickering of torches, the mob was smaller than he had expected. He saw no uniforms, no military weapons. There was no commanding officer. There were even women among them. They were just a crowd of scummy people from the slums, stinking of sweat and alcohol and waving improvised weapons like butchers' knives and sharpened wooden stakes.

When they became aware of Aulus, they began jeering. One man stepped forward.

"Well well, who do we have *here*?"

Was he their leader? He was broad and thickset, with a dirty, scarred face and a low forehead. He was much shorter than Aulus—would that make him more dangerous, or less?—and he was twitching nervously.

Aulus tried to sound impressive.

"I am Faustus Pomponius Atticus, son of the Lord Governor of the North, who is a Senator of the Blues"—at this point his voice cracked—"and a personal friend of Lord Naevius."

The man laughed.

"I know who you are, sonny! And I don't see any fucking Blue Senators round here." He turned to his friends. "Do you see any Blue Senators?"

"Nah!"

"What I see is a fucking faggot who hides behind his big Blue daddy." He leered up into Aulus's face. "And sucks Red cock."

"What?!"

"You've got Sextus Placidus in there, haven't you? You're hiding that cunt in your house! He's on our list. Bring him out, or my boys'll go in and fetch him!"

"What list? I don't see any list. Show me the list!" (That was stupid—why did he say that? He must be panicking.)

The mob had been quieter while their leader was speaking. Now they started baying and jeering again. Oh, they would definitely show him something, the pansy boy. They would stick it right up him, and it wouldn't be a list! Their fun was about to begin…

Suddenly the crowd swayed forward slightly, as if it was being augmented, or pushed from behind. Aulus took a step backwards. Then he saw the reason.

Another group of men with torches had come up behind the mob. Some of them were in uniform, and carrying spears: they were Prefectural police. And he recognized his uncle, and Davus. Sol be praised!

Now his uncle was speaking. He could be impressive without even trying.

"I take it that you are the spokesman for these good people? Do you have any legal authorization to threaten my property? Or to intimidate my nephew?"

There were a few isolated shouts from the back of "Green cunt!" and similar, but the leader of the mob was respectful.

"We are looking for Sextus Placidus, my Lord. You know who that is, don't you? We have reason to think he may be in your house. He's on our list."

"No, he's not on your list. Because you don't have a list, young man. *I* have a list. I put my name to it, along with my colleagues Marcus Naevius and Quintus Naevius. Yes, Sextus Placidus is on that list, and I give you my solemn word that I would never shelter him in my home. Now, take your friends and leave, so that loyal Citizens can go to bed and get some sleep."

The Prefectural guards brandished their spears. Servo had also come out onto the street. He was by far the biggest and angriest man in sight.

There was some more abuse and threats from the mob, but not as loud or self-confident as before, and emanating from the safety of the second or third row. The thugs began to drift away. This time they had been frustrated, but there would be other victims. The night was not over yet. Within an hour or so they would be taking out their disappointment on some poor creature in a neighboring street.

The Senator thanked the guardsmen for providing him with an escort. No, they could leave now, it would not be necessary for them to watch the house. Then he led Aulus and Davus inside.

"We'll go to the library. Beltran can bring us wine."

Inside the entrance the house-slaves were still gathered, wide-eyed and trembling. The Senator thanked them for their loyalty, singled out Servo for particular praise, and told them to return to their duties, or their beds.

"This has not been a good day," he said, after Beltran had served their wine and left them. "Terrible things have been done, yet we really had no choice. If only the General were here! But he can't leave the frontier, and Quintus and his bullies know that they can do whatever they like until he returns." He added, in a quieter voice: "You know what they say: when the dogs are loose, you run *with* them or *from* them."

He had no wish to discuss the proscription lists, and Aulus didn't press him. His uncle must be very tired, but he too was completely exhausted. The life of action was not for him! He begged the Senator to excuse him.

There was one more thing, his uncle said. He had spoken to Senator Naevius and requested a civic appointment for Aulus.

"But uncle—"

"Yes, I know. You don't want to go into the Senate. But this is for your safety. You will take whatever he offers you. It will make your parents very happy," he added, with a slight note of bitterness in his voice. "The choice of faction is yours, of course, though I would recommend your father's party, the Blues. For obvious reasons."

Aulus returned to his sleeping cubicle and put himself to bed, without troubling any of the slaves. He slept uneasily, dreaming of men with torches rushing about on dark streets looking for someone. Were they looking for him?

For the second time that night he was shaken awake.

"No, Beltran, let me sleep. I can't do it. Isn't my uncle there?"

"Your uncle needs you, sir. In the library."

It wasn't Beltran, it was Davus.

"Have they come back?"

He couldn't hear anything. The house was quiet. It must be deep into the night. Even Servo and his dog would probably be asleep.

"We have visitors. And your uncle needs you."

Davus escorted him to the library. The Senator, wearing a house-robe flung over his nightgown, was pacing up and down. Against the long wall of shelving for stacking the scrolls stood their visitors, three cloaked and hooded figures: Sextus Placidus, Cornelia, and—Fannia!

"This is my house, Aulus, but these are *your* visitors. Sextus Placidus is not welcome here, and I have given my word that he will not be sheltered under this roof. As soon as he has eaten, and if the street outside is still empty, he will be leaving. Only Servo has seen him. You understand? *Sextus Placidus has not been here tonight.*"

Aulus was horrified.

"Uncle! You can't drive them away: you've seen what's happening out there on the streets."

Sextus took a step forward. Under the hood, his face was caked with soot or dirt, but his eyes were gleaming.

"Don't worry, Aulus. I'll take my chances. And I have to look for someone. I found these two, but my sister is still out there, and in greater danger. Because of her name. Which happens to be my name as well."

"Uncle, say something! Do something!"

"No, he is right. He can't stay here—it's a question of personal honor. And if your name was Placidus and you had a sister, you would be out on the streets searching for her too. That would be a matter of *your* honor. Yes, I know you would do that, Aulus. I saw tonight how brave you can be."

Aulus hung his head. He wasn't so sure about how brave or honorable he was. But he said to Sextus: "I'll help you, I'll come with you!"

Sextus and the Senator said "No!" simultaneously, and Sextus added, "You can't help me tonight, but one day you will be able to, I'm sure of that."

The two young women were bedraggled, and besmirched with dirt. Fannia looked resolute; Cornelia was sniffling quietly.

As if he could read his nephew's thoughts, the Senator said, "The two girls can stay here, under my protection. Lady Cornelia's father is being held at the Palace, but for the time being his life is not in danger. Her mother has left the City and is now in safety, I hope."

Cornelia collapsed into a heap of sobbing misery, and Fannia bent down to comfort her. Before Aulus could speak, she said, "Your uncle is a noble gentleman. Both his gods and Cornelia's will reward his courage!"

The Senator reached out and patted her shoulder.

"I doubt it, my dear. And this is not a gesture, but a calculation. Naevius needs the General, which means that he needs *me*. I say, again: for the time being. Perhaps we must all learn such a new way of living: to live just for today, for the moment, and take tomorrow as it comes."

Cornelia looked up at him, with tear-filled eyes.

"We must learn to trust in the Slave!"

"Yes, my dear, this is a time for trust. And for courage. I trust all of you, and I trust my slaves, but sooner or later Naevius will find out where you are. So for that reason I shall tell him tomorrow, quite openly, that you are here, and that I am holding the two of you under house-arrest."

"Uncle, you are condemning them both to death…"

"No, only male members of the Red families have been proscribed. Since all the property of Red Senators that is within reach is being confiscated, the problem of their wives and daughters—out on the streets, unprotected, without money, hunted by the mob—that problem will I fear resolve itself very quickly. He will let you stay here, Cornelia, because that gives him a hold over *me*. And he doesn't need you, because he already has your father." Then to Fannia: "You, on the other hand, are a person of no consequence to him. But don't be offended, my dear—be truly grateful for that!"

Sinica would show them to a room where they could sleep, and find them clean clothes. Some water would be heated for them to wash with; tomorrow, the bath-house would be at their disposal.

The Senator had some news for Aulus, but it could wait until the morning. He wished the young people a good night, and left.

Sextus and Fannia embraced tearfully. Aulus, who could no longer look his friend in the eye for shame, slipped away back to his room. He threw off his clothes and lay on the sleeping couch, thoroughly miserable and unwilling to confront the thoughts going through his head. Sleep, when it came, was a relief.

Much later that night he was woken for the third time. Someone had come into the sleeping cubicle with a lamp, and placed it in the corner of the room. A figure loomed over him.

"Uh?"

"Shh! Move over, and be quiet. We don't want to wake the slaves."

It was Fannia. She slipped under the blankets with him. She was naked.

"What…what are you doing?"

"You're a sweetie, Aulus. You're a brave, kind man. I've seen the way you stare at me! I just thought I'd say thank you in my own way."

"But…Sextus?"

"Sextus doesn't need to know…" She giggled. "Or Cornelia. That girl is quite keen on you. Now, my dear…"

She took his hand and guided it to all the places that he had dreamed about so many times. He felt the large, firm breasts; he moulded the roundness of her bottom; he discovered the treasure waiting for him between her plump, soft thighs.

"Oh, Fannia," he gasped as she placed his fingers inside her.

"Take it, Aulus, it's all yours. Whatever you want. However you want me."

The gates of paradise were wide open. And the sword was ready.

He moved on top of her.

But it didn't work. Somehow the couch was too narrow, his knee kept on slipping off on one side or the other.

"I don't think…"

"Shh. Let *me* go on top."

She pulled him round so that their positions were reversed. It should have solved the problem, but it didn't. Suddenly, his weapon was unprepared for battle. She massaged him, but too vigorously. It didn't help.

"That's not so good."

"I can see that, Aulus! I'm not stupid. Very well, let's try something different. You can take me from behind, like a boy." She turned away from him and got on her hands and knees, offering him the delightful sight of her bottom. "Is that better?"

"Oh yes."

It might indeed be easier if he couldn't feel her looking at him.

But it wasn't better. Esbus, what was wrong with him?

"Oh, come on, Aulus, just do it! You must have fucked a boy or two! Hey, do you prefer boys? That might be the problem. Of course, if you really want to—"

Nothing helped, and everything she said only made it worse.

"I'm sorry, Fannia. It's been a long day…"

They lay side by side, not wanting to touch but holding on to each other to avoid falling off the couch.

"Never mind. Perhaps you're just not such a gifted swordsman as Sextus. You know, he doesn't only write about all those things, he does them too! No, don't cry. You're a sweet boy, and we're so grateful. Cornelia will say thank you, too. Not like this, of course! Oh, Aulus, don't be upset. We can try again some time, if you like. Naturally, you mustn't tell Sextus, you know he's awfully fond of you."

"Yes."

His whole body was stiff—except for the small part that had needed to be.

"Very well, I think I should be getting back to Cornelia. I hope she's still asleep."

"Yes."

All he wanted was for this to be over.

She got up off the couch and retrieved the lamp. After she had left the room he hid himself under the blanket and sobbed bitterly. He was so ashamed of himself, and disappointed.

But there was even worse to come.

Again someone slipped under the blanket with him, and held him expertly in her arms. It was Sinica!

"There, there, master. We all love you. You were so wonderful to-night."

She held him, and caressed him, tenderly smoothing away the hurt that he felt. He felt safe, and loved. Her hands roamed gently over his body, and in response his moved over hers until—oh, the dreadful shame of it!—everything that he had wanted to do with Fannia he did with the slave-girl, not once, but twice, before he fell asleep in her arms.

When he awoke the next morning he was alone, deeply confused, and with a terrible headache. Beltran came to dress him, and told him that his uncle asked to speak to him—urgently. He was waiting for the young master on the summer breakfast terrace.

Aulus prayed to Sol and any other gods who might be listening that Fannia wouldn't be there. And that Sinica wouldn't be serving the breakfast. He wasn't sure which of them he would *less* like to see. He couldn't face the embarrassment.

He had no wish to see Cornelia either.

Fortunately, none of them were there. Nor was there any breakfast on offer. Instead, his uncle served him up two surprises.

The smaller surprise was the news from the night before: the news that could wait. Yet another fire-beacon message had arrived from Aulus's father, and Lucius Atticus was working himself up into a fury about it.

"Really, my brother is abusing the system. In Sol's name, to send us a list of slaves! The fire-beacon is intended for urgent messages about military matters and affairs of state, not tittle-tattle! Bad enough when he sends us personal news like his last message, even though that was short and cryptic. But now, now that his friend Naevius is running the show here in the City, he believes that he can send us detailed gossip, every day, just as he pleases! "

"What does my father want?"

Aulus asked politely, though he had no interest in what his father might or might not have to say to him. His life was falling apart, and he felt ashamed of himself, and useless, and worthless. No breakfast was being served, and for once he didn't care.

"It is about those 'two presents' that were on their way to you. Such an important matter! Huh! They're not wedding gifts. Castor, his secretary—do you remember him?"

"Yes, certainly I do."

"Castor has died, and bequeathed you his two slaves. Their names are Phrygillus and Mara. And *that* news requires a fire-beacon message across half the Empire? Really, I ask you! Whatever next?"

Half the Empire was a slight exaggeration, though his uncle did have a point.

So—Aulus was about to become a slave-owner. So what? How would that solve his problems?

His uncle rambled on. Strictly speaking, as head of the family his father would have been within his rights to retain the slaves for his own use, but he had behaved honorably in respecting Castor's wishes.

Aulus was barely listening.

What were those names again?

"Phrygillus." He hadn't seen Castor for many years, but he remembered that the secretary had resolutely preferred the company of men. Whatever it was he had got up to with them, or they with him, it had been done discreetly. Phrygillus would probably be a handsome young male attendant, graceful, tactful, well-trained and accustomed to looking after his master's daily needs.

He might be a good replacement for Beltran! A slave who would fuss over his clothes and belongings and make himself useful about the house. (Aulus wouldn't ask more of him than that, it went without saying.) His uncle could hardly disapprove of such an addition to his household.

But "Mara"? What sort of name was that? It was a woman's name, and it sounded distinctly barbaric to Aulus. But why should Castor have needed a female slave, in a house that was full of maids and cooks? And what would the fastidious, highly-educated secretary have wanted with a barbarian? Especially some hairy monster like those Sueni women you saw working in the cheap wineshops.

Had he won her at dice? Or in betting on races at the hippodrome? Castor hadn't been known to gamble, and even more than Davus he had never had patience with those who wasted their time in trivial pursuits.

Oh, what did it matter anyway?

Lucius Atticus must have noticed that his nephew had stopped paying attention. He broke off his rant about the Lord Governor and announced that he would now tell Aulus the far more important piece of news, which affected him directly.

And *that* surprise was massive.

A courier from the Palace had brought instructions. Aulus was to report there at once. Faustus Pomponius Atticus Junior, young adult male of the Senatorial Class, resident in the City and of no known permanent occupation, was required to fulfill his "civic duty". He would be leaving the City almost immediately, as a member of a delegation to the East.

The gods had indeed been listening. With a vengeance.

VII

DECIMUS IS GIVEN A NEW TASK

The Great Provincial Road, and Maidunum.

A few hours north of Maidunum, Decimus caught up with a detachment of Citizen soldiers who were heading in the same direction. Sore from riding so far, and with his destination so close, Decimus allowed himself the luxury of dismounting and walking for a stretch. Leading his horse, he marched alongside the commanding Sub-officer, who seemed not averse to some conversation.

Senex was a battle-scarred veteran of the Eleventh, one of the divisions stationed on the Northern Shore. Decimus introduced himself as a low-ranking member of the General's staff.

What were they doing so far south, he asked? They were marching fast, with no wagons, only a line of pack-mules for their tents and gear. Had they been sent to join the army that the General was gathering to confront the Blood-Drinkers?

It was no secret: the news had soon spread that word had gone out to all the Lord Commanders in the cold north to come at once. They were to bring every division that they had, leaving behind only auxiliaries and naval forces. If stripping the Northern Shore of its regular troops meant letting in the pirates and raiders, so be it. The pampered settlers had enjoyed the protection of the eagle's wing for long enough—let them now see to their own defences.

Senex grunted, and spat out whatever it was that he was chewing.

"Every division, eh? Does this look like a division to you, young man? It's barely half a unit. No, we set off a week earlier, before the order came through. The rest will now be on their way, sure, but these lads won't be rejoining them."

Decimus had been engaging in polite conversation, but now he became genuinely curious.

The Sub-officer explained that there had been constant fighting between some of the units in the Eleventh. Only the young men, not the veterans. Everywhere you went, young men were always the same. There wasn't a lot to do in camp, the local whores weren't up to much, and the weather was always shit up there in the far north. For the older men it was different: you had a nice girl of your own and some kids and your loyal mates around you, guys that you'd served with for fifteen years or more.

"The lads were bored, right? Our pirate friends were quiet after the last sea-battle, you remember, when they lost half their ships? The land was peaceful for once. Life was quiet. You couldn't really expect the youngsters to just sit around, could you? Young men need action."

When the message arrived asking for volunteers willing to transfer to the Ninth, because that division's numbers were down, Lord Commander Ovidius had used the opportunity, picked out the worst of the hotheads and told them: "You're volunteering! And Sub-officer Senex here will take you to your new home. Don't fight on the way, though— save that for your new mates!" And they'd been as bright and cheerful as Sol's golden helmet ever since.

"But if you'd waited…?"

Senex spat again, even more ferociously.

"Then we could've marched together, the whole division, and we'd be staying together too. You know, we met some cavalry on the road and they told us about the marching orders that had gone out. Fuck! I didn't say a word, mind you, but when they'd ridden on, I picked out one of the boys—that grinning idiot at the back, I can always find a good excuse for laying into *him*—and I kicked the crap out of him. He's used to it though."

"But aren't you pleased? For Sol's sake! You're getting rid of your hotheads, and after you've said goodbye to them you'll soon be back with your old division."

"You're not really a military man, are you, Decimus?"

"No."

"Do you think, once we've settled in, that our new Company-commander is going to let me go back to my old division? He's getting my boys, *and* the guy who trained them and knows how to handle them. His lucky day!"

"But what's wrong with staying in the Province? You know: the place where the living is easy? Where fruit falls off the trees straight into your mouth? It never gets too hot, but the sun shines nearly every day? The wine is better than drinkable? And the girls aren't crazy barbarians? That sounds pretty good to me!"

"Oh, nothing much. Just this: I've got a woman and two little girls back on the North Shore. We stay away too long, and they'll find themselves another daddy. And next year some pirate may be raping them anyway. No. When we've sorted out the fucking Blood-Drinkers, and my division goes back, I want to go with them." He paused. "That's reason enough, isn't it?"

"Yes, that's a good reason," Decimus said, adding, with an exaggerated show of ruefulness, "I haven't got a woman, and I haven't got any kids." Let the man feel sorry for him—that might take his mind off his own problems!

Even if Decimus had wanted to, his work for the General wouldn't allow him to settle down—he didn't say that, though.

For a while they marched on without talking.

Senex finally spoke, blurting out: "And there's another reason: it's the *Ninth* we're talking about here! The fucking Ninth, may their dicks drop off!"

The "Unlucky Ninth" had the worst reputation of any division in the Citizen Army. Even the "non-military man" Decimus knew that. No other division had suffered so many defeats. No other division had "mislaid" its standards so often. No other division had been in so many "tactical withdrawals".

It was no coincidence that since the time of Maximus the Great the Ninth had been stationed in the Province, which was the cushiest posting in the Western Empire. There were no barbarians to worry about, no throat-slitting Sybarite rebels, no pirates. Just routine police work— knocking heads together when some local festival like the Day of the Two Riders or the Feast of the Horned One got too lively.

"And your boys don't know about the Ninth?"

"Of course they do! But *they* don't care. They think about all that other stuff, you know, what you just said: food, and sunshine, and the girls. They're not proper soldiers yet. I *am*, and I do care. I don't want to end my soldiering days ashamed to tell anyone which division I was in."

The Sub-officer called a halt, and the soldiers stepped to the side of the road to rest for a few minutes, stacking their shields, spears and javelins in best regulation Citizen Army fashion. *He* might not be happy with them, Decimus thought to himself, but, Sol, his young soldiers were fit and well-disciplined! He'd seen far worse.

There was dust rising nearby. Decimus noticed it first, and pointed it out to the Sub-officer.

"Hey," he said, "I don't like that. I don't like that one little bit." Then he yelled "Back into formation! *Now!*"

His men were not yet back in line when there was a "ping!" as an arrow glanced off someone's armor. Then another. And then a loud scream. One of the men had taken an arrow to the neck. Shields went up, just in time, as the first riders charged up on their shaggy ponies and released more arrows into the soldiers' midst from close range.

"Tortoise!" the Sub-officer shouted, and to Decimus: "Get behind them! Stay down!"

The soldiers created the famous shield formation—their bodies were now fully protected.

"Hedgehog!" he yelled, and the formation bristled with spears.

Decimus, sheltering behind the soldiers but outside their shield-wall, realized that his life wouldn't be worth a Maximian if they were surrounded and attacked from all sides. He knew how to fight—oh yes, Sub-officer Senex would be astounded to see how well!—but his sword was of no use in this situation, and he had no shield with which to ward off arrows.

Fortunately, it was only a small raiding party of scavengers, a mere handful of riders. There were too few of them to carry out the fearsome maneuver that the Blood-Drinkers often practiced, where two circles of horsemen would ride around their foes in opposite directions, shooting arrows quickfire into their ranks. Even the shield-walls of the Citizen soldiers had been known to crumble under such an onslaught.

The soldiers' formation was impressive, but purely defensive. They massively outnumbered their attackers, but couldn't reach them. Their spears weren't for throwing, and they couldn't hurl their shorter javelins very effectively while the shields were locked together. The Blood-Drinkers for their part were keeping out of spear-range and trying to pick off the soldiers with arrows.

It was like that point in a board-game where neither player is able to win, but neither is willing to give up.

The stalemate was ended by the arrival of a troop of Sueni cavalry. With much whooping and hollering and ineffective brandishing of swords they galloped up to the Blood-Drinkers from behind. The troopers' horses towered over their enemies' steeds, but the little ponies were nimble-footed and the Blood-Drinkers were easily able to escape, even releasing a few parting shots as they left.

Not a single one of the attackers had been killed. Two Sueni troopers had managed to fall off their horses, one of them injuring himself quite badly. The pack-mules had ambled away, followed by Decimus's horse; it took a while to round them up again. That was good luck, since normally the Blood-Drinkers would have stolen the horse, and killed or hamstrung the pack-mules (unless they were carrying something of value).

Several of the soldiers had minor injuries, and the one who had taken an arrow in the neck was dead.

He was a follower of the Slave, Senex said, so his body must be taken to Maidunum, where there might be a priest, a Slave Man, to perform the obsequies. (Or maybe not, thought Decimus: the people of the Province still worshiped the old gods, who had been there long before Sol the Radiant or the Blessed Slave.)

The Sub-officer was really angry.

"Shit! He was one of my best men—we can't afford to lose men like him."

And he was annoyed by the way the Sueni troop-commander kept on congratulating himself for having saved the Citizen Army once again.

"See?" he said, twirling at the ends of his mustache, "I pull your meat out of the fire for you real good!"

Then he and his men rode off, leaving behind the injured trooper, who would have to be transported to Maidunum for medical treatment on a pack-mule.

A few hours later they saw their destination glinting in the distance, and soon afterwards they reached the outskirts of the huge tented encampment of the Ninth Division. Decimus took his leave of Sub-officer Senex, introduced himself to the guards at the gate of the city, and was informed that the General was at the city hall.

Maidunum, "the city of gilded porticoes", wasn't a favorite of his, despite its excellent libraries. He liked it even less than he liked Fanum Fortunae. While Fanum was a straightforward, modest place (with plenty to be modest about), Maidunum's inhabitants gave themselves preposterous airs. Their city was no better than a dusty market town, and it wasn't even a provincial capital like Fanum.

What Maidunum did have was a fancy academy. Many generations ago, scholars and learned Senators fleeing from the mad cruelties of Severian the Evil had taken refuge in the little town. For want of anything better to do, they had set up a School of Higher Studies there that soon became renowned.

That was *then*. Today, Maidunum lived off its ancient reputation, and the commercial aspect was paramount. The School attracted the sons of Senators or wealthy merchants to its expensive courses in philosophy, rhetoric and mathematics. Young Aulus had briefly been a student there, which is how Decimus had come to know (and dislike) the place. Its most famous son in modern times was the windbag Terebinthian—which as far as Decimus was concerned said absolutely everything that you needed to know about Maidunum—and many of the professors currently teaching there had been contemporaries of his as students.

For reasons no-one understood, the northernmost city of the Province received very little rain. It was an uninviting dust bowl in a region otherwise known for its lush farmlands and pleasant little country towns. Maidunum was both emphatically Green and close to the North, which made it a good place for Ogilo to set up his campaign headquarters.

The General was staying at the villa of a wealthy Green supporter, but a meeting had been called at the city hall to welcome and to negotiate with a delegation from the capital. Was that seen as being more neutral ground? By the time that Decimus had reached the hall and passed through a sequence of security checkpoints, he found that the meeting had already begun.

Ogilo acknowledged his arrival in the crowded conference room with a barely perceptible nod, and Decimus took up a standing position by the side wall, from where he had a good view of both parties. He had learned always to take in as much information about a new situation as he possibly could. One day it could mean the difference between life and death.

The General was flanked by two Lord Commanders, neither of whom Decimus recognized. Lord Rhaetius wasn't present; nor, unexpectedly, was Aulus's father. Was that an intentional snub? The Lord Governor and the General were known to destest each other. Or had Ogilo sent word that the Lord Governor's attendance wasn't needed (what contribution could Pomponius Atticus make, beyond getting on everyone's nerves?).

The men ranged to the General's left and right, or standing behind him, were also unfamiliar to Decimus. Judging by their dress some of them were Staff Officers, while the rest were plainly civilians. Some of the latter would be advisors; others would be officials responsible for finance, supplies and suchlike bureaucratic matters, perhaps freedmen like himself.

Sitting opposite the General were the members of the delegation. In the middle was an arrogant, hawk-nosed face that Decimus recognized at once: the Blue Senator Marcus Vulpeculus. Now that *wasn't* a surprise. Since Naevius couldn't risk leaving the City himself, he had sent the best man that he had. Not his thuggish son, not the doddery City Prefect, or his equally doddery brother Lentulus Pulcher, but the cunning and ruthless Vulpeculus.

Next to him sat the tall, thin figure of the White Senator Terentius Ager, a nonentity even by the standards of the Senate. All three factions that were in alliance against the Placidi were thus represented at the meeting.

The other members of the delegation were presumably secretaries.

The introductory greetings and formalities were already over, and Marcus Vulpeculus was now elucidating the details of a contract that he had likely brought with him and which lay on the small table between the two parties. Decimus noticed how, every time that he came to a point that was more controversial, his upper lip twitched slightly.

"That you will remain Master of Horse and Foot, with total command of all the armies of the Western Empire, goes without saying," he announced smugly. "Although I *am* saying it, General. I am saying it loudly, and in public, so that there be no misunderstandings among those who are unable to see the written agreement."

Ogilo smiled sweetly.

"Yes, it goes without saying, Senator—unless you yourself were planning to take the field against the Blood-Drinkers? Or your master? No? I thought not. So that unenviable task will continue to be *my* burden."

"But perhaps you are missing the point, General? The supreme military command will remain yours even after you have crushed and annihilated the barbarians."

The Senator's upper lip had twitched. Decimus translated: the supreme military command will remain yours after you have dealt with the barbarians for us but only until we have an opportunity to murder you.

"The agreement," Ogilo replied smoothly, "does no more than reflect the realities of the present situation."

Decimus noted how neither man was prepared to address the other as "my Lord". It was well known that there was no great love lost between them.

"Indeed, General, and exactly the same can be said with regard to the next point, namely, that Senator Naevius is with immediate effect to become Imperial Guardian. Firstly, because his Imperial Majesty will soon be marrying into his family, and, secondly, in order to guarantee the security of the capital against the southern rebels, since as you know the militias under his control are the only military force of substantial size presently in the City." He added: "You will notice, General, that I am quoting almost word for word from the document in front of you."

He had barely finished speaking when there was an outbreak of angry shouts and incredulous laughter from the men facing him. Even the General, a man not given to emotional outbursts, was smiling and shaking his head.

The Lord Commander to his left had gone beetroot-red and looked as if he was about to burst.

"Militias? What fucking cheek! How can you call those poxy bands of gangsters and petty criminals a military force? That is an insult to the Citizen Army!"

"No, come come, my Lord," Ogilo said, tapping the man's forearm gently. "What they call themselves, or how Senator Vulpeculus describes them in this document, which I imagine he himself formulated—"

Vulpeculus nodded in confirmation.

"I had some small part in the drafting of the agreement—"

"—or even how *we* choose to describe them now is of no importance."

"No?"

"Truly, my Lord, it isn't. What *is* of consequence is how they acquit themselves when the City comes under attack from the Placidi. Because until the Blood-Drinkers are turned back we will have no regular troops to spare for its defence."

The Lord Commander sat back, nodding in agreement. Momentarily Vulpeculus had looked uncomfortable, but he resumed again in his best lawyer manner.

"Wisely spoken, General! In these dangerous times we must keep hold of facts, and necessities, and not give way to partisan emotions, or resort to abuse." He paused. "Though I do have to say that I noticed that you too were...*amused*. Might I ask you why, General?"

Ogilo leant forward, no longer smiling.

"I have studied this text most carefully. If I might say so, it's a typical lawyer's contract, full of cunning traps for the innocent, and weasel words to confuse the well-meaning. The words don't matter to me, Senator. Like you, I prefer facts. And the facts are: you hold the City; my armies hold the north." Then he leant back, smiling again. "But I admit that I *was* slightly amused, Senator. Because for all your undoubted skill with words, your document has one serious flaw, an ambiguity that will cause confusion that benefits neither of us."

Vulpeculus stared at him.

"That text was drafted with great care, by experts..."

"Then let us see. How did it go? Ah, yes. 'Senator Naevius is with immediate effect to become Imperial Guardian. His Imperial Majesty will be marrying into his family.' Correct? You see, I know the contract too! I think I'm quoting more or less accurately from it. Well, Senator, as the text stands, it is likely to be understood as saying that Senator *Quintus* Naevius is to become Imperial Guardian. That would be logical, wouldn't it? He will soon be the Emperor's father-in-law, will he not? If that is *not* your intention, it's rather sloppy drafting, I have to say."

There were thumping gales of laughter from both sides of the room. Decimus was laughing too. The sheer thought of the brutal, loutish Quintus holding such a serious and dignified office was grotesque. But the mistake was understandable—it was easy to forget that Quintus, even though he never attended sessions of the Senate, was a Senator just like his father.

The only person who was not laughing was Marcus Vulpeculus. He was struggling to keep his emotions under control. The lip was twitching! He had been made to look ridiculous, and when they returned to the City Terentius Ager could be expected to tell all his friends about it, so that the whole Senate knew. Clever-boy Vulpeculus had made a fool of himself! It was an insult he would not quickly forgive or forget.

But Ogilo ignored the Senator's displeasure and insisted on pressing ahead with the minutiae of the agreement.

He accepted that swift action had needed to be taken by Senator Marcus Naevius to deal with the allies and supporters of the Placidi. The lives of all male members of the Placidus family were forfeit (though none had so far been apprehended). Agreed. However, all surviving Red Senators and their adult sons would merely remain in custody until the extent of their involvement in the events had been established. No more executions, therefore, without due process. Vulpeculus nodded. Their property was forfeit, yes, but their wives, daughters and underage sons would be allowed to leave, or to remain in the City if they could support themselves through honest labor. ("By working as whores?" someone asked.) There would be no need for further proscriptions.

Military matters were also discussed in some detail. The defence of the City should be coordinated between the Imperial Guardian, the City Prefect, and the Commander of the Imperial Guard. Quintus Naevius was not mentioned.

The worship of Lord Sol the Radiant would remain the official religion of the state, with his Imperial Majesty as Chief Servant of Sol. The High Priest of Sol and the High Priestess of Luna would continue to occupy privileged positions in public life and government. No special status was to be awarded to the Lesser Worship of the Blessed Slave, despite the clamor of its adherents. Vulpeculus frowned—his master would not be pleased with that, he pointed out—but made no further objection. Other religions might be practiced without disadvantage or interference.

For Decimus, the most interesting aspect of the whole discussion was the calm with which the General had accepted the loss of his position as Imperial Guardian. Had nobody else noticed how he had not advanced a single counter-argument, or made any protest? How could he not be angry? Naevius had seized control of the Emperor's person, and of the capital, in a violent coup, and there was no gainsaying that. These were facts that the General couldn't alter—for the moment. But, as they say, the game is not over until it's over.

A few changes needed to be made to the text (the belated insertion of the full name of Senator Marcus Naevius being the most important one).

The reconstitution of the Imperial Council was discussed. How should its role be defined? It was agreed that its role would be minimal. Affairs of state should be left to the two most powerful men in the state: the Imperial Guardian, and the Master of Horse and Foot.

The clerks and secretaries would work late into the night, revising the draft and preparing a number of identical copies: two for Naevius (one of which was to be sealed, the other left open), the same for the General and for each of the other members of the Council, and one sealed copy for the Imperial archive in the great Temple of Sol.

Next morning, all the copies would be checked and double-checked, and then the ones that were to be retained for legal reference would be closed with the personal seals of Vulpeculus (in his capacity as legal representative of the Senate and of the Imperial Guardian-to-be) and Ogilo (in his capacity as former Imperial Guardian and past-and-future Master of Horse and Foot).

The General's seal, taken from his signet ring, bore a standing lion; the Senator's showed the forepart of a fox, seen from the front. Vulpeculus suggested that they might also follow the newly fashionable procedure of signing their names in ink on every document, and the General concurred.

Under "any other business" Vulpeculus mentioned that a delegation was already on its way to Neopolis, to deliver an invitation to Emperor Theodore to attend the forthcoming Imperial wedding. It was purely a formality. No-one of any significance at the Eastern court was likely to take up the invitation.

"The delegation is led by my able colleague Gaius Ambibulus Necro of the Whites, accompanied by Faustus Pomponius Atticus."

Decimus was not the only person in the room who was puzzled. How could that possibly be? Lord Governor Pomponius Atticus was at Fanum Fortunae, surely? How could he be on his way to the East? Though that might explain his absence at the meeting.

No, it was the younger Faustus Atticus that he was referring to, the Senator's son. Or "Aulus Atticus", as he foolishly called himself.

"Ah, this time no-one can accuse you of inexact use of language, Senator!" Ogilo said with a laugh. "You gave us the boy's correct name, and we assumed, wrongly, that you meant the father, though that would have been most unlikely. So now we are even. But why Aulus Atticus? He's not a Senator yet."

Vulpeculus pointed out that, as the son of a Blue Senator and the nephew of a Green, young Atticus was of Senatorial status and could conveniently represent both the other factions.

"And so we avoid having to waste two further members of the Senate, in addition to Necro, on an expedition of such little consequence!"

Clever, the General agreed.

Decimus thought: how will poor Master Aulus survive? The journey will be long and exhausting, and he hates strenuous activity. And for weeks he'll be trapped with Necro, who'll bore him to death before they even reach their destination.

"Incidentally, talking about Aulus Atticus has reminded me of something, Senator." Ogilo turned to look in the direction of Decimus, and beckoned him to step forward. "This is Decimus, a freedman of that same young gentleman. He is now a trusted member of my staff, and will be accompanying you back to the City, to represent me there."

Vulpeculus was markedly displeased, and the discussion became more heated.

"Is that necessary, General? Your interests there are well-served by Senator Lucius Atticus, who will soon (we hope) be rejoined by his esteemed colleague Senator Terebinthian."

"No, you misunderstand me! Decimus won't be in the Senate, or on the Council. He'll be in the Palace. *That's* where he'll represent my interests."

"Ah, I understand now: he is to be your spy!"

"My dear Senator, that is hardly necessary. My spies in the Palace have already been in place for a long time." The expression on the Senator's face showed that he didn't find that funny. "No, don't be alarmed, Senator, I was only joking! Decimus will be your contact with me on practical matters. You will allow him to send me messages by fire-beacon—which you may read beforehand, of course, since, I repeat, he is not my spy—and he will bring you any information that is, let us say... too *sensitive* to be revealed to a wider audience."

"And what will his official function be? What reason do we give for his presence in the Palace?"

The General shrugged.

"That is entirely up to you. You might consider attaching him to the Imperial Guards as an advisor. He is skilled in matters of protection and security, and he knows several of the barbarian tongues. He is on good terms with Senator Lucius Atticus of the Greens, and he will be on his very best behavior, if that is what you are worried about."

Vulpeculus made no further comment, and the meeting came to an end.

Decimus had been given no forewarning of what the General intended for him. It would be a challenging task. To his mind, the Palace was the most unpredictable place in the world.

He was worried rather than frightened. Unpredictability meant danger, and the Palace was a place where death didn't charge at you honestly, riding a shaggy pony and wielding a sword, a bow or a spiked lasso. Instead, it lurked behind a shining tapestry, or in a dark corner, or it lay in wait for you, hidden in your food or in your drink. Death could be instant, or agonizingly slow. It could be at the hands of a man, a woman, or a eunuch—or it might strike you so quickly that you would never know where it came from.

VIII

MARA SHOUTS FOR HER SUPPER

�֍   *The forest.*

The Little People took them deeper and deeper into the forest. They carried Phrygillus on a stretcher of interwoven branches and vines that they had brought with them. How long had they been watching the two intruders? Had they prepared the stretcher while they were waiting?

They showed no anger or violence towards them. One of them approached the horse, holding out a handful of grasses and making a clucking noise. It must have been a delicacy that no horse could resist, because the "demon" instantly became as docile as a child's pet.

Another offered Mara his tiny, fine-boned hand, and she too allowed herself to be led.

Their captors were far smaller than Mara and of a size with little Phrygillus. As it grew lighter she was better able to observe them. Their skin was so dark that, while not quite black, it shone like a deep, dark blue. Their eyes were indeed red, but not because they were devils. Later, at their encampment, she saw Little People rubbing a powder into their eyes. Why should they do that? Did it help them to see in the dark?

She had no way to ask them. Their tongue was unlike any that she had heard before, a high twittering that was interspersed with clicks and grunts. It wasn't unpleasant to her ears, but utterly incomprehensible.

Mara had lost some of her natural shame at the slave market in Fanum Fortunae. She hadn't lost all of it, though. The men of the Little People wore no clothes, even though summer was ending, only a thong of vines and leaves twined around their loins. Judging by the time that they spent elaborately rearranging their costume, it may have been intended more as decoration than as a covering.

The women went completely naked. (Except that later she saw older or pregnant women wearing "clothing" not unlike that of the men.)

At first she didn't know where to look. What did help was to think of them as children, she found, which was easy to do because of their size and because they had no hair on their bodies, only on their heads.

By the time that they reached the encampment it was fully light. Phrygillus was given over into the care of a very old woman, who was treated by everyone with noticeable respect. (So they had wise women too, just as the Horse People did!) Mara was presented with food—fruits and nuts, and a peculiar kind of bread seemingly baked from vegetables—and water flavored with fruit-juice.

She never saw any of the Little People eating meat. After a few days at the encampment she yearned for food that was more satisfying, though she was grateful that they were being treated so kindly. The Horse People also had a tradition of kindness to strangers, let it be said, but it was a tradition that was seldom put to the test, since very few strangers who were eligible for kindness ever came visiting. Strangers who were from the Free People, or who were thieving Sueni, or Citizen soldiers, or Blood-Drinkers, were obviously *not* eligible.

The Little People had no tents or houses. They lived under and between the trees, in shelters created out of existing branches, into which other branches, giant leaves, vines and ferns had been woven. To sleep at night, they climbed into narrow pits dug out of the earth, keeping warm under mountains of leaves. She was sure that they must have warmer clothing for the winter, but she never saw any.

The Little People washed themselves in a nearby stream, which was on the other side of the encampment from the place where they went to shit. That was good! And men and women had separate areas, whether it was for washing or for shitting. There was great excitement whenever Mara accompanied the women to the stream. They were fascinated by her body: her huge size, the color of her skin and its texture, which was much rougher than theirs, and her body-hair, since they had none.

Yet they were even more fascinated by her clothes—the plain slave's garments that she had been given in Fanum Fortunae—stroking the fabric and admiring the simple clasp of her traveling cloak.

Mara used the opportunity to wash her undergarments, a procedure that caused some puzzlement. She put them out to dry on a convenient rock, in a patch of sunlight that was shining in between the trees. Then she went to find Phrygillus. His clothes would need to be washed too.

The boy's fever seemed to have gone. He was playing with some of the children, who were barely half his size, and making himself understood most effectively by using signs. They were petting a tame fawn, giving the smallest of the children rides on it (Phrygillus would very possibly have broken its back if he had climbed onto it). They were kissing and stroking the silly animal, Mara noted with disgust. Soon they'd be giving it a name! It obviously wouldn't be called Demon.

When *she* looked at the fawn, what she saw was that it could provide a small feast of roast venison, if the Little People would only realize that…

Phrygillus was quite content to give up his clothes and run naked with the children. He had no shame, the little beast.

On her way back to the stream she stopped to greet the horse, who was peacefully grazing, thereby doing his demonic name no honor. She washed the boy's few garments in the stream, but when she took them to dry on the rock in the patch of sunlight (now no longer so bright, she noticed), she saw that her own clothes had disappeared.

She should have expected it: all the women had been so obsessed with her undergarments. What was she to do? She had no change of clothing, and no wish to wear just her cloak or run about naked like the Little People. The other clothes that had been packed for their journey to the City were probably still in the wagon, left behind at the ruined watchtower where Victor and Lelia had attacked them.

But how could she explain this to the Little People? For them, her undergarments were a rare and fascinating treasure; for her, they were a necessity. She would use signs! If Phrygillus could do it, so could she.

The Little People lived in the open, everyone constantly under the eyes of the whole community, even more so than among her own folk. (Among the Horse People, if you retired to your tent that was a clear sign that you wanted to be alone, and then only your family, your relatives, your neighbors and your friends were allowed to disturb you—which was admittedly quite a lot of people.) That gave her good reason to think that if someone had stolen from her, someone else would have seen it. Did the Little People even have belongings? She hadn't seen anything that she would describe as possessions. How would the thief hide what she had stolen?

Gathering an audience was the easy part. She was the overwhelming object of interest for everyone in the encampment (except Phrygillus and his new friends, who were still playing with the fawn). She struck up a "look at me!" pose, and when there was attentive quiet she gestured and grimaced vigorously, making shapes in the air to convey her meaning.

There was a guessing game among the Horse People where you acted out a particular object—"Haimo's sword", say, or "a dog turd", or "the Great River"—without words. She had always been good at that game, unlike her slow-witted cousins.

But here it didn't work. Some of the gestures that she made caused high-pitched merriment. Did the Little People attach quite different meanings to those gestures?

Finally someone realized what she wanted. A tiny woman stepped forward, and beckoned Mara to follow her. Accompanied by a large crowd, she led her out of the encampment in the other direction from the stream. Wending their way between the trees, they stepped out suddenly onto a small sunlit meadow and there, spread out on a patch of dry ground, were Mara's undergarments.

The woman had taken them to a place where they would dry more quickly!

And they were nearly dry. Mara added the boy's clothes to her own, but she felt bad. She was embarrassed that she had mistrusted their tiny hosts (she could no longer think of them as their captors), who had offered them only kindness. Her embarrassment must have shown itself in a way that the Little People understood, because they encircled her, making soothing noises, and two of the women embraced her. They each took one of her hands, and led her back to the encampment.

When they arrived, Phrygillus rushed up to her and demanded to know why she'd left him on his own.

"You can't do that, I'm your *seflar*!" he piped shrilly. "You're charged with guarding and protecting me. That was in my master's will. I heard it!"

Yes, yes, she said, and cuddled him, although he was still naked. Lord Castor had charged her with looking after him, and she would do that.

What she didn't say was that she had also sworn an oath to do so, on the spirits of her ancestors, the honor of her clan, and the secret name of the God Who Cannot Be Named. That counted as much more than a promise made to an old man, or words in a lawyer's document.

After all, what use had the Horse People for lawyers, except to piss on them? On the other hand, the thought of what would happen to her if she broke her oath made her shudder.

That day she helped with the gathering of fruit and the preparation of food for the evening meal. As it grew dark fires were lit, and the men of the tribe made themselves comfortable on beds of leaves. Phrygillus, now reunited with his garments, was invited to join them. When everything was ready, the women moved among the men, serving them with food on wide, thick leaves that could also be eaten. Not until all the men had received their food did the women, sitting down opposite them, begin to eat too.

Between the two groups sat the old wise woman who had looked after Phrygillus when they arrived at the encampment. She held a large, strangely-shaped stone. Whenever people spoke to her they always said "Ja-neh". Was that her name? Mara hadn't heard the Little People using anything that sounded like names. Maybe it was a title of respect?

Men took it in turns to speak. The first man was chosen by the wise woman, who handed him the stone. After that, the stone was passed on to another man, and then another, and whoever received it would speak. Mara guessed that they were telling stories. Some evoked laughter or loud comments; one story caused tears and gentle moaning.

She wished that she could understand what they were saying. She knew only the Tongue (which was how the Horse People referred to their own language) and the Citizens' Tongue, she had a rough grasp of Sueni; and Manasa had taught her a few words of Sybarite. It would be so useful to know more! She was sure that she would learn quickly.

Now the men were silent, and looked across to the women: it was *their* turn to entertain the company. But the women didn't tell stories. They sang, at first in chorus. Mara had never heard anything like it. It was a fierce, rhythmic chant that grew louder and louder, gradually filling the darkening forest like a challenge: We are here! *Ker-chuck, ker-chuck!* We are the Little People! We rule!

The chanting stopped abruptly, with a tremendous grunt of satisfaction. Silence enveloped them, and people turned to their neighbors and nodded, as if to say "that was good".

Next, the wise woman handed the stone to one of the younger women, who sang on her own, a weird, eerie keening. After her, other women sang. Their music seemed to slide in and out of the trees.

Then, to her horror, the stone was given to Mara. From all sides she sensed that red eyes were watching her. It was her turn. *She* had to sing.

The Horse People had many beautiful songs, with swooping melodies and complicated trills, sung by the womenfolk for the entertainment of the menfolk. Mara had never enjoyed sitting with the women to darn the men's clothes or repair the tents, which was when such songs would be learned and practiced. In fact, she had often been out playing with the boys when she should have been sitting (and singing) with the women of her family. So she had never mastered the women's songs, and her voice was unsuited to them anyway.

When her aunt spoke to her about it, Mara answered her back cheekily, saying that in her honest opinion the songs had very stupid texts. (Which they did.)

Her aunt complained to her father, and her father laughed. But he pretended (for her aunt's benefit) to be angry with her.

So she had never learned the women's songs as she should have done. The men's songs, however, she knew only too well. They were epic accounts of the deeds of heroic ancestors, with endless repetitions of the heroes' violent exploits. They were far more fun, and easier to sing. You could even shout them if you wanted to, which was as much as most of the boys could manage anyway. (And Mara too, for that matter.)

Some of the songs were about contests between the young men of different clans, involving boasts and mockery and challenges. A girl might be abducted—and, if it was a good-natured song, as such songs usually were, quickly won back before she could bring dishonor on her family. Sometimes her brother would defeat the abductor in single combat, but then graciously spare his life. The defeated foeman would praise the young warrior's nobility and beg for the hand of his sister, because she would doubtless breed great champions like her brother. Their father would grant the plea, and the two families would feast together at the wedding and for ever after be linked in honorable kinship.

It was assumed that the girl would happily accept her fate (she was never asked).

While women might be stolen away, horses never were. There was no honor involved in that, only despicable shame.

Other songs were light-hearted, making fun of the ridiculous Sueni, who provided endless material for humor. They were called the Dream People because they walked around in a constant stupid daze. A bit like the idiot boy of the Speaking Bird clan, who lived off scraps, and slept between the dogs, and gabbled nonsense! Not that you could understand the Sueni either, whatever tongue it was they were using, because of their thick, syrupy accent. They never washed, and (Mara had heard it claimed) wiped their backsides with whatever they happened to be wearing. Ugh!

Even worse than the Sueni were the Free People, who had been sworn enemies of the less numerous Horse People since the beginning of time. Despite their name, they weren't "free": they had abandoned the freedom of the open plains, and exchanged their tents for broken-down settlements and a life of scavenging and stealing from their neighbors. Not many Free People were ever killed in the songs, because they always ran away so fast! If the Horse People were like lions, the Free People were like carrion-eating hyenas.

Mara had never seen a lion or a hyena, of course, but her father had told her many stories about them. Hyenas were the most dangerous animals she might ever encounter, he said, but they deserved no respect.

There were songs about fabulous monsters and wicked sorcerers, but there were none about the Blood-Drinkers. They had been unknown to the Horse People of earlier days, and they were not a fit topic for a song around the campfire at night.

What might the Little People enjoy? Mara launched into one of her favorites.

Let every warrior praise his name!

There is no foe he cannot kill,
There is no horse he cannot tame,
On steppe or valley, plain or hill.

He took his horse, his sword and spear,
And rode as fast as eagles fly
To join the battle raging near:
A warrior unafraid to die!

He called his challenge to the foe
And soon his sword a foeman found,
Splitting the man from head to toe,
Spilling his guts upon the ground!

And there were many more verses about the bloodthirsty adventures of the hero.

A dreadful fire-breathing beast bars his way. *Snicker-snack* goes his sword, and the beast's head is off!

A beautiful but wicked witch invites him to gaze into her eyes. If he does so, though, he will be turned into stone. He whispers a word to his horse, and it rears up and stamps the wicked witch into the dirt!

He encounters three huge champions of the Free People, who challenge him to single combat, in three bouts one after the other. No, he cries, I need no unfair advantage, and he attacks and kills all three of them in one go!

Mara knew and loved every single verse. Since none of the Little People could understand what she was singing, she would continue belting out the song until she noticed that they were getting bored.

It did briefly cross her mind that the hero—and it was always a "he"—might well have been a great champion out on the Plain or in the hills, but he had never made it to the forest. Or into the city.

She had now done both! Would the Horse People one day be singing (or shouting) songs about *her*, so that she would be remembered for generations to come?

Her audience remained attentive and appreciative until Mara was sinking with exhaustion and her voice had begun to croak. Finally, a few of the Little People started slipping away to their leafy beds and Phrygillus was seemingly already asleep; only then did she bring her epic performance to an end.

IX

THOMASIUS IS WELCOMED
BACK WITH A FEAST

✠ *Cascantum.*

Thomasius didn't enjoy the journey, but although his whole body was aching from the jolting of the wretched cart, he went looking for the Lord Commander as soon as he reached Cascantum. He was told that Rhaetius, himself newly arrived back in the fortress, was supervising the interrogation of prisoners out on the small parade-ground, the one that was used for drilling recruits. The troops had returned with a handful of Blood-Drinker prisoners in tow. Blood-Drinkers weren't captured very often. They would want to make the most of this, and extract as much from them as they could.

When Thomasius found the Lord Commander, a prisoner was being "interrogated": a Sub-officer was hacking the man's fingers off, one by one. Thomasius was glad that *he* hadn't been ordered to do it.

Although he was chained around the body, two soldiers were needed to hold the man still, while a third pressed his hand down onto a wooden chopping-block, the fingers splayed out. The Sub-officer worked in-between the soldiers, carving at the prisoner's hand with a specially sharpened knife. An Army interpreter, Gracchus, who had helped Thomasius when he had begun to learn the Tongue of the Horse People and who presumably also had a smattering of the Tongue of the Blood-Drinkers, stood close-by. All of them had been spattered with blood.

Thomasius knew the gruesome procedure only as a penalty for thieves, in lawless frontier areas that were under military control. (The civil code prescribed flogging, which could often be avoided with a bribe to the magistrate.) He had never been charged with carrying out the gross punishment, and he was happy that, with five men surrounding the prisoner, he had no uninterrupted view of what was being done. (Sol be thanked for that.)

Yet he heard the screams.

Talking to Decimus in the inn at Fanum, he had said that the Horse People or the Sueni felt pain just as much as Citizens did, but that he wasn't so sure about the Blood-Drinkers. These were the screams of a human being, though.

The others were standing in a wider circle round the interrogation. Only Rhaetius was seated, on a magistrate's stool of office. When someone of Senatorial rank sat on such a stool, no-one who was not a Senator was supposed to sit, unless given express permission. Even sitting down, the Lord Commander dominated the scene with his physical presence.

Grim-faced, he was giving instructions to the Sub-officer.

"Take another finger! Cut slowly, man, make it hurt!"

Suddenly the Blood-Drinker flopped together.

"He's fainted, my Lord!"

"Fires of Esbus! Stick some ginger up him! No, leave him, we'll take another one, and give this animal some time to look at what's left of his hand when he wakes up."

He ordered a break in the proceedings. The men must return when the horn-blower blew the shortened version of the command "Assemble!" In the meantime, the Lord Commander had business to attend to. He had spotted Thomasius in the circle of soldiers, and given him a short, fierce stare, with raised eyebrows. Thomasius was to follow him. *Now.*

"I won't order any refreshments for you," he said, when they had adjourned to the map-room and Rhaetius had dismissed his attendants. "But you're wounded, so you may sit."

He gestured towards an uncomfortable-looking, carved wooden stool—typical military furniture! There was no other stool or bench in sight.

"Thank you, my Lord, but with your permission I'd prefer to stand in the Presence. That's what we're trained to do."

Rhaetius snorted.

"Well, more fool you! I shall sit."

He eased his muscular bulk down onto the stool. Thomasius heard a distinct cracking sound, as if the stool was protesting. The Lord Commander got up again.

"Or maybe not."

"With your permission: we have a right, my Lord, to expect the highest standards of Citizen Army furnishings. I don't believe that that stool meets them!"

And both men laughed.

"No promotion for you yet, Sub-officer. You didn't find the horsey-girl. And you've spent a lot of the money that I gave you. I hear that you have even acquired a new slave-girl, a little Sybarite bed-warmer. That was not with my money, I trust?"

"Oh no, my Lord. I won her at Doghead. I threw a Goddess at just the right moment."

"I didn't have you down as a gambling man, Sub-officer. Unlike your colleague Grassica—"

"It was Grassica who taught me all I know, my Lord! Begging your pardon."

He was aware that he had interrupted the Lord Commander. Few people ever did that.

"I know all about the famous game of dice in Fanum. I have an outstanding source of information—Staff Officer Petronius. That gentleman never ceases to amaze me with his knowledge of everything that goes on within these walls, and even in distant Fanum Fortunae."

"Yes, my Lord."

"Your little Sybarite has apparently been looked after by Grassica's housekeeper. I haven't seen her yet. She'll provide you with refreshment and tender attention. Is she a good fuck?"

Thomasius was nonplussed.

"We haven't actually… Well, I was intending to ask her, my Lord, when—"

"Sol's holy bollocks! 'I was intending to ask her'? What sort of talk is that? Have you perhaps found your way to the bosom of the Blessed Slave since I last saw you? *Ask* her? You put the bitch on her back and you mount her! That's all there is to it! And she'll thank you for it afterwards, believe you me. Ask her, for Sol's sake—whatever next?"

"I'll heed your advice, my Lord."

"You do that, or I'll take the girl into *my* personal service. Petronius told me that she had craved an audience. If you hadn't arrived, I might be interviewing her right now, and then—who knows? Ah, how *do* I miss all these women? By the way, Petronius's housekeeper is quite the little sex-kitten, too. She's completely wasted on him. How could I possibly have overlooked her as well?"

Thomasius put on his most serious face.

"Your responsibilities leave you no time, my Lord, for such distractions."

Rhaetius looked at him very sharply indeed.

"That wasn't irony by any chance, Sub-officer? I'm not well-known for my sense of humor. You can be *demoted* just as easily as promoted. In any case, you'll need to do some more groveling and ass-licking if you want to make it to Company-commander."

"No irony, my Lord, I assure you. Never." But he couldn't resist adding: "That's way above my present pay-level."

"Hmm. You know your place. Good to hear it. But to return to the matter of responsibilities and duties: tell me now what you *did* achieve, or find out, while you were spending vast amounts of my money! And when you've finished, you can run along to your Sybarite woman and put my good advice into practice."

Thomasius told him everything that he and Decimus had found out.

Rhaetius showed very little interest in the fate of the horsey-girl, Mara—there were now far more urgent matters to be dealt with, such as the tens of thousands of Blood-Drinkers that were about to enter the Empire, with most unfriendly intent. But there were still cavalry patrols out looking for her, and if they found her she would be returned to her father.

"We have to keep the Horse People on our side in the coming conflict. Of course it's slightly embarrassing that she should have become the property of young Atticus, who is the son of one prominent Senator—that idiot in Fanum!—and the nephew of another. Whenever Senators are involved, it always takes longer. And now she is on the run, with a little bum-boy. Best place for her!"

"Is she safe, my Lord? This man Victor has sought to kill her twice: once in the house of the Lord Governor, and once at the ruined watchtower, the place where Decimus found the dead bodies of the slave and the two soldiers. And she has stolen his fancy horse. He'll be angry about that. Humiliated. He'll want to put that right."

Rhaetius hammered a huge fist into his thigh.

"He killed two of my men! May Esbus swallow him up for that alone! We must find the man, before he causes any more trouble. We know that he works for Issachar of Maritima, and that he is a slaver like Issachar We now also know that he is a Sybarite assassin, and that he serves the Cause. Does that mean that there is a connection between *Issachar* and the Cause? Issachar isn't from the south. Why should he be sentimental about Sybaris? He's a trader. But find Victor, bring him here to me, and we shall soon have answers!"

Thomasius mentioned the Sleepless Ones. And the starfish tattoo. What Manasa had told them had been new knowledge to him, but it hadn't been new to Decimus.

The Lord Commander also seemed to be familiar with the sinister organization. The tattoo, he said, signified membership of the Cause.

"Or at least support for it. Apparently they are committed to restoring the former greatness of Sybaris. What a ridiculous idea! Who knows, though. The Placidus brothers both have such a tattoo, but does that make them Sleepless Ones? Gnaeus Placidus is a thoroughly disgusting, indolent man, who would never miss an hour's sleep, unless it was to fit in an extra banquet! In his case, I have always held the tattoo to be no more than an affectation: a way to gain favor with the old Sybarite nobility, perhaps, or with the southern merchants. Perhaps that is Issacher's motive, too."

"A Sub-officer that I once knew, my Lord, a Sybarite: he had such a tattoo as well. I didn't know then what it meant. I thought it was just a star. He was a Red supporter, I suppose, aren't all the southerners? But he was always loyal."

"See! There you are! We shouldn't leap too quickly to sinister conclusions. My dear colleague Cornelius Rufus actively supports the Placidi, but I went to the bath-house with him once, after a long debate in the Senate, and saw that he had no tattoo on any part of his body. Not even on his dick! He may be a Red, but he is a decent man, and he wouldn't send assassins to murder people treacherously in the night."

"Victor also tried to kill *me*."

"Good!"

Thomasius almost forgot himself.

"Good, my Lord? *Good?* He almost succeeded!"

"Excellent! You've seen him face-to-face. Who else here has? And he has marked you for life with his sword. You'll never make the mistake of underestimating him—"

"No, my Lord, I most certainly won't."

"Which means that you are the right man to catch him! I gave the freedman Decimus instructions to find Victor, but by now he will have made contact with the General, and he may have been given other duties. So—finding Victor is now *your* task, Sub-officer." He raised his hand, unnecessarily. "No, don't thank me! I appreciate your gratitude, and I shall show my generosity when you have fulfilled this commission. Unfortunately there is no vacancy at present for a Company-commander here in Cascantum—although if you wish I could enquire about a transfer to the Ninth—"

"The Ninth? No thank you, my Lord."

"I thought not. And I would have been disappointed if you'd said yes. I've already assigned your unit to a new man. They're still out on field duty, but when they return you must vacate your quarters. Since I can't use *you* in the field until your wounds are properly healed, I have no option but to find other duties for you—like this one. It's an outstanding opportunity for you to cover yourself in glory!"

And to get myself killed, Thomasius thought to himself. But he said, "Thank you, my Lord, you are too generous."

"Now go to your little Sybarite, Sub-officer, and enjoy what is left of the day. Tomorrow we shall discuss what needs to be done in more detail." And, with a wave of his hand: "Go. You are dismissed."

Thomasius left. He was beginning to have doubts that the promotion was ever going to happen. Was the Lord Commander just leading him on, like a man training his dog with the promise of a juicy tidbit? Nor did he quite understand of logic of "You are too weak for field service" coupled with "You are fit enough to chase a vicious assassin, who has already had one go at you with his scimitar".

And where would he (and Manasa) be accommodated when his men returned from the field? Some dingy corner of the storerooms, no doubt.

How he would miss his men—some of them, at least! A Company-commander had a different relationship with the lower ranks, it wasn't like the close, fatherly contact that a Sub-officer had.

Fatherly? Maybe that wasn't the right word. Older-brotherly, perhaps? Nobody would ever say that Company-commander Decius was like an older brother to his men. "Ass-wipe" was Grassica's favorite way of describing him, and that was mild compared to what the men in his company called him. Thomasius would try to be different.

After going first to what were still his own quarters and finding no-one there (though he noticed that everything looked remarkably tidy and well-swept), he went to Grassica's, where he found Manasa with Grassica's girl Gemma; they had just returned from a visit to the bath-house. Grassica arrived soon afterwards.

Manasa greeted her master in the old-fashioned way, by touching his feet. Oh! He had not expected that. And she kept her eyes cast modestly downwards when he spoke to her. What in Sol's name was going on? Had Gemma been training her in good behavior? Was she intimidated by the atmosphere of the fortress? He much preferred the old Manasa.

And, sure enough, when Grassica and Gemma weren't watching, he caught her looking at him sideways, one eye-brow cocked, and the hint of a smile on her lips. This is only for *their* benefit, she seemed to be saying.

But again she reacted unexpectedly when he recounted what he now knew, from Decimus, about the assassin Victor and his female companion, both of them murderers! She looked shocked, and upset, but she wouldn't tell him why.

She changed the subject, and they were soon distracted by another topic. It was late, but if they hurried they could lay on a feast in his honor. Gemma and Manasa would do the cooking, and they would invite Gemmella, too. Perhaps Petronius would also deign to share their food, even though (as he had often let it be known) he didn't make a habit of dining anywhere other than at the Lord Commander's table, as was his right as a Staff Officer.

The extra dining couches that they would need had to be brought over from Thomasius's quarters. It was agreed that the men would be served first, as was customary, and that the women would join them on the couches afterwards, rather than eating in the kitchen.

"Manasa, too?" Gemma had asked. "With her master's permission of course."

She was, let it not be forgotten, only a slave.

"Why not? There's plenty of room on the couch," he had said (and imagined how there might even be some cuddling after the food and the wine had done their work…).

Alternatively, she could share a couch with Gemmella, if Staff Officer Petronius didn't show up?

No, there would be no need for that. He wasn't some great nobleman, Thomasius said. His parents had been farmers, lowly, plain-living people. And even Emperors had been known to share their couch with a beautiful slave, as a special mark of favor. Although Severian the Evil, he added, might on a whim have the boy or girl mutilated the next day.

Gemma had not commented on that, but given him her "oh-dear-what-strange-people-the-Citizens-are" look.

It was agreed, however, that, should Petronius appear after all, Manasa must slip off the couch before the Staff Officer noticed her, and become the humble serving-girl once again. A senior Staff Officer of Senatorial rank could hardly be expected to dine with slaves!

The food would be excellent. Grassica had happened to acquire a plump hare that one of the Sueni cavalrymen, riding out on the Plain, had killed with a lucky slingshot. He hadn't wanted to keep it.

The Sueni were great fish-eaters, but they only ate their local river-fish, which Manasa, who was from a land where men harvested the rich bounty of the ocean, found disgusting. And they were ridiculously fussy when it came to meat.

The cow, for instance, was taboo, because of the Sacred Earth Cow. That was hard to understand. Among the ancient gods who were still worshiped in much of the north, the Great Mother was also often represented as a cow, and her consort was the sacred bull that was sacrificed once a year, but none of that stopped people from enjoying their beef. The Sueni were different, though.

Similarly, the hare was the totem animal of one of the leading clans, and associated with the Moon Hare; it too was worshiped by the Sueni more often than it was eaten.

The cavalryman, practicing with his sling, had foolishly mistaken the hare for a rabbit. (Wasn't almost everything that the Sueni did foolish?) There were no taboos about eating *them*. Rabbits, in fact, were something of a plague, and plentiful out on the Plain. The man had sold it quickly and fairly cheaply—for half a Maximian—before his comrades noticed what he'd done and cursed him for bringing bad luck down on them.

Most northerners liked eating meat, and it was a regular part of the Citizen Army diet, but what was served tended to be bacon of decidedly poor quality, supplemented by other meats "as and when available", or so the regulations stipulated. If you wanted something a bit special, how did you obtain it, when you were cooped up in the fortress all day? Unless you were tempted by the thought of rat- or dog-meat. There was a plague of rats, too, and they were easily found. Otherwise, you had to spend your own hard-earned money with the local shop-keepers.

The hare would make a nice stew. Gemma was a practical girl, and not obsessively pious. She would cook whatever Grassica asked her to, but she and her sister wouldn't eat any of the meat, thereby leaving more for the men. (Even a very plump hare wouldn't amount to much shared between five or, including Petronius, six people.) They would eat the vegetables, however, of which they had plenty, and the broth in which the meat and vegetables had been cooked.

A *very* sensible girl, to Thomasius's way of thinking.

He asked Manasa whether they ate hare in Sybaris? Yes, naturally they did, she said, the Sybarites cooked and ate everything, and she had also eaten it at feasts when she was a slave among the Horse People. She would have to make sure that Gemma added enough fish-sauce to the stew. The Citizens used it in almost every dish, as did the southerners, but the swamp-people had no way of making the sauce themselves from their ugly riverfish, and it was expensive if you bought it from traders, so it was not part of their diet.

They would have freshly-baked bread from the unit's kitchen, and for dessert there would be a tasty patina of pears, Grassica's favorite. For that, apart from the pears, you needed honey and white wine, salt, pepper, cumin, oil, eggs—and fish-sauce, naturally!

Pepper and cumin? They were spices from the south: weren't they very costly? Yes, they were, but Gemmella had obtained a small quantity from the slave who cooked the Lord Commander's meals. This was on the understanding that Petronius would ostentatiously praise his cooking to the Lord Commander on every possible occasion—because Rhaetius had several times complained about the food, and threatened to send the man to the mines if he continued to disappoint him.

The patina was a recipe that Manasa didn't know, and she was very curious to learn how to prepare it. Grassica had learnt it from his mother, who had learnt it from *her* mother, and he had taught it to Gemma (this wasn't a dish that you would ever encounter among the swamp-dwellers).

The pears, brought in by a trader, were from the Valley. Thomasius liked to eat them raw, but for the patina you had to peel and core them, and cook them for a bit in water. Then you mashed them up and added the other stuff, stirring in the eggs. Finally the dish went in the oven.

Grassica hovered anxiously in the background, concerned that they get it right. Thomasius observed with amusement how the women fussed over the cooking, while Grassica fussed over the women.

"I don't know why he doesn't trust me," Gemma said, "It comes out just as good as his stupid mother always made it. Doesn't it? *Men!*"

The cooking was well under way when Manasa disappeared into one of the other rooms, and then came back shortly afterwards and approached Thomasius, saying to him in a loud whisper, "Please come to the sleeping cubicle with me, Master."

Sol in the heavens, what a pleasant surprise!

But he felt obliged to say, "It wouldn't be right, would it? These are not my quarters."

"We have permission."

Very well!

He set off, and she followed him docilely into Grassica's sleeping cubicle. It was well-lit: she must have gone into the room previously to light not one but two oil-lamps. Lamp-oil was not cheap. She could only have done that with permission from Grassica.

Once inside the room, her manner changed completely. She faced him, her legs planted firmly apart, and her hands on her hips. Staring at him boldly, she announced, "Here in this room, you are the slave and I am now the mistress. Now, slave Thomasius, take off your clothes!"

This was very unfamiliar to him, although he had heard that there were couples who derived pleasure from such peculiar games. The few women that he had bedded had behaved quite differently to this, however. With most of them, their love-talk had begun with a demand for money from him—in advance. Then they had rushed to get him "finished", as they put it, and objected if he requested a second bout. ("No, dearie, that wasn't what we agreed. Though for a small additional payment…")

Others had wandered off into a dream world of their own pleasure, in which they had only noticed him when they were telling him to do this, or not to do that, or to put his thing *there*. ("Yes, that's right. Oh , that's *so* good!")

But if this was how Manasa wanted to do it, well, that was fine with him. And she looked really keen.

He took off his clothes, slowly and carefully, because of the wounds, which were healing well but which he still felt. All the while she watched him, but made no effort to remove her own clothing.

His body was tingling, and it wasn't from the wounds. He was very conscious of his nakedness and of her presence. She looked very beautiful in the lamp-light.

"Aren't you going to, er...?" he asked her huskily.

They had seen each other without clothes before, but this was a different situation.

"To undress? No."

"No? But I thought you wanted to...?"

She smiled at him.

"What *you* want to do is quite plain to see! And I am happy that the Master's patron god has so clearly not deserted him."

"My patron god? Sol?"

"No—the Lord of the Gardens."

She was making fun of his erection!

Forlex, the little Lord of the Gardens, was a fertility god whose outrageous statue graced every garden and orchard in the Province and the Valley: a tiny, grinning figure with an enormous phallus (or, in extreme cases, an enormous phallus attached to a tiny, grinning figure). All the old gods had names, which were known but should not be spoken, except during sacred rituals. Forlex was the exception. Small children were fascinated by Him, boastful young men swore by Him, whores gave Forlex amulets to their favorite customers ("So you'll remember your mighty performance tonight, and come back to me soon!"), and He was particularly popular with fruit-growers and the owners of orchards. He had doubtless watched over the ripening and plumping of the pears that they were about to eat.

Even as he laughed at her joke, the outward sign of Thomasius's dedication to the god was subsiding.

"Yes, but didn't you...?"

Fires of Esbus, why couldn't he finish his sentences?

"I have much respect for the Lord of the Gardens. He is a mighty god, known even in Sybaris! Yet I have more concern for my Master's health. When were these wounds last dressed?"

She removed the dressings, and tut-tutted over the appearance of his wounds, but in a proprietary manner. Actually, they were more or less healed, as she promptly admitted.

"Yes, the stitches can come out soon. I feel fine."

"The doctor of the soldiers will see you tomorrow. Lord Grassica arranged it. The doctor can cut the stitches, though I also know how to do it. I will wash the wounds and change the dressings, however."

Everything that she needed for that was laid out ready to be used.

This was why she had lit two lamps rather than one! It was not to light their lovemaking; it was so that she could better see what she was doing as she tended his wounds.

He was disappointed, certainly. But the gentleness with which she touched him told him that she cared for him, and that made him feel good in a different way to the way he normally felt after he had just ploughed a woman.

When she joined him on the couch, she served him wine and later, when he had eaten and was happily full up, tried to serve him with yet more of the dessert. He told her to eat her food now—there was plenty left, and she had worked hard. She must be hungry.

He lay back contentedly, feeling her body against his. Oh, she had nice breasts! He was tired, and sleepy. The journey from Fanum had been thoroughly exhausting. Perhaps a mule would have been a better choice than the jolting trader's cart, which had stunk of dried fish. Dozing comfortably, he didn't hear Petronius arrive until the man was already speaking. Or rather shouting.

"Get up, man! Put on a uniform or something—at once!"

"Sir?"

Manasa was already gone. Had he seen her on the couch with him? He must have done.

"The Lord Commander demands your presence. Hurry!"

What was so urgent that it couldn't wait till the morning? And why did the Lord Commander need *him*? At that moment he couldn't have looked very military. He didn't *feel* military at all. But Thomasius would pull himself together.

He staggered to his feet and offered the Staff Officer a belated salute.

"In the map-room, sir?

"No. Not in the map-room. The Lord Commander is waiting for you out on the small parade-ground. Bring the Sybarite girl with you. She may be needed."

Thomasius was so bewildered that he tottered, lost his balance and fell back onto the couch. Grassica pulled him back up onto his feet, hissing "For Sol's sake!" into his ear.

He managed to steady himself, and apologized to Petronius, "Sorry, sir, it's the wine. I've had too much," adding "But we're both off duty!"

Grassica seemed not to have been so affected by the wine.

"The night air will sober him up, sir!" Then to Manasa, who had suddenly popped up beside him, "Take your master back to his quarters and get him into his uniform."

Petronius waved his arm dismissively.

"No, no, just give him a cloak. And make the girl decent."

Manasa's tunic had slipped down on one side, revealing a succulent breast. Why was that? Had he been pawing at it? Thomasius couldn't remember doing so. Surely he would have remembered it if he had been?

"Yes, sir. At once, sir."

That can't have sounded very convincing! Thomasius couldn't decide whether he was feeling exhilarated from the wine, or queasy.

Gemmella was now tugging at the Staff Officer's arm.

"Do they really have to go? Look, there's still so much food. You'll love the dessert, it's Grassica's favorite—"

Petronius ignored her, looking straight at Thomasius.

"Hurry! There is something that you need to see, out on the parade-ground. And it's not a pretty sight."

X

DECIMUS SPENDS SOME OF
THE GENERAL'S SILVER

✠ *The Great Provincial Road, and Caledunum.*

If Decimus was apprehensive about what might be awaiting him at the Palace, his first problem was the journey back to the City, in the company of a man who had shown himself to be distinctly hostile. He believed, though, that he could "read" Marcus Vulpeculus.

The Senator was an opportunist, and a pragmatist. He was also a man who could barely control his upper lip—particularly interesting was the way that it twitched whenever he invoked the "Blessed Slave". Vulpeculus might be a Blue, but his religious commitment must be only skin deep! Not all the Blue Senators were fanatically spiritual: Quintus Naevius wouldn't recognize a moral precept unless it got up and punched him on the nose.

Once they had left Maidunum and were on their way, Vulpeculus became much friendlier towards Decimus than he had been at the meeting. To Decimus's amazement, they were traveling alone, on horseback, with only a small escort of bodyguards, and with the original contract in their care. And they were traveling fast.

Far behind them on the road was Terentius Ager, carried in a litter like old woman. Also, on mules, the secretaries belonging to the delegation, and with them the numerous copies of the contract that the secretaries had spent a long night redrafting, writing out, correcting, and preparing for signing and sealing.

Only the original contract was needed in the City, as proof of Marcus Naevius's enhanced role in the new order of the Western Empire and confirmation of his authority. Vulpeculus meant to get it to him as quickly as he could.

Decimus was impressed. It wasn't as though he liked the man, or trusted him enough to turn his back on him for more than a bat of an eyelid, but he had to admit that Vulpeculus was an excellent horseman, and that he was well-organized. He had even left his own personal slave behind, to travel slowly by mule with Ager and the secretaries. (Although there would be servants enough to see to his needs at the different inns they would be using.)

The Senator ignored the escorts, but treated Decimus almost as an equal. Yet, like the lawyer that he was, he probed him with questions about the General and his plans.

"Ogilo commands our armies, yes, but can he move his troops away from the frontier? No. As long as the Blood-Drinkers are massing beyond the Great River, he is trapped where he is. He has power, yes, but can he use it? No. And he needs Marcus Naevius to hold the City for him, to protect the person of the Emperor, and to fend off the Placidi. Or do you see it any differently?"

Decimus was not going to allow himself to be drawn on the subject of the General's intentions. He knew a certain amount about them, probably more than Vulpeculus did, and he knew that Vulpeculus knew that. He would be insulting the Senator's intelligence if he pretended to be ignorant.

"No, my Lord, I believe that that is an accurate assessment of the situation."

"And Marcus Naevius, for his part, needs the north to be secure, so that he can concentrate the limited resources that he has on dealing with the rebels."

"Indeed, my Lord."

Aha, so the Placidi were rebels? Vulpeculus had already used that word at the meeting, and the General had not chosen to correct him.

The City had been full of armed men, yet it was Naevius who had reportedly struck the first blow. Had he merely preempted the Placidi? They might have been hatching a similar plot, but they had been slower. And the gods favor the speedy. Very well, the Placidi were rebels and traitors. Ogilo was prepared to accept that account as the public version of the events in the Palace, and in the City. He had hinted as much to Decimus, at a brief private meeting that took place shortly before the departure of the delegation from Maidunum.

History was never written by the defeated, and the damage had already been done. After all, when the cup falls from the table, what is to be gained by pretending that the wine is still in it? Both factions had made a bid for power, and the General had tried to play them off against each other—without success. The bride-show had not gone to plan ("That damn eunuch!"), and it was the Naevii who had made their move first. They had seized power by force, but since the Emperor was seen to support them their actions could hardly be described as a rebellion.

Like it or not, Ogilo and Marcus Naevius were now tucked up in bed together, despite their loathing for each other. They could fight each other, but for the moment the fight would only be over how they were going to share the blanket.

Decimus's task would be to position himself as close as he could to where the decisions were now being taken in the City. To watch, and listen, and report back to the General.

That wouldn't be by official fire-beacon, of course! Ogilo had joked to Vulpeculus that his spies were already in place in the Palace—which was true. Decimus would not be working with them, however, unless it was absolutely necessary. They were less reliable than he was, and they might compromise him. Or, the General said, if he made a mistake, he might compromise *them*.

When did I ever make such a mistake? Decimus had thought to himself, feeling slightly offended. But the General was right.

As for the sending of information, there were other resources available: men who were paid well to risk their lives. Since greed on its own was not a good basis for trust, these men had been chosen (in preference to others) because they happened also to have personal reasons to hate the Blues—especially the vicious Quintus Naevius. His men had bullied, plundered and murdered in the more lawless parts of the City for as long as Decimus could remember. A man whose shop had been pillaged, his wife humiliated, and his daughter spread-eagled and raped: such a man would not be so easy for the Naevii to turn as a man who was working against them solely for money.

There were questions, some more sensitive than others, to which Ogilo wanted answers.

What had really happened at the bride-show?

Had the eunuch been seduced with silver, or persuaded with threats?

Had Maximillus willingly agreed to the marriage?

Had the Senate been cowed, or could Whites and Greens still act with a modicum of independence if they so chose?

And—had the Reds been destroyed completely, or was there still some southerner of influence left in the City whom the General could talk to? The Placidi might yet be useful as a counterweight to Naevius.

Most of the answers to those questions would be found at the Palace, but Decimus would still need to go into the City, and for that he would need a pretext.

It would be accepted readily enough that he would have occasional business (on the General's behalf) at the homes of Green Senators like Lucius Atticus and Terebinthian. Out of loyalty to his former master, his visits to the Atticus household might be quite frequent. He was also known to appreciate being given access to private libraries like those that the wealthier Senators (such as the two prominent Greens) sometimes owned.

In addition, he could make long-drawn-out visits to taverns and brothels in the slum quarters.

"But I don't do that," Decimus had almost said.

It would only be a cover. In the slums it would be easier to lose whoever was tailing him.

Decimus hadn't been convinced. He had pointed out to the General that it was in the poorest parts of the City that the Naevii had most of their followers and supporters. Wherever he went in the slums, and for whatever reason, there would inevitably be one of Quintus's men somewhere nearby.

Then, said the General, he should pick a *respectable* house that he could visit regularly, a house which had a second, hidden entrance or an escape passageway (such as many wealthy merchants and Senators had quickly added to their homes in the time of Severian the Evil). In that household, there would be a slave-girl or a freedwoman that he could pretend to be visiting. He could use the long hours of his "assignation" with her to slip out, preferably disguised, and make other visits—though even in those parts of the City where there were fewer supporters of the Naevii he must take care, and trust in Sol that he was not spotted by chance.

The master of the respectable house must be informed, and the girl rewarded for her cooperation, and her silence, in good silver. (And, yes, the General would give him sufficient money. Had he ever stinted with money in the past? Decimus said nothing. But the money was not to be spent on whores. "Or not too often, at least.")

The journey had barely begun, and Decimus had already dipped into the purse to pay for a girl to share his bed. It had happened on the second night.

The first night had been spent at a comfortable inn in a small town south of Maidunum. They had traveled fast, and were deep inside the Province, that part of the Western Empire that (to Decimus's mind) had the pleasantest climate. It would be a good place to settle down one day, he thought, when he was old.

Many would have preferred the Valley. It was fertile and delightful, he had to admit, and the winters there, in the shelter of the mountains, were very mild; but there were no towns worthy of the name. Which meant: no libraries, no booksellers, and, in his experience, fewer opportunities for civilized conversation The Province, on the other hand, had many charming small- and medium-sized towns (Maidunum *not* included), and the population, still loyal to the old gods, seemed to live in a sensible, practical but comfortable way.

That couldn't be said of the people of the City and the surrounding areas. Many there were devoted to the Lesser Worship of the Slave, which discouraged pleasure and self-indulgence and encouraged constant soul-searching and feelings of guilt. (This, at least, was the public face of the cult, though in reality its followers, behind their noisy piety, were often incorrigible hypocrites.)

Added to which, the countryside around the City was barren and infertile, parceled up into tiny farms on which the peasants could barely scratch a living. Many of them had long given up, sold their land to a speculator from the City, and become hired men on his property, or, worse still, bonded laborers—the lives of bonded laborers being harsher than those of many slaves.

That process was even further advanced in the south, where most of the fields were worked by slaves and belonged to a handful of fabulously wealthy plantation-owners like the Placidi. The way of life of the free Sybarite population (or what was left of it) was exotically different, and highly interesting, but Decimus, despite his dark coloring, was a northerner, and the climate of Sybaris was simply too hot and sticky for him.

At the first inn they stayed at, Vulpeculus had instructed their escort to bed down in the stables, and guard the horses. The innkeeper wouldn't dare to charge the noble Senator for sleeping space for his entourage in the straw. Besides, why waste money on them? Vulpeculus took the best room, of course, from which an indignant traveling merchant had first to be evicted, and he gave orders that the room next to it be given to Decimus.

Would it be wise to have the bodyguards sleeping so far away from the Senator?

"You are skilled in matters of protection and security," Vulpeculus had replied, with an ironic smile. "Or so I have been informed by your master. I shall feel perfectly safe with you in the next room."

Though tired, Decimus had had trouble getting to sleep that night. The separating wall between their rooms was thin, and the Senator was obviously and loudly bedding a woman.

Or, to judge from the sounds coming from the next room, he was torturing her.

On the second night they stayed at a more modest inn, the Apple Tree, in a little town called Caledunum. Vulpeculus ordered similar arrangements to be made for their accommodation. This time, the rooms were of about the same size, and Decimus was delighted to see that the bed in his room was large, clean and comfortable-looking.

The maid saw him staring at the bed, and winked at him.

"Why doesn't the master give it a bounce to try it out? No bed ever got softer just by looking at it."

And she laughed. Cheeky girl! She was tall and well-built, blonde, and light-skinned, and she was quite pretty, too, in an open-faced, gap-toothed kind of way. She was a typical girl of the Province, the result of centuries of rutting between the Citizens and the friendlier barbarian tribes. Her name was Jenufa, and for a small consideration she was available, she said, to make his overnight stay even more pleasant…

He imagined her young breasts, and strong, muscular thighs. She was a robust, healthy girl. She looked clean. He was tired from the journey, but—why not?

"If you don't demand too much riding from a tired horseman, you can tuck me up tonight. Drop the 'master', though. I'm—"

He wasn't sure how to put it.

"You're a freedman, aren't you? I can always tell."

That was unexpected.

"What makes you so sure?"

She smiled at him. The gap in her front teeth was truly most endearing!

"You won't be angry?"

"No, tell me."

"You freedmen—you always try harder. And you never relax. Like there's someone watching you." Before he could say anything, she added quickly: "But I like that." And after a pause, during which she looked him boldly in the eye: "You're not angry, are you?"

"Oh no, my dear, not at all!"

And he meant it. Tired or not, he was looking forward to the evening's entertainment.

She would come back to his room after her other duties were finished, she said. And he mustn't feel that he had to perform for her. There was no need for him to be like one of those famous charioteers from the hippodrome, boasting about all their victories! (Actually, they'd had one of those guys staying at the Apple Tree once, and her friend Licia had said that he didn't perform *at all well*.)

Jenufa was as good as her word. He had left the door unbolted, but stayed awake until she came, though he didn't think they would be in much danger in Caledunum. She slipped in quietly (maids had a talent for opening and closing heavy wooden doors without as much as a squeak!), bolted the door behind her, stripped off her clothes, and climbed into the bed beside him.

Her body was firm like a peasant-girl's, and sweet-smelling (an unusual quality among the serving-girls at inns). Had she washed after she finished work? She was gentle and undemanding with him, and her gentleness actually stimulated him to be forceful. However, she had asked him not to spend himself inside her, and he was careful not to do so.

Afterwards, they lay pleasantly entwined, and it was only then that he heard the noises from the next room.

The sound of blows, and sobbing; curses, and a half-suppressed scream of pain.

Vulpeculus.

Jenufa whispered, "The great lord is taking his pleasure."

"What is he doing to her?"

"All men have different needs. His needs are…more difficult than yours."

There was another scream, this time louder.

"That is terrible!"

"No, it's more common than you think."

"He must be hurting her."

He wanted to stop what was happening in the next room—but knew that he wouldn't. Jenufa must have realized how agitated he felt, and how helpless. She gripped his shoulders and looked into his face, her eyes glinting in the darkness.

"Hush! He is a great lord, and you are a freedman. Let them be. Licia knows about men like that, and he'll pay her well. He'll have to pay her—she's not a slave. But I should have gone to him instead. I'm much stronger than she is. I can take it better than she can."

Decimus felt ashamed. He changed their conversation, away from what mattered, to harmless, inconsequential chatter.

"Licia. That's a traditional Citizen name. She must come from an old Citizen family. I wonder how she came to be a maid in Caledunum?"

And more of the same.

Soon afterwards, mercifully, he fell asleep in Jenufa's arms.

The next morning he woke early, even before the maid (and maids have to be early risers). He placed some good silver coins on the table, and left the room to search of the latrine. A girl, smaller and more slightly built than Jenufa—Licia—came out of the next room. One of her eyes had been blackened, and there was blood caked below her nose. She walked with hunched shoulders, as if in pain, and she was trembling.

He looked away, and neither of them spoke.

When he returned to the room, Jenufa had already got up and dressed herself. She had taken the silver coins, but had left one of them on the table.

Their eyes met.

"That coin," she said, "you should give it to someone who needs it. A small act of kindness? Do it in the name of your gods, or mine—whichever you prefer."

"And you don't need it?"

"No! I'm not some miserable slave-girl, saving up copper coins to buy her freedom. There's a shopkeeper here who's asked me if I'll be his woman. He's a lot older than me. He wants me badly, but he hasn't seen more than my tits so far. I'll say yes, if he agrees to marry me. I'll have to pay for the wedding, though—he's too mean. In other ways he's a good man. *That's* why I'm saving. One part of the money will go to the Great Mother, though. I swore an oath to Her, and I'll make him swear one too. She will bless our marriage and watch over me, so that he'll never dare to treat me badly! Because the Great Mother never forgives an insult to one of Her women. Our future will be a good one. There'll be children— I know that—and when I die I'll die satisfied with my life. May the gods so bless you, that you will be able to say the same!"

Decimus had never heard such a long speech from a maid. He could easily imagine her holding her own with a dull-witted provincial shopkeeper.

When the little party took to the road again, and after the first greetings had been exchanged, there was an uneasy silence between Decimus and the Senator. It was Vulpeculus who finally broke it.

"You had a woman in your bed last night! I hope that you slept the better for it, and that your master's money was well spent? I saw the girl leaving your room: a fine-looking creature. Strong limbs. If we pass through this town again…"

Decimus found that thought extremely distasteful.

"Thank you, my Lord. I hope that you too slept well."

"Oh yes. I slept well, and I had a good fuck too. You may have heard us?"

Decimus found himself speaking through gritted teeth.

"Yes, my Lord."

Vulpeculus reached across suddenly and grasped his arm, so that both horses started, and then slowed. He looked at Decimus intently.

"A word with you, freedman! I'm being open with you now, you realize that?" He released Decimus's arm, and smiled. "Though why in the name of any of the gods I'm being so honest I really don't know! What other Senator would speak to a freedman with such frankness?"

Decimus thought: Lucius Atticus, for one. But he didn't say it. Lord Commander Rhaetius, for another. Quintus Naevius, for a third. Not that you'd ever want to get into a cozy chat with Quintus Naevius.

"Not a single one, my Lord. I know that, and I respect your kindness."

He had chosen the word intentionally—to provoke. The Blessed Slave enjoined His followers to show kindness to the weak and helpless. It was the best-known of all the moral precepts of the cult. Even Aulus's father made an occasional effort to live up to it.

But Vulpeculus only laughed, a brutal, masculine guffaw that startled both horses and caused the escort riding ahead of them to swivel round and stare at them.

"*Kindness?* I kicked seven circles of Esbus out of that girl, and fucked her silly as well. It wasn't just her nose that was bleeding, I'll tell you! But I'll tell you this, too: I gave her a gold half-piece. That's twelve heavy silver coins. Not bad, eh? She offered me a service, and I paid her for it. A fair transaction, wouldn't you say? How else can a little whore like that come to gold? She knows the value of money because she has to work for it. Hard. On her back or on her knees. Just as I worked hard for my money too. I'm a rich man, but it's not 'old money' that I got from my daddy or my granddaddy. Not like the fortunes that fell into the laps of most of those old farts of colleagues of mine in the Senate. Oh no, it's what I spent half a lifetime earning. And because I earned it, I have the right to spend it on whatever happens to give me pleasure. As I did last night. By the way, what did you pay yours? A couple of Maximians? A handful of coppers?"

"Slightly more than that, my Lord."

"Well, you could afford to be generous—it wasn't your money you were giving away."

Decimus wasn't sure where this "frank" conversation was leading.

"I'm always careful with money that's been entrusted to me, my Lord."

"Yes, I don't doubt that, but you've never had much money of your own, have you? When Faustus Atticus manumitted you, did he settle money on you? No. Did he set you up in a business? No, I thought not. Did he give you anything at all, except a parting sneer and a kick up the backside? I notice that you don't honor him by bearing his name."

"I was grateful to him for my freedom, but since the day of my manumission I've always looked after myself."

"You mean: you chose to work for Ogilo! Which was not a bad choice. If I was a gambling man, there was a time when I would have put my money on his colors, too. But I wouldn't do that now."

"My Lord?"

Vulpeculus lowered his voice.

"Come to *me*, freedman. I'll make it worth your while. Lots of money to spend, on whatever you like! The General's good fortune is on the wane. Our friends the Blood-Drinkers are soon going to come crashing over the Great River, and they'll ravage the north. Can Ogilo stop them? And if he can't, how long will he remain General? Even if by some wonder he does survive, he'll have been so weakened that Naevius and the Blues will quickly snuff him out."

"That is a possible outcome, my Lord. There are many possible outcomes."

"Don't piss me about. Where will you go when the storm breaks? As break it surely will! With gold you can go wherever you like. The world is a big place."

"I'll continue to do my duty, my Lord, as I've always done."

"Listen carefully: you would be *my* man, not Naevius's. Yes, Marcus Naevius is an impressive figure, we can all agree on that. Twenty years ago he would have made a fine Emperor. But he's *old*. And afterwards? His son has more enemies than a Sueni blanket has fleas. I wouldn't want to be in his sandals when the mob turns on him. Emperor Quintus the First? I think not!"

Vulpeculus seemed to find the idea very funny. And there was no sign of movement of his upper lip.

"It's difficult to look so far ahead, my Lord."

"Of course, of course. But wise to do so. And nobody's talking treachery here, are they? It's good to have options for the future, and that means putting arrangements in place for a day that might (or might not) come. Only the foolish leave everything to chance. And that day will be a day for new men. Men like myself—and you as well. Why not? We have time before we reach the City. Think on it."

"I shall, my Lord."

"Oh, and before I forget: just so as you know, I have my friends, and I have my enemies." He paused. "There is nothing in between. That makes this complicated life that we all lead so much simpler. Remember that, freedman."

Decimus now understood what the Senator had meant by "frankness".

For the rest of their journey to the City, Vulpeculus entertained a maid at each of the inns that they stayed at. Noisily.

Decimus said nothing more to him about the matter. He was too busy with other thoughts.

XI

MARA DREAMS OF HORSES

※ *The forest, and the Great Plain.*

The next morning there was a bustle about the encampment. The Little People may have had few belongings, but what they had was now being packed. The tribe was on the move!

Mara and Phrygillus had barely finished eating their morning fruit and nuts when tiny hands pulled at them to get up. They joined a column of little blue-black figures making their way between the trees, and tracked through the forest for the rest of that day. Mara estimated that they were going south.

They continued this slow southward march for many days, finding a suitable place to sleep when it grew dark, and continuing onwards the next morning; eventually they made a proper encampment, and stayed there for perhaps a week; but then the southward march was resumed. Such was the pattern.

Mara led the horse, and Phrygillus was allowed to sit on its back; he even persuaded one of his new friends to join him. With Mara's help the boy was heaved up, with much banter and giggling, though when the "demon" started to move he screamed with fright and threw himself off. Phrygillus was more at ease now with the horse, but he couldn't ride it on his own. What would he do when they reached the Horse People? Mara would have to teach him to ride, on the smallest, oldest horse she could find. How the other children would mock them!

They would laugh, too, if they knew that he had been helping her with her plaits. It was important to her that people should see her hair and know who she was (by "people" she meant the Horse People, of course—if they happened to meet any of them). She couldn't do the plaits properly on her own. Manasa had helped her on the march to Fanum Fortunae. Now Phrygillus proved to be remarkably skillful. It was not a skill that boys were expected to master, any more than that they should understand how to darn clothes or feed babies.

They made a second encampment, and stayed there even longer. Mara was concerned that they were getting further and further away from the Great Plain. They were now deep inside the forest and she was uncertain how long it would take before they reached the end of the trees and the beginning of the grasslands.

They could set off alone before then—her newly acquired knowledge of forest fruits and how to prepare them meant that they wouldn't starve—but how would she, Phrygillus and the horse be able to find their way through to the Plain? The forest here was dense and gloomy, and the sun not always easy to see.

How far did the Little People intend to go? It was apparent to her that they were moving away from the autumn cold and as far south as they could. But how big was the forest? She didn't know. It seemed to go on forever.

The gloominess was beginning to prey on her spirits.

Phrygillus was also unhappy. He had lost much of his fleshiness and now looked more like a child of the Horse People, even if he didn't behave like one. He was covered in scratches and bruises. In the evenings he still played with the children of the Little People, but he spent a lot of time whining and complaining that he was bored, that he didn't like the forest, that he wanted to go the bath-house, and, above all, that he wanted to eat meat again. Lots of it. And sweets. Did the Horse People have sweets?

Mara assured him that the Horse People were great meat-eaters. She tried to keep off the topic of sweets.

He was insistent.

"Don't you have honey?"

She didn't want to give him a direct answer. In the Speaking Bird clan they knew about honey, which they sometimes bought from passing traders. It was too expensive to give to children, though. The wise women employed it as a medicine.

"The *Sueni* have lots of honey, because they use it to flavor their beer." (How disgusting!) "If honey is so important to you, perhaps you would prefer to go and live with the Dream People of the swamps, instead of with the Horse People?"

No! He knew all about *them*: Togulus, the gatekeeper at Fanum, was a Sueni, and he was a nasty rotten pig who had shouted at Phrygillus and thumped the end of his spear on the floor. Phrygillus didn't like him at all.

"What about dates?"

Mara had no idea what he meant. He was now on the brink of tears. "Figs?"

She shook her head.

And he couldn't hold back the tears any longer. He wanted to go *home*, he wailed. Did he mean Fanum Fortunae, she asked herself, where he had been a slave?

Yet she hugged him, and promised that, at the first opportunity, as soon as they caught a glimpse of the end of the trees, they would make a run for it. He must jump up behind her onto the horse, and off they would ride. The Little People wouldn't be able to catch them. Besides, when they reached the edge of the forest, would their hosts dare to leave the shelter of the trees?

They had nothing. Just the horse, and the little knife. How long could they possibly survive out on the Plain? Her plan would only succeed if the Horse People were very close by, but she feared that they had already marched so far south that her clan would be many, many leagues away.

They had been traveling now for weeks rather than days.

Mara's father had taught her how to calculate the passing of time as the Citizens did, giving the days names and forming them into groups of seven called weeks and into bigger groups of moon-cycles called months. The months were also given names. Some of the names were silly, she thought (Emperors from long ago) and she found it difficult to remember all of them, or put them in the right order. But the weeks were a good idea. It was so much easier to count large numbers of days by forming them into groups of seven.

Among the Horse People, only the seasons were named, and there were moon-cycles, several in each season. More important, though, were the feast-days, like the Day of the Foals, which was a beautiful celebration for small children, or the Feast of the Sacred Mother of Horses, when there was a great horse fair and the young men would show off their riding skills to impress the unmarried girls.

That was how Hengilo had first caught her eye: by trying out a trick that he hadn't properly mastered, and falling off his horse!

You knew when the feast-days were, because they would be so many days into the first (or the second or third) moon-cycle of a particular season. And if you forgot, well, the wise women would always remind you.

Mara had marked the passing of time in the forest in the manner of the Citizens. The riding-cloth was folded over on two opposite sides, and the folded edges sewn together, except where there was the little pocket, fastened with tiny hooks, in which they had found the knife. There were tassels on the other two sides.

The way Mara did it was as follows: she made the tassels on one side represent days, those on the other, weeks. As each day came to an end, she would knot a tassel on the first side. When she had seven of these, she would unknot them but knot a single tassel on the other side.

Their first attempt to escape was a disaster, because Phrygillus saw a big, stripey-colored bird (he told her afterwards) and failed to see Mara's signal. Mara acted the innocent, slipping off the horse's back and pretending that she had been playing with it.

Once she was sure that the Little People accompanying them hadn't noticed anything, she glowered at Phrygillus.

He didn't understand why she was upset.

"Why are you angry? The bird was so pretty! And it was hopping up and down, like this."

He tried to imitate its movements.

Mara brought her anger under control, before any of the Little People became suspicious.

She had thought of it as an "escape", but was that what they were trying to do? Were the Little People holding them prisoner, against their will, or were they simply guests who could leave whenever they wanted? Mara had no way to find out. The strange, twittering tongue of the forest folk was impossible to understand.

The reason why Mara had given the signal was because she had seen, through the trees, a treeless plain spreading out into the distance. Phrygillus, who was not staring into the distance like her, but busy with children's things, had seen only the fascinating, stripey-colored bird.

The column now turned away into the depths of the forest again, and no further opportunity offered itself for several more days.

Phrygillus realized that he had let her down, and he promised to pay attention next time. During the day he did his best to behave, but at night he cried, and said that he wanted meat, and sweets, and above all that he wanted to go *home*.

Home? They weren't going back to Fanum Fortunae, though she didn't tell him that. Would he ever be able to make the Horse People his home? And would the clan of the Speaking Bird be willing to accept him?

Mara wasn't even sure whether *she* would be welcomed, if she came home to her clan with a story of a respected warrior's treachery and betrayal that no-one would want to believe, however convincingly she told it.

Once again she turned the riding-cloth into a little sack, this time not for stones but for carrying fruit for them to eat once they left the forest. Who knew whether they would be able to find any food at all once they were out on the Plain? She might have been good at braining the rats and crows that hung around her father's settlement (though Phrygillus wouldn't believe her), but any large wild animal that they encountered would be harder to bring down with a stone—assuming that the beast hadn't already attacked and eaten *them*.

They would have to speed across the Plain and hope to encounter some riders from the Horse People. This far south, there was no chance that they would find a settlement, or even a temporary encampment, though the clans would be moving southwards, sending out small parties of scouts ahead of them. Her people were moving out of the path of the Blood-Drinkers, who brought death with them. That was why the Speaking Bird clan had crossed the Great River many moons ago and now grazed their horses within the realm of the Citizens, with permission (her father had said) from their great lord.

Was that lord the same man whose house she had been in in Fanum, the house where Castor had been murdered? Or had it been some other great man of the Citizens who gave the order?

The Lord Governor in Fanum had not looked to her like a great man. He was flabby and foolish, and he was was bullied by his own loud, bad-tempered woman (what strange customs the Citizens had!). Mara was sure that he would soon fall off any horse that was worth riding. How could that weakling have fathered a child? He was not a chieftain, a man who gave orders that other men rushed to obey. Instead of commanding "It shall be done thus!" he had fussed over the scroll that Castor had written, making her (and Phrygillus) the property of his son. Among the Horse People, even women had more dignity.

The son was no doubt another flabby man, frightened of horses and bullied by women!

Who cared, though, what foolishness was written in their documents? Those were the ways of the Citizens, whose miserable lives and cruel cities she had seen for herself. Phrygillus might be a slave, but she was not. She had known another, a better life. She was a free woman of the Horse People, a chieftain's daughter, and soon she would be out there on the Plain, riding a magnificent horse, feeling the wind and smelling the air, and on her way back to the people of her own clan.

When they saw the "demon", how envious they would be! Naturally she would offer the horse to her father. He was a man who deserved to ride such a fine animal. First, however, she would show everyone that *she* knew how to ride him. And after that, there would be no more fillies for her—only huge black stallions!

Mara was so deeply engrossed in these thoughts that she almost missed the second sighting, through the trees, of the Great Plain. This time, however, she caught Phrygillus's eye, clambered onto the horse's back, held onto its mane and, with the help of a conveniently placed fallen tree, succeeded in pulling the boy up behind her.

Even so, it was an awkward maneuver: Phrygillus had been given the responsible task of carrying their bag of fruit, and almost dropped it. Happily he didn't—it was all that they would have to eat.

No-one tried to stop them or attack them. In fact, she had never seen the Little People with weapons. Why should they need them? They lived off what they found in the forest, and they never killed any animals. Maybe there were different tribes, and the tribes battled with each other over the best places to gather fruit. Or over women. You would need weapons for that. But perhaps there was only the one tribe. Or there were many tribes, but they never fought each other.

No-one chased after them as Mara guided the horse carefully between the trees. And then they were out in the open, and the light hit her like a blow from the fist of a warrior. She sucked in the air. How wonderful it was!

The way that they were riding was uncomfortable for them, and probably for the horse too. Once it was certain that no-one was following them—the forest was still in sight—they dismounted and allowed the horse to graze.

Mara looked about her. The Plain stretched out to the horizon, the flatness broken only by ridges of very low hills and occasional clumps of trees. She hoped that, somewhere, there would be streams. She couldn't see any horsemen or encampments. It looked much like the grasslands from which she had been abducted, but they must be far distant.

A flock of large birds flew southwards, a sign that colder days were coming.

Phrygillus started unpacking the bag of fruit. She stopped him. No, she understood that he was hungry, but this was all that they had to eat. It had to last. If there were streams (and she was sure that she would find one), with water and with the fruit that they had they could live for many days, until they found friendly people who would feed them and help them. But they had to be careful with the fruit.

"Can't we eat grass, like Demon?"

No. You could suck broad-leaf grass, she explained, to still your thirst. It didn't fill your stomach, though. And there were some grasses that you could use as herbs, or cook slowly in a stew if you had nothing better to eat. Their most realistic chance of finding food out on the Plain would be where the clumps of trees were—because perhaps there would also be bushes with berries, if they were very lucky indeed.

Phrygillus looked downcast. She tried to cheer him up.

"You know, the horse might accidentally tread on a rabbit? A very elderly, slow, overweight one, with lost of meat on it? Or maybe even two fat, elderly rabbits, going out for a stroll?"

And he laughed.

Their best hope, though, was to find *people*.

They might not be Horse People, so far south. But there were other groups who lived out on the Plain, and shared some of the customs of the Horse People, trading with them and occasionally attending their feast-days. Some of them were remnants of once great tribes, now reduced to a few families and their tents and livestock. Others were Sueni who had chosen to live with horses, in the fresh air of the Plain, rather than in their stinking swamps. And then there were the renegades, runaways from the Citizen army or from Citizen justice. It might not be so good to meet *them*.

Apart from the outlaws, all such people would recognize and respect the name of Mara's grandfather, who was a member of the Council of the Horse People, and maybe her father's name, too, even if he was no more than a clan chieftain.

They would know that they could earn the undying gratitude of the Horse People (and some silver coins) by helping Mara; and that they would harvest hatred, pursuit, and revenge if it were discovered that they had failed to help her, or had even caused her harm.

They might meet traders, and then they could buy food, if only they had something to buy it with. Selling the horse was unthinkable; other-wise, they had only the clothes they were wearing, the riding-cloth, and the little knife. The knife was a pretty object—maybe they could sell it to someone?

They rode on, to the nearest of the clumps of trees, where Mara had decided they would camp for the night. It was some considerable dis-tance away, but they had no other choice: they mightn't have reached the next one before nightfall.

Disappointingly, there were no bushes with berries. However, there was some soft undergrowth beneath the trees that would make a comfort-able bed.

Supper was a quick, modest affair. Because they had no water yet, she picked out the juiciest of the fruit. The next morning, she promised, they would look for a stream, and while they were searching she would show him that trick with the broad-leaf grass (which would be easier to find).

Did he need to "go"?

No, he didn't. (Well, thank the Thousand Names of the Horses in the Sky for that, at least!)

They cuddled up together to keep warm. There were a few fallen leaves, though not enough to cover them like a blanket. It wasn't too cold yet for sleeping, but it would be chilly in the morning hours.

He asked her for a story. Did she have one that *wasn't* about horses?

Mara was rather hurt. She had told him every single story that she had ever heard as a child, and, naturally, the children's stories of the Horse People were about horses. What was wrong with that? Horses were wonderful, beautiful animals. Not that you should be sentimental about them, like giving them names or whatever.

Well, if he didn't want one of her stories about horses, what *would* he like? He should make a suggestion.

He had no idea.

"It's your job to tell me stories. You promised to look after me. And the lawyer said you have to."

How often he had reminded her of that! Cursed be all lawyers, and all their documents! Esbus had a deep pit of burning excrement waiting for them.

"Why don't you tell *me* a story? You must have heard a few stories that weren't about horses. From Lord Castor, perhaps, or—"

She was about to say "from Lelia", but bit on her tongue.

He sniffled.

"Can't remember any."

She had another try.

"Then why don't you tell me some stories about yourself? Like: where did you live before you came to Fanum? Do you remember any nice people, or animals?"

He pondered over that.

"There was a man who brought me to Castor. He stroked me, and gave me sweets, and told me to be good and do what I was told. I can't remember. It's so long ago!"

"Was he a nice man?"

"No. But he was very rich! Everyone treated him with lots of respect. They were all frightened of him. When I grow up, I want to be rich, too, and give everyone orders!" He gave Mara a coy smile. "The way I give you orders!"

"What was his name?"

"Issachar!"

She knew that name. And if she had not yet noticed the night growing colder, now she felt the chill on her skin.

Issachar! What had Manasa said? That anywhere where people were being hurt and frightened, Issachar wouldn't be far away.

"Come here, little *seflar*."

And she hugged him as close to her as she could, until he fell asleep, as she did soon afterwards.

Her sleep was troubled by vivid dreams.

Horses with waving manes and gleaming eyes were circling her. She tried to escape the circle, but there was no way to get past them. She called to them, but they galloped ever faster.

Something was out there, beyond them. It was calling to her. She was aware of a face, but couldn't see its features.

Let me out, she told the horses. No, they told her. We mustn't.

I want to go, she said. She sensed the face. Now it had eyes. It was calling her. It wanted her.

We want you too, the horses said, and they whirled faster and faster.

We are protecting you.

Protecting me? From what?

She tried to raise her arm to strike the horses, but her arm wouldn't move.

Now the face had eyes! It was—

At which point she woke.

Her arm was being pinned to the ground by a foot in a leather riding boot. She looked up into the broad, grinning face of a cavalryman.

"Good morning! You sleep well, eh?"

He was speaking in Sueni. He *was* a Sueni. She turned her head, and saw another one, standing behind him, holding the "demon"'s bridle and grasping Phrygillus with his other hand.

"A horsey virgin—just what we were looking for! Hey hey, this must be our lucky day."

XII

MANASA EXPLAINS THE
MEANING OF A MESSAGE

✠ *Cascantum.*

The night air was fresh, quite unpleasantly so, as they followed Petronius out onto a small, open courtyard—the "small parade-ground", he had said. Manasa regretted having to leave the little supper-party. She hadn't eaten so well for a long time. When would she get another such opportunity?

Thomasius, she could see, was sobering up rapidly. During the supper he'd had too much wine, and he had pawed at her breasts in a friendly and exploratory manner. She hadn't pushed his hands away: he was her master, after all. He'd been very unassertive and sleepy, and Grassica and Gemma were engaged in doing more or less the same.

She'd felt sorry for Gemmella, who in the absence of her own man had busied herself with preparing and serving the food and drink.

Out on the parade-ground, which was lit by soldiers carrying torches, a man was waiting for them. He was powerfully built: his legs were set like tree-trunks, and his massive arms were folded in front of him. Petronius and the two Sub-officers saluted him.

This must be the famous Lord Commander Rhaetius.

"My Lord!"

Rhaetius stared right past them—at her, but with the darkness and the flickering of the torchlight there was too much shadow for her to be sure about the expression on his face.

"This is your Sybarite girl, Thomasius?"

"Yes, my Lord."

"Hmm! Not bad. What tongues has she mastered?" He paused. "No, let her answer that!"

She didn't think that Thomasius had been about to say anything, but now he shoved her forwards, and onto her knees, whispering "Be careful". Or had he said "Be honest"? She would be both, as best she could.

"All the tongues of the south, my Lord: Sybarite, Xinga, and the lesser tongues of the neighboring peoples—"

"Good."

Manasa had deliberately *not* mentioned Old Sybarite, which was the evil tongue of Esbus, and of sorcerers. But she wasn't finished yet.

"The Tongue of the Horse People. And the Citizens' Tongue that we are speaking now."

"Don't try my patience, girl, by stating the obvious!"

His voice was harsh. Thomasius kneed her gently in the back by way of warning.

"Forgive me, my Lord!" She bowed her head tactfully. "If it pleases my Lord, I also have some knowledge of Sueni, of the Tongue of the Free People, and of the Eto."

"But not of the Tongue of the Blood-Drinkers?"

"No, my Lord. I have had no opportunity to learn their tongue."

Rhaetius stepped towards her and, cupping her chin in a huge paw, lifted her head so that their eyes met.

"What a pity. For so many reasons."

What did he mean by that?

He looked up again and spoke to the two Sub-officers, pointing at something that was lying in the darkness at the edge of the parade-ground. They should take a look at it. Petronius had already seen it.

He beckoned for torchbearers, as the four men walked across to whatever it was, Manasa following closely behind. (No-one had told her not to, had they?)

The object was the dead body of a man, stripped to the waist. His limbs were stretched out. He was spread-eagled, *arranged* in a careful way that she had seen somewhere before.

Thomasius was the first to react.

"Oh no—that's Gracchus!"

Who was Gracchus? And what was so special about him, to make the great Lord Commander haul his Sub-officers out of their supper-party?

"Yes, that is all that is left of my best interpreter. The killer has done me great harm. We have other interpreters, but not one of them has such a good command of the Tongue of the Blood-Drinkers as Gracchus did. I was hoping that your Sybarite girl might have some knowledge."

Manasa shrank back just a little, in case they should all stare at her, but no-one did. They were too fascinated by the sight of the dead interpreter.

His throat had been gashed, from ear to ear, with a smooth, thin cut such as only a Sybarite blade could produce. The upper part of his body was bare, and there were letters carved into his chest.

She formed the letters silently with her lips.

K-A-F-Λ.

Oh no! This was very bad. It was worse than bad, it was horribly dangerous, and she was the only one who would understand why. Should she speak?

Rhaetius pointed to the letters, and invited their comments.

"Kafl," Grassica said, pronouncing it "kaffel". "Not a word that I'm actually familiar with!"

According to Petronius, on the other hand, it wasn't a word at all but a name, clearly of barbarian origin, and as barbarous as the behavior of the man who had cut it into the body of the unfortunate interpreter.

"Perhaps Gracchus owed this Kaffel money," he added, "and this is a warning to others to remember to pay their debts?"

The Lord Commander snorted.

"Do we know of any money-lenders named Kaffel? And why should our interpreter, Sol give him peace, need to borrow money? Did he keep a woman? Did he gamble?"

Grassica: "Neither, to my knowledge."

Rhaetius laughed: "And you would know about the gambling if anyone would! Gentlemen, think this through. If it was a small debt, why should this Kaffel take the risk of murdering a soldier in the very heart of the fortress? And if was a large debt, what hope does Kaffel now have of retrieving his money, after doing *this* to our poor interpreter?"

Manasa cleared her throat, loudly. But to no avail: she was ignored.

"It's a funny business, my Lord," Thomasius said. "The first three letters are from our script, but the last one, the 'L', is from the Eto. Or some other tongue that uses the eastern letters."

Manasa cleared her throat again. Rhaetius turned and stared at her.

"Ah, the girl! Tell us then, might it be in Sybarite? Although it is not written in a script of the south."

"Yes, my Lord, it—"

But before she could go on a soldier rushed up to the little group and saluted the Lord Commander. He had an urgent message for him.

Rhaetius took the man aside and listened to what he had to say. They spoke for some time, and then the soldier was dismissed. The way that he left the parade-ground, briskly and purposefully, made Manasa sure that he had been given important instructions. Rhaetius didn't move, however, but just remained where he was standing, looking thoughtful.

She didn't dare to continue.

Finally, the Lord Commander spoke, though it was to Thomasius, not to her.

"Sub-officer, your girl is freezing. She's from the south, man, don't forget that. Give her your cloak."

Thomasius wrapped his cloak over her shoulders. Yes, she had been feeling the cold.

"Thank you," she whispered.

"That man's throat was slit with a Sybarite blade, are we agreed? Our Citizen weapons don't make cuts like that. And it seems that we have had Sybarite visitors within the fortress walls tonight. One of the stable-boys reported to the duty officer. He saw two young men, small, dark-skinned, one bearded, both in black, slipping out of the stables. That description doesn't sound much like Sueni cavalrymen!"

"Or like anyone local, my Lord."

"And that came to pass, my dear Thomasius, many hours ago. The duty officer didn't consider it worth following up, because the stable-boy, he said, was a notorious drinker. Company-commander Decius—"

"Decius? Well, well! He's hardly an enemy of the wine-cup himself!"

"Shut up, Grassica, that's a superior officer you're talking about. And at the moment I need every man that I've got, even the drinkers. Though when this business is over, I shall have some serious words with Company-commander Decius, I promise you that. My best interpreter might still be alive if he had bothered to order a proper search for the two intruders. Instead, he let Sybarite killers run amok inside the walls of Cascantum. Two deadly young men, dressed in black—or a man and a girl!"

Manasa's heart sank, but it was Thomasius who spoke.

"You mean: Victor, and the Lord Governor's maid?"

"Yes: Victor, the same man who tried to kill you in Fanum. The girl might be his lover, or perhaps she is merely his creature. But both of them serve the Cause." Now he turned to Manasa again. "So, we have two Sybarite murderers on the rampage in my fortress. I am not happy about that! The writing on this man's chest is in the Tongue of Sybaris, or so you were about to tell us, I believe. What do the letters mean? Your master and I are very curious to find out."

Manasa was torn between revealing everything that she knew—or revealing nothing at all. A small, insistent voice from within her was telling her to remain silent. If she did, one person very dear to her might be saved. *Might.* But for everyone else, including herself, and Thomasius, who had been kind to her, the final consequences could be terrible. And she knew that it was the road of evil—a road that she wouldn't take.

She would tell them, but try to hold back what was most precious to her, for as long as she could.

"It is a Sybarite word, but you mustn't speak it, my Lord! No-one must speak the word, or they will die!"

Rhaetius wasn't impressed.

"What nonsense is this? Words don't kill. It's swords that kill. Spears. Arrows." He held out his clenched fist. "And I have killed with this more than once." But then he asked, more quietly: "What is this *word* that can kill?"

"It is not in your tongue, my Lord, but it was written in your Citizen script so that you could read it. Sybarite letters are shaped differently, with many curves. Not many northerners can read them."

The Lord Commander laughed.

"And they're also more difficult to carve into a man's flesh, eh? These are just straight cuts. Much easier. But go on. What does this word that can't be spoken *mean*?"

"It means 'soon'."

"'Soon'?"

"'Soon', or 'again'. It is only used as a threat."

"You mean like: I'm coming to get you!" Rhaetius found that very funny. He turned to his officers. "I'm absolutely *wetting* myself, boys! Give me one good reason why we should be worried."

Oh, there was so much that he didn't know. And if he did, he wouldn't be so amused.

"This Victor is an educated man, my Lord, surely?" Thomasius looked perplexed. "Well-traveled, at least? So why has he mixed letters from two different scripts? To what purpose?"

"Sons of Esbus, how should I know? Perhaps the girl wrote it for him?"

She would need to tell them more.

"My Lord?"

"Yes?"

"It is a message. And a threat." Her voice dropped to a whisper. "And it is a spell. The word is Old Sybarite, the tongue of the sorcerers. Whoever speaks the word, disaster will come to him. It is a double magic, my Lord. First, because it is written in blood. Blood calls up the demons, and binds them to your will…"

"Yes, and?"

"And, secondly, because of the letters. The third letter is not truly 'F', my Lord. There is no such letter 'F' in Old or New Sybarite, but a sound like 'F' is made by another letter, which also exists in the Eto, though not in the Citizens' Tongue. You would write it as 'PH'."

"So why didn't he write 'PH', then? Again, was that 'P' too awkward for him to cut? Too curved?" He paused. "Kafl: that has a meaning in Sybarite? Or have I just put a spell on myself by speaking the word?"

Manasa would have smiled if she had dared.

"No, my Lord, and the word that you spoke has a different meaning." She hesitated, expecting them all to laugh. "It means…'carrot'."

None of the men reacted immediately. There was silence, broken only the spluttering of the torches. She waited. It was Grassica who laughed first, then the others.

"Carrot? What a terrifying curse!"

"Speak the word, and you will be poisoned with a dish of carrots!"

"You will choke on a carrot! You will die after being poked in the eye with a raw carrot!"

"Carrots will come for you in the night!"

But Rhaetius wasn't laughing, and he ended it with a gesture ("Enough").

"My Lord, the word 'kafl' was not intended. The last letter is not an 'L', in the Eto script, but an 'A', in the script of the Citizens, with one stroke missing." She added quickly: "Please don't try to speak the word!"

"So he was interrupted while he was cutting poor Gracchus, and couldn't finish it—this word that I mustn't speak?"

"No, my Lord, it was deliberate. There had to be eleven cuts, not one more and not one less. Whoever wrote this hoped that someone would speculate, as you just did, guess that one last cut wasn't made, and then blurt out the word. The spell comes to life when the word is spoken."

"But why eleven?"

She told them unwillingly. There were evil things, things of the darkness, that could be woken simply by naming them. Better not to speak of them.

"Because eleven is an awkward number, like thirteen or nineteen."

"Awkward numbers? Why are they awkward? What is the girl talking about?"

Petronius stepped forward.

"She means prime numbers, my Lord: numbers that can't be divided, except by one and by themselves."

"Well done, Staff Officer, it would be embarrassing if four experienced officers of the Citizen Army knew less about mathematics than a slave-girl! This is one of the fruits of your studies in Maidunum, I take it?"

"Yes, my Lord, one half-day a week was devoted to mathematical studies, in addition to philosophy, rhetoric—"

"Yes yes, quite enough of that! You've established that you're a clever boy. Now tell us what is so dangerous about eleven. Why not nineteen? If he'd made nineteen cuts he could have sent us a longer message!"

"I have no idea, my Lord."

This, too, Manasa had to explain.

The awkward numbers were numbers with magical properties, and which were therefore reserved for the use of the gods. Two was the number of the Great One and His consort; three stood for the Sacred Triad, every child knew that; five is the number of good-omen: the Star of Fortune has five points, and the hand raised in blessing four fingers and a thumb; seven was the natural number of all that mattered, from the days of the week to the wonders of the world...

As the first of the magic numbers were being assigned, the Lord of Esbus grew impatient that He had not been given one, and He declared, "The next number is for *me*!"

And since then, eleven had been the number of dread and ill-omen.

"And what with the other awkward numbers after eleven?" Grassica asked her.

No, she said, the Dark One made no claim on them. One number would suffice for all His fell purposes.

Rhaetius was angry.

"So our friend Victor is trying to lure us into provoking the Lord of Esbus? He is playing with us. I want this man's head on a stake! And the girl's head, too—but not until every man in the fortress has been through her, twice. Then we'll see who's laughing!"

Manasa said nothing.

Petronius stepped forward. His handsome face was quivering with heroic eagerness.

"*I* shall find them, my Lord! I shall find them, vanquish them, bring them to you in chains, and throw them at your feet!"

He would do nothing of the sort, Rhaetius replied.

"You are my senior Staff Officer (Sol help us all) and we are about to be overrun by Blood-Drinkers. I need everyone, even Staff Officers."

"Then permit me to set extra watch-parties, my Lord, and organize patrols to catch these intruders."

"That has already been done. What do you think I was telling that boy who brought me the message?" For the first time the Lord Commander sounded tired. "Those searches have been going on while we were speaking. Inside the walls of the fortress. And at first light patrols will go into the township, and search there too. From house to house. That is all we can afford to do, with the manpower that we have."

"Sir—"

"No! I can't spare you. But I do have an experienced Sub-officer who is still unfit for duty, who is currently without a posting, and who knows the man. Thomasius! And a girl who speaks their tongue and understands their magic. *You* will find these Sybarites for me! They can't be far away."

Thomasius stood aghast. His jaw had dropped. Manasa felt much the same, and she hoped that she didn't look as stupid as he did.

Grassica spoke up for his colleague.

"My Lord, Thomasius is barely back on his feet again, and this man is an experienced killer."

"Rubbish! *All* my men are experienced killers, or they wouldn't be serving in the Citizen Army, would they? I won't stand for such talk! But if it will set your mind at rest, I'll give Thomasius another man to hold his hand and watch his back. You said that his stitches were coming out tomorrow? Have it done quickly, and after that, he and the girl can join the patrols searching in the township." He switched his attention to Thomasius. "The girl might see clues that the soldiers would miss. And I didn't say *kill* them, I said *find* them. When you've found them, corner them, like rats, and then…persuade them, trick them, overwhelm them. Whatever has to be done. I want them alive, though. And you won't need to fight the man on your own. Now: go to bed. And no more wine."

But no-one was in the mood for drinking.

If Manasa had known how to make them, there were special potions that she could have prepared that gave you courage and the ability to forget every danger. She was now deeply oppressed by her thoughts.

Despite what she had said, the trap that Victor had laid was not intended for the Lord Commander, or for any of his officers. How would they ever have known how to decipher the puzzle? No, it had been intended for *her*.

Yet the Sleepless Ones had surely not sent him just to kill a slave-girl. What did *she* matter? She was of no significance to them. Victor was there for some other evil reason, some greater purpose. But because in Fanum she had stood over Thomasius and had brandished his sword at the attacker, she—a mere woman!—had cheated the man of his prey, and this was now something *personal* between them.

Victor had known that she was in Cascantum, and he had counted on their seeing that the deadly cut that had killed Gracchus had been made by a southern blade, not by a heavy Citizen sword. To make sure, he had allowed a stable-boy to see two dark young southerners. He had expected Rhaetius to then show her the body, with its cryptic message, and to ask her what it meant. How many southerners were there in Cascantum whom he could turn to for help?

And he had counted on her recognizing that it was an incomplete Sybarite word that had been cut into the interpreter's chest, and on her making the deadly mistake of completing the word and speaking it out loud.

What he hadn't counted on was her having some slight knowledge of the darker magic. How could he know *everything* that was in her past?

But there was much more that was troubling her. She needed to talk to someone, and that person would have to be Thomasius.

To tell him these things, she would need to be very close to him. He had wanted her, when they were sharing the couch. Then let him now have his way with her—they would hold each other tight, and whisper, and she would be able to tell him!

But Thomasius remained sunk in his own thoughts, and when the time came and she slipped into bed beside him, naked, she found that he was already fast asleep, and snoring quietly.

XIII

FLORIANUS MEETS ONE OF HIS TRAVELING COMPANIONS

※ *The Imperial Palace, in the City.*

Julian would bleed to death, and it would serve him right! Florianus was not an excessively vindictive person, but he believed in paying his debts—and Julian had caused him pain and public humiliation. The time had come to settle accounts.

The thought of having Julian castrated had crossed his mind often enough, especially when he had given his master that sneering "I am a complete man" look that Florianus knew so well. He had seen it often enough on the faces of courtiers or Guardsmen (and occasionally Palace servants too, if they were under the impression that he wasn't watching them).

Florianus was always watching, though, and the servant's insolence would be rewarded with a well-deserved beating.

Back then it would not have been difficult for the High Chamberlain to arrange a castration, even of a free man like Julian, for was Julian not poor, and without friends, and completely dependent on him? However, Florianus would have waited until a specialist could be organized to carry out the delicate operation. Afterwards, Julian might have thanked him for liberating him from the burdensome cravings of the flesh.

No such solicitude now! A plan for revenge had shaped itself in his mind on that day that Julian had defiled him, on a couch in the Golden Rooms, for the entertainment of the Emperor. Now he had been encouraged to put his plan to the test by an opportune visit that he received soon after Senator Naevius had rescued him.

He had been given temporary quarters in the Palace in a section of underground rooms that were used to accommodate the servants. Some of them—the loyal ones!—came to commiserate with him. Among them was Calixta, who was in charge of the maids, and whose husband was the chief executioner (and torturer).

Florianus had a good relationship with the dreaded Calixtus, although the man was a drunken incompetent. On several occasions he had bribed him to spare some miserable victim the worst of the horrors of torture or execution; or, if it was a flogging, to reduce the total number of lashes to what human flesh could actually stand, or to substitute a simple whip (such as traditional-minded Citizen husbands used to discipline their wives) for the fearsome punishment whip, which was studded with sharp fragments of bone and tiny spikes of metal.

Calixtus and his assistants were not themselves sadistically cruel. To his knowledge, they derived no twisted pleasure from the torments they inflicted. For them, it was all part of the day's work. They did what they were told to do and paid to do, and so they could also (if one exercised suitable discretion) be told and paid to do it slightly *differently*.

Florianus was very cautious with the executioner's wife, though. Calixta was a hard, selfish woman, of the kind who would bear a long-term grudge from even the smallest of slights. And, unlike her husband, she would probably have reveled in what for him was just a routine job.

She was just one of several Palace servants who complained to him about his successor. Julian was treating the maids, and even some of the younger female cooks, as his personal property. He would waylay girls in the corridor, or pounce on them while they were working. They had to obey him, he said, not only because he was the High Chamberlain but because he was also the bosom friend of the Emperor! ("He said *that*? How interesting…") And then he would show them his "love-tool", as he called it, and bend them over the edge of a bed or table. Very few had had the courage to push him away and flee.

"He's like a rutting donkey. Or an ape. He hit some of my maids, and he took one of them back to his room. While she was there, *I* had to do her work for her! He kept her there for hours, and when she came out she couldn't walk properly."

"Yes, that's really terrible—but what can *I* do about it?"

Calixta nodded in irritation, acknowledging that Florianus was no longer in a position to help her.

All the women told him more or less the same about Julian. But it was Calixta who asked: "Why do my girls have to put up with this? He doesn't even pay them for it. How can they be expected to get their work done properly? And you know what will happen? In the end, I will be blamed!" And then: "*But isn't the High Chamberlain always supposed to be a eunuch?*"

Yes!

He assured her that this was indeed the ancient tradition of the court, and that Julian would no doubt soon be willingly undergoing the little alteration. It was a necessary qualification for anyone who hoped to occupy such a high position permanently!

It would do no harm for Calixta to draw her husband's attention to the fact that he might soon be needed to carry out the operation. Bearing in mind that Senator Naevius was terribly busy, and that he was not familiar with court etiquette. While it would hardly be a deliberate snub if the Senator brought in a stranger from outside to perform the task, it would still be a loss of face for her husband. Nor would he receive the generous fee for the castration.

From the glint in her eye, Florianus deduced that she knew exactly what he was up to. She would be an all too willing accomplice!

The next step was to persuade the Senator. Calixtus was unlikely to be able to approach him directly (though he might well talk to Quintus Naevius). Florianus could therefore scarcely believe his good fortune when Senator Naevius himself gave him an opportunity to broach the subject.

The Senator had summoned him to the small conference chamber to discuss the mission to Neopolis. No servants or guards were present, he noted, only Naevius, his son, and Florianus himself.

While Quintus looked on, picking his teeth with the point of a dagger, the Senator told Florianus how important his role would be. The invitation to the upcoming wedding was no more than an excuse—a screen behind which to hide the real reason for the expedition, which was to gather information. That would be the task of Florianus.

In audience, Necro would do all the talking. Although he was a blather-mouth and a bore, he would find the right words to flatter the sensibilities of the Eastern heretics. It would help that, as a White, he was not a known adherent of the Slave in either of the manifestations of that worship, neither the rightful form practiced in the West nor the perversion indulged in in the East, or of any other cult other than that of Lord Sol, to which he was drawn by his fascination for ritual.

Necro's lack of religious fanaticism was the only positive quality that Florianus had discovered in him so far.

The "handful of diplomatic gifts" to which Necro had referred so disparagingly would be entrusted to the eunuch, until the moment came for them to be formally presented by the Senator. The most significant of them, a direct gift from Emperor Maximillus to his Imperial cousin, was nothing special to look at: a plain silver ring, with the device of a handclasp.

"His Imperial Majesty extends the hand of friendship, which is grasped in acknowledgment of the concord and harmony that shall reign over both halves of the Empire. A symbolic handclasp. This is the ring that Emperor Maximus wore whenever he gave audience, and which he showed to his sons as he lay dying. He made them swear on it that, even though he was dividing his realm between them, they would never forget that the Empire was one and indivisible, and built on trust and fraternal affection. That kind of thing. Let Necro make the speech, though."

"Isn't that a very precious gift to give his Imperial Majesty of the East? A historical heirloom?"

Quintus answered for his father.

"You think we're stupid? It's only a fucking copy!"

"Though that is information that stays here in his room, between the three of us. You understand that?"

"Perfectly, my Lord. I will swear any oath that you require of me. My loyalty to you is as reliable as the rising and setting of the sun."

"Do your work well, and there will be a rich reward for you. A new position, away from the Palace. You served his Imperial Majesty well, and how did he reward you?"

Quintus guffawed.

"I bet it hurt! That man is built like a stallion! And you should have seen his face while he was screwing you—I thought his head was going to burst."

The Senator motioned to his son to be quiet.

"That's enough, Quintus. I'm pleased that I wasn't there to see it. Disgusting! But his Majesty has a peculiar sense of humor, and he has taken an unfortunate liking to this Julian. I truly hope that he can carry out his duties as High Chamberlain adequately. You trained him well enough, I'm sure, but I already have my doubts. Is there anything we should bear in mind?"

No, Julian had attended him for so long that he was completely familiar with the etiquette and rituals of the court.

"He is excellently qualified to be my successor, except for one small detail: a formal requirement..."

Quintus butted in, grinning broadly.

"And I know what that is! We had to spend some time this morning with that asshole Rufus. Calixtus and I."

His father wasn't amused.

"I hope that you didn't torture Cornelius Rufus? He's a Senator, and we may yet need him. It's bad enough that your men beat him so badly. I expressly told you—"

"Yes, father. You do so much take the fun out of life." He yawned. "And, no, we didn't torture him. Just showed him the instruments. Tried to get some names out of him. You know, Calixtus has this sweet little device like a nutcracker... Fascinating. But even that didn't help, though we told him which nuts we'd be cracking with it!"

"Quintus!"

"Don't worry, Rufus is still in one piece."

"I'm pleased to hear that. But what is the point you were trying to make?"

"Oh, yes, Calixtus told me that any time we needed him, he and his boys were ready to do the cutting."

"The cutting?"

The Senator seemed to have no idea what his son was talking about.

"Julian needs to be...*cut*."

The Senator still didn't understand. This was the cue for Florianus to step in.

"My Lord, if I might? There is an ancient tradition that the High Chamberlain has to be a eunuch."

Quintus: "And Julian obviously isn't, as you found out the painful way, ha ha!"

The "ancient tradition" didn't exist, Florianus had invented it, but who was there to contradict him? Only Senator Necro and possibly his Holiness the High Priest of Sol might know a little about this aspect of court procedure—or they might not. And Necro was about to disappear, while his Holiness would probably object indignantly to being asked to discuss such a trivial and distasteful subject.

"The tradition is rooted in practical necessity. The High Chamberlain has unrestricted access to the Imperial ladies in their private quarters. For obvious reasons, he needs to be a eunuch. There have been no Imperial ladies at the court of the present Emperor, but that is about to change. Your granddaughter, my Lord—your daughter, of course, my Lord—will soon be Empress. That is a new situation that requires a reconsideration of many of the practical arrangements at the court."

Quintus was quicker to react than his father was.

"You see? We hadn't thought about that, had we? Now I don't give a toss of a Maximian about any ancient-fucking-traditions, but that man is a wet, dripping phallus on legs. None of the maids is safe from him. We can't have him slipping in and out of Naevia's bedchamber whenever he likes, brandishing his weapon in front of the ladies! No, he'll have to be cut. I'll do it myself!"

And he twirled the little knife that he had been using on his teeth.

It was agreed that Julian should be castrated as soon as possible, if only to "calm him down", as the Senator chose to put it, so that he could concentrate better on his duties. He had already disappointed Naevius on several matters.

For instance, it was planned to present Quintilianus Asper (whose weakness for boys was notorious) with a pretty cup-bearer as a gift, and Florianus (who probably knew his former master's taste better than anyone in the West) would be asked to find a suitable catamite. But the new High Chamberlain had rushed off to the slave-market without waiting for anyone and had made a spectacularly expensive purchase.

If he had intended to impress the Senator, he had not succeeeded. Quintus was less critical.

"Be fair, father, when did *you* ever show any interest in boys? So who are you to judge? On a dark night, one boy is as good as another. This one's pretty enough."

Florianus had made no comment. On a dark night, one boy was *not* as good as another, or Asper, who considered himself an esthete, would not have paid a small fortune for little Florianus, and had him cut in the hope of preserving his beauty and his tractability.

Even without examining the boy, he doubted whether he would be up to much—it was the wrong time of year to make that kind of purchase. The merchandise on offer was mostly leftovers from the summer sales.

Julian would be castrated at the first opportunity. While he was recovering from the operation, his duties could be carried out by the eunuch Photon (a harmless creature from the secretariat). The responsibility for the procedure would be placed (on Florianus's recommendation) in the capable hands of the chief executioner, Calixtus.

Capable hands! May his hands be *exceptionally* shaky that day! Florianus was very satisfied with the results of the meeting so far.

He was told that he would be allowed one servant to accompany him on the journey and see to his needs. One servant only. The Naevii might control the City, and thereby the state coffers of the Western Empire, but those coffers were almost empty. The Emperor was poorer than more than one of his richest subjects, and he had so many expensive commitments. What money could be scratched together would be needed to hire mercenaries to ward off an attack from Sybaris. And a lavish wedding celebration was imminent. There was no money left to waste on diplomatic fripperies.

So much for the "grandiose entourage" that the Senator had promised!

Florianus later heard that Necro had been most unhappy when he was informed about this. As an Imperial ambassador, an emissary between the thrones of the West and the East, he had expected to travel in style. He had wrangled with Senator Naevius over the number of attendants he would be permitted, complaining so bitterly and at such length that the younger Naevius eventually got up and threatened him with violence.

"No, have patience, Quintus," his father had said. "I am sure that

Senator Necro will let himself be persuaded to make a few small compromises."

In the event, the compromises were that Necro would be attended by a substantial entourage of servants and that the other principal members of the delation—Florianus and young Atticus—would be granted one attendant only. Atticus was not a Senator, and why should the eunuch ("a mere Palace servant without rank") need to have a servant at all? The eunuch (wherever possible, Necro avoided using his name) should also carry out all the necessary secretarial duties, so that no scribe would need to be added to the party either, allowing a further attendant to be assigned to the only Senator in the group.

On that last point Naevius had refused to budge. Whatever the formal rank of the eunuch Florianus might be, his *duties* would be considerable and he should not be distracted from them by having to carry out routine secretarial tasks.

Something had to give. The military escort would therefore be reduced to a minimum of one single white-cloaked Guards officer, an impressively-mustachioed but slow-moving Sueni, who was nearing the end of his career and would be of little use in any upcoming battles with the Placidi.

The mustachio-twirler would be instructed to commandeer protection for the delegates from the chief magistrate of every town that they passed through, and once they had crossed the border their security would be a matter for the Easterners.

If Senator Necro felt that these arrangements were insufficient, he could always hire additional men at his own expense. And he should ensure that some at least of the numerous attendants who would be escorting him were armed bodyguards, rather than cup-bearers or flute-players!

Those last comments had come from Quintus Naevius and were intended as an insult, since flute-players were popularly associated with brothels and orgies. Necro had veritably dribbled with annoyance, but had given his word that his attendants would be chosen with suitable care.

Florianus would be allowed one servant, to be paid for from the purse of gold and silver pieces for the expenses of the journey that would be entrusted to his (not Senator Necro's) care.

Excellent! Florianus decided on the spot that he would take Minnermus with him, but manumit him just before they departed. There was no danger that the old man would run off, hopping and dancing with joy, to savor his new freedom. He had nowhere else to go other than his master's little household. Besides, he really enjoyed fussing over Florianus, and seeing to his needs like a mother hen.

Minnermus had become quite doddery of late, and he was too old now to serve his master in that particular way that had sometimes been required of him in the past. However, since his recent brutal and humiliating encounter with Julian in the Imperial Presence, Florianus had lost any desire for physical contact of that kind.

Perhaps Minnermus would die from the rigors of the journey? If so, a replacement could easily be found in the slave-markets of Neopolis. And it wouldn't be necessary to pay the old man, meaning that the money thus saved could be used for other purposes.

If the footman happened to survive, and they all got back to the City safely, Florianus would offer him a small amount of money as a reward for his many years of faithful service. With that gift, he could buy himself an old woman if he so wished, to nurse him and warm his bed, and she could even be given a place in Florianus's household, to help out as a cook or a maid.

There was also a meeting with young Atticus, who had been called to the Palace to be informed about what was expected of him (which was very little). The duty of informing him was left to Florianus, neither of the Naevii being willing to waste their time on the "spoilt brat" (as Marcus Naevius described him) and "stupid little cunt" (the view of his son Quintus).

Quintus Naevius had reluctantly agreed to remove the boy's name from his "list".

It was strange that the lad should chose to call himself "Aulus", a distinctly outmoded name. What was wrong with Faustus Pomponius Atticus Junior? That was a name redolent of Citizen history, of status and privilege, a name that would win attention and open doors in both halves of the Empire and across the political factions. (Which was a major reason why the miserable boy had been chosen for this mission in the first place.)

It was rumored that Aulus had ambitions in the direction of poetry, like his wretched friend Sextus Placidus. Unlike the doomed Placidus, however, no-one had seen examples of his work. Did they even exist? Florianus had made the effort to read some of the Placidian outpourings, and he had been underwhelmed. Granted, he felt little affinity for the groans and desperate yearnings of sexually confused young men, but leaving aside the question of the poems' subject matter any fool could see that these were works of no great technical merit.

Perhaps (unlike his friend) young Aulus had had the intelligence to realize that his poetic works were rubbish, and had therefore refrained from inflicting them on the world?

Florianus doubted that very much. The behavior of the two young men at the bride-show—flouncing about like cockerels, and wearing more perfume and makeup than a Sybarite whore—was hardly evidence of good sense or good taste.

But when the boy arrived, Florianus was pleasantly surprised. Aulus—yes, he would have to get used to calling him that, if only to irritate Necro—was timid and sheepish, and hadn't paid much attention to his appearance.

Had he just crawled out of bed? Had the journey through the streets of the City, even under the protection of a small escort of Guardsmen, unnerved him? Quintus's thugs were everywhere, and the boy's name had previously been on his "list".

He mentioned that he had met Necro at the gate of the Palace, had greeted him respectfully, and had been ignored by the haughty Senator. That was very hurtful, he said. Was it because he had links to the Green and Blue factions—he put the Greens first, Florianus noticed—while Necro was a prominent White?

Florianus nodded in agreement, though he didn't think that that was the reason. What obligation was there for Necro to like the boy? In his eyes, Aulus was no more than a self-indulgent wastrel who had tried to evade his proper civic duties as a member of the Senatorial class.

Yet, then again, was there *anyone* that Necro didn't behave unpleasantly towards?

The thought that it was "only" about politics seemed to cheer Aulus up.

"Well, that's all right then!"

And he gave Florianus a bright smile, which for the first time lent his rather undistinguished-looking face a touch of charm.

Young Aulus plainly had no interest in factional politics. Good for him! This was a most satisfying start, Florianus thought to himself. The boy was polite and respectful. He would be a natural ally against the Senator. Florianus had to have *someone* to talk to on the journey, since Necro probably wouldn't deign to talk to him (unless it was absolutely essential); Minnermus was friendly, but slow-witted and lacking in education; and the magnificent-looking Guards officer Urgo expressed himself mostly in aggressive grunts.

Florianus had been considering which of the Palace scribes he could suggest be selected (the principle qualification being that it should be someone with moderately intelligent conversation). That was now no longer so urgent. He and Aulus already had a good topic—their shared antipathy for Gaius Ambibulus Necro—and literature could be another possibility (if the Senator's son was willing to listen to advice from a well-read eunuch).

He might even be useful in attracting attention away from Florianus, while the eunuch was making his discreet enquiries into certain matters of interest to his new patron, Marcus Naevius. Aulus was not a great beauty—in profile, you noticed the weakness of his jaw—and he was definitely not a heartbreaker, but if he returned to dolling himself up so ridiculously, he might yet cause a modest flutter among the court ladies in Neopolis. (And even among some of the male courtiers.)

Fashions were markedly different there. The Greater Worship favored in the East showed a much greater tolerance of color and pageantry, for instance, than was acceptable to those followers of the Slave who adhered to the Lesser Worship, the dourer version of the cult that was practiced in the City. (Both movements regarded the other as heretical, and their mutual dislike extended to questions of personal style.)

Florianus remembered how male courtiers in Neopolis had poked little golden rods (sometimes studded with precious stones) through fleshy, even very private, parts of the body, secured them with tiny clips, and worn these impractical items as male jewelry or intimate accessories.

Ugh! What would the High Priest of Sol make of *that*?

In contrast, Western noblemen and Senators tended to cultivate the "Citizen style" of robe and tunic (or the toga, where appropriate), evoking those distant times when their ancestors had ploughed their own fields, subscribed to the ancient virtues, and dressed with rough simplicity. Everything had been so much better then! Granted, breeches of the barbarian variety (in rough fabrics) had achieved a degree of acceptance in recent years, for practical reasons, but silks and feathers? Sybarite gowns in all the colors of the rainbow—for *men*? Body piercings? The ancestors would have been appalled!

Aulus Atticus, mocked as an effeminate popinjay in the City, might find himself more fully appreciated at the court of Neopolis. If that kept people's attention fixed on him, rather than on Florianus (eunuchs were in any case two to a copper coin in the East), it would be all to the good.

XIV

DECIMUS IS ADVISED TO
KEEP HIS HANDS TO HIMSELF
AND HIS MOUTH SHUT

✠   *The City.*

There is nothing more exciting than entering a great city at dusk. The lamps are being lit, decent folk are making for home, the smell of ovens announces the preparation of evening meals, and painted creatures of the night are beginning to take to the streets. After traveling for days or weeks across desolate country, and through grubby little towns and sleepy villages, it was thrilling to be plunged into the heart of the metropolis.

Decimus was almost overwhelmed by the sounds and smells, the bustle all around them, the shouting and good-natured banter. If this was a capital city that had just undergone a violent seizure of power, followed by the "cleansing" of the supporters of the defeated faction, not much of that was immediately in evidence.

Nor was it a city that seemed to be living in any fear of attack. Blood-Drinkers? Who were they? The narrow streets between the North Gate, from which he had left the City and through which he and Vulpeculus had re-entered it, and the Palace, towards which they were now heading, were like one long, uninterrupted party. There were no obvious signs of burning or looting. There were no trembling survivors of beating or rape, cowering in corners in fear of their lives. There were the usual desperate beggars on display, but not in greater number than they always were.

But, then again, this part of the City was a Blue stronghold, and the Blues had much to celebrate.

In the more affluent parts of town, where the prominent Reds had once lived, or in the densely-packed slum quarters where migrants from the south were housed in crumbling tenement blocks, it would be very different. And in every part of the City there would be fear, Decimus knew, bubbling uneasily under the surface until some event caused panic to break out.

Although night was falling, the city gates had still been wide open. A handful of Prefectural police manned the North Gate and asked them for their names. They officiously demanded to know the purpose that had brought them to the City. Vulpeculus was visibly displeased to be treated in this manner, and not to have been recognized.

"Don't you know who I am?"

But before he could say any more, the policemen were swept aside, with vigorous shouts of "Fuck off!" and "Stupid pricks!", by a gang of fearsome-looking bully-boys wearing blue scarves and ribbons. With much noise, and with energetic abuse and shoving about of passers-by, they were escorted by this ragtag bodyguard to their final destination.

On the way, Vulpeculus exchanged bawdy comments with the leader of the thugs, whom he apparently knew. This unappealing creature was short and scar-faced, powerfully built, and with an insolent, threatening manner. He fed the Senator with the latest news, sometimes dropping his voice so that Vulpeculus had to lean down to hear matters that were only for his ears.

He seemed perfectly at ease with the man, and seemed very pleased indeed with what he was being told.

Decimus wondered what that could be.

That the family of Senator So-and-So had been completely extinguished?

That they had just burned down a famous library full of scrolls of Sybarite literature and philosophy, precious, irreplaceable texts?

That there were tenement properties which had formerly belonged to proscribed Senators that Vulpeculus could now acquire for a most reasonable price?

Decimus was too tired to care, but he was far from happy to see that the mob not only ruled the streets, but controled the gates of the city too.

The Senator had insisted that they go straight to the Palace, however late the hour. He was bearing news, and a certain document, both of which would greatly please the new masters of the capital. For Decimus's benefit he pointed out that it would show respect, and demonstrate their loyal fervor, if they delivered these at once. Naevius, despite his advanced age, was not a man who slept much, and if it was a matter touching upon state business, or security, he would expect his attendants to wake him.

In that he was very like the General.

It was also an opportunity to present Decimus to those in power, and to allow him to commence his posting in the Palace more auspiciously.

Under normal circumstances, his presence there as Ogilo's man would have been viewed by Naevius as unnecessary and inconvenient, in fact, as an insolent provocation. Now, their relationship could begin in a warm glow of friendly approval. They should take full advantage of that.

Approaching the North Gate, Vulpeculus had asked him, one last time, whether he had considered his offer, and Decimus had said yes: when the time came, the Senator could rely upon him. But he insisted that he not be asked to betray his master directly and publicly. He had sworn loyalty to him.

Vulpeculus was amused by his squeamishmess.

"Well I never, a freedman with scruples! Whatever next?"

But no-one would demand that open act of betrayal of him—not yet, at least. The General was still needed, in fact needed far more (Vulpeculus whispered) than the pathetic Emperor was, or the vicious, uncontrollable Quintus Naevius. One had to be practical, and patient.

"If I do ever ask that you betray Ogilo, it will be because the man *deserves* to be betrayed, for the good of the Empire. But that day has not come yet. For the time being, you will simply be serving two masters, whose needs are not in conflict with each other."

Decimus felt flattered by the Senator's interest. Serving two masters would be a dangerous game, yet if he won the confidence of Vulpeculus it would bring him very close to those whom he should now be watching on the General's behalf. And the knowledge that he gained would make it easier for him to decide, when the time came, which way to jump—if he ever had to make that choice.

He would prefer to serve the General, whom he respected. Liked? No, Ogilo wouldn't allow anyone close enough to him for that. And Decimus couldn't say that he would never, ever, betray him.

There was only one person about whom he could say that: Aulus. That wasn't because his young master had been kind to him. Aulus was kind to everyone. As a child he had worried himself silly about birds that the kitchen cats had caught and mauled. Nor was it because Aulus had gone to his father and asked—demanded, even—that Decimus be freed. It was because Aulus had given him his affection, and his trust, when he was still a slave.

In second place would be Lucius Atticus, because he had always treated his nephew's freedman with courtesy and with respect. He couldn't claim to be the Senator's friend (as that other freedman, Davus, certainly was), but he knew that Lucius Atticus liked him. Decimus would not willingly do anything to cause harm to Senator Atticus.

The General came third, a long way behind.

Some might find it sad, Decimus thought, that he had no family to be loyal to, and no woman. But then this was the path he had chosen for himself.

The street that they were now going down was becoming impossibly crowded. At first, kicks and curses from their escort had sufficed to clear a way through, but now the road was blocked, with wagons carrying baskets of chickens or piles of firewood, with porters loaded down with the wares of shopkeepers, with the hand-carts of refreshment vendors, and with bad-tempered people on foot who were just trying to get home.

"This is shit," the leader of their escort declared. "We'll go round the back way." Clutching the reins, he guided their horses down a narrow side-street where there was very little traffic. Their new route caused them to double back towards the city wall, and they passed by another gate, the Gate of the Winds, which was named after a well-known local landmark, an elaborate monument dedicated to the Four Winds. The whole area was gaudily lit, like the scene of some rich man's midnight party, and the gate itself yawned wide open, with people passing through it in both directions and no police controls.

Decimus was furious. The General's suggestion, that he might advise the Commander of the Imperial Guard on matters of security, now looked less like an excuse for him being in the Palace and more like an urgent necessity.

He said something about it to Vulpeculus, adding, "If there were Blood-Drinkers out there beyond the gate, they could ride into the heart of this city whenever they liked. They could stable their horses in the Temple of Sol, and no-one would notice them!"

To his amazement the Senator laughed, and then said, "Too late, I'm afraid: the Blood-Drinkers are already inside the city."

"*What?*"

The leader of their escort stared at Decimus unpleasantly.

"You heard the gentleman. You think you're so clever, freedman, but you don't know *fuck* about nothing."

Decimus made a mental note to teach the man a painful lesson in manners one day if he ever got the chance. But how could the Blood-Drinkers already be inside the city? What had he missed?

Vulpeculus put him out of his misery. Among the pieces of information that the man had fed him was the news that a delegation from the Great King had arrived, and was now at the Palace.

"To negotiate?"

Vulpeculus shrugged.

"How do you define 'negotiate'? More likely, to tell us what they want. And to frighten us, of course. All the more reason for us to get to the Palace quickly. Naevius may need my advice. I shall introduce you if the situation allows it. Otherwise, all of that must wait till tomorrow."

They reached the Palace and dismounted. Ow, that hurt! For the first time Decimus noticed how sore he was from the days of riding. It would be so good not to have to get onto a horse for a while. Their escort told his men to deal with the horses, and then pointed cheerfully to a row of heads spiked on the outer railings of the Palace gate.

"Red assholes," he told them. "Placidus shit." He paused, before turning to Vulpeculus (and away from Decimus) and adding politely: "My Lord."

Even if there had been far more torches, it wouldn't have made it much easier to identify the decomposing heads, to which crows had obviously been giving their attention.

"But not the brothers themselves, I assume."

Vulpeculus seemed very sure that the heads of Gaius and Gnaeus Placidus were not part of the display.

"Nah." Their friend spat dramatically, shooting his spittle away from the Senator but intentionally close to Decimus's feet. "We didn't get them. But we will. We got that Rufus, didn't we? And we had some good fun with him, too."

"Is he—"

"Nah. Some fucking white-cloak pussy boy stuck his nose in, just when it was getting interesting. But the high-and-mighty Senator's in the deep cells now, and he won't be coming out."

They were searched and disarmed—here the security was not so lax—and promptly hustled through the outer parts of the Palace complex towards the Golden Rooms, handed on from one team of Guards to another. Vulpeculus was instantly recognized by all of them. Decimus, on the other hand, was a less familiar face, though he had been to the Palace often enough. But it was sufficient for the Senator to glance at him each time and nod. Vulpeculus had been expected, and anyone who was with him was not considered to be a likely threat to the Imperial Person.

Besides, there was a more obvious danger alive and awake within the Palace walls. As they crossed one of the outer courtyards they saw a handful of Blood-Drinkers—the bodyguards of the delegation?—surrounded and held in check by Guardsmen.

Dismounted, they were disappointingly small, and they too had been relieved of their weapons. But they still looked frightening. The Blood-Drinkers were laughing and joking among themselves in their guttural tongue, quite unimpressed by their guards. Decimus would have dearly liked to stop and observe them more closely, because that is what you should always do with your enemy: watch him, and learn everything you can about him. But they were hustled onwards.

Quintus Naevius and a bevy of his men met them at the door to the throne-room.

"Well done, Senator, not a moment late and just when you're needed! Once again you show up at the right place, at the right time. You're as reliable as my morning shit. How *do* you manage it?"

A good question. It was the same gift, Decimus told himself, that rats had with corpses, or flies with rotting meat.

"This," the Senator said, pointing to him, "is Decimus. He serves the General, and is carrying the document that your father has been waiting for so keenly."

Quintus looked him straight in the eye.

"I know exactly who he is. He's a little shit. Ogilo's favorite cocksucker."

Quintus's men and some of the waiting courtiers and eunuchs sniggered. Decimus immediately looked down. Show politeness, don't challenge him, this is a dog that bites, a beast that you shouldn't provoke without a good reason.

"My Lord," he said in a respectful whisper, at the same time holding out the contract.

"Very nice. Daddy will be so pleased," Quintus said, with a sneer. "Don't lose it, freedman. Hold it tight, or play with your prick. But whatever you do—keep your hands well to yourself, and your mouth shut. We'll be watching you."

Then he led them into the room.

The Emperor was enthroned at the front. Senator Naevius, standing below the dais, saw his colleague at once and beckoned to him to come forward. As they advanced, however, their progress was cut off by a pompous little eunuch, who indicated that the Senator should take up a position to the right of the dais, where a number of other Senators (all Blues) were already in position. Decimus could stand behind him, but at the side of the hall. Even from there, though, he would be able to see and hear everything that was about to happen.

He saw a handful of White Senators and other dignitaries to the left of the dais, including the High Priest of Sol and the City Prefect. If any Greens were present, they must be in the body of the hall, and well-hidden.

Seated beside Maximillus, but on a simple chair rather than a throne, was the Empress-to-Be.

The famous envoys from the Great King had not yet been admitted to the throne-room. There had been a protocol problem, it was whispered. One of them was apparently refusing to make the full obeisance. Who did he think he was? What a disgrace!

While everyone else was therefore scanning the room for a sighting of the notorious Blood-Drinkers, Decimus used the opportunity to take a longer look at the unequal couple on the dais.

He had glimpsed the Emperor on frequent occasions over the years, at public ceremonies and on his visits to the Palace to report to the General. Maximillus had been a graceless, unattractive child, and he had grown into a graceless, unattractive youth. He looked pale and sweaty. Had he been drinking, and had they inconveniently been obliged to wake him for the arrival of the emissaries? Was he suffering from a late summer fever? Or had the Emperor simply overtaxed his strength in the bedroom?

If that last was the case, the reason was probably sitting beside him.

He looked at Naevia with genuine curiosity. She was older than Maximillus, and when they both stood up she might even be taller than him. And, yes, she was a redhead.

Redheads were feared and despised. It was a coloring that was seldom encountered among the Citizens, but found often enough in some of the barbarian tribes.

In ancient times, Davus had told him, redheads were regarded as monstrous freaks and (if they hadn't already been done to death by their parents) forced to live in squalid settlements close to the walls, along with lunatics, crippled beggars, and the incurably diseased, all of them impure creatures to be kept at a distance from the temples of the gods.

Today, redheads were merely scorned, and for the most part excluded from polite society. Neighbors would whisper maliciously that the redheaded child was a reminder of how the mistress of the house had once been shagged by a barbarian hostage, or by her flame-haired Sueni gatekeeper.

Yet instead of masking the color of her hair and the teint of her skin with dyes and cosmetics, as other women would have done, Naevia had chosen to accentuate her hair- and skin-coloring, and her girls had achieved this with consummate skill. Her appearance might be unusual, yes, but she was undoubtedly beautiful. She would make an impressive Empress, worthy of a better consort than Maximillus.

She was looking about her, with lively interest. Suddenly, her eyes caught those of Decimus. Or did they? Surely not! He was not standing close enough to her. Or was he? Had he stared at her for slightly too long? Maybe he had been the only person looking at *her*, and not for the Blood-Drinkers, and she had seen that.

He tried to blend himself back into the group of Senatorial attendants around him, all of them, unfortunately, much shorter than he was.

And now she was smiling. Esbus! This was really bad—his task was to *see*, rather than to be noticed by others. Under no circumstances should he attract unnecessary attention to himself. How could he have been so clumsy? But perhaps he was imagining it all.

Another eunuch, this one wearing a chain of office, now waddled towards the throne. "Photon," someone whispered. But who was he? And where was the new High Chamberlain, Julian, who had replaced the disgraced Florianus? He was nowhere to be seen.

Photon prostrated himself most expertly and, upon being invited to rise, informed the Emperor that the envoy of the Great King was now waiting to attend upon his Imperial Majesty. He was forbidden by the "ancient laws and traditions of his people" (several Senators snorted very loudly upon hearing this improbable formulation) to make the full obeisance before anyone but the Khan of Khans (more mutterings—what kind of title was *that*?). His refusal should not, however, be understood as showing a lack of respect; and his deputy, and interpreter, who was of a different race though he had been in the service of the Great King for many years, would make the full obeisance on the ambassador's behalf.

Would his Imperial Majesty be so generous as to accept this diplomatic compromise?

The Emperor replied, with his wonted grace and charm, "Fuck it! Just get it over with! I want to go to bed."

The eunuch signaled that the envoys now had his Imperial Majesty's gracious permission to approach the throne.

XV

MARA LOSES A HORSE, FOR THE SECOND TIME

✠ *The Great Plain, and beyond.*

This, she realized, had happened to her once before: two brutal men holding her trapped, with the grasslands all around her, and no hope of rescue. It had led to slavery, humiliation, danger and murder.

No, she wasn't going to let it happen again! She wriggled, and twisted round, sinking her teeth into what she thought was the man's leg, but getting only a mouthful of leather boot.

Esbus, why wasn't Phrygillus trying to help her? He was standing there, held loosely by the other cavalryman, and doing nothing to break out of his grip.

Very well, let him do that, he was a slave and he had never been anything else, but she *wasn't*. Not any more, she wasn't.

With her free hand she grabbed suddenly at the man, hoping to startle him into moving the booted foot that was holding her down, but instead he eased down onto her, pinning her with the weight of his body. She was now helpless, and he could do what he liked with her.

She was gulping for breath. She expected the man's hand to begin to defile her in some revolting way. Instead, though, he stroked her hair and said, in a rough version of the Tongue of the Horse People, "There, there. Keep still, sweetheart. No bad!"

"She's the one, isn't she?" the other man called over in his own tongue. "But who is this little fellow?"

"Who cares? A runaway slave, I'm guessing. We'll get a bounty for him too."

"What, from the old bastard? Never! He'll just sell him on. But what about the horse? Just look at him! This beauty is worth real silver. Gold, even."

The "demon" whinnied, and nuzzled amiably at the man. Another traitor! Was she the only one who was willing to resist?

Who were these men? Were they slavers, or were they horse-thieves? She wasn't sure which would be worse.

"Who are you?" she asked, in her own tongue. Better that they didn't know that she could understand them.

"You are Mara, the 'happy one', and we, my dear, are your happiness!"

What?

"You know my name?"

"Of course. We were sent to find you, and bring you back to Cascantum—"

The other man broke in: "And collect a big fat reward from old man Rhaetius!"

Now they were both speaking Sueni.

"If we're lucky—we've been gone a long time, and he'll want the skin off our backs. But if we bring him this bundle here, that should put him in a better mood."

"We could even have some fun with her on the way!"

Her captor glared at his companion.

"No, forget it! We were told to find a horsey virgin, and what do we have here? One horsey virgin. Complete with her fucking plaits! And she stays that way. Plaits and all."

Mara silently thanked all the gods that she had taught Phrygillus how to do her hair, and that he had proved to be so skillful.

"She's a good-looking piece, though. So how come she got to keep her cherry, if the slavers had her?"

"Use your brain: because that makes her worth more. And it makes her worth more to us, too, if she keeps it." He stroked her hair again. "Besides, I've got a girl her age. I hope she's still got *her* cherry! How would you like it if it was your kid?" The other man shrugged. "But you've got a boy, haven't you? You don't have to worry about all that, you lucky bastard." Then to Mara, in his crude Sueni-version of her tongue: "The Lord…the big man made a promise to your father. That we find you. And bring you back to him. So no fear. No bad."

He released her, and she got up and put her clothes straight. She explained to Phrygillus that the men meant them no harm, hoping that that was true. The man who was holding him said "That's right, little guy!" in the Citizens' Tongue, and let him go.

At first Phrygillus didn't move, or say anything; then, all he said was "I want some food! I'm hungry!"

The two cavalrymen shared their food with them. The nicer man, the one who had held her down, but who had also stroked her hair and who had a daughter, was named Geto; the not-so-nice man was Orogo.

Mara admired how efficiently they prepared a simple meal, and was amazed how many cooking and eating utensils they were carrying with them. They even had water. Geto lit a fire, while Orogo searched expertly for reasonable-sized stones to support a pan. Then they added a small amount of water to some grain, stirring it in and making a thick, gooey porridge. They also had dried biscuits, and some salty bacon.

Geto said, "This is Citizen Army shit, but we have something rather special that will make it *much* more tasty!"

With a beaming smile he produced some vile pieces of dried fish and added them to the porridge. Mara didn't like the fish at all—it was the horrible stuff that the Sueni enthusiastically dredged up out of the swamps of the Great River. They esteemed their fish very highly, and often tried to barter it to the Horse People, but the Horse People scorned it and would only eat it only in times of need.

Choosing a moment when neither of the Sueni was watching, Mara picked the pieces of fish out of her porridge and slipped them onto Phrygillus's plate. Phrygillus, she had noted, was wolfing everything down as if it was the last meal he would ever have.

The two cavalrymen discussed in their own tongue what they should do next.

They must take her back to Cascantum and claim the reward—that was clear. It seemed that they'd lost the rest of their troop in the early fog one morning.

How ridiculous! The Horse People never lost each other like that.

Or had they lost themselves deliberately, so that they would be the ones to find Mara and claim the reward? That seemed to be what Orogo was saying. Her knowledge of the Tongue of the Sueni wasn't so good that she understood every single word.

But what was to be done with the boy?

Geto asked him suddenly, "Who was your master?"

Phrygillus, intent on his food, muttered "Castor".

Castor? Who was he? They'd never heard of any Castor.

Mara was furious with him. How would this help them in any way? The Sueni didn't need to know so much.

Geto held out a particularly fatty piece of bacon.

"And anyone else?"

"Atticus," the boy muttered again, and grabbed the bacon.

Ah! Now that was a name they knew. Atticus was an important man, and a well-known this-or-that (Mara didn't recognize the word, but guessed that it might be something unfriendly like "fuckface"). The "old man" (whoever that was) hated his guts. So if they took Phrygillus back with them, he would never be returned to his master. And they wouldn't get their money.

Atticus. They obviously thought Phrygillus had meant the Governor, that flabby man in Fanum who let his wife order him about, and who was an "important man", and not his stupid son, who probably wasn't. Well, if they wanted to be rude about either of them, that was perfectly fine with her.

Orogo: "Or we go to Fanum first, and deliver the boy personally!"

"Teats of the Earth Cow, are you totally out of your mind? They already think that we're runners (deserters?), and you want to arrange it so we get back even later? And what if a patrol just happens to pick us up and we're *not* on our way home? I like my back the way it is."

Geto added that (fuckface?) Atticus hated all the military, and might not give them a reward anyway, just to be spiteful.

"You're right. I hadn't thought of that."

But there was, it seemed, a fixed bounty throughout the Empire for all lost or runaway slaves—not much, maybe, but better than having a rat chew on your testicles (Geto's charming way of putting it). So all they had to do was deliver the boy to some bloody magistrate and claim the money. Then off they'd go, and the magistrate got to sort it all out.

Mara didn't like the sound of that. Phrygillus was in her charge. She was responsible for him.

"And we can sell the horse while we're there!"

Orogo wasn't happy. He wanted to keep the horse for himself. Geto told him that he was crazy—again. It was a nobleman's horse. The old man would just take it from them and give it to one of his favorite officers. End of story.

Anyway, why was Orogo so sure he could even ride it? It was a big animal.

"You're not a better rider than me!" he replied. "You spend half your time picking yourself up off the ground! When did you last see *me* fall off a horse?" Then, before Geto could answer, he asked Phrygillus, "The horse—what's his name?"

Phrygillus, still gulping his food down, grunted, "Demon."

Demon or no demon, Geto said, the horse had to be sold. After selling it, for just a portion of the money they got for it they could buy a cheap mule for the girl to ride—they needed to get back quickly—and they could sell the mule in Cascantum afterwards. Maybe even for a profit...

May She with the Talons take them! It made Mara really angry to have the horse stolen from her. Among the Horse People, no-one stole horses. Yes, she had taken the "demon" from Victor, but he was a murderer who would have killed her, and Phrygillus, given the chance. He was an enemy, and you could do bad things to your enemies—as the songs of the Horse People so vividly described!

Did these men see her as an enemy?

It also made her angry how they talked about "money" all the time. Money couldn't turn you into a better horseman, or earn you the respect of your clan. It couldn't buy you honor. Or true friendship.

She had heard the slaves in Fanum say that you only ever needed one single silver coin: the ferryman's fee to pay for your passage on the Final Journey. But Manasa had told her that slaves were always looking for ways to earn money, by one trick or another, to save up to buy their freedom.

Although Geto seemed to be a kinder man than Orogo, she shouldn't have expected more from either of them. They were Sueni. They happily filled their lungs with the filthy air of the swamps, and they had been changed for the worse (if there had ever been a time when they were better, that is) by living side-by-side with the Citizens, who worshiped money.

The Horse People could only avoid that fate by staying on the grasslands forever, where the air was fresh and in the clear light you could see what you needed to do to protect your honor. No dirty, narrow streets, no houses locking you in with their walls and gates, no money, no thieving, no murder or treachery.

Then she remembered, with a great pang of sadness, the treachery of Gisso, which had thrown her into slavery. It was too late. The evil ways of the Citizens had already reached her clan!

Where should they go? The nearest town, Geto said, was Kesta (or something like that).

Kesta was a shithole, according to Orogo.

All those towns, said Geto, were complete shitholes. It couldn't be any worse than Cascantum, though. Fuck all that Citizen shit! How he longed to be back in his home beside the Great River...

Mara, after her experience of Fanum, agreed with the first part of what he had said, but not with the last bit. How could they even *breathe* properly in the swamps?

"What about Lorrinum?" Geto asked.

Orogo definitely didn't want to go *there*.

"That's in the fucking Riverlands! Last time I was there, they (some word she didn't know) my drink and took everything I had. May the Earth Cow shit on them!"

Geto laughed.

"While they were at it, they didn't help themselves to your pretty backside, by any chance?"

Orogo didn't see the joke.

"Who cares about that? All my fucking money, every single copper. You want to go to fucking Lorrinum? Then be my guest! But without me, comrade, without me. And just watch what you drink."

They finally agreed on Kesta.

The two men packed up the cooking gear very quickly. What they *didn't* do—typical Sueni!—was to make sure that the fire had been put out. Mara did that for them. Swampies might not care, but the Plain belonged to the Horse People and although the hot days of the summer were gone no-one wanted a raging fire that would eat up the grasslands.

Kesta wasn't far away, Geto said. If they hurried, he told Orogo, they could sell the horse, dump the boy and collect the bounty, buy a mule, and be out of the town before nightfall.

Mara said nothing to Phrygillus. What was she to do? She had sworn to protect him, and now these men were planning to "dump" him—she hadn't misheard them, it was almost the same word in the Tongue of the Horse People.

Would he be safe in this place, Kesta? Did he want to remain a slave, and be returned to the stupid son of that stupid man in Fanum? Perhaps he would even be happier there than among the Horse People of the Speaking Bird clan, which is where Mara had been taking him.

Yet how could anyone be happier as a slave, trapped by walls and dark rooms, than enjoying the wind and the sunlight and breathing in the fresh air of freedom out on the Plain?

She hadn't forgotten that it wouldn't be easy for him, but she would be there to help him. She would make a tough young warrior out of him yet!

The Sueni didn't trust her completely (although they were taking her to freedom, they said); neither could they agree on which of them was going to ride the "demon". Their solution was that Mara rode the horse, but with her mount and Orogo's lashed loosely together; Phrygillus rode with Geto.

It took them longer to reach Kesta than Geto had planned. The sun was already dipping. It was a smaller place than Fanum, with an outer palisade and earthworks, such as the Horse People had occasionally been known to build, rather than a proper wall.

Kesta would not be difficult for a determined enemy to capture!

Mara was uneasy at the thought of having to go into the narrow streets of the town, and she was relieved when they stopped just inside the gate at what Geto called a "nice house" (he couldn't find the right word in her tongue, but it was obviously a place for eating and drinking).

He would now take the "demon" to find a new owner (she noticed that he was going to lead the horse, dismounted, rather than try to ride it on the cobbled streets); Orogo would stay with Mara and Phrygillus.

And he mustn't drink too much!

No no, of course not.

But the moment Geto was gone, Orogo ordered wine for himself. He was already on his third beaker when he suddenly remembered that he wasn't alone, and asked them what *they* wanted?

Phrygillus immediately said "Food". Orogo ordered soup for them all, and bread, without waiting for Mara to say what she would like.

She didn't like the place. It was smelly and noisy, and the men sitting at the other tables looked unpleasant. Without being invited, the inn-keeper sat down beside them. He asked Mara if she spoke the Citizens' Tongue and, when she nodded, pointed to her plaits and leered.

"You still a virgin? Hanging out with a couple of Sueni boys and you've still got your cherry?" He grinned at her. "Come on—if you believe that, you'll believe anything."

Orogo leaned across the wooden table, and belched.

"You got some kind of problem with the Dream People? I don't mean to be rude, but…you…can…fuck…off!"

The innkeeper got up, giving Orogo a contemptuous smile, and went about his business.

Orogo was drinking too much—Mara could see that. It was what warriors did, even among the Horse People, though whether it was right to call Orogo a warrior she couldn't quite decide. He was spending coins generously, and this attracted some of the other drinkers. They came over and sat on the wooden benches around them.

One man tried to touch Mara, until Orogo growled at him and the man whipped his hand away. Orogo might be a stupid swampie who'd had too much wine, but he was still a soldier and he was carrying a sword. The Sueni were known to be rough and quarrelsome.

Another man was paying a great deal of attention to Phrygillus, stroking his hair and whispering to him what a handsome boy he was. How stupid the Citizens were!

Mara was quite relieved when Geto returned. He looked mightily displeased at the company clustered around them, and promptly pushed one man off the bench in order to sit down himself.

He ordered wine, telling Orogo in Sueni "Just one beaker. And nothing more for you, you've had enough!"

Orogo muttered something that sounded very rude, but then: "How did it go? Did you get a good price? Gold?"

"Not here!" Geto hissed. But it was too late—someone must have known a few words of their tongue, or at least the word "gold". There

was a buzz of interest, and their new "friends" clustered even closer.

Phrygillus's attentive admirer chose this moment to slip his hand between the boy's legs. When Phrygillus squealed, Geto grabbed the man by the throat with one hand and hit him in the face with the other.

In Mara's opinion, it was actually more of a smack than a punch. It drew blood nevertheless. The man clutched at his nose.

"I'm bleeding!"

"You touch the boy, I touch *you*. Got it?"

The innkeeper appeared at the side of the "injured man". Were they friends?

"We don't need any bad feeling here, gentlemen! This is a friendly town."

"Town full of faggots, more like it," Geto muttered. "Just get away from us, all of you."

"This is my wife's brother," said the innkeeper, "and I'm sure he meant no harm."

"Oh yes? He can suck *your* dick, if he likes, but he leaves the boy alone, or I'll stick him up his Citizen bum with something long and hard that he's *not* expecting."

Mara saw how the innkeeper took a step backwards, drawing in his breath. He looked angry. Their "friends" were also shifting away from them slightly.

Bang! Someone had kicked open the wooden door of the inn. There was a flurry of movement. New faces were looking at them. Who were these people?

A small, plump man in a plain toga was staring down at them. (Only just—if Geto got up, he'd be twice the man's size!) Behind the little man were two much bigger men, carrying spears.

"I'm looking for a Sueni thief and troublemaker, and I think I've found him! It'll be one of you two, so you'll both come with me now."

Geto gawped at him in amazement.

"And who might *you* be, when you're not in your kennel?"

The little man drew himself up to his greatest height, which was not impressive, and announced, "My name is Portho, and I am first deputy to the magistrate. I am also chief inspector of markets, and a member of the city council of Kestai!"

The men accompanying him brandished their spears, as if to emphasize what he had said.

Were they going to fight? This was what happened when young men drank too much wine! She must keep Phrygillus out of range of the spears and swords. She didn't think much of the Sueni in general, but she reckoned that these two would be more than a match for the two guys with spears.

But instead of pulling out his sword, Geto smiled.

"What is troubling you so badly, O deputy inspector of this beautiful town?"

"What is troubling me is the money that you stole from an honest citizen: a whole bag of gold coins."

"What?" Geto looked shocked. "What are you talking about?"

"Do you deny that you are carrying a purse containing gold coins?"

"Fuck!" That was Orogo. Geto glared at him.

"No, I don't deny it. That's the money I got for my horse. A big, black horse."

Now Portho smiled. He looked about the room, at the customers, the innkeeper, and the serving-girls.

"Does anyone here see a big, black horse? I don't. There is no big, black horse within the walls of this city" (he meant palisade, surely?) "but I *do* see a thief with a bag of gold coins."

Suddenly Geto switched from the Citizens' Tongue to that of the Sueni. Why should he do that?

"Come come, my lord, as one Sueni to another I swear on the Spirit (?) of the Earth Cow that I'm telling the truth. But you do have a thief and a liar in your town, someone who tells you falsehoods—"

Portho was confused.

"What is he gabbling?"

"He is speaking in Sueni, honorable sir," the innkeeper helpfully told him. "He thinks you're a swampie!"

Portho had been irritated, but now he was indignant.

"What?!"

And Geto was also angry.

"Your name is Portho, isn't it? That makes you one of us!" (Mara had to admit that "Portho" did sound like a Sueni name.) He turned to the innkeeper. "And what do you mean by 'swampie'? Are you so tired of life?"

Portho was outraged.

"You think I'm a barbarian? I'll have you know that my name is Quintus Calendarius Portho, and that the menfolk of my family have been free Citizens for many generations!"

Geto laughed from his belly.

"How come you're called Portho, then, if someone like my grand-daddy *didn't* get to fuck your grandma?"

And then everyone was shouting at the same time. Tables and benches were pushed over. A lead beaker was thrown, missing its target, but hitting a serving-girl painfully in the face. Threats were made. As Geto pulled his sword from its scabbard, the two armed men went for him. He beat down the spear of one of them, and stabbed the man in the thigh, but the other man's spear pricked into the side of his throat. He dropped his weapon with a clatter.

Someone grabbed Orogo from behind, so that he couldn't draw his sword at all.

The innkeeper gave a signal, and a couple of thuggish-looking men stepped out of the shadows and secured the two Sueni with ropes.

"Find the purse!" Portho instructed, and when the purse of gold coins had been found and handed to him, he shouted pompously, "Take them to the council chamber! Secure the boy and the barbarian girl, too. This is a serious matter! This is a criminal gang!"

All four of them were pushed through the darkening streets, the two Sueni receiving a few well-placed blows along the way.

I hate towns, Mara told herself. Every time I go to a town bad things happen to me. Why do people choose to live in towns?

When they reached their destination, Portho ordered that the Sueni be given a sound beating "to teach them manners". The two guards started slamming into them with the butts of their spears, while the innkeeper's thugs joined in with enthusiastic kicks and punches.

Soon the Sueni were howling.

Beating men who were tied up and helpless was not honorable. She didn't like Orogo, but she felt sorry for Geto. Finally, the little official signaled for his men to stop. He told the Sueni to answer his questions honestly, and without insolence, or they would regret it bitterly.

Who were they?

Geto first spat out some gobbets of blood, and a broken tooth, and then told him who they were. He added that it was *he* who would regret mistreating men of the Citizen Army, honest fighting-men who were traveling on official business and were under the protection of Lord Commander Rhaetius.

"This Lord Commander of yours: isn't he the man in the north? But here the military take their orders from the two Lord Commanders in Gladium, not those in Cascantum. More to the point," and Mara thought she could see him swelling up a frog, "the military have no jurisdiction within the walls of Kestai. Here, it is the chief magistrate who decides everything! On the basis of Citizen law. And I am his deputy."

"Then take us to the fucking chief magistrate! And give me back my money!" (Orogo whispered: "*Our* money.")

That, the little man insisted, would not be possible, and he told them why. He was a man who greatly liked the sound of his own voice; Mara decided.

His Excellency Olympiodorus Postumus Tryphaenatus, chief magistrate and principal benefactor of Kestai, was entertaining important visitors from the City and must under no circumstances be distracted from his duties. He, Portho, had been left in charge, and he intended to waste no further time on them.

They would be locked up for the night, but separately from the two children, since they were obviously desperate and probably degenerate characters. In the morning, they would be taken (as they wished) before the chief magistrate, where the least they could expect would be a flogging. And if they proved to be deserters, their eventual fate would be most unpleasant indeed.

As for the money, that would be returned to the honest fellow they had stolen it from. He was a close friend of the deputy magistrate, and Portho would hand it back to him personally. Let it not be said that he was not a man of his word!

Runaway slaves—yes, there was indeed a bounty to be earned, that was correct, but first the identity of the slave's owner had to be established, which was a thoroughly complicated business, involving a lot of expense and bureaucracy. And why should good, hard-earned silver from the meager coffers of the municipality be doled out to passing vagabonds, with no guarantee that that silver would ever be refunded to the decent people of Kestai?

Furthermore, were these actually slaves, or were they simply frightened children who had been kidnaped as part of a wicked scheme to extort money from the authorities? (Mara hoped that she didn't look frightened; Phrygillus certainly didn't, in fact he had a bored, "I've-seen-all-this-before" look on his face.)

And the story that Mara was a chieftain's daughter whose fate was the concern of Lord Governors and Lord Commanders... Well, Portho had never heard such a ridiculous tale in his whole life. The magistrate would soon get to the bottom of it, though, he was a man of huge experience and great authority, and woe betide them if they tried fooling with *him*!

No-one had seen a large, black horse. Their own horses would for the time being be held by the innkeeper.

XVI

DECIMUS IS NOT PRESENTED
TO THE EMPEROR AFTER ALL

✠ *The City.*

All necks were craned to see the exotic visitors. And they made an even more unequal pair than the Imperial couple on the dais.

One of them, dressed in a flowing black robe, was immensely tall, the tallest man Decimus had ever seen, and exceedingly thin, with a long, wispy beard; the other, wearing dirty, fur-trimmed riding clothes, was small, bandy-legged and squat, and clutched a battered leather bag and a riding-whip.

That was a weapon, surely? Why had he been allowed to bring a weapon into the Imperial Presence?

Some of the court ladies were tittering: an exotic-looking, dirty little man with a whip! How exciting! Perhaps they would have the opportunity to get to know him more closely?

The tall man slipped smoothly to the ground in prostration. This must therefore be the interpreter. He had already found his feet again before Senator Naevius had finished saying "Someone tell the man he can get up."

"No need, my Lord. I speak your tongue fluently."

He introduced himself as Alumgar, trusted advisor to his Majesty the Great King. He would interpret for his Majesty's ambassador. He was familiar with many tongues, including that of the Citizens, because as a Priest of the Dead he had traveled to countless places and conversed with their wisest men. He had sought out the Sueni in their swampland sanctuaries of the Earth Cow, he had been to the Tower of the Sky many times, to debate there with mages and necromancers, he had visited the court of the Emperor of Sin, whose subjects were more numerous than the grains of sand on the beaches of Sybaris, he—"

"Yes, yes," Naevius told him, "you are an excellent choice to interpret for the ambassador. Now introduce him to us, if you would, and tell us what brings you to the court of Maximillus, First Citizen and Imperator!"

The Senator, Decimus noted, had not included the Emperor's title of "Chief Servant of Sol". The High Priest of Sol would not be pleased.

Alumgar drew himself up to his full height. He was much taller than the Senator, who was no certainly no small man, and he would have dwarfed the Emperor if he had been allowed closer to him.

Very well, he said, he was honored to present the great lord Khan Darkhon, maternal first cousin to the Khan of Khans, victor of countless battles and sacker of innumerable cities. As it happened, Khan Darkhon also understood the Citizen's Tongue very well, having learnt it from Citizen whores and slave-women, but he preferred not to have to voice what he considered its ugly sounds.

And as if to illustrate what his interpreter had just said, Darkhon interrupted him with a short comment.

Alumgar allowed him to finish, and then translated his words with a provocative smile.

"My master says that many of those cities, before he reduced them to ashes and rubble, were larger and more beautiful than this one, and that he took the best of their women to his tent for fucking."

There were shouts of rage from all sides. Darkhon himself was grinning smugly, like a little god. His skin was sallow, and his eyes were mere slits. He was enjoying the effect that his words, translated by the interpreter, were having on this assembly of Citizens. Yet despite the shouting, no-one tried to lay hands on him. Quintus, who might well have done, was standing guard outside the door to the throne-room.

Maximillus, his sweaty white face now flushed with anger, squawked with fury.

"Ah," said Alumgar, "so *this* is the Emperor! So honored!" (Though he didn't repeat the obeisance.) "Though I was looking for a somewhat taller man, more of a warrior."

Naevius lifted his hand for quiet, and the throne-room gradually fell silent. When he then spoke, it wasn't necessary for him to raise his voice.

"You have come a very long way, interpreter, to insult a great prince in his own throne-room."

"I see only a boy sitting on a chair. If my master is to convey the message of the Great King, he must convey it to a man. No matter. You are such a man, Senator. You will listen, and we shall tell you the commands of he who is Khan of Khans."

Maximillus had jumped to his feet on the dais, but seeing that the interpreter still towered over him he had sat down again very quickly.

Naevius was far from amused.

"Interpreter, ask your master the ambassador, please, what punishment would be inflicted by your people upon a man who offended the Great King in front of his nobles?"

The interpreter shrugged.

"There is no need to consult him. Every child knows it. The Khan of Khans would strike the insolent man dead with one blow of his mighty fist. But there is also a traditional punishment, one that is likewise known to everyone. It is called the Punishment of Left or Right."

"Left or right?"

"Yes, that is the question that the man would be asked. And he would be punished according to his answer."

If he said "left" (far the wiser choice), his left eye would be scooped out with a sharpened, heated spoon, his left ear would be severed, his left hand (or perhaps the whole arm) would be cut off, his left testicle would be bitten off by a specially trained slave, and his left foot amputated.

If he said "right", the same mutilations would be carried out, but on the other side of his body.

He would then, however, be left in peace, to continue his life as best he could, a constant reminder to all who saw him of the merciful and generous nature of the Great King.

"Fuck mercy!" Maximillus shouted, his voice breaking. "Do that to *him*—now! Do *both* of them! One 'right', one 'left'!"

With unexpected smoothness, Naevius turned away from the Blood-Drinkers, stepped up onto the dais, made a brief genuflection. and whispered into the Imperial ear.

Decimus could guess what he was saying.

Like it or not, the person of an ambassador was sacrosanct, however offensively he might behave. Oaths that had been given to the gods, promising the emissary safe passage, should not lightly be broken. And the future safety of our own envoys, and of any hostages that the enemy might have, should not be endangered.

Besides, kill them now, and we would maybe never find out what they wanted. The contact, a contact that might later be needed, would be lost.

On the other hand, with clever questioning much could be learnt from their words and actions, perhaps more than their master wished to have revealed.

An angry, emotional response showed nothing but weakness, and fear. A strong man laughed off insults—there would always be time for vengeance later.

And so on. Naevius was an experienced statesman, and he knew what he was doing.

He bowed again to the Emperor, and in one careful movement slipped down from the dais and turned to address the envoys. Decimus admired how well this was done: it would have been a catastrophic loss of face for him if he had stumbled.

"His Imperial Majesty has graciously agreed to forgive your insolence. You are not familiar with our ways. Tell us now what your master the Great King requests of us."

Alumgar laughed thinly.

"I know your ways only too well, Senator! Which is why I was chosen for this mission. And the Great King has no *requests* to make of you. Requests are for women, for eunuchs, and slaves. You Citizens may *request* each other to suck your cock or lick your shitty behind. The Khan of Khans *commands*. And today he has two commands, both of which you will obey, or he will bring you death and annihilation. His first command is the payment of a million gold pieces."

After the initial shock, with the whole room momentarily struck silent, there was a buzz of excited chatter.

A million gold pieces! That was an immense amount of money. No-one had such a sum. The Placidi, perhaps, but they were gone. How could such a staggering sum be raised?

"And the second...*request*?"

"The Great King wishes to shed his mercy on your realm by taking as a wife a princess of the Imperial blood. But she has to be young, and... I can't find the right word in your tongue... Fuckable? Is there such a word?" He pointed past Naevius to the Senator's granddaughter. "Like her, the woman sitting there beside the boy." He added: "But not a red witch. Is she his concubine?"

"That is my granddaughter, and our future Empress!"

The interpreter shrugged.

"No matter. I believe we have already established that your ways are different to ours? But whoever is chosen, it would be a very great honor for her. My master has a hundred wives, and a thousand concubines. But your princess would share the noble rank of Second Wife with a princess of Sin, the eldest daughter of their Emperor."

"*Second* Wife?" Naevius briefly looked flabbergasted, before recovering his composure.

"Yes. First Wife is not possible. So sorry! My master's First Wife is the mother of the eldest of his sons. Her status therefore cannot be changed. Unless the queen dies. As women often do, even queens. They are such weak creatures." Darkhon said something to the interpreter, grinning salaciously and making an unambiguously filthy gesture. "Aha! My Lord the ambassador has reminded me how much your princess will enjoy being fucked. My master is very potent. Women everywhere will greatly envy her!"

At first no-one spoke. What was there to say? There was no money. And there was certainly no "princess of the Imperial blood" available—unless Naevia produced one soon. Though it was a boy, a future Emperor, that was wished for.

Or did Maximillus have some female cousin, dull and ugly, hidden away and never before seen at court? Could it be that the Blood-Drinkers had been misinformed about the size of the Imperial family? Or had they just assumed that Citizen Imperators took as many women to bed and spawned as many offspring as the Great Kings apparently did?

Maximus the Great had indeed been known for his insatiable rutting, but his successor had been a miserable excuse for a man, who might even have left it to a favorite servant of the Empress's (rumor had it) to help him to a son and heir. And Maximillus—

Decimus's chain of thought was interrupted, as Senator Naevius finally replied.

"Ask the ambassador what your master will do if his Imperial Majesty agrees to his two requests. And then, what he intends if the Emperor says no."

The two Blood-Drinkers discussed what the answers to Naevius's two questions should be. But surely they already knew what to say? Had something that had been said earlier perhaps created an uncertainty? Or were they merely discussing the wording of the response? Or deciding how much (or how little) should be revealed by the interpreter's answer?

Finally Alumgar spoke.

"Hear this! No mortal refuses the command of the Great King, and it not for us to dare to circumscribe his designs with our words. His will must be obeyed. It is our *belief*, however, that our master, after he has received your gold and has anointed your princess with his godlike scepter of manhood, will turn the horde eastwards to punish Neopolis. Once before we stood beneath its wretched gates; this time there will be no escape for the Easterners. When your Citizen mare foals, if it is a healthy male child you will be bound in eternal and honorable kinship with the Great King. But your Emperor must first swear loyalty, and obedience."

Naevius cleared his throat before responding.

"And otherwise?"

"The horde will come to *your* gates, and blow your city away like the storm-wind in the fall that smashes the nests of the birds. Can any eye encompass the immensity of the horde? Stand on your horse in our encampment: it stretches as far as the eye can see. Then go to that furthest place on the horizon, and stand on your horse again, and again you will see no end to our camp. And again. And again. And those are just the warriors, and not their women and their slaves and the levies of the subject peoples. The horde sweeps everything before it, turning the land black. You will know only death, darkness, and crows, and your miserable realm will be a wasteland for twice a thousand years."

It was surely time for someone to put the Blood-Drinkers in their place, at least with words. Or did Naevius plan to capitulate immediately? Though with no money and with no princess, how could he possibly agree to their terms?

Naevius stood his ground.

"Remind your master," he said, "how you were held back at Neopolis by Ogilo. How on that memorable day you left thousands of your dead and dying on the battlefield, before fleeing back to the northern wastes with your tails between your legs. Be in no doubt, that same Ogilo will stop you again!"

It was strange to hear Naevius calling on the General, of all people, the nephew whom he hated so much. It didn't ring true.

The interpreter simply laughed.

"Ah, the General! Your dear, dear friend the General... Where is he now? Do you know, Senator? *We* know."

"And I suppose you are going to tell us?"

The two Blood-Drinkers consulted for a moment, before the interpreter replied.

"Why not. Why shouldn't you be told? The General has concentrated his troops, few that they are, along the road between your little city of Fanum and the bridge that carries that road south. He has pitifully few men. At Neopolis he had the forces of both your realms, and the high walls of a fortress at his back; this time he is alone, and in open country. What do you think his strategy could be? What would *yours* be?"

"It will be a wise strategy, be sure of that."

"Oh, Senator, how you disappoint me! What can the poor man possibly hope to achieve? He wishes to protect Fanum, and to block the road south. *But when did the horde ever need roads?* When we wish to go south, we shall ford the river upstream and go past him in the night. And how will he stop us? By attacking our flank with his few units of Sueni cavalry? Assuming, that is, that the Sueni remain loyal. Or by sending his poor Citizen soldiers to run after us on foot? Sweating and stumbling and falling over their spears? I think not! But what my master does next will depend on your answer, Senator. We offer you hope. If you obey my master's commands, he will take the horde east, far from your city walls, to our usual winter pastures, and then turn south in the spring for a campaign against Neopolis."

"And if not, you will attack the West."

"Yes. If you disobey, the lands that you call the Valley will make an excellent winter pasture for our horses. Ogilo has already abandoned the people who live there. Next year it will then be the turn of the Province. We shall come south, at our enjoyable leisure, until we reach the gates of this city."

"The General will not allow that."

"Ogilo would be foolish to offer him battle, but if he does my master will crush his army like a wild aurochs trampling a flower. Yet be assured, on the battlefield he will spare the life of your nephew, though *his* life only. And do you know why? Because he has sworn a blood-oath not to kill him."

Judging by the gasps and whispered comments, Decimus was almost the only person in the throne-room who was not astounded by what the interpreter had said. It was no secret, and many knew that Ogilo as a young man had been a hostage among the Blood-Drinkers. Perhaps a few others among those present knew that he had also won the friendship of the Great King's nephew, Khan Horkhon. But only Decimus would have known that their friendship had been so close. That they were actually blood-brothers…

Naevius was shocked, and now visibly confused, but not as much as the Emperor was. Maximillus jumped up excitedly, shrieking at the assembled Citizens.

"The General has already betrayed us! He is a barbarian, and we can expect no help from him. He has betrayed us! And *you*," he added, glowering at the envoys, "you have just come here to deceive us and delay us with empty talk, knowing that we will refuse you. And then Ogilo will march on the City at the head of both armies, his own and yours, and your master will make *him* Emperor!"

Naevius tried to calm him.

"Your Majesty, you know that the General—"

"No!" Maximillus yelped. "He wants to kill me! He's always hated me! He wants my throne!"

Decimus was astounded by the way the Emperor had spoken. Ogilo leading an army of Blood-Drinkers murdering and pillaging across the Empire? What a ridiculous idea—it was utter nonsense! There were muffled shouts and mutterings of astonishment, puzzlement and even indignation all around him, but before any voice could speak up clearly there was an unexpected distraction.

Khan Darkhon began cursing, and flailing out with his bandy legs. The Emperor's tiny dog was yapping around his feet, leaping up with amazing energy in its attempts to snatch the leather bag that the Khan was holding. Inevitably, foot met dog, and the animal was projected squealing into the group of Guardsmen escorting the two Blood-Drinkers.

"Porphyrius!" the Emperor cried out, even more distraught than he had previously been. "Don't hurt him!"

There was general laughter as one of the Guardsmen caught the indignant dog, was bitten for his pains, but bravely managed to deposit the animal back on the dais, where it ran about in circles, barking furiously, before returning to its master.

When Maximillus bent down to stroke it, the dog ignored his attentions and piddled copiously over the end of his robe.

Porphyrius! That was the name of a popular entertainer, a singer of vulgar sentimental ballads who was idolized by the unwashed of the slums. What a well-chosen name!

Alumgar took the leather bag from the Khan.

"You do well not to trust your General! And whatever his plans or wishes might be, they are of no concern, because he is helpless now. You will obey my master, or you will feel his anger. That is all that remains to be said." He paused. "Though my master in his kindness has sent you this gift."

Reaching down into the bag, the interpreter carefully brought out…a severed head! He held it up for all to see. It was foul and quite unrecognizable.

The laughter had already ebbed. Now it died completely, and there was a deathly quiet.

"Whose head is that, interpreter?" Naevius asked. His voice was shaking.

"His name was Ovidius. He was a Senator, or so I have been told."

Ovidius, Lord Commander of the Eleventh! One of the divisions from the Northern Shore that had been marching to reinforce the General.

Understandably, it was the Senators who were present in the throneroom who were the most loudly outraged. Ovidius had been their colleague—his faction didn't matter anymore. Friend or political foe, the poor man had been murdered by the filthy Blood-Drinkers! There were calls of "Kill them!" and "Send them back in pieces!"

"He was on his way to join your nephew. He had to select a mountain pass. He chose the wrong one."

Naevius fixed the interpreter with a grim look.

"Under our laws, the killing of a Senator is repaid with death. Now *I* have no choice but to put you both in chains and bring you to the Senate Chamber, where that sentence will be passed on you, and carried out immediately."

Neither of the Blood-Drinkers looked at all concerned. Alumgar shrugged noncommittedly.

"We would gladly die in our master's service. And we would happily give you the killer of this man—if we knew his name. This Ovidius chose to march his troops through the territory of the Free People, who have sworn fealty to my master. But my master did not command them to do *this*. They did it of their own accord, in order to win his favor. The Free People are not your friends, it would seem." He added, "You should be grateful to my master. He ordered the remaining parts of the unfortunate man's carcass to be secured, and had them burnt honorably. Tell his family that no blood magic was done with the body."

The expression on the interpreter's face suggested that he actually expected to be thanked. Instead, Naevius shouted "Get them out of here!", and the audience broke up in chaos.

The Blood-Drinkers were escorted from the throne-room, for their own safety. Unbelievably, the Emperor and his bride-to-be had already slipped away during the uproar. Senators were milling about, shouting hysterically.

About the million gold pieces that needed to be found. Would they be asked to contribute?

About the disastrous military situation. Who was it who would get to the City first, to murder them all and rape their wives and daughters? Would it be the Blood-Drinkers, or the Placidi?

And about the miserable barbarian Ogilo, the so-called General who had let them down with his foolish strategy, or deserted them, or sold them to the enemy.

Naevius, deeply shocked, had stumbled away to convene an emergency meeting of the Imperial Council, which consisted (without Ogilo) of Naevius himself, the City Prefect, the High Priest of Sol, and three Senators from the White, Blue and Green factions.

"I have been invited to represent the Blues," Senator Vulpeculus informed Decimus as they left the throne-room together. "A great honor, don't you agree? So we'll present you to the Emperor tomorrow, my boy—if his Imperial Majesty is not indisposed, that is, after all the excitements of the evening. It's given us a lot to think about, wouldn't you say?"

And, to Decimus's surprise, he smiled. He didn't look like a man who had just been confronted with the possibility of utter destruction, and threatened by Blood-Drinkers with death, darkness, and crows.

XVII

AULUS BRAVELY RESISTS TEMPTATION

✠ *The road east.*

Aulus had already had enough of Senator Gaius Ambibulus Necro to last several lifetimes, and they were still nowhere near the border of the Eastern Empire.

Those two statements were closely connected. Despite his shaky grasp of the geography of the West (let alone of the East, those enticing lands that he so desperately looked forward to experiencing), even Aulus was aware that they were wasting time by going to Neopolis the long way round.

Aulus had also looked forward to the first sea-journey of his life, but, no, Ambibulus Necro was having none of that. It would have meant traveling to Portus and taking ship from there, and, as everyone apparently knew, Portus was infested with cut-throat supporters of the Placidi.

"Oh, I didn't know that," Aulus had said, and afterwards, when he told Florianus, the eunuch had confirmed that it was indeed complete nonsense ("Unless the sailors and the whores have all turned Red").

It might not worry *him*, Necro had replied—after all, young Atticus was known to be a bosom friend of the degenerate would-be poet Sextus Placidus, and his uncle was harboring two Red females of dubious moral reputation under his roof. But a prominent White Senator like himself… Necro would be an obvious target for Red assassins, with whom the streets of Portus were known to be swarming.

Then why couldn't they travel overland to Trebenna and embark by ship from there?

Was Aulus out of his mind? The Riverlands were a hot-bed of Green support, and as for Trebenna, where that barbarian oaf who called himself "the General" had been brought up, well, enough said!

So, if they weren't going to get on a ship, how would they ever reach the East?

Necro had decided that they should take the (safe) "merchants' road" north across the mountains into the Province, negotiate the well-guarded Stone Gates Pass, and then travel east to the border, crossing the Great River either at the fortress of Gladium, where there was a bridge and where one of Necro's cousins was a senior Staff Officer, or lower down the river and closer to the ocean, where there were ferries (in which case Aulus would get to enjoy his sea journey, ha ha!).

After which they would follow the coast road to Maritima and on to Neopolis.

This plan had the advantage that they would never be in what Necro opined was "dangerous" territory. There was open country between the Pass and the Great River, but it was criss-crossed regularly by military patrols.

Relations between Necro and Florianus were even less cordial. The Senator and the eunuch had from the start barely exchanged a single word. It obviously irked Necro that a eunuch had been entrusted with the money for paying the expenses of *his* delegation. Since the two were hardly speaking to each other, Aulus's main role, or so it seemed to him, was to play the messenger-boy for the Senator whenever he needed something from Florianus.

If that was his principal role, a secondary role was to assist the Guards officer Urgo in arranging armed escorts for the delegation at every stage of the journey. To do this, someone had to speak to the chief magistrate of each town that they passed through and to the officer commanding any military unit that they encountered.

While Urgo's appearance was magnificent, his mastery of the Citizens' Tongue was less than impressive, if only because of his impenetrable Sueni accent. That was why Aulus was needed.

Urgo would bellow at the magistrates, and Aulus would then say more politely what it was that they wanted. This worked reasonably well. They had a travel warrant authorizing them to requisition bodyguards, but it was never required.

When it came to the military, however, Urgo sensibly allowed Aulus to do the talking. Citizen Army Sub-officers didn't have much affection for barbarian Guardsmen, however big their mustaches were, and they wouldn't take kindly to being bellowed at. Besides, when the soldiers were told that this was Lucius Atticus's nephew, it had a magical effect (his father's name tended to produce a less positive reaction, except with some of the magistrates).

The bodyguards, Florianus pointed out, were only necessary because Necro had insisted on having a ridiculously bloated entourage of servants and attendants to minister to his needs. Florianus had had to make do with one freed slave, Minnermus; Aulus was being looked after by

Beltran, his uncle's footman.

He wondered how useful Minnermus and Beltran would be if the Senator's nightmare became reality and they were attacked by vicious Reds, or by murderous Greens, or even (Sol preserve them!) by a horde of Blood-Drinkers. Admittedly, Aulus wouldn't be much use either—Decimus had tried to teach him all kinds of fancy stuff with swords and bows and arrows, but he hadn't liked being whacked by the heavy wooden practice sword whenever he was slow in getting out of its way, and his arrows had never landed where he had intended them to.

If they were attacked, his probable response would be to run away (or, preferably, to ride away on his mule). No doubt it would be more heroic to stand and face the enemy, however fearsome. Yet what would it benefit anyone if he was skewered or hacked to bits, with his sad remains being thrown into a ditch for the local dogs to feast on?

There were few circumstances in which he could imagine himself fighting. If the attackers were *very* small, or fairly elderly, or physically decrepit, if they were already dying of their wounds, or wielding swords that were blunt and not too long, or even wooden swords. Weren't there barbarian tribes in the far distant north who still went into battle without weapons made of metal?—he might exchange a few blows with them.

Otherwise, he could count himself lucky that he had been assigned a young, frisky mule. It might be an awkward animal to ride, but it would fly like the wind if there were Blood-Drinkers about, he was sure of that.

No, fighting was not for him. Aulus Atticus would be a warrior with *words*, like Sextus or Terebinthian, though the famous Green Senator was dreadfully boring, it had to be said, even if everyone did claim that he was a great orator. On no account did Aulus want to be boring. He would overwhelm his enemies with eloquence, and with glorious tropes and metaphors! Even the Blood-Drinkers would quail in the face of his ardor!

Aulus and Florianus found themselves thrown together on the journey, partly because of their shared dislike of Necro, and partly because of the lack of any other suitable conversation partners. Urgo was impossible to understand, and the scribe was gossipy, but unpleasant and spiteful. Nor would it be the done thing for Aulus to spend all his time talking to Beltran (even if Beltran had any serious conversation, which he didn't).

Florianus asked him what he thought of the handsome young creature that Julian had bought at the slave-market as a gift for Quintilianus Asper. He couldn't imagine that Asper, who had a highly developed esthetic sense, would be especially pleased, but what did Aulus think?

How should Aulus know? His knowledge in that area was almost non-existent. His earlier forays into the slaves' quarters had included encounters with young women, but none with boys. Except for Decimus, there hadn't been any young male slaves in his father's household, and Aulus wouldn't have known what to do with one anyway.

The boy's name was Gorth. "What kind of name is that for a catamite?" Florianus had asked. "He should be called Opalinus, Florus or Servidor, the way I was renamed Florianus." The boy was slim and well-proportioned, with pale skin coloring and straw-colored hair. He had pleasant freckles—his best feature. He was from the Fish People of the north (Aulus could ask him about those wooden swords!).

According to Julian, who had bought him, he was "unspoiled". Someone should ascertain whether that was true. Florianus obviously couldn't. Would Master Aulus like to take him to his bed, for some chaste but exploratory embraces...?

Certainly not! Aulus had no wish for any explorations of that kind.

"Though perhaps Senator Necro would like to?" he suggested, trying to be helpful. "He has no woman attending him, and he hasn't asked for a maid at any of the inns that we've stayed at." The eunuch looked at him quizzically, so he quickly added, "My man Beltran! He is very observant in such matters."

Aulus hadn't asked for any of the maids either. For a start, he had only a small amount of money, given to him by his uncle for the personal expenses of the journey. Nor (after his encounters with Fannia and Sinica) had he any real desire for such adventures, at least for the present.

Florianus's only comment on this information about the Senator's nocturnal behavior was that Necro was so deeply and passionately in love—with himself—that he felt no need to share his bed with anyone else, male, female, slave or free.

Gorth was undoubtedly pretty, with regular features, but the overall effect was spoiled by the expression (or, rather, the lack of one) that never left his face, except when food came into view. The boy's nose ran slightly, and he sniffled a lot. Were all the Fish People like that, Aulus wondered, because of having to live in such a dark, cold, rainy land? Would he too be like that if he lived on the Northern Shore?

He couldn't decide which he found less appealing: Gorth's runny nose, or Ambibulus Necro's dribbling.

Florianus was of the opinion that Asper wouldn't be too pleased with his present—he would more likely feel insulted.

"Which will rebound onto the Senator, and onto the new High Chamberlain, but not onto you or me, Master Aulus," he pointed out, and seemed not to be overly worried at the prospect. "However, the Master of Horse and Foot is the most powerful man at the Eastern court, and if he *is* offended, that will make the work of our little delegation that much more difficult to carry out. We should bear that in mind."

Aulus wasn't sure what, when they finally reached Neopolis, his own role in the work of the delegation was going to be. Or how it might or might not be affected by the great man's displeasure.

As for Gorth's innocence: a few days later, Beltran confided in his master (without any encouragement) that the swampie Guards officer, Urgo, had slept with one of the maids, the one with a cast in her eye, and had refused to pay her afterwards; that she had told the innkeeper, who had complained to the Senator; that the Senator had paid the girl with silver from his own purse, and was now very angry with the Guards officer; oh, yes, and that the fishy-boy Gorth was bedding down with the scribe, Philotas, in return for extra food.

So much for his being "unspoiled"!

Aulus had been longing for wild and strange encounters with the previously unknown (provided that these didn't involve too much danger), but thanks to Necro's insistence on their taking the safest route possible the journey so far had been remarkably uneventful—greatly to Aulus's disappointment. One small town was much like another. The same could also be said of the inns that they stayed at.

Necro took every opportunity to demonstrate his own importance. Wherever they went, he encouraged the civic authorities to celebrate the presence in their little town of such an august figure from the capital. He reveled in the flattering attention paid to him by the dignitaries.

They would allow him to preside over council meetings, and to adjudicate in minor legal cases (although Necro, unlike Terebinthian or Marcus Vulpeculus, was an expert on protocol rather than a renowned lawyer). Necro insisted that Aulus join him on these tedious occasions. The boy intended to become a Senator, did he not? Then he should start learning what this entailed!

If the chief magistrate was also chief priest of the state religion of Sol in that particular town, or chairman of the board of guardians of the temple, he would invite the Senator (as a prominent White) to join him in the performance of the obligatory rites and sacrifices.

And if the chief magistrate happened in addition to be the wealthiest citizen of the town (as was often the case), and his mansion or villa suitably luxurious, Necro would relocate himself, and as many members of his entourage as possible, to the home of the magistrate, leaving Aulus and Florianus to fend for themselves at the local inn.

The inns along the road through the mountains had catered for years for large numbers of travelers, and were comfortable enough; those in the Province were likewise of an acceptable standard. But there were no hostelries in the winding Stone Gates Pass, only signaling watchtowers and small military blockhouses, a reminder of how many Citizen soldiers had once been needed to pacify the mountain tribes of that region.

Those days were long gone, and today it would be quite possible (even exciting, Aulus thought) to camp out beside the road. A night under the stars! Yet according to Necro there were bands of robbers and renegades still at large in the area, and so the Pass had best be negotiated in a single day's journey, without an overnight stop.

Aulus felt sorry for Necro's litter-bearers, who sweated and gasped to keep up with the riders. How tempted they must have been to tip the litter and its contents into a ravine! Or over the side of the horrifying cliff that so often appeared to left or to right of the road. Aulus was happy that his mule was not only frisky, but also nimble-footed. The animal had every intention of getting itself and its rider safely to their destination.

That destination was the townlet of Cestae, at the eastern end of the Pass.

Cestae had originated as a fortress, not much larger than the block-houses, and grown steadily into a municipality as services sprang up to meet the needs of the garrison. It wasn't a true market town, for the land around it was little better for farming than the dull grassland of the Plain into which it merged, but it served as a modest administrative center for the villages that nestled in the shadow of the mountains.

Word of their coming had already reached Cestae by fire-beacon, and the town's only decent inn had been cleared of all other guests so that it could accommodate the delegation. A messenger informed Senator Necro that he was humbly invited to attend a late supper in his honor at the home of the chief magistrate, a certain Olympiodorus Postumus Tryphaenatus.

"That name positively reeks of freed slave," the Senator sniffed contemptuously, "either the wretched man himself or his father." (Aulus's uncle, who had no prejudice against freedmen, would merely have said, "The bigger the name, the smaller the man.")

Necro had begun to speak more freely to Aulus, now that he saw him as a Senatorial aspirant, granted a most unpromising one, and himself in the role of the wise mentor. He would even occasionally talk to Florianus—when he needed something from him badly enough. Aulus had proved to be an unsatisfactory go-between. And when Necro had tried sending his slaves to require the eunuch to hand over money, Florianus had indignantly and quite rightly refused to give it to them purely on their say-so if their master himself happened to be in the close vicinity.

Or had the Senator simply grown tired of having no-one to talk to but his servants, Urgo, and the scribe?

Necro graciously offered to take Aulus with him to the magistrate's house. When Aulus suggested that "for practical reasons" Florianus should also attend the supper, the Senator speculated loudly whether the presence of a eunuch at the magistrate's table would be deemed *appropriate* (a favorite word of his), or *decorous* (another one), but eventually relented, with ill-grace.

"They might even recognize each other," he sneered, "from the day when they were on sale together in the same slave auction!"

A torchbearer came to escort them. From what they could see of Cestae on their short, torch-lit walk, the magistrate's house was the largest and most solidly built structure in the town. Their host was waiting to greet them at the main door, flanked by house-slaves and members of his staff.

Olympiodorus Postumus Tryphaenatus was a great mountain of a man, his fleshy body barely contained by an old-fashioned Senatorial-style toga (though without the purple stripe worn by proper Senators). He greeted Necro effusively, bowing and scraping in front of the eminent visitor.

"Our little town is so honored by my Lord's presence! A second springtime has come to Cestae, at the end of summer!" he burbled, and more of such nonsense.

Necro allowed him to continue, and when he was satisfied that the magistrate was genuinely and unreservedly cognizant of the honor that was being bestowed upon him, he at last deigned to introduce Aulus. He presented him as "Faustus Pomponius Atticus Junior" (Aulus winced, as always, at the word "Junior"), "the son and nephew of Senators".

Later, they discovered that the fire-beacon message to Cestae had included the size of the delegation, but mentioned only Ambibulus Necro by name. The civic authorities were already groveling obsequiously at the feet of their distinguished guest. Did Necro somehow imagine that by introducing Aulus by his real (and more impressive) name it would ensure even more fawning and sycophancy?

Aulus was just about to introduce Florianus when one of the magistrate's attendants suddenly called out to him and Tryphaenatus most rudely turned away to address him. He beckoned to the man to come forward, and the two of them held an agitated, whispered conversation.

Necro was affronted by this behavior, so much so that he did the completely unexpected: he introduced Florianus himself!

"If I might have your attention, magistrate? May I introduce the treasurer and secretary to our delegation, Florianus, formerly High Chamberlain at the Imperial court?"

Tryphaenatus apologized profusely. An unexpected case had arisen, an awkward situation involving questions of jurisdiction. Bullying threats had been made. All those concerned had now been put in chains, and thrown into a dungeon reserved for such worthless people.

"I shall deal with the case personally first thing tomorrow. In fact, would the Senator perhaps do me the immense honor of sitting with me in judgment in the matter?"

Necro indicated his willingness with a brusque "Of course, of course" and a dismissive chop of his hand. Although Necro was an experienced public speaker, the movement reminded Aulus more of someone swatting a fly than of a gesture from the repertoire of an orator.

Tryphaenatus sighed with gratitude. In the meantime, nothing should be allowed to disturb the small supper that his cooks had prepared for them. Would the noble Senator please grace his home with his presence?

The magistrate led them to the dining-room of his house, where other guests—the social elite of the town, presumably—were waiting for them and the tables were spread with a truly startling number of dishes.

Fine! Aulus was a seasoned trencherman, and used to all-night feasting. But he was also accustomed to being able to sleep off the effects of too much food and wine the next day. Necro didn't strike him as being a devotee of pleasure, though, and what if the Senator insisted that they move on from Cestae after breakfast, and the court case? Aulus didn't fancy a long day on mule-back without having had a good night's (and morning's) sleep first.

Ideally, Necro would forget to drag him along to the court proceedings, and the silly judicial case might with luck stretch to hours or even days! Sol let it be ridiculously complicated, full of legal and procedural complexities! Necro would then be like a dog with a fresh and juicy bone.

Still, to be safe Aulus should try to exercise restraint in the face of whatever temptations he was confronted with.

Tryphaenatus had introduced his guests to the visitors, starting with his brother, Olympiodorus Postumus Gannex, the municipal treasurer (probably the *second* wealthiest man in the town, Aulus said to himself). Gannex was a slightly shorter but even more voluminous version of his brother. His main interest in life was soon apparent, as he wittered on interminably (ignoring the line of local worthies waiting patiently behind him) on the subject of the delightful food that they were going to be served.

Gannex recommended the honey-cakes ("Leave plenty of room for them!", an eventuality for which he personally was well prepared). They were a renowned specialty of the region ("We have so many bees, because of the nearby grasslands, and the mountains"). Was it a coincidence that as well as being town treasurer he was also chairman of the Apiarian

Guild, the confederation of local honey-producers and -merchants?

The worthies, when their turn finally came, proved to be wholly lacking in good looks, dress sense, or any obvious charm of manners or conversation.

More memorable was the magistrate's wife, Fortunata, who introduced herself, pushing aside several of the worthies in the process.

In size she was a match for her husband and brother-in-law. Her overall appearance reminded Aulus somewhat of a crumbling wall that had been shored up in desperate haste. It must have been the product of many hours of frantic attention to the noble lady's hair and make-up by her hardworking slave-girls.

She took an unwholesome interest in Aulus.

"My Lord is the son of a Senator? Ah! And himself so distinguished-looking! But too young to be married, surely?" Aulus unwisely confirmed that that was so. "Might I then introduce our daughter, Olympiodora, who has been *dying* to meet you?"

Oh, you fool! But Olympiodora was already bearing down on him, a glint in her eye. She was smaller than her mother, but with the obvious potential to one day swell up to the size of a professional wrestler.

On his night-time excursions in the City Aulus had met many girls like her—plump, lustful puddings, greedy for pleasure, not one of them "unspoiled"—and he had bedded several of them, without ever returning for a second portion of the pudding. Olympiodora was undoubtedly there for the taking. There was even something of Fannia in the challenging way that she looked at him. (Esbus! Why did he have to think of *her*?) You didn't marry girls like that, though, even if that was what Lady Fortunata might have in mind for him.

You never married them, unless they trapped you, if a quick spend in the course of the night's amusement produced unwanted consequences, and the girl's father was too influential to be ignored.

But this was a temptation that was easy to resist. He didn't want any amusements or adventures, not after that disastrous encounter with Fannia. And he didn't want to get married either, whatever his mother might say. Not even to Fannia.

Now it dawned on him how foolish he had been! His infatuation had been a fever of his emotions. Fannia would never be at the center of his life, as he had once dreamt she might me. His passion for her had been no more than unfulfilled lust, and he had had his chance to enjoy her, and hadn't taken it.

Clouds moved away, the sun shone through; at last his thoughts were clear. Thank you, Olympiodora, thank you!

Naturally he didn't say that, but he must have looked at her very strangely, because she gaped at him and said nothing.

He didn't know what to say either, and he didn't get a chance to say anything at all, because Necro now did the completely unexpected for the second time that night.

He was suddenly at Aulus's side, breathing heavily and staring at the magistrate's daughter.

"But who is this vision, Lady Fortunata?" he gulped. "What costly treasures, what rare jewels, has your fine city been withholding from us?"

Aulus had never before heard him speak so unctuously. And little Cestae a *city*? He glanced at him: the Senator's eyes were gleaming, the dribble was sliding from his mouth.

What was the man doing? Necro was *married*, for Sol's sake! (It was hard to believe, and hard to envision him in any kind of intimate relationship, but, yes, there was a spouse, "Even worse than him", according to the scribe Philotas, "Lady Death on a lead platter.")

Simultaneously, Olympiodora and her mother began to simper. Aulus felt their attention shift from him to the Senator—and a weight was lifted from his shoulders.

When they were invited to take their seats, he was able to secure a place on a couch safely out of reach of the two dangerous ladies. It came at a heavy price: throughout the whole meal, he had to listen to Olympiodorus Gannex explaining how the various dishes that they were served had been prepared, which dishes could only be offered at a particular time of the year (such as the apiarian's own favorite, asparagus), how to dress artichokes, and many other equally exciting topics.

He caught himself nodding off several times, and it was not because of the wine.

Necro, he observed, was completely preoccupied with the charming Olympiodora. It therefore came as no surprise to Aulus when the Senator beckoned him across to his couch and suggested that he and Florianus might prefer to leave, since the next day would be strenuous for everyone.

As a favor to Tryphaenatus, he had a tiresome judicial duty to perform, but after that they must resume their journey. The magistrate would provide them with an armed escort, Urgo should be informed, however (he had obviously not been invited to the supper), and he must discuss their route with the escort. This would be for Aulus to arrange.

He himself had been invited to stay at the magistrate's home that night, and had already been made to feel very welcome. It would be rude to decline the offer, and he would therefore not be accompanying them back to the inn.

Aulus was happy to be able to go back, even though it meant missing out on the fabled honey-cakes. He couldn't resist the thought that Necro urgently wanted Florianus and himself out of the way. He could then pursue his dalliance with Olympiodora, without fear of either of them telling embarrassing stories about him when they had all returned to the City.

Florianus, it seemed, was more than content to leave. He had been placed in a far corner of the dining-room, among the least distinguished guests, and promptly ignored—eunuchs were not part of the polite social scene in Cestae, and no-one had been eager to engage him in discussion. Every time that Aulus had looked in his direction, he had been toying morosely with his food, while the conversation passed him by.

On the way back to the inn they discussed the Senator's peculiar behavior, but in a whisper, so that the torchbearer couldn't hear what they were saying.

"There are men who are upright and virtuous in public," Florianus said, "while in private they are the dirtiest of all. Because they are so ugly in their behavior, they do their fucking in the dark—I mean that as a metaphor, Master Aulus, you do understand?—or they wait until they are in some little provincial nest, some backwater like Cestae, where no-one who matters can see them."

Nevertheless, they both had to admit that Necro was more complicated, and more cunning, than they had previously thought. It might be dangerous to underestimate him.

XVIII

THOMASIUS ACCOMPANIES A SEARCH

�֍   *Cascantum.*

Thomasius's sleep was fitful, and disturbed by extraordinary dreams. Numbers battled with each other. One of them (was it a five?) shouted "I'm awkward!", while the others replied "No you aren't!" The numbers jumped about, pushing him down so that he was lying uncomfortably on top of one of them. Or was he trying to make love to it? It must be that five! Was five female? Maybe that's why it was awkward?

Gradually he crawled back into a waking state, and realized that he was lying on top of a lump in the bed.

But at least he was back in his own bed, which was very good. And Manasa would be there. Maybe she would like an early-morning cuddle? He reached across to where she ought to be, and found nothing to embrace.

He was disappointed. But she was no doubt already up and about preparing his breakfast, as a good woman should...

He rolled over again to enjoy a final snooze.

"Get up! Get dressed!"

That was Manasa, and it wasn't a "Good-morning-I've-made-you-breakfast-dear-master" sort of voice. In fact, she sounded distinctly short-tempered.

He rubbed his eyes. She was there in front of him, and was already dressed in plain, everyday clothes, not the light, revealing tunic that she had worn the evening before.

Worse still, there was a man standing behind her!

Instead of offering to help him get dressed, Manasa disappeared, leaving him to the mercy of the stranger, a young Sueni cavalryman who introduced himself as Turgulo. He was reasonably clean and presentable—for a swampie—but he wouldn't shut up.

He volunteered the information that, in the Tongue of the Sueni, Turgulo meant "fit".

"Fit? Oh, yes? You mean, er, athletic?"

"That, too. But you know what I mean, boss," he said, with a friend-ly leer, "fit...for the ladies!"

His mother had had great hopes for him, he declared, twirling at the ends of his meager mustache, and he hadn't let her down. Give him a job, and he'd get it done. Whether it was the weapon dangling from his belt or *the other one*, the beautiful one that the Sacred Earth Cow had bestowed on him at birth, he knew how to use both those weapons ex-pertly—whether cutting or *thrusting*, he was no mean swordsman!

Oh, and he could hurl a javelin as well as any infantryman, and he knew all the wrestling throws and holds, even the deadly Sueni death-grip. (What in Sol's name was that? Thomasius had never heard of it.)

Bleary-eyed, and trying to get himself dressed, Thomasius let this nonsense flow over him like the wash from a barge on the Great River. Or the gush of horse-piss from one of the Suenis' mounts. He noticed now that his head was thumping from the wine—he wasn't such an ex-perienced carouser as some Sub-officers that he knew.

Who *was* the man? And what was he doing in the Sub-officer's quar-ters?

Finally Turgulo told him. He was Thomasius's new "bodyguard".

Oh, that! His heart sank. Fires of Esbus, the Lord Commander had indeed promised him someone to "hold his hand and watch his back", but he had expected it to be a battle-hardened, broad-shouldered Citizen Army brute, wide enough to shield him from the odd arrow, and not some chatterbox ladies' man who couldn't even grow a proper mustache.

How had it come about, Thomasius asked, that *he* had been chosen for this duty?

Well, apart from his well-known fighting skills, Turgulo said, he had also mastered the Tongue of the Sybarites, backwards, forwards, up, down, and round the corner! He liked those southern girls, yes indeed, and they'd taught him a thing or two when he was a youngster, and not just their funny lingo.

Manasa came back in and glared at both of them.

"If Master would please hurry up, and Swampie Boy would kindly *shut up*, there is a detachment of soldiers waiting for us outside."

"Sorry, boss. Duty calls, and we must answer. Ah, the ladies are al-ways right."

He winked lewdly at Manasa and exchanged words in Sybarite with her.

(She told Thomasius later, when he asked her, that Turgulo had said "You can't win them all!" and that she had replied with the Sybarite equivalent of "Fuck off!", which sounds particularly bad, because the tongue of Sybaris is normally so elegant and melodious-sounding. He was from Urtho's cavalry-troop, and they had met once before in Fanum. He was probably harmless, she said, but Sueni men had never been very high on her shopping-list. Remembering Urtho, Thomasius didn't press her any further on that subject.)

Only a handful of infantrymen were waiting for them. Holding torches, they were hopping from foot to foot in irritation because they'd had to wait so long while the Sub-officer got himself out of bed. As they made their careful way down to the South Gate, the section-commander who was in charge told Thomasius that the rest of his section would be meeting them in the township, at the Street of Silver. That was the first area that they would be searching, house by house. Other sections had been assigned to the other areas, and they would keep in touch by means of runners.

The Lord Commander wanted the Sybarites taken *alive*, so if they actually found what they were looking for the girl's knowledge of the Sybarite tongue might prove to be useful.

"Mine too!" Turgulo said.

The section-commander gave him an icy stare.

Thomasius was thinking to himself that they didn't really need *him* at all. And hadn't the plan been that someone was going to take out his stitches first? But it was still dark, even if the dawn couldn't be far off, and though a Sub-officer like himself could be hauled out of bed early they weren't going to disturb the precious sleep of an army doctor, were they? (Because if you did, he might remember you next time you had a nasty wound that needed seeing to.)

The Street of Silver! A beautiful name that suggested a broad, paved thoroughfare, lined with silversmiths and fancy jewelers' shops, and thronged with young bucks buying trinkets for their mistresses and wealthy old ladies seeking to purchase yet another item for the jewel-casket.

In reality, the Street of Silver was just a narrow, filthy lane. There were no silversmiths to be seen. The "street" wound its considerable length through the festering slum that had sprung up to house the soldiers' whores and camp-followers and their bastard offspring. An astonishing number of people lived there, crushed together and constantly treading on each other's toes and interfering in each other's business. Not a situation that encouraged peace and harmony!

The other main "streets", of Gold, Copper and Bronze, were no better. Their residents had decided that they needed names, and they had chosen to name them after metals. ("Dirt", "Mud", "Filth" and "Dogshit" would have been more appropriate, Thomasius thought.) Of course, the names were not recognized by the authorities, and the "streets" weren't even laid out in the proper grid-pattern, but the local people liked them and they had even erected painted wooden signs as if their slum were part of a great city.

Some of the men in Thomasius's unit—no, what had formerly been his unit, he would have to get used to the new situation—kept women, some of them with children, in the Street of Silver. They weren't bad people just because they lived in a cesspit. The soldiers in the detachment wouldn't be brutal, or unnecessarily rude to them. These were the families of their comrades, and maybe even their own, whose hovels they'd be searching.

Soldiers can't help making a noise, and by the time they'd arrived the inhabitants of the Street of Silver were all wide-awake and busily engaged in hiding whatever they had that was precious. Which was sensible: though the soldiers were looking for two dangerous people on the run, and not for forbidden items, valuables did have a certain way of getting mislaid whenever a search was carried out, however carefully a section-commander might watch his men.

Many of the "houses" were no better than one- or two-room shacks or sheds, and even the larger ones were very primitive constructions. There were no multi-storey tenements here, of the kind that you found in proper cities. Who would build them? It rained a lot, and solid, expensive foundations would have to be laid if a larger building was going to be safe to live in. How long would it then take the owner to recoup his expenses? These people wouldn't ever be paying much rent.

Besides, taller buildings weren't permitted anywhere near the walls of the fortress, for obvious reasons.

There were only two moderately sturdy-looking buildings in the whole township: a simple but comfortable inn called the Fighting Cocks, and a cheaper hostelry named the Stallion, both of them half-way down the Street of Copper. They were the only two-storey buildings beyond the walls of the fortress.

Thomasius had once been interested in one of the maids at the Fighting Cocks, so he'd been there quite often before she finally took up with an amber merchant and told the Sub-officer to get lost. The Cocks was known as *the* place to go in Cascantum for assignations. In truth, where else could you take a girl if you wanted her to think you were serious?

The Stallion was smaller and dirtier, but it did have a regular gaming circle, and over the years Sub-officer Grassica had honed his skills there, relieving passing travelers of their Maximians.

Cascantum's other inns and taverns were all disgusting beyond description.

Anyone who counted in this place, whether they were in the Citizen Army or working for it, would wish to have their normal accommodation *within* the walls of the fortress, and not outside them.

Their search of the Street of Silver didn't amount to what Thomasius would have considered to be an efficient house to house search.

It wasn't just because Turgulo held them up by talking all the time, to anyone who was happy to listen and to many who weren't.

It wasn't just because there was a maze of mucky footpaths, yards, drains and chicken-coops behind the "houses", all of which really ought to be searched (inevitably some of them weren't).

And it wasn't because they found anything remotely significant, or encountered any opposition.

No, it was because the soldiers regarded the whole business as a tiresome chore for which they had been selected, most unfairly, while their more fortunate comrades could stay inside the fortress and not get their feet muddy. If they had to do it, then they might as well enjoy themselves, so they were taking an inordinate amount of time over the searches, chatting up the women, finding out whose girl a particular trollop was, and poking around inquisitively in people's belongings.

At long last they reached the end of the Street of Silver and met up with the detachment that had been searching the Street of Copper. Did *they* have anything to report?

Well, some of their comrades had apparently abandoned their women and were keeping new doxies, so the former "wives" had given them a proper earful to take back to the fortress with them and pass on to their "exes". For instance, there was that section commander…

Thomasius interrupted the flow of gossip in exasperation.

Yes, and? What about the two inns? Had they searched *them* properly?

They were even better! At the Stallion, they had caught one of the Staff Officers making out with a Sueni boy.

Now that really was a sensation—not because of what they were up to, but because the Staff Officer was doing the boy, and not the other way round as they would have expected! Also, because of where they were doing it.

"Mean fucking ponce! Typical! Too bloody mean to pay for a decent room at the Cocks!"

To his eternal shame, Thomasius heard himself enquiring which Staff Officer it had been. (Was he perhaps half-hoping that it might be the fragrant Petronius?)

No, it was some new Staff Officer, recently arrived.

"So it wasn't Petronius?"

The soldiers looked at him in amazement.

"What, *him*? Of course not! Why would he need a swampie boy? Haven't you seen his little bed-warmer? She's quite something, that one!"

Oh, and there was a couple that had been shagging at the Fighting Cocks early that morning, a trader and his slave-girl.

"Did you check *their* identity?"

Not exactly. The gentleman had been so energetically busy, it would have been a pity to interrupt him. And the only weapon that they saw was the one he was using.

"And it looked bloody dangerous to me! And as for her, well…"

Thomasius persisted.

"Were they from the south?"

"Hard to say, in that light. But she was blonde-haired, definitely. And he was really giving it to her."

But that had been early in the morning. They'd be long gone by now.

"And if they aren't," one of the other men added, "and they're still doing it, he's a better man than I am!"

There was no point. The men in both patrols were tired, and wanted to get back. They'd been offered plenty of drinks, home-brewed beer, which they weren't supposed to accept, but obviously had done, whenever Thomasius and the section-commanders weren't watching. But no-one had offered them any food, so they were hungry.

Thomasius was hungry, too, but even more than that he wanted to get away from Turgulo for a while. The man had stuck to him like a leech throughout the day, offering what he thought were witty comments on whatever was going on.

Manasa was now loudly bad-tempered, for a host of reasons (apart from Turgulo). One reason was that she wasn't wearing robust shoes, which meant that her feet were bruised and scratched and her legs were caked in mud to well above her ankles. And she had found the soldiers' search-and-gossip activities even less enthralling than Thomasius had.

A runner found them, bringing the news that the other patrols had also failed to find any Sybarite killers, although in the Street of Gold they had stumbled across an interesting cache of contraband trading goods.

By the time that they got back to the fortress, and the men had been dismissed, it was closer to supper-time than to the time of the midday meal. Manasa responded insolently when her master decided that, before returning to his quarters, they should report to the Lord Commander.

"What is there to report?" she asked with a yawn, adding, with a sideways glance at Turgulo: "That one of his Staff Officers fancies hairy, smelly Sueni boys?"

"Enough of that! Not another word!"

He would have to be stricter with her. He was angry, though if he was honest with himself he would have to admit that it was Turgulo who had got on his nerves—all day—rather than Manasa.

Rhaetius would likely be in the map-room, Thomasius thought, but the Lord Commander wasn't, and the door was locked and guarded.

"No entry, Sub-officer!" the guard bellowed, but then relaxed. "The old man isn't there anyway. He went off on a secret mission. And Lord Commander Memmius isn't back yet."

Really? Maybe Petronius, the ranking Staff Officer of the Seventh, was the man to talk to, especially as Thomasius knew him, whereas he didn't really know any of the Staff Officers in the Fourth.

As if he had been summoned by magic, Petronius now approached, followed by two soldiers in full battle-gear, and with a look of amazement on his face.

But he wasn't looking at Thomasius. *He was looking at Manasa.*

And it was Manasa that he spoke to, not Thomasius: "What are you doing here?"

Without understanding the question, Thomasius intervened.

"Excuse me, sir, we've just come off patrol—"

"I know that, man!" the Staff Officer snapped at him. "But what is the slave-girl doing here?"

"She accompanied us, as the Lord Commander instructed."

Petronius stepped back. Then he turned to the soldiers and told them to withdraw to the corridor outside. Turgulo too, and the guard on the map-room door.

He waited until he was alone with Thomasius and Manasa before speaking again.

First to Thomasius: "You should take the skin off this girl's back! And then sell her to the mines."

"*What?*"

Then, ignoring Thomasius, to Manasa: "At this very moment, you are supposed to be shagging the Lord Commander, behind your master's back. So where is the Lord Commander, then? Why hasn't he returned? And what are you doing here?"

Manasa was obviously stunned, and lost for words; again, Thomasius spoke for her.

"That can't be true, sir. She's been with me all day."

Now it was Petronius's turn to be baffled.

A boy from the Fighting Cocks had come, he said, with a personal message for the Lord Commander. It was from the Sub-officer's Sybarite girl. She could meet him at the inn, if he came at once. He had left immediately, taking two trusted men with him and leaving Petronius in temporary command. Since it was a private matter, only Petronius and the two guards knew about it.

"You know what the Lord Commander is like with women, Sub-officer. And your girl was flirting with him, leading him on."

That wasn't true, and yet it didn't matter. Petronius might be slow-witted, but Thomasius wasn't.

"There's only one other Sybarite girl in Cascantum, and she's here to kill the Lord Commander. We must go *now*!"

Leaving the Staff Officer gawping after him, Thomasius rushed out into the corridor, followed by Manasa. He ordered the three soldiers to surrender their javelins, took one for himself, and gave one to Turgulo and (for what it was worth) one to Manasa. Swords—his Army sword and Turgulo's cavalry sword—might not be enough.

Staff Officer Petronius would soon be coming with dramatic orders for them, he said, but *he* had no time to waste.

The three of them sped as fast as they could to the South Gate, and Thomasius told the section-commander on duty there to get half his men armed and follow them to the Fighting Cocks. Without waiting, he led Turgulo and Manasa down into the township, slipping and sliding in the muddy lane until they reached the inn.

It was quiet, and there was no-one there.

Inns are *never* quiet, and there is *always* someone there.

All the rooms on the ground floor were empty, even the kitchen, though food had recently been prepared—the oven was still warm. Had everyone fled?

They would need to go up to the first floor, where most of the rooms for guests were, using the rickety wooden staircase. Whoever was up there would hear them coming. And when they reached the landing and began to search the rooms, the creaky wooden floorboards would give away every single step that they took.

Should they wait for reinforcements? No, not if they wanted to save the Lord Commander's life.

Watchfully, but very noisily, they climbed the stairs.

Although it was still afternoon, there was very little light inside the inn, with most of it coming in through cracks in the wood. The small windows on the corridor were for air, not for light, and they had been covered with sacking material to keep out birds and insects. Specks of dust danced in the beams of light shining in through larger cracks.

The two soldiers who had accompanied the Lord Commander lay sprawled at the top of the staircase, their throats slashed and their limbs spread awkwardly in attitudes of death. The floorboards around them were slippery with blood.

Out of the corner of his eye Thomasius caught a flash of movement, more like a shadow than a shape, at one end of the corridor. He couldn't run too fast to where he'd seen it, because it might be a trap: the shadow could be the girl, and Victor might be lying in wait, sword drawn, in any of the doorways that he had to pass.

When they did reach the end of the corridor, there was much more light. The "shadow" had gone into the last of the guestrooms, clambered onto a table and out through the small, high window, and dropped onto the roof of the shed below. It was now, with unbelievable agility, escaping across the roofs of the township.

Only a cat could have achieved all that, but it wasn't a light-footed cat that was leaping and springing acrobatically across those flimsy roofs, it was a man: Victor.

Neither Thomasius nor Turgulo could have squeezed through the window. Manasa might conceivably have managed it, but carrying only a short-sword, not a long-sword or javelin. And could she have followed him, equally nimbly, across the roofs of Cascantum? And if she had caught up with him, what would have happened next?

"If that is Victor," Thomasius said, "where is the girl? And where is the Lord Commander?"

They returned along the corridor, checking each of the rooms and finding nothing. Beyond the top of the staircase there were two more guestrooms, but this end of the corridor was very dark and gloomy.

There was nothing in the first room, except an unmade bed.

The second room was larger, and would be used by more important guests. What Thomasius saw there made him pull back instinctively, bumping into Manasa.

There was a massive body stretched out on the floor and lying deathly still. It wasn't a felled ox, it was the Lord Commander. Nails or tent-pegs had been hammered through his hands into the wooden floorboards. Two more protruded from the sockets of his eyes.

Hunched over him, like a beast gloating over its prey, was the slight figure of a girl. She had cut first her victim's clothes open, and then his body. Both her hands were deep inside the huge wound, and moving in a frenzied way. Was she mutilating him? Cutting out his organs? Blood was dripping from her mouth. Was she *eating* parts of him?

Whatever dreadful task she was engaged in, she was so preoccupied with it that at first she didn't notice them.

Paralyzed, Thomasius gazed at the horror in silence, but Manasa shouted, "No!"

The girl looked up. Thomasius took in the slim, pretty face, scarred on one side and smeared with blood; and the blonde wig lying beside her. As the girl lifted her hands, he saw that she was holding a small knife in one of them and a piece of human flesh in the other. Her face was blank of any expression, but her eyes glowed blood-red.

Manasa had already pushed past him and was reaching out to the girl.

"Lelia! *Maneira?* Don't you remember me? My name is Manasa." She made no response. "My name is Manasa. *Sero e'Manasa.*"

The girl finally looked at her, and spoke in a voice devoid of any emotion.

"Sero en al-kraak."

And then she sprang to her feet and hurled herself at Manasa, the knife outstretched.

Thomasius was too shocked to move; Turgulo wasn't. There was a sudden rush of air past Thomasius's head and the attacker was flung backwards by the force of the javelin striking her chest.

Her body hit the floor with a thud.

Manasa threw herself onto the girl, cradling her head in her hands and talking to her in a torrent of Sybarite words. Lelia gasped and shuddered. It was clear that no doctor would be able to save her.

Pulling out the javelin would kill her immediately, but she would die anyway. Thomasius had seen such injuries on the battlefield, and once in a training exercise. There was nothing that could be done. Turgulo, he thought grimly, had not been exaggerating when he'd boasted of his skill with the javelin.

When she died, moments later, Manasa wept. And she turned on Turgulo.

"Why did you have to do that?" she asked, between sobs. "She was my sister! My sister Lelia."

Turgulo spoke softly, to Thomasius: "She was going to kill her. I had to do it."

"What did the girl say to her?" Thomasius asked.

"Sero en al-kraak. My name is Death."

XIX

DECIMUS EXPLORES THE PALACE

✠   *The Imperial Palace, in the City.*

The following morning, his Imperial Majesty *was* indisposed, and no audience took place. Vulpeculus had important business to attend to, he said, but Decimus should remain in the Palace and act as his eyes and ears. Then he disappeared, and didn't return.

Decimus spent a frustrating day, neither seeing nor hearing anything of great interest. The Blood-Drinkers, for example, had been carefully hidden away.

The next day followed the same pattern, although Decimus allowed himself to explore the Palace a little.

On the third day, Senator Marcus Vulpeculus formally presented Decimus to the Emperor, at his considerably delayed morning audience.

It was so late that it was almost an afternoon audience.

First, they had to wait outside the audience chamber. The eunuch Photon, who was standing in as High Chamberlain in the absence of Julian—an absence for which no-one was seemingly prepared to offer a reason—was managing the event. He was making himself important and only allowing small groups to enter, "so as not to over-tax his Imperial Majesty's strength", he said. Neither Senator Marcus Naevius nor his son Quintus were in attendance. The eunuch told Vulpeculus and Decimus that, when their turn came, they should "keep it short, please, very short", as his Imperial Majesty was somewhat tired.

The Senator gave Photon a withering stare. He wasn't used to being given instructions by eunuchs.

While they were waiting for admission to the audience chamber, Vulpeculus told Decimus that the Emperor had not attended the emergency midnight meeting of the Imperial Council. Nor had he been seen very much since. He had failed to appear for two morning audiences, and had presented himself for this one much later than was customary. No-one, it seemed, had dared to wake him, but when Maximillus had eventually woken up he had been greeted with catastrophic news that had reached the Palace by fire-beacon just before dawn. Gnaeus Placidus had outwitted or subverted the Citizen divisions in the south, and was advancing northwards with a sizeable army. He was already distressingly close to the City.

Gnaeus was grossly obese, but he was a cunning and experienced military commander. As a young Senator, he had volunteered for the unpopular task of crushing an uprising of slaves and bonded laborers in the countryside south of the City. Though he had been jealously starved of troops, ostensibly because of financial constraints but in reality for political reasons, he had brought the rebellion to a swift, cruel end, with the bodies of thousands of crucified or impaled rebels rotting along the roads into the capital.

Gnaeus might be lazy, but he would make the right strategic decisions and then delegate tactical command to well-chosen and more energetic subordinates.

With Ogilo unable to leave the north, who was there to take the field against him? And, more to the point, with which troops?

Alternatively, could the City hope to withstand a siege? There were still Red traitors within the walls.

In the outer corridors of the Golden Rooms the disturbing news from the south was now the only topic of conversation: the alarming speed with which Fat Placidus was approaching, and the speculation about what would happen to them all when he and his men arrived in the City, with so many outstanding scores to be settled.

As a loyal Council member, Vulpeculus had already been briefed.

"Since you and I have reached an understanding, freedman," Vulpeculus said, "I am telling you everything that I know. Naturally, I shall expect you to return the favor."

Without believing him, Decimus nodded in agreement, and then pressed the Senator for more details about the emergency Council meeting.

Nothing of import had been decided, Vulpeculus said. After all, what was there that the *powerless* could possibly decide? Gold and an Imperial princess were what was needed now, and neither was immediately available.

There was no money with which to pay off the Blood-Drinkers. Given time, the million gold pieces could presumably be raised—by squeezing the Senators, the merchants, the priests of Sol and everyone else of any wealth and position in the City.

It could be done, for sure, but it wouldn't be wise to do it. Because although Quintus could control the capital by terror—for a while, maybe—in the longer term his father, who had no army at his disposal, could only maintain his hold on power, and stave off the threat from Placidus, with the active support of those very same Senators, priests and merchants.

And there was no princess of the Imperial blood, "fuckable" or otherwise, to offer the Great King. In nine to ten months there *might* be a little princess, however, whose sad destiny it would be to be sent to appease the demons from beyond the Great River, poor child.

From the point of view of Naevius, in both instances the only sensible course was to play for time. The negotiations must be made to last as long as possible. Darkhon could be kept happy with whores and strong drink. There were also ladies of the court eager to make his acquaintance. Alumgar, though, would have to be offered more than that. He would need to be fed with ideas and proposals, and with hints of a princess "on the way" (if Maximillus would only do his duty!). But would mere promises be enough to turn the horde away from the City, and eastwards, towards Neopolis?

Decimus thanked the Senator for sharing his thoughts with him so generously.

No! Vulpeculus replied, Decimus was quite bright enough to work it all out for himself. If he wasn't, the Senator wouldn't have wasted his time on him.

Then, almost as a test, he asked Decimus what he would do, if *he* were the Khan of Khans?

"I would ignore the General, my Lord, and move north into the Valley for winter pasturing. There I would bide my time, to see what Naevius produced by way of gold and princesses."

Vulpeculus waited until he was sure that Decimus had nothing further to add, and then asked, "You would do that, despite the risk of Ogilo also growing stronger, and maybe trapping the horde there against the mountains?"

"No reinforcements of Citizen troops that are available to the General will make him strong enough to want to offer battle. There is only one development that could cause Horkhon to lose a little sleep."

"Aha! And that is?"

"A great alliance of the Citizens with all the northern tribes: the Sueni, the Horse People, even the Free People. Then Ogilo would finally command enough cavalry to restrict the horde in its movements, to harrass its flanks, to force it back across the Great River or maneuver it towards a battle-ground of his own choosing."

"Hmmm. Clever boy. It won't happen, though." Vulpeculus marked the points one by one with his fingers. "The loyalty of our Sueni cavalry has never been certain. The Free People have already made their choice. And the Horse People are restless, and dissatisfied. But, like you, I see the Blood-Drinkers moving up into the Valley for the winter. Who wants a winter campaign?"

And that would help Naevius, he said, provided that a deal with the Blood-Drinkers was eventually forthcoming, because it would weaken Ogilo, who would forfeit the respect of the Greens, just as it would also weaken the Greens, who would lose one of their main power-bases.

"But the Empire would lose the revenues of a rich province, too. Is that such a good outcome?"

Well, Vulpeculus said, there was always a price to be paid in life, wasn't there? And who knew what might yet happen in the days and weeks to come? Even the *cleverest* freedmen couldn't know or predict everything!

"Trust me: there will be surprises. Surprises that you could never have foreseen. Everyone is watching the lions, the bears and the wolves, and waiting for them to rip each other apart. But who is watching the fox? You won't regret your loyalty to me."

Had his upper lip twitched? Decimus couldn't be sure. And at that moment Photon came out of the audience chamber in order to usher them into the Sublime Presence.

The Presence was not looking very well. The Imperial shoulders were hunched, the Imperial eyes were red, and Maximillus had notice-able difficulty concentrating on what was going on. Naevia was not with him.

Both men made the full obeisance, Decimus with practiced smooth-ness (slaves learned to adopt the postures of subjugation very easily), Vulpeculus stiffly, conscious of the humiliation that was entailed in grov-eling in front of such a despicable man.

At eye-level, Decimus could see the dog Porphyrius playing at the Emperor's feet, yapping, jumping about, and tugging at the Imperial robe.

"Get up!" Maximillus shouted, and Photon leant over them and tapped on their shoulders. "There is no need to tell me anything at all, Senator. You are too late! Your colleague Naevius was exceptionally well-informed. And why shouldn't he be, since you went to *him* first, before you came to me?"

He gave Vulpeculus a spiteful look. This was a clear reproach.

"Your Imperial Majesty—"

"No! Enough! I've been bored quite enough for one day."

"The contract—"

"If Ogilo is a traitor your precious contract is worth shit! And now

Fat Placidus is coming to kill us all, because of all those southerners that you and your Blue friends murdered. Which wasn't *my* idea. Why should I have to pay for your mistakes?"

So much for the "warm glow of friendly approval" that Vulpeculus had promised the document would generate! But the Senator was not going to give up so soon.

"Your Majesty, much as I share your dislike of the General, his loyalty to the throne cannot be doubted. And despite his personal loathing for the man, Senator Naevius has surely told you the same. Ogilo is still our best hope against the Blood-Drinkers—"

"Ugh!" Maximillus shuddered. "Enough! Don't mention those disgusting creatures, and don't let them near me! I don't want to see them again!"

"—and he remains a bulwark against the Placidi. As a gesture of good faith, he has sent his close confidant, the freedman Decimus, to your court."

He nudged Decimus, and Decimus stepped forward and presented himself with an elegant half-obeisance.

"Your Imperial Majesty."

The Emperor looked past him, ignoring him, and spoke only to Vulpeculus. He was working himself up into a massive tantrum.

"Keep *him* away from me too! He's just a spy. Or he'll try and tell me what to do, like everyone else. 'My master Ogilo says do this', 'my master Ogilo says do that'. I'm *tired* of being told what to do! First it's Ogilo and flabby old Florianus. And the High Priest of Sol, too, that ghastly old man. He never shuts up! Then it's Naevius and his creepy son. Now it's you and Ogilo again. He's a fucking barbarian—and he has the cheek to send a freedman to tell *me* what to do? I'm the Emperor—no-one tells me what to do. No-one!"

While the Emperor was ranting, Photon hopped about beside the throne like a plump little bird, flapping his hands and clucking "Oh, your Majesty, please, your Majesty."

Photon wasn't just concerned about the Emperor getting over-excited. The Imperial remarks about Naevius and his son had been tactless, to say the least. In the Palace, the walls had ears.

Then the dog yapped once too often. Maximillus lashed out—and missed.

"Get rid of that! Get me another dog, one that doesn't crap so much!"

Photon seized the unfortunate Porphyrius. He handed the delinquent animal to a slave who had come rushing forward, only too happy to play his part in ending the reign of the yapping, crapping little monster. Porphyrius was taken away, never to be seen again.

The eunuch then made a fluttering gesture to Vulpeculus and Decimus, effectively indicating that they should better leave.

With Maximillus in such a mood, nothing could be achieved, and so they took the eunuch's signaled advice. Decimus was relieved that his part in the audience was over, but the Senator was angry and perhaps also frustrated.

"That *creature*, that little degenerate," he whispered, the moment that they were safely outside the audience chamber and out of hearing of any courtiers or Guardsmen, "is the glorious ruler of the West, our First Citizen and Imperator, and the Chief Servant of Sol! What have we come to?"

He had another session of the Imperial Council to attend, which had been called to discuss the "Placidus problem". Naevius would be there, but nothing would come of that meeting either. Just as there was no gold and no princess with which to buy off the Blood-Drinkers, there was also no army to send against Gnaeus Placidus.

"Does that mean a siege, my Lord?"

"Maybe. Who knows? We shall all have to make our own little arrangements. I won't forget that we have an agreement."

And with that Vulpeculus left him to his own devices.

The Senator had made no further mention of Decimus's "duties" regarding the security of the City. Perhaps Decimus could find the Commander of the Imperial Guard and introduce himself? That shouldn't be too difficult.

With the City Prefect (who was, after all, a member of the Senate) it would be harder. He could hardly walk up to him and brazenly declare that he, Decimus the freedman, would now be offering him advice on how best to do his job. To meet the Prefect, he would first need an introduction.

It was too late to visit Senator Lucius Atticus, so Decimus decided to continue exploring the Palace, or at least those parts of it where his entry wouldn't be blocked by Guardsmen or officious eunuchs. There were the Silver Rooms, for example, which housed the offices of the Imperial administration, and where there were guesthouses for visitors and functionaries.

As an avid reader, he would most of all have liked to visit the Palace library, except that it didn't really exist.

Over the centuries, successive Emperors had built up a fine collection, which had reached its apogee in the reign of Severian the Evil. Severian had been very learned, but his personal taste had been more for the obscure and the exotic (some would say the obscene) than for works of conventional scholarship. For instance, he had added to the library such connoisseur items as a supposedly philosophical text entitled *The Infinite and Ineffable Glory of Copulation*. Lavishly illustrated treatises on love-making had also been purchased, at huge expense, from such distant places as the court of Sin, and transported halfway across the world by camel.

When Severian had been overthrown, the outer parts of the Palace had burned, and the great library had burned with them. Subsequent Emperors had been too busy fighting usurpers and barbarians to have had much time for reading, and most of them were in any case too poorly educated to have any inclination in that direction.

Maximus the Great had been a notable exception—a warrior who considered himself to be a man of learning (and who would have dared to contradict him?). He had rebuilt and restocked the Imperial library, albeit with a large number of unreadable works of Slave "scholarship". His son, however, had been dull-witted, and as for his grandson...

Immediately adjacent to the Palace was the Senate, and there was an excellent Senatorial library that Decimus would love to use. There was one small snag: the librarians were unlikely to give a freedman access to the collection without the warmest letter of recommendation from a high-ranking Senator—a letter such as Lucius Atticus had written for Davus. Senatorial librarian was a profession that seemed to attract pedants and fanatical sticklers to the rules!

Decimus must ask Senator Atticus whether he would be so kind as to write him such a letter.

There was only one more or less public library to which he would have no difficulty in being admitted: the Imperial and City archives. But these were housed in a building in the compound of the Temple of Sol, which was some distance from the Palace.

He was still considering where to go next when he heard a whisper, "Decimus?"

He spun round. It was the fussy little eunuch from the audience with the Blood-Drinkers. Speaking so softly that Decimus could barely understand him, he introduced himself as Philoxas.

"Isn't that the name of a flower?"

The eunuch tittered, his chins wobbling.

"What a charming thing to say! Please come with me, my dear boy. There is someone who wishes to meet you. Someone very important"

He led Decimus down several small side-corridors, and then opened a door, cunningly built into wooden side-paneling, that Decimus would otherwise have overlooked. It opened onto a long, narrow, very dark corridor that must have been built to facilitate just such surreptitious movement about the Palace.

Philoxas urged him to be very quiet, and not to touch the walls, where there were further hidden doors that might spring open if a careless hand happened to brush unintentionally against a tiny switch or lever.

This was what Decimus had most feared! Darkness, treachery, shadows, danger lurking in wait… But the General had sent him to the Palace for a reason, and he couldn't shirk his duty now by refusing to take a small step into the unknown.

Without a weapon, he felt naked. Maybe, if danger appeared, he could improvize, by seizing a torch, say, or a small piece of furnishing, or an artwork. Perhaps some loose wall-fitting like a metal torch-bracket. Whoever attacked him would have the advantage of being armed, though, and of knowing the layout of the rooms and the corridors.

He had no choice but to take the risk.

Who could the important someone be? Not the Emperor, surely? He had already made his distaste for Decimus very clear. Senator Naevius, perhaps?

Philoxas opened yet another door. He pushed Decimus through into the room beyond, saying "This is where I must leave you for a short while."

He stumbled, momentarily blinded by the brightness of the room after the darkness of the outer corridor. He was aware of someone standing in front of him.

It wasn't a vicious killer—it was a naked girl.

She grinned at him, and said, "What kind of a gentleman keeps his own clothes on when the lady has already removed hers?"

Decimus gave a sigh of relief.

She was small, slim, and very young, not much more than a child, and pretty rather than beautiful, with a cheeky snub-nose and freckles. She was a northerner, but he could see that her pale skin was unusually smooth, and that she had been expertly plucked of all her body-hair.

He didn't recognize her. How could this be an "important person"?

He should please undress, she said again, or did he require her help?

The room was dazzlingly bright because of the remarkable number of torches and lamps, whose light reflected off the surface of the exquisite mosaics that covered the walls and the floor. Decimus had never seen such a room—it must have cost a fortune to construct. Surely they were in the very heart of the Golden Rooms!

The mosaics were of the finest quality and showed heroes slaying demons, heroines taming fierce monsters, fabulous winged creatures, hunting landscapes, and scenes of love-making. Such delightful mosaics had not been produced for hundreds of years. The skill of artists and craftsmen in the West had declined, and no longer was there anyone remotely capable of such masterly handiwork.

Sunk into the floor at the far end of the room was a bath, with gleaming surfaces of blue and gold mosaic squares that shimmered and glinted beneath the water. Beside the bath was a table, on which were laid out flasks, no doubt containing unguents and scented oils, some scrapers and massage tools, and cloths for drying; there was also a low couch.

Over the bath there were yet more impressive mosaics, showing the great rulers of earlier days and their consorts, who gazed down benignly on whoever was now using the bath-house.

Decimus stripped off his clothes and allowed the girl to bathe him. She took pleasure in stimulating him with her hand, but she wouldn't allow him to touch her in return. Afterwards, she dried and massaged him, rubbing him amorously and even taking his man-part briefly between her lips.

"This is a noble weapon!" she giggled. "I trust that its owner knows how to use it!"

"Most certainly," he replied, but he made no further attempt to prove it to her.

Decimus felt aroused, yet also uneasy. What was going on here? He was conscious of the eyes in the mosaics looking down at him, and he couldn't help feeling that some of those eyes might not be of stone.

The Palace was renowned for its spyholes and secret windows.

Instead of permitting him to put his own clothes back on, the girl dressed him in new clothes that had been hidden below the couch. There were soft undergarments, and an elegant, dark-colored tunic of the finest Sybarite material, cut low and short to show off both his chest and his legs, and with fashionable sleeves. There were expensive, perfectly-fitting sandals of soft leather.

She dressed and perfumed his hair, and rubbed him with scented oil.

Someone had arranged all this with great care. He was being prepared for a meeting with that someone. A powerful older woman? A lover of young men?

"You'll do," she said, and added: "Your old clothes will be brought to your quarters."

That was reassuring! They would hardly take such trouble over his clothes—even though they were his very best set, worn to make a good impression on the Emperor—if he was about to meet a sticky and painful end.

The girl put on her own tunic, a diaphanous item that revealed more than it covered. Then she pressed a hidden switch in the wall. A different hidden door opened, and Philoxas the eunuch appeared again. He smiled in appreciation of the freshly-bathed and scented Decimus.

"Oh my, what a honey-cake! Unfortunately he's not for me. Or for you, Cassia. Please come with me, my dear."

And he led Decimus out through the door through which he had just entered, the girl, Cassia, following close behind.

This time there was no shock of dazzling light, just a plain corridor. They passed through another door, not even a secret one, and stepped into a well-furnished, medium-sized reception room. It contained only a dais, and a couch.

On the dais sat Naevia, the Empress-to-be.

Cassia rushed over to her and placed herself like a favored pet at her mistress's feet. There were no other attendants, nor were there any Guardsmen or bodyguards such as Decimus would normally have expected.

He stepped forward and made an obeisance, even before the eunuch could remind him.

Naevia looked at him with curiosity.

"What do you think of my maid?" she asked. "Cute little thing, isn't she? Squeaks like a field-mouse if you touch her in the right places." She glanced down at the girl. "Isn't that right, Cassia?"

"If you say so, my Lady."

"I don't say so, I *know* so." And turning again to Decimus: "Freedman? Don't you agree?"

"She's a most pleasant young lady."

Naevia snorted.

"*Lady?* Now that's going a bit far. She's not a slave, mind you—not even a freed slave like yourself. She's a local girl: a product of the slums of our beautiful City. Or, as the poet puts it, 'A jewel scooped up from the muck.' My father says that he found her somewhere. Actually, I think she might be one of his bastards. There are so many of them! Which makes us half-sisters, I suppose. But you're not interested in her?"

"No, my Lady."

Decimus was uncertain where this was leading. Was she trying to compromise him, to turn him away from serving the General?

Did she want him to "perform" with Cassia, for her amusement?

"Good", she said, "because I'd like you to concentrate your attention on other matters. I wouldn't want you wasting your energy ploughing this little animal, however 'pleasant' she might be." She paused. "And do you know why not? Because I want you to be doing that to *me*."

XX

FLORIANUS HAS AN IDEA

✠ *Cestae.*

Florianus was used to being woken at any hour, however uncivilized. A chamberlain must be available day and night. He preferred to be woken gracefully, however, and he had trained Minnermus not to thump or shake him, or shout into his ear.

But now Minnermus *was* shouting into his ear. What was he shouting? That one of Necro's servants had brought an urgent message?

"Yes?"

But it was a message for Master Aulus, not for him.

Aha!

Florianus, High Chamberlain that he had once been, considered himself a man of quick responses, even before breakfast. He made the connection, and knew why *he* was being woken too.

Minnermus had realized at once that young Aulus was out of his depth.

How appropriate that image was, Florianus mused as he was helped to dress. Swimming was a rare skill, and one that he himself had never mastered, but it did throw up such useful metaphors!

He could already hear the hubbub from the next room.

When they went next door, he found that Aulus, far from being merely out of his depth, had already gone under. The tiny room was so crowded that at first he could barely see Aulus, who was cowering on his sleeping couch.

Everyone was either moving or talking, or doing both at the same time: the messenger who had come from Necro, the young master's slave Beltran, the innkeeper (what was he doing there?), Minnermus, who had led him into the room, and two maids.

Two maids? He hadn't as yet seen even *one* maid in his own room—but then, he was just a eunuch, and not a charming young nobleman from the capital.

He ascertained that there was no-one there whom he couldn't allow himself to shout at.

"Out! At once! All of you!"

When he was alone in the room with Aulus, he asked him what had happened.

Necro had (it seemed) returned in the early morning hours and gone straight to bed, though not before ordering one of his servants to instruct Aulus to make appropriate apologies to the magistrate for him (the stress of the journey, the lavish feast of the night before, etc.) and then represent him at the legal proceeding that he had been invited to attend.

Aulus should wrap up the nonsense quickly, thank Tryphaenatus for his hospitality, and return to the inn. After which they would leave Cestae at once. Urgo had already been informed, and would make the necessary arrangements with their escort.

"But I can't do it!" Aulus wailed. "I'm not a lawyer! I'm not a magistrate!"

Florianus had to laugh. So the honorable Senator was doing a fuck-and-run on the voluptuous Olympiodora, and had no wish to spend the morning with her father? He was briefly tempted to advise Aulus to refuse, leaving Necro well and truly in it, so to speak, and up to the neck.

After all, the boy wasn't legally trained or qualified. However, the magistrate *was*, and all that Aulus would actually have to do was stay awake, nod, agree, make polite comments, recommend clemency, and so on...

It would have been fun to watch Necro squirming with embarrassment, though!

Aulus would have to bite the leather and do it, he was afraid, but he would come with him, and give him support and encouragement. It would soon be over, and afterwards Necro would owe them a very big favor!

In the meantime, Beltran and Minnermus should get the packing done.

A footman was already waiting to take Aulus to the council chamber (which was what the innkeeper had been trying to tell him all along). When they arrived, they were met by Tryphaenatus, who greeted them effusively but was clearly upset that the esteemed Senator wouldn't be joining them.

"I was so hoping for the benefit of his advice, for expert instruction from such a distinguished legal mind!"

He remained friendly—young Faustus would soon be a Senator, too, would he not?—and nothing in his manner suggested that his daughter had already left her bed and spoken to her father.

Or was he simply putting a brave face on it? It wasn't as if Olympiodora had lost her innocence that night! And she might even have enjoyed being poked by Necro. (On second thoughts, that hardly seemed likely.)

The day's business wouldn't take long, the magistrate reassured them. Sordid, trivial matters, albeit somehow interconnected. They had no fewer than four delinquents in custody: two drunken Sueni thieves, a barbarian girl, and a runaway slave. But with his, Faustus Atticus's, help they would all get what they deserved.

His deputy, Portho, would shortly be bringing them up from the cells. In the meantime, if the young Senator-in-waiting would kindly take a seat with him on the dais? There would be refreshments later. No, on the camp-stool, please? No disrespect was intended, of course. But they only had one magistrate's stool, which had been specially crafted to take his, Tryphaenatus's, er, more substantial frame. He didn't think that he would fit on the camp-stool! Whereas young Faustus, such a slim, handsome young man, certainly would.

Should he so wish, his man could attend him on the dais?

"His man." The cheek of it! But Florianus swallowed his indignation. This way, standing behind Aulus, he could whisper into his ear if required.

They took their places on the dais, and Tryphaenatus clapped his hands.

Nothing happened.

He clapped his hands again, and coughed very loudly.

Again, nothing happened.

Finally, a side-door of the council chamber creaked open and the four prisoners were brought in, their wrists and ankles in chains. They were accompanied by two municipal heavies, who prodded them, unnecessarily dramatically, with their spears. A little functionary in a provincial toga led the way.

The functionary—who reminded Florianus somewhat of a frog, or of a smaller version of Julian, ugh!—ordered the prisoners to salute "his noble Excellency Olympiodorus Postumus Tryphaenatus, chief magistrate and most glorious benefactor of Cestae". Let it be known that their fate was now in his hands!

The prisoners looked cowed, momentarily, and each of them made some kind of half-hearted attempt to obey the instructions. Their night in the cells under the council chamber can't have been particularly comfortable.

Tryphaenatus now opened the proceedings with a long-winded formal statement in which he explained the extent of the jurisdiction of his court, which powers were vested in him, and so on and so forth. While he was doing this, Florianus studied the four criminals.

Two of them were indeed Sueni cavalrymen. Florianus had had plenty of experience of the swamp-dwellers, in the form of Guards, Palace servants, porters, in fact any role that required brawn rather than wit, and these two were more or less what he would have expected.

They were battered and bruised, with bloodstains on their clothes. So they had resisted arrest! The slightly more impressive specimen was called Geto.

The other man, Orogo, was smaller and more obsequious. He plainly saw that they were in danger of serious punishment, and he had perhaps decided to try to lessen that danger by behaving in a servile manner.

Then there was a barbarian girl, quite young but bigger than most Citizen girls of her age would be. She was one of the Horse People. They were not as venal as the Sueni, it was said, but more primitive, having had less contact with the civilized ways of the Citizens.

And there was a slave-boy, grimy, snot-nosed and unkempt, but angel-faced. At once, an interesting thought came into Florianus's head.

Tryphaenatus had begun with the two cavalrymen, who were accused of stealing a purse of gold coins.

"How many gold coins were in it?"

The question was addressed to Portho.

"Three full gold pieces, your Excellency," he replied.

Both the Sueni reacted at once. The one called Orogo blurted out, "*He* did it!" and pointed at his companion, who ignored him and bellowed at Portho, "It was four, you cunt! Four gold pieces!"

Tryphaenatus gestured to the spearmen *not* to hit the insolent barbarian, and then told Geto to watch his tongue. He pointedly reminded him that Cestae was under civil, not military, jurisdiction. While he had no powers to actually execute the two cavalrymen, there were other severe penalties that he could impose that they would not enjoy.

"Whether it was four gold pieces or whether it was three, how did you come by such a large sum of money?"

Geto said that he had obtained the money by selling a horse…

Portho interrupted, asserting that there was no horse and that Geto had brutally stolen the purse, from a good acquaintance of his named Sponsorus. Sponsorus had then come to him for help.

Sponsorus? The magistrate wasn't aware of any Citizen of that name in Cestae.

"I'm sorry, your Excellency, his name is normally written in the Eastern style and pronounced *Sponsoros*. He is a resident of Maritima."

"Is this person Sponsoros present in this court today to claim his money?"

"No, your Excellency, he has already returned to Maritima. But he has entrusted me with his claim!"

How peculiar, Florianus thought, and the magistrate seemed to agree with him.

"Your friend is owed so much money, yet he disappears *overnight*?"

Geto muttered, "And with my fucking horse!"

Portho insisted, "There was no horse, your Excellency, there is only a thief and a liar."

Suddenly the boy spoke up.

"There *was* a horse, and his name is Demon!"

His high-pitched voice was full of passion, and his whole body quivered. What a beautiful object he was, Florianus decided. He was supposedly a runaway slave. Had he run away from his master's lust, or his mistress's jealousy, or from both?

Portho glared at the boy, and began saying that he was obviously an accomplice of Geto's, a dreadful little vagabond, and no doubt himself an experienced criminal who—

The magistrate waved him to be silent.

"And what is *your* name, child?"

He didn't sound unkind. Perhaps he had noticed the boy's attractiveness. Many people become gentler and softer in the face of beauty.

"Phrygillus."

"Oh!"

Aulus had almost jumped backwards. He had shifted violently on the camp-stool, bumping against Florianus, who was standing close behind him.

Tryphaenatus was also startled by the young man's reaction. He touched him lightly on the arm.

"My Lord? Are you well?"

Aulus leant across and whispered to him, so that even Florianus could barely hear him and no-one else in the room would have been able to.

"Ask her what her name is! It should be Mara. If it is, she and the boy are my property, I think."

"Why don't *you* ask her, my Lord? Would you like to continue the cross-examination yourself?"

"May I? Oh, well, I can give it a try!"

Aulus seemed flustered, but he got to his feet and stepped hesitantly to the edge of the dais—and nearly fell off. Recovering his balance, he positioned himself carefully directly opposite the girl.

"Umm, might I ask what your name is, my dear?"

Sol in the heavens, the lad couldn't make himself sound less Senatorial if he tried! She was a barbarian girl. No horsey warrior would ever talk like that! She must think Aulus was some kind of idiot or joke.

"My name is Mara," she replied, in a firmer, louder voice than his.

Aulus turned back to the magistrate.

"You see," he said with a grin. "I told you! I told you so!"

This was becoming deeply embarrassing, and Florianus might himself have intervened if Tryphaenatus, whose court it was, hadn't taken hold of the reins again.

"Please sit down, my Lord, and let me continue. These are formal matters that we are dealing with."

"Yes, of course. Sorry."

And Aulus sat down again so abruptly that he must surely have hurt himself on the camp-stool. Florianus, whose bottom was larger and softer than those of most complete men, was very aware of the dangers posed by uncomfortable wooden furniture.

Showing no interest in the horsey-girl, the magistrate spoke to Phrygillus once again.

"You, boy, are accused of being a runaway slave. Tell us who your master is, and why you ran away from him."

The boy stared back at him.

"No."

Tryphaenatus was quite taken aback.

"What do you mean: no?"

"We got lost, and this nasty man wanted to kill me, and we were in the woods, and we saw all these little people, and stripey birds. Then these two men came and took us, and they stole Demon as well!"

Geto butted in.

"Hey, what about the bounty? We was bringing you the boy for the bounty!"

The magistrate glowered at him.

"Be silent! I won't warn you again! And be happy that the boy is corroborating your story about a horse."

Portho: "My Lord, I must insist—"

"No. You were not a witness to whatever happened, or didn't happen, regarding the horse—if that horse ever existed. Your testimony is hearsay at best. It is therefore this man's word, and the boy's, against the word of...Sponsoros. And Sponsoros is not present in my court."

"So *we* get the gold pieces for the horse? Hey? Ow! Leave off!"

One of the spearmen had thumped Geto.

"No. On this matter I rule, provisionally, as follows. The boy claims that you took the horse from him and the girl. The ownership of the horse is therefore contested. If the horse belongs to the boy or the girl, it is not theirs, strictly speaking, because they are only slaves. It belongs to their master. But since the horse, if we presume its existence, is not to be found, it is only the three gold pieces, purportedly used to purchase the horse, that need concern us, and these, pending my final decision, will remain in the safekeeping of the court." He turned to Portho. "If, on the other hand, we presume the *non*-existence of the horse, we are left with the matter of gold pieces that belong either to a man who is unable to claim them, or to the two defendants, who still face a number of other charges, I believe?"

"Yes, my Lord, damage to property, assault, abuse of an officer of the court..."

"For which fines may be imposed, and compensation may have to be paid! Again, the three gold pieces must remain with the court until all these questions have been resolved."

Well done, Florianus thought to himself. This was what had made the Citizens great—not military power, but enforcing order and justice within their dominions. Necro could hardly have done it better! Tryphaenatus was a finer man than he looked. (Just as Florianus himself was, he liked to think.)

The two Sueni were less impressed. Orogo grunted, and Geto said, "Fuck!", though barely audibly.

"Furthermore, in the matter of the bounty, it is true that a small sum in silver is payable to those who return runaway slaves to their master or deliver them into the custody of a magistrate. In the latter case the bounty becomes due after the identity of the slave has been determined and that of his master confirmed. Since the initial payment is made from the public treasury of the municipality, there are lengthy procedures that need to be followed. I doubt whether your commanding officer would permit you to remain in Cestae until the final conclusion of those procedures; it would therefore become necessary for you to return to Cestae at a later date."

"Shit!"

The magistrate raised his finger.

"But...do we really need to go down that tiresome road? It seems to me that no delivery of the slaves in question actually took place. You made no obvious effort to deliver them; instead, you were busily engaged in the dubious matter of the horse, and in causing mayhem in a local hostelry! Did you even *intend* to deliver the two slaves to me, or were you simply on your way to Laurinum to sell them in the slave-market there?"

The two Sueni were outraged, and needed to be restrained by the spearmen.

"Is this what you call Citizen justice?" Geto shouted. "Bastards!"

And he felt the butt of a spear in the ribs.

"No, you will receive justice! In fact, instead of accusing you of what would be a very serious offence indeed, I shall give you the benefit of the doubt. You had intended to deliver the slaves, but you failed to do so so. The slaves were found and taken into custody by an officer of this court! A bounty payment is therefore out of the question, although the owner of the slaves might be willing to give you a small reward for their return. Finding him may be more more easily done than you realize." He smiled. "Phrygillus, let me ask you again: what is your master's name?"

"Castor."

"Are you sure? That is a slave's name."

The boy looked sulky.

"Atticus, then."

"Ah, now that is a well-known name, and I can think of several very prominent Attici. Are you referring to Senator Faustus Pomponius Atticus, Lord Governor of the North?" The boy didn't reply. "Or the noble Senator Lucius Pomponius Atticus? Atticus Dako the merchant of Trebenna? Atticus the charioteer? Or someone else altogether?"

"No, that first one: we was in his house. He had an angry woman. She wasn't nice to me! She didn't like me!"

Phrygillus stopped, as if he had already said too much and expected to be beaten for it.

"Yes? And?"

"But he didn't want us. Mara and me. He sent us to his son."

"Faustus Pomponius Atticus the Younger?"

"The slaves called him Junior. But we never got there."

"The gentleman sitting beside me is that person. Phrygillus, this is your master: greet him respectfully!"

The boy stared at Aulus, his head turned slightly to one side.

"Hallo," he simpered, with mock shyness.

Sol, the beast was fluttering his eyelashes! He was flirting with Aulus! What a little minx! He had obviously read young Atticus as an easy touch, a soft master who would spoil and pamper him. So he had cunning, as well as beauty!

Atticus was meanwhile doing everything he possibly could to confirm the boy's impression of him: he was stammering something incomprehensible, shifting awkwardly on his camp-stool, and turning first to the magistrate, then to Florianus, for help in this unexpected situation.

Here was an opportunity: he would definitely help him, oh yes! Aulus Atticus might not know what to do with the boy, but Florianus had a very clear idea. Washed, trimmed, and carefully prepared, he would be a choice morsel indeed. Little Phrygillus was a gift from the gods—a fitting gift for the most powerful man in the East. He would stir the ageing loins of Quintilianus Asper, even if he couldn't warm the evil lecher's cold heart!

Without knowing it yet, Master Aulus was going to make a very substantial contribution to the success of their undertaking. What divine providence was it that had brought together, in such an unexpected way, a master and slave who had never even seen each other before? If their little party had reached Cestae a day earlier, or a day later, or if they had taken a different route, it would never have happened... The gods had been truly gracious.

Tryphaenatus had now come to the horsey-girl—who was an irrelevance, of course. as far as Florianus was concerned. Here, too, the Sueni apparently had hopes of some financial reward. They had been sent out by their Lord Commander, they said, to find the girl, who had been seized illegally by slavers, and they must therefore take her back with them.

"Must", however, is a word not to be addressed to magistrates.

Tryphaenatus expressed the view that their assertion might amount to no more than bare-faced opportunism. Was the girl not likewise intended for the slave-market of Laurinum, where she would fetch much more on a white-washed block than Lord Commander Rhaetius was ever likely to give them?

Geto denied the charge vehemently.

Florianus doubted that the girl would fetch a decent price. The market at Laurinum was not a busy one, the summer sales were long over, and there would be little going on there. Who would buy her, except a blind man or someone with most peculiar tastes? Yet the cavalrymen might not know that. And one part of their story was certainly plausible—Florianus had been told by the General himself that such illegal slaving raids were being carried out.

So why not let the wretched Sueni have the girl? She would be of no use at all to the expedition. In fact, Necro would create a huge fuss about another extra mouth to be fed. It would even need to be made clear to him how important the *boy* would be to them.

To make up for this, perhaps the miserable fishy-boy could be sold off along the way. (Were they planning to go via Laurinum? He couldn't remember. But there was a huge slave-market in Maritima.)

Florianus was waiting for a chance to slip in some practical suggestions of his own—politely, and without giving offence, of course—when the magistrate was interrupted by the firm, resonant voice of the girl. Her use of the Citizens' Tongue was excellent, and her accent, though noticeable, was much pleasanter on the ear than the horrible sounds that the Sueni produced.

"They are not good men, and I won't go with them." Everyone stared at her. "If Phrygillus won't come with me, I will stay with him." She paused. "But I am *not* a slave."

XXI

DECIMUS MAKES AN UNUSUAL DISCOVERY

✠ *The Imperial Palace, in the City.*

The shock was so great that Decimus stepped back involuntarily.

"My Lady? What do you mean?"

It was a stupid question, but he needed time to think. Naevia was understandably not too impressed.

"Come on! You're a fine-looking man, and I've heard excellent report of you, Decimus. Were they all completely wrong? Don't tell me that you're a fool after all! Ploughing. If you prefer, call it screwing. Or poking. Shafting. Shagging. *Doing* it. Fucking. Am I making myself clear?"

Decimus never panicked—but now he did. This woman would soon be Empress. What awful, unspeakable things would they do to him, what monstrous, agonizing, lingering death could he expect, if he were ever caught in her bed?

"My Lady, what you are suggesting…the punishment would be… unimaginably horrible. If your grandfather were ever to learn of it. Or your father."

A smile flickered across her face.

"My father, you say?"

Decimus felt the presence of the man behind him just a fraction of a moment before he heard the man's voice.

"Correct!"

It was Quintus Naevius! Decimus had whirled round, to find the master of the streets of the City standing directly behind him. How had he succeeded in slipping in so quietly? It was good that Decimus wasn't carrying a weapon, or one of them might already be dead or wounded.

"My Lord," he managed to croak.

"Her grandfather the Senator wouldn't be overwhelmed with joy, true enough. According to his friends, Senator Naevius is a man of unflinching conservative principles; his enemies would say that he's an unimaginative asshole. Her *father*, on the other hand, the other Senator

Naevius, would give you his blessing—and maybe even ask to watch!"

"Father! Don't be so disgusting!"

"My Lord—I don't understand?"

Quintus grinned at him. He was tall and muscular, and renowned as a street-fighter. For his age, he was in magnificent physical condition. He moved like one of those beautiful, deadly beasts that had once fought in the Great Arena, before the Senate suspended such entertainments. Could Decimus take him? He wasn't at all sure. It would depend on the situation, the weapons, which of them was able to land the first blow...

"No reason to be ashamed: how *could* you understand? This is a new world for you, freedman, isn't it? Princes, and courts, power, intrigue, lust. We do things differently here." Then, to his daughter. "Will you tell him, or shall I? It would amuse me more to hear it from your lips again, my dear. With *all* the dirty details!"

Naevia sighed.

"No, father, without the details." And then to Decimus: "In a nutshell, my future husband can't do it. The 'ploughing'! Though he wants me to give him a son and heir, he says."

Quintus interrupted, "We *all* want you to have a son. To secure the great Maximian Dynasty."

Oh yes, Decimus thought: to secure the dynasty. Sure. Or, as soon as a male heir had been produced, to dispose of Maximillus, so that Naevius and his son could rule the Western Empire for twenty years as regents for a child!

"We have tried, but his Majesty only wants to have what he calls 'fun'. Hurting people makes him excited. If we had Cassia here tortured," she was stroking her maid's hair, then suddenly yanked it so that the girl squealed, "*that*, he said, would make him really stiff. It might even be worth a try."

"Mistress!"

Naevia boxed her ears.

"Stupid girl, I'm only joking." She paused. "But my dear husband-to-be certainly wasn't."

"If all that he needs is a torture show to get himself into the right mood," her father said, "that can easily be arranged. It'll be like the days of Severian again! The cellars and prisons are packed with Red supporters, and their wives and children."

"Though not the Placidus girl, the little cripple?"

"Unfortunately, no. Not yet."

"When you do catch her, father, leave that young lady to me. *That's* a show I'll be only too happy to arrange for his Majesty's entertainment."

"If it would help to produce what is required..."

"It might, but it would certainly be for his enjoyment—and mine too. However excited it made him, though. it still wouldn't get me with child. Since his Majesty can't bear to be *touched*, how is he going to make a baby? Answer me that! By magic? Someone is going to have to make the baby for him. It's been done before. Isn't that how Maximillus was sired?" She paused. "And why shouldn't it be someone like *you*, freed-man?"

Her stare was so fierce that Decimus turned away, and addressed Quintus Naevius.

"What does your daughter mean, my Lord? Why me of all people? I am the liegeman of your father's worst enemy!"

"You mean: why you, rather than some young cockerel of a Senator, who would boast about it afterwards in his cups? Or some dirty slave? Or a barbarian Guardsman, maybe? No, we want a child that is healthy, strong, and intelligent—as you are claimed to be, though I'm beginning to have my doubts." He spread his arms out in a dramatic pose and gazed upwards. "In the name of the fucking Slave and all the other gods, the Lord of the Gardens in particular, am I going to have to do this myself?"

"Father!!"

"Since when have you been so shy?"

He smirked, and Decimus saw something in the locked gaze of daughter and father that spoke of a complex relationship.

"Enough," she whispered.

Decimus had to escape from this web that was about to trap him.

"My Lord, if his Imperial Majesty never touches your daughter, he will know that any child she bears cannot be his."

"True—"

"I thought of that, father. So I'll slip quietly into his bed and play with him, when he has the morning stiffness but he isn't properly awake yet. For a few sleepy moments he won't notice me, and if I'm lucky he'll mess himself. If not, I'll have a flask with something sticky to smear the bed-linen with. Afterwards I'll tell him that he was a lion, ripping me apart with his majestic weapon. He won't remember much."

"My Lady, if you are capable of bringing him to satisfaction by such a trick, surely with a skillful hand there would be a chance—"

"Oh, you are *slow*! Do you think I *want* to be touched by that crea-ture? Do you you think I *want* his seed inside me, or to bear *his* child? It could be a monster! Every single Maximian has been worse than the last one."

Quintus added, "And any man could father a better child on her than that little piece of shit. But Maximillus at least has to *think* it's his."

"Yes, my Lord—but again, why me?"

"Because you are ideal for this purpose. If there is gossip—and in the Palace, there often is—no-one will believe it. As you said, you are the creature of our hated enemy, and at our recent meeting I believe I made my feelings about you clear enough, didn't I? Besides, you have nowhere to run to: the bastard Ogilo would never forgive you for betraying his trust. Do your job, and you will be rewarded for your labors with a large amount of gold, and ship's passage to any distant shore that you choose"—or with a blade between the ribs, Decimus told himself—"and, finally, if that is not enough for you, there is my daughter. A beauty, is she not? She knows how to please a man. Are you not sorely tempted? I certainly would be!"

Decimus swallowed hard, and gave an honest answer.

"Oh yes, my Lord."

He was indeed tempted, and not merely by the thought of enjoying the proud redhead. He had been told to gain access to sources of information, hadn't he? Wasn't he supposed to make new friends in powerful places, and to get as close as he could to the new rulers of the City? He had never dreamt he would get as close to them as this.

"Good. In any case, you have no choice. You now know far too much for your own safety—unless you are working for us, of course." He turned to the maid. "Come, Cassia, here are two young people who want to...*get to know each other better*. We're not needed here. But you and the eunuch will stand guard. My men will be at the far end of the corridor. If there is any untoward interruption, you will warn my daughter, and the lovebirds will have plenty of opportunity to disappear through the room at the back."

After her father, the eunuch and the maid had left, Naevia rose to her feet and walked slowly towards Decimus.

What should he do? Take her in his arms? Throw her on her back? Amuse her with witty conversation, whilst all the while caressing her to make her aroused? He had never before been in a situation like this one, or with a woman quite like this.

Her physical charms were undeniable. He had never fucked a redhead before. They were supposed to be like demons from Esbus when you pleasured them.

But instead of touching Decimus as he expected her to, she circled him, stopping and looking him up and down from different angles.

"Not bad! I like what I see. Strong limbs. A tight ass. A straight back. Most freedmen crouch and creep like the slaves they once were. Do you like women? Or do you prefer boys? It's not important! *Your* enjoyment doesn't matter—you have a job to do. Ignore my father, this is between you...and me. I want you to plant a baby in me. The time of the month is auspicious. We mustn't make too much noise. It has to be done silently, and quickly. Can you do that?" Then, after a pause: "Yes, I think you can. Then let's go to work! Take off your clothes."

He stepped towards her.

"Then you too, my Lady." His voice was hoarse. "*Naevia.*"

She slipped off her jeweled stola and stood naked in front of him, as they said she had stood naked at the bride-show in front of the whole Imperial court.

Decimus removed his own clothes, and took her by the hand to lead her to the couch.

"No," she said. "You must get down first. I am an Empress, and I am not to be mounted by a freedman. *I* shall mount *you.*"

"Very well, my Lady."

He lay back on the couch, and she joined him there. They were both aroused—it was easy for her to slide down onto him.

And that was where the problems began.

Fine, this was a form of love-making that Decimus knew, and normally enjoyed. It was one of many different ways of making love. He was a considerate lover, and he derived pleasure from pleasing his partner. If this was therefore how she wanted it, so be it…

But his own pleasure also mattered.

Ever since the day he had been freed, Decimus had arranged his life so that, wherever possible, *he* could be in control. He wasn't a slave any more, and he wouldn't let himself become a half-slave either, like those pathetic freedmen who were constantly groveling, or scurrying about to satisfy their former masters' wishes. He had therefore chosen *not* to serve Faustus Atticus, but to work for the General, who gave him tasks but allowed him to fulfill them as he, Decimus, saw fit.

Naevia had pinned him down, and was moving on him. As she thrust downwards, she was twisting her body slightly to increase her own enjoyment.

He became aware of her smell, not only the smell of sex that was coming from between her legs but her personal aroma, which was subtly different from what he had expected. It was both arousing and off-putting at the same time.

He had been trapped into rutting with this woman because her gross husband-to-be was unable to. He had been used, and threatened. Whatever Quintus promised, he knew that from the moment that she was with child his life would be worthless, and he would probably be on the run. How could he then carry out the task that the General had set him?

Naevia's eyes were glazed over with lust, and she was straining not to make a noise, though she couldn't stop herself panting and moaning softly.

He must finish this, and in his own way. He gripped her by the hips and, as she moved upwards slightly, held her there against her will, while making his own fierce thrusting movements into the depths of her body. She grunted in surprise, looking into his eyes for the first time. As she acknowledged him, he grabbed her buttocks, pulled her down onto him and spasmed joyfully as he spent himself deep inside her.

"Aaah," he whispered, "that was good."

"Was it?" she said, looking at him with distaste. "Was it really?" She climbed down from the couch, looking for a cloth to wipe herself with. "If I need you again, freedman, I'll send the eunuch for you. I hope it won't be necessary, though. Now get out!"

A door opened and Philoxas entered without having been called. Had he been watching them? He picked up Decimus's clothes, pushed them into his arms, and led him quickly into another room. It contained a small marble wash-basin, decorated with inlaid semi-precious stones. The eunuch waited while Decimus cleaned himself and got dressed.

"Follow me, my dear. And let me give you some advice. You have never been here. You have never spoken to Lady Naevia. And you remember nothing, because there is nothing for you to remember. Do all that," he said with a gentle smile, "and stay alive."

Then, through a maze of corridors and antechambers, he escorted Decimus out of the Golden Rooms. He left him in the main entrance hall of the Palace, to find his own way back to his temporary living quarters.

His head was reeling. Decimus had never felt like this before after mounting a woman. Then again, he *hadn't* mounted her, had he? She had mounted him.

As if he was already following the eunuch's advice, he found that he couldn't remember much of what had happened. What had her skin felt like? And her breasts? What had it felt like when he was inside her?

But he couldn't remember, and when he tried his thoughts for some strange reason turned of their own accord to the girl at the inn in Caledunum. Jenufa. He remembered *her* well enough. Her hefty thighs, her smile, the gap in her teeth, her friendly laughter. He had a clearer picture of her in his mind than he had of Naevia, whom he had left just moments before.

The entrance hall was crowded, and busy. Decimus had lost all sense of time, but if so many people were leaving the Palace the daylight outside must already be fading. The streets were less safe now than they had ever been. No-one wanted to have to find their way home in the darkness, with so many Blue thugs and fugitive Reds infesting the streets, and Blood-Drinkers already within the City.

The important people who were leaving all had bodyguards or armed servants.

The not-so-important people didn't, and they were therefore collecting the swords, clubs or staves that they had checked in at the gatekeeper's lodge. Normally, it was forbidden for private citizens to carry arms within the confines of the city walls, but that rule had not been enforced for a long time for the escorts of Senators, and now it seemed to be in complete abeyance.

If they wanted to enforce the rule now, they would have to disarm every single one of Quintus's bullies, for instance, and who was going to try and do that?

On the other side of the entrance hall he saw Senator Vulpeculus, also about to leave, giving some final instructions to a footman or messenger.

He was leaving alone, it seemed. And without a weapon.

How could that be? Something was not quite right. Vulpeculus was a strong man, and very fit, as he had shown when they rode together for days (and he had still had enough strength left to abuse the maids at the inns, night after night). But he was also far too sharp-witted to wander about the streets of the City after dark, unarmed, and on his own.

No, something was definitely wrong. Was he planning to meet someone very close by? Someone that he couldn't be seen talking to at the Palace?

Decimus was curious. He needed to know what the Senator was up to. *This* was what the General was expecting him to do: to sniff out danger, and find out what murky plots and intrigues were being hatched in the shadows.

Vulpeculus might be unarmed, but Decimus couldn't be. He didn't know whom he might encounter once they had left the Palace, and he remembered that the clothes he had been given made him look like a rich, effeminate courtier—an ideal target for any prowling cut-throat.

Fortunately, his new tunic was of dark material. What he needed was a weapon, and a dark cloak to hide it under.

He found both of these at the gatekeeper's lodge. In a small room at the back, weapons of all kinds and cloaks and mantles of different shapes and sizes were piled, invitingly unattended, against the wall.

The gatekeeper had left them unguarded!

He was being harangued by a City merchant, whose cloak he had mislaid. The Sueni gatekeeper, a prize example of the type, had apparently made the mistake of not taking the man seriously when he complained that his large, *light-gray* mantle had been lost and that he had been fobbed off with a small, dirty, *dark-brown* cloak of inferior quality.

Wasn't there supposed to be a system of wooden dockets to show which item belonged to which person?

The Sueni replied that he was only standing in for the proper gate-keeper, who was sick, and that he didn't understand the fucking dockets!

Yes, but even so, couldn't the wretched man tell one cloak from another? He had handed the merchant a cloak the color of shit that no self-respecting Citizen would be seen dead in! Only a slave would wear something like that.

Or had the man deliberately withheld his expensive cloak, in order to sell it later?

The Sueni took that last remark rather badly. He brandished his spear at the merchant and told him where he intended to put it.

The merchant in return informed the Sueni that he was a respected purveyor of sweetmeats to the Imperial court and a personal friend of several of the most influential Palace eunuchs (all eunuchs loved sweets) and that he would not allow himself to be intimidated.

Despite all the bluster on both sides, Decimus could see that nothing was going to happen for a while. Those in the queue directly behind the merchant were becoming impatient and abusive for having to wait so long, and in addition to them a crowd of the curious but uninvolved had begun to gather to watch the entertainment.

With everyone's attention fixed on the two adversaries, it wasn't difficult for Decimus to slip in behind them unobserved. He helped himself to a dark, moth-eaten cloak (he wasn't as choosy as the merchant) and an Army-style stabbing-sword, easy to hide under the cloak and more suitable for close-fighting than a longer weapon would be.

He saw that Vulpeculus had already left the Palace, but that he hadn't got very far. He was keeping to the outer wall of the complex. After a few hundred paces, the Senator reached an area of buildings that had been ransacked and partly burnt out by the mob that overthrew Severian; it had never been rebuilt.

Suddenly he dropped out of sight.

Decimus rushed forward. Where had he gone?

There was a gap in the outer wall. The ruins behind them were cut off from the main Palace complex by an interior wall, and had been abandoned to the rats long ago. Normally, human rats would use them, too, as a place to sleep and crap; however, Decimus knew that these buildings had once housed Severian's dungeons and personal torture-chambers, and that they were reputedly haunted by the tormented, vengeful spirits of his victims.

Rats might not care about that, but people would hesitate to enter the ruins, even in the daytime. And in the dark, the crumbling buildings would be completely unsafe to walk in.

Vulpeculus had entered them without a torch! Either he knew them well, or he was expecting to be met.

Decimus decided to follow him. He passed through the gap in the wall and walked cautiously into the main building. Inside, it was pitch-dark.

He slipped, and almost plunged down a stairwell. If he had done he might well have broken his neck, and he would certainly have dropped his sword with a clatter as he fell. Decimus took a deep breath and clamped his eyes shut. When he opened them again they were better adjusted to the darkness, and he could see vague shapes at least. He wouldn't miss the next stairwell.

Which way should he go? He listened carefully…and heard faint footsteps from somewhere below. Very well! Vulpeculus had gone down the steps without breaking his neck. Decimus would do the same.

He could only *feel* his way down the staircase. When he had reached the bottom, he found that the corridor went off in opposed directions, but he knew which way to go because he could still hear footsteps, very faintly, in the distance, and he could also make out a glimmer of light.

That meant that someone else was there. Someone who had been waiting for the Senator.

Decimus must now be extremely careful. If he was discovered, there was bound to be a fight. There would be no time for asking or answering questions—like rats in the darkness, it would be kill or be killed.

Why should he fight anyone, until he knew what was happening? He only wanted to know what Vulpeculus was doing. He had no wish to confront him, because if he did the Senator would assume that "the freedman" didn't trust him and was probably still working for the General. Nor did he want to kill or maim the man by accident.

He crept closer towards the voices and the light.

The Senator was standing talking to two men, both of them bigger than he was—and Vulpeculus wasn't small. That meant thugs, body-guards, perhaps off-duty Guardsmen that the Senator had bribed. They were holding torches, and clubs, and each of them had a barbarian long-sword strapped to his belt.

That there were now three of them was good. Three men make more noise, interact more, and cast more shadows than two, and they are less likely to notice a fourth man. (And, though he didn't want a fight, if there *was* one three men would tend to get in each other's way.)

They were stood beside a door to the room at the end of the corridor. The corridor itself went off to left and right in front of the room, forming the cross-beam of a "T". There was a huge metal padlock on the door, which one of the men was struggling to open with a large key. He cursed, as he perhaps cut himself or broke a fingernail, speaking with a guttural accent that Decimus didn't recognize. Finally, the padlock squeaked noisily open.

One of the men pulled at the wooden door, which scraped reluctantly against the floor of the corridor before giving way. The three men entered the room, with a great effort pulling the door shut behind them.

The corridor was plunged into darkness again.

The door was a mixed blessing. They wouldn't be able to open it quickly and surprise him; however, there was also no way that Decimus could sneak into the room behind them. If the room led to another corridor, he had lost them—he couldn't risk going any further, and attracting their attention.

He crept cautiously up to the door. It was a battered old construction, and it had long cracks and even holes. He put his ear to the largest of these and heard the voices, muffled yet reasonably clear. He still couldn't make out what the thugs were saying, but he heard Vulpeculus say "yes", "no", and "payment". The Senator said "two days", and one of the two men finally said something that Decimus could understand: "days." Vulpeculus grunted, and said "yes".

And then a woman spoke!

She said "animal" (or was it "animals"?), in a small, sweet-sounding voice, and he heard the men laugh.

She had been locked inside the room. Vulpeculus was keeping a woman hidden, or captive, in a ruined outbuilding of the Palace!

But why not at his home? The City was full of desperate, fugitive women. Many of Quintus's thugs were probably holding a woman or a young girl prisoner in a cellar or outhouse, and playing their nasty games with her at leisure. No-one would think twice about it if a mighty Senator like Vulpeculus did the same. Decimus had learnt how the man behaved with women. He could be raping the poor girl nightly at his home, in comfort, rather than in a dark, dirty cellar.

Which meant that, whoever the woman was, Vulpeculus needed to keep her existence a secret!

Decimus was desperate to know more, but he couldn't see through any of the tiny holes in the door, and he didn't recognize the woman's voice. Her accent was educated, though, like that of Vulpeculus himself.

The corridor to the left of the door was pitch-dark, but to the right there was a faint, diffused shimmer of light. He felt his way slowly along the wall. It was damp and porous. Somewhere there must be a crack or a hole that was letting some light through—and he found it. It was a sizeable crack, very high up, but there was a moldering, slippery wooden beam at the base of the wall that he could move slightly and stand on if he was extremely careful. Even then he needed to stand on tiptoe to see into the room properly. He could have made the hole larger by scratching at it with his sword, but he didn't want to risk drawing the attention of the men inside.

He looked down into the room.

He saw three men confronting, and laughing at, but not touching, a young girl. She was tiny, more like a doll than a woman, and her hands were manacled. A thin chain around her waist was attached to a metal ring set into the wall.

He heard Vulpeculus say, "So now you know, my Lady! It's for your own good." And she replied: "Never!"

As she spoke, she raised her head defiantly, and he saw the perfect oval of her face, and her exquisite features. She reminded him strongly of someone that he knew, but who was she?

"You will learn patience," the Senator said. "You will be *taught* patience."

"And you will burn in Esbus!"

All three men laughed again, and she stepped backwards, dropping her head—in resignation? And stumbled.

Or had she? Her feet weren't manacled. He looked at her as intently as he could, squinting down through the hole in the wall. No, she hadn't stumbled—she had a deformed foot.

And then he knew. Though he had never seen her before, he had heard the descriptions of what she had looked like when she appeared at the bride-show: it was Julia Placida!

XXII

MANASA TELLS HER MASTER ABOUT THE SPIDER'S WEB

Cascantum.

The soldiers and officers surged around her, shouting, asking questions, making accusations of negligence, incompetence, conspiracy. The Lord Commander was dead! The great man had been lured into a trap by a treacherous Sybarite slave-girl, murdered, and mutilated.

For a few moments, all that she could think was: what did she care? For so many years she had searched for her sister. Finally she had found her, and then…*this*. What did anything else matter any more?

She was soon pulled back to her senses.

She was a slave, and she had been a slave for most of her life. There was no changing that. If they want to survive, slaves learn quickly that emotions are a luxury that they can't afford. So, even as she wept, and grieved inside, Manasa was watching herself. Don't be a fool, girl! Life has to go on. *Your* life will go on, but only if you are careful what you say or do next.

Lelia might have been her sister, but she was also a killer. She had chosen the path of evil—which is a choice that even the humblest slave is free to refuse. Manasa herself would never, ever, make such a choice, not even if by doing so she could reclaim her sister from the realm of the dead (which was a gift that the Sleepless Ones were rumored to have within their power).

The other thing that brought her back to reality was more immediate.

She felt herself being hugged, though rather awkwardly. A voice was trying to comfort her, and doing that clumsily too. It couldn't possibly be Turgulo—from *his* lips, honeyed, well-chosen words would now be flowing. He would be telling how how he had saved her life—which was true—and inviting her to cry on his shoulder (while gently maneuvering her towards his bed).

It was her master, Thomasius.

Well, he wasn't the sort of man she had ever dreamed of or lusted after, but he was decent, kind, and honest, and he meant well by her. For the moment, at least, she needed a harbor to take refuge in from the storm. A rock on which to plant her feet.

He would have to be that harbor; that rock.

Petronius appeared, and if anything the presence of the Staff Officer made the confusion worse, rather than better.

Then, suddenly, there was silence. Manasa looked up. Petronius was saluting a man who had just arrived. He was smaller than Lord Commander Rhaetius, but he could otherwise pass as his brother: he had the same bull-like stature, the same fierce expression. This could only be Memmius, the Lord Commander of the Fourth Division.

Rhaetius was dead, so Memmius would now be the Military Commander of the North. He had only just returned, and was sweaty from many hours in the saddle, but he was already giving commands, and men were rushing to obey them without question.

Manasa had a story to tell, but no-one wanted to listen. Instead, she was ordered back to her master's quarters, and she was not to leave them under any circumstances. Two men would be placed on guard there.

They suspected her! They must believe that she was part of the plot to murder Rhaetius. After all, the killer was her sister, and she was a Sybarite too. The "invitation" that had lured the Lord Commander to his death had been in her name.

Or were the men there to guard her, in case Victor returned to kill her as well? He had a personal score to settle with her. But the Sleepless Ones hadn't sent him all the way to Cascantum to take *her* life.

To hold her fears at bay she had to keep herself occupied, so she busied herself with preparing some food for the evening, and with sweeping and tidying Thomasius's quarters. There wasn't actually a great deal that needed to be done. There would have been much more such work in his colleague Grassica's quarters, where Gemma would have been faced with a lot of clearing up after the supper-party. Of course, she and Gemmella would probably be finished by now, but, if not, she could perhaps offer her help? It would be a welcome gesture.

However, the guards wouldn't let her take even those few steps outside her master's quarters.

It was a relief when Thomasius finally returned.

He waved aside her offer of food.

"Sit down. We have to talk."

His stitches had just been removed, but before that he had attended an emergency conference with Lord Commander Memmius, Petronius, and the other Staff Officers, from both divisions, who were still in Cascantum—a comparatively small number, because every unit that could be spared had been sent to reinforce the General. Not even Company-commanders were present. It was a great honor for him, a mere Sub-officer, to be invited to attend!

On which subject, he must try to find a way to tell the new Military Commander of the North that his predeceesor had promised to promote him to Company-commander. Unfortunately, it seemed that Rhaetius hadn't informed his colleague of his intentions, and all that Memmius had said was that he would need to be assigned a new unit. Unit, he had said—no mention of a new *company*.

There had been tensions at the meeting. Petronius was annoyed that he hadn't been placed in temporary command of the Seventh until the General appointed a new Lord Commander. He was the senior Staff Of-ficer of the division, wasn't he? Yet Memmius had preferred to appoint his own ranking Staff Officer from the Fourth, on the grounds that he himself could run his division blindfold and with both hands tied behind his back, which made Trebellius available for other duties.

Petronius and Trebellius loathed each other. And now the obnoxious Trebellius had been appointed over his head! That would be fun to watch, even if it would only be for a short while until the new man arrived.

Yet he couldn't expect Trebellius to promote him either. He would have his favorites from the Fourth, whose careers he would try to further, if and when a vacancy for a Company-commander came up.

None of this interested her very much, so to shut him up Manasa declared that she ought to look at and clean the places where the stitches had been removed. New dressings, perhaps? All that was hardly neces-sary, but while he was mulling over her suggestion she asked him what had been decided at the meeting about Victor.

"And," she said quietly, "about *me*."

He apologized for forgetting how upset she must be feeling.

(A master apologizing to his slave—well, that was something out of the ordinary!)

Among the Staff Officers there had been loud voices (not Petroni-us's, he quickly added) demanding that an example be made of her. A Lord Commander had been murdered, and someone should be seen to be paying for it, slowly and painfully. Why not her?

She was Lelia's sister.

With or without her knowledge, she had been part of the plot to lure Rhaetius to his death.

She was an accursed Sybarite.

And she was only a slave-girl.

She would do.

Manasa was terrified. If she hadn't already been sitting down, she would have collapsed in fright.

"No, no," he reassured her. "It won't happen."

He had spoken up for her, he said, even though it had meant butting in quite forcefully on an exchange between two of the Staff Officers.

He had told them how he had been sent to find Mara—and had found Manasa. How she had helped him in his search. How they had encountered Victor, and how she had saved his life by risking her own. How, badly injured, he had had to entrust her with a message for Lord Commander Rhaetius, and how loyally she had fulfilled her task. (It had been no fault of hers that her master had reached the fortress himself before she was able to deliver her news to Rhaetius.)

He had told them how she and her master were ordered to continue the hunt for the two Sybarites. And how she had been constantly by his side during the long hours of the township search during which she had (allegedly) sent her deadly invitation to the Lord Commander.

If she was guilty, he, Thomasius, must obviously be guilty too!

And he had even dared to thump the table for emphasis.

He would have said more than that, and all of it in her favor, but Memmius had ordered him to stop, and it wouldn't have been necessary.

Because Memmius was not Rhaetius. He wasn't as great a fighter, and (it was said) he wasn't as sound a tactician. His enemies knew this: Victor had been sent to kill Rhaetius—or, at least, to kill Rhaetius *first*. But Memmius also had far less of his colleague's cruelty. He had ordered impalings and crucifixions, he had commanded torture and mutilation, but never with the obvious pleasure shown by Rhaetius.

More importantly, he believed in doing what was lawful. Slave-girl or not, Memmius had said, Manasa was innocent until she was shown to be otherwise. Thomasius trusted her, and he trusted Thomasius. That would suffice for him, and it was his decision to make, and his alone.

The Sub-officer must have his stitches removed, and then he should continue with the task that Lord Commander Rhaetius had set him: to find the Sybarite assassin. The slave-girl Manasa might yet be of great use to him.

Admittedly, her relationship with the dead Sybarite girl was a murky matter, but since her sister was now dead she was no longer in danger of being tricked or compromised into treachery. And being a Sybarite didn't necessarily make you a traitor—at least one of the Staff Officers present was a southerner, was he not? And more than a few of the junior officers, all of them known to be loyal.

There would be no "show executions", at least not until the assassin was captured. And if Manasa needed to punished for any reason, that was entirely up to Thomasius.

She cast her eyes down demurely.

"Really? He said all that, Master?"

"Yes!" he replied, giving her an untypically stern look.

In her experience, there had only been two kinds of master when it came to beating her or (more often) flogging one of the other slave-girls: the cruel, energetic kind, and the kind who started half-heartedly and soon threw the whip aside. In both cases, the "punishment" normally concluded with the master taking his pleasure, either with brutal relish or with caresses and feeble endearments.

You hated the first kind of master, of course, and you despised the second.

Thomasius didn't seem to her to be of either type. And he proved it by now reminding her almost shyly about the food that she had offered him when he arrived. No refreshments had been provided at the meeting and he was, it seemed, quite hungry.

While he was eating, she told him everything that she had previously held back, for lack of the right opportunity. He didn't interrupt her, but several times he put the food down and stared at her.

Much of her tale he would already have known, or could have pieced together. She hadn't been born into slavery, but when she was very young her father had lost his fortune and been threatened with horrible consequences by his creditors. He had then done what many fathers (not only in Sybaris) would have done: he had sold two of his three daughters, Manasa and her younger sister Maneira ("valuable like jewels"), into slavery, keeping only the baby girl, her parents' favorite, who had died soon afterwards.

It was a sad but familiar story, which must have been repeated a thousand times throughout the known world, and without giving anyone particular cause for thought. Only one small detail was perhaps worthy of mention: that Manasa and Maneira were not the two girls' birth-names, but names that they were given when they were sold, though that too was nothing extraordinary.

This was how it had been explained to the little girls at the time—Maneira would have been too young to understand—and this was the version that Manasa had grown up believing.

Until one cold winter's day when she was sent out to chop wood, because the kitchen-boy, whose task it normally was, had been taken sick with a flux.

The woodland belonged to her master, but two vagabonds came to steal wood that day, and when they saw Manasa they seized her, beat and stripped her, and began to abuse her. She was rescued by the old charcoal-burner who guarded the wood—he may have been old, but he was as tough as the handle of his ax. He took her back to his hut, where his woman gave her food and comfort.

She was a Sybarite. And she was one of the wise ones, adept in the old lore and in forbidden knowledge. She laughed when Manasa recounted her story. She knew exactly what had happened—the names told her *everything*.

Manasa's father must have been a supporter of the Cause.

In ancient Sybaris, before the hateful conquest by the Citizens, every noble family had been expected to sacrifice their first-born male child in the burning kilns to She (not to be named) who is the consort of the Dark One. The Citizens had even used this harsh tradition as an excuse for attacking Sybaris. Exterminate them! Raise Sybaris to the ground! A people of such monstrous cruelty had no right to exist! They were not human!

Today, the Sleepless Ones still took the eldest son from their followers, not in order to sacrifice him, but to raise him as one of their own and to train him for their sinister purposes.

Victor would probably have been such a child.

And if a family had no son to offer? Then the Cause would take money. And if a family had no money, but did have daughters, *two* children would be taken, or rather the money earned by their sale in the slave-market. The girls would be given names that recorded and celebrated the dutiful loyalty of their parents.

After that, Manasa made an arrangement with the kitchen-boy to do the wood-chopping for him, so that she could spend more time with the old woman.

She learnt Old Sybarite from her, much of the old wisdom, and even a little of the darker magic. Only a little, because the old woman told her that, although there were deeper and far more terrible things that she could teach her, Manasa was much too young to understand the nature of the price she would have to pay for them. If, when she was older, she eventually chose to take that path, there would be no going back.

The charcoal-burner showed her what to with the ax if the two vagabonds ever attacked her again. And some other useful tricks for dealing with men.

Then her master died, in those same woods, in a hunting accident, and she was sold on, to a new master. She never saw the two old people again.

She was curious to know what had become of her sister, "Maneira". And, if she was patient, there was a way for her to find out.

Did her dear master know about the Spider's Web?

No, Thomasius had no idea what she was talking about.

If he would bear with her, she would be honored to tell him.

Slaves, she said, knew much more than their masters realized. They attended them constantly, and were present during their conversations, whether they wanted to listen to them or not. If they were sensible they listened, because it could have painful consequences for them if they were caught not paying attention.

A trusted slave might accompany his master (or her mistress) to another house, where, sooner or later, they would be banished to the kitchen, to be fed, or just to be kept out of the way, until the time came when they would escort master or mistress home again. Sitting in the kitchen, they would exchange whatever knowledge they had, or gossip that they had heard, with the slaves of that household. Some of the slaves that they spoke to might in turn find themselves visiting yet another house, nearby or far away, taking that same body of knowledge and gossip with them and passing it on.

Visits to the bath-house were another opportunity to obtain and exchange news, since the slaves would often sit together waiting while their masters enjoyed the attentions of the bath-house whores.

What had no doubt begun as chance, as a banal part of the everyday life of slaves, had blossomed into a tradition that was consciously supported and actively encouraged. And it offered slaves their only possible opportunity to discover what had happened to a brother or sister, a son or daughter, a parent, or a friend.

They could hardly ask their masters, could they?

In this way a great accumulation of gossip, facts and fantasies, stories, rumors and speculation spread like a vast net or web over the world of the slaves. They could access it only very occasionally, and seldom did it provide the tidbit of news that some poor creature was yearning for, as an item of casual knowledge suddenly became a vital piece of information.

But it did happen...

"Did you hear anything from Trebenna? Your master was there for the Feast of Sol, wasn't he?"

"Yes, some of the merchants' wives have been cheating on their husbands."

"Well, that's nothing new, is it? Did he hear any names?"

"No, he didn't say. I don't think he's as interested as other men would be. I think he secretly prefers boys! I wonder if the mistress suspects him yet..."

"And that was all?"

"He said the prices in the markets were very high. And there was bad feeling among the stall-holders, between the Slave followers and the followers of the old gods. They all went and complained to Serenus the city councilor, and he found against the Slave worshipers, so the Slave Men, you know, their stupid priests, went and accused him of taking bribes—"

"Don't they all?"

"—and of maltreating his house-slaves."

"Oh, that's interesting! Did they punish him?"

"No, of course not! But the council told him to treat his slaves better. They say that in his household he's got a woman from Sin, and another woman with eleven toes!"

"What? Did you hear what her name was?"

"The Sin woman? I dunno, some funny name."

"No, the other one!"

"Something with a 'D'. Druva? Druvina?"

"Druvinna! But that's my mother! What more have you heard?"

And so on.

Thomasius laughed. He had had no idea. But he didn't see…?

She begged him to be patient. It was hard for her to talk about her sister, but now she would tell him.

The information provided by the Spider's Web was never much, and it was often distorted, confused, or incomplete, and always out of date, but it was all that the slaves had. It had therefore become a deep obligation, respected by almost all slaves, to acquire and pass on as much knowledge as you could, because one day, perhaps, you too might benefit from the Web.

If there was anything unusual about a slave, something that made them stand out, they were more likely to be mentioned. Like the woman from Sin, or the woman with eleven toes. And so it came about that Manasa, over the years, had heard news of her sister on two separate occasions.

The first news was that the owner of a young Sybarite slave-girl had renamed her, divesting her of the honorable name Maneira and calling her Lelia instead. "Lelia" was a name for a whore, or the sort of name a girl might give her doll.

The Sleepless Ones would be deeply offended.

This was such suicidally foolish behavior on her master's part— why didn't he just go ahead and kill himself instead?—that it was much talked about, and the news spread. It reached even the household where Manasa was now a slave, although Manasa never heard what (if anything) consequently happened to her sister's owner at the hands of the Sleepless Ones.

The second news, a few years later, was that a beautiful slave named

Leila or Lelia had been disfigured when her mistress, angry with her for some unknown reason, had held the side of her face against a brazier.

Because she was now too ugly to have in the house, her master had had to sell the girl at a great loss, and he had taken his bad temper out on his wife by thrashing her with a leather belt.

The bit about the master beating his own wife had circulated very quickly on the Spider's Web, and had caused merriment in the kitchens of numerous households. The slave-girl's name had been no more than an incidental detail, but, sad as it was, it was still news of Manasa's sister.

That was the last that she had heard of her, until Thomasius was told about a certain kitchen-maid named Lelia, "with bad burn-scars on one side of her face", by the Lord Governor's steward in Fanum Fortunae. And then Decimus had discovered that she and Victor were traveling— and murdering—together.

"He must have discovered her on one of his visits to the Lord Governor in Fanum. A Sybarite girl, bitter, and well-placed to do harm. And he somehow seduced her into his wickedness."

Probably with kindness, Manasa thought. It was easiest to seduce a slave-girl with kindness.

But what she said was, "He used magic. Her eyes were glowing red! He had rubbed powdered anchor-root into them to help her see better in the dark, as she hunted and killed. He's been trained in the ancient knowledge. He must have given her potions that destroy fear, and pity, and turn you into a beast. She didn't know what she was doing."

"They told me that she had been injured in the fight. The Lord Commander would have fought them like a wild bull. She was too badly hurt to follow him across the roof-tops, so Victor left her there and made his own escape. He used her, and abandoned her." He paused. "But what was she doing to the body?"

Manasa knew only too well what ritual mutilations her sister had been carrying out on the corpse, and why, but if she told her master it would rob him of his sleep. Some things you truly don't want to know. There is frightening knowledge that is only too easy to plant in the mind, but impossible to uproot.

Instead, she said, "It was Victor who killed my sister, not the Sueni boy, and I am going to kill *him*."

"No," her master said, "*we* are going to kill him. We shall leave tomorrow."

"Leave? But he is still here, in Cascantum!"

No, Thomasius said, no-one believed that. Victor's work in Cascantum was done. He had been sent to murder Lord Commander Rhaetius. And why? To weaken the defence of the Empire against the Blood-

Drinkers. For those who wished the Empire ill, Memmius, fine soldier that he might be, was a less serious threat, and therefore a less interesting target. Besides, a hornet's nest had now been stirred up in Cascantum, so that it would be harder for Victor to find a way to kill the Lord Commander and more difficult for him to avoid capture.

But there was another, far more tempting, target, one that was less than a two-days' ride away: the General.

"His forces are shielding Fanum and the road south. That is where we are going now. Victor has a score to settle with you. If he sees you, that might distract him. And it might help us to protect the General."

She wasn't going to *distract* Victor; she was going to kill him. In fact, she would do much more to him than kill him.

Her sister's body wouldn't be treated with respect; in fact, they would probably leave it for the dogs. If her sister was to find peace in the realm of the dead, there were grim rituals that she must perform—if possible, on Victor's living flesh.

She wouldn't tell Thomasius, however. If he knew her intentions, he wouldn't want to share his bed with her that night. And the time had now come to bind him to her.

XXIII

AULUS CONTINUES HIS JOURNEY

✠ *On the road eastwards from Cestae.*

Aulus was only too glad to see the back of Cestae, but was far from being satisfied with the present state of affairs, even though Florianus had been most supportive.

And *only* Florianus. Almost everyone else seemed to resent the sudden enlargement of their expedition.

Necro had been furious. If he had gone to the council chamber after all, this would never have happened. Why did Aulus need *three* slaves? Two of whom were useless for normal purposes, and totally peculiar. Who was going to pay for their food? They would need mules—who was going to pay for them? *He* wasn't, and the delegation shouldn't be expected to.

And where were the two new ones, a barbarian girl and a pretty-boy, going to sleep, when the party stayed at inns which had a dormitory to accommodate the servants and litter-bearers, all of whom were men? And at other inns, without a dormitory, would they need a room of their own? More expense!

They ought of course to sleep in their master's room, but Aulus was generally assigned a room that was barely big enough for himself and Beltran (who would sleep on a pallet at the foot of the bed or beside the door).

Necro had even spoken to Florianus about it. That in itself was a sign of how urgent the crisis was! With Sol knew what arguments and flatteries, Florianus had finally succeeded in calming the Senator down, to the extent that he now accepted the presence of the boy Phrygillus at least. Cleaned up, the child would make a pretty cup-bearer or attendant when Necro was invited somewhere civilized to dine. And the little fellow would consume less than the girl.

(Actually, this proved to be completely wrong: the "little fellow" was even greedier than the insatiable Gorth, while the long-limbed horsey-girl ate very moderately.)

Perhaps the Senator had no inclination for a fight or a long discussion—the vengeful Tryphaenatus might appear at any moment, demanding justice for his daughter!

Beltran was sent out at once to purchase mules, of the cheaper variety—Aulus had been made to understand that he would have to pay for them—and in a hurry. And as for the sleeping arrangements, rather than taking on the expense of an additional room, everyone (except the Senator, of course, and Aulus, if he really insisted) would simply have to squeeze up a bit more.

That proved to be most unpopular news.

For the rest of the journey, for example, Urgo the Guards officer would have to double up with the scribe Philotas, who would no longer be able to lure Gorth to his bed (just as Urgo would find it harder to entertain any of the maids).

Necro had to be persuaded that the three "children" would need to share a small room, though he agreed that they couldn't sleep in a dormitory room. This wasn't so much because of the danger of their being raped—which was an everyday risk for slaves—as because their mere presence would lead to fights, and knives being drawn, and injuries. Necro was in no two minds about that—to have a single one of his litter-bearers incapacitated by a stab-wound would be a disaster. It would endanger the whole expedition!

Beltran was noticeably sulky, and concerned about his privileged position, even though neither Mara nor Phrygillus could have replaced him as the young master's personal servant.

Some of the members of the expedition resented the "bum-boy" (one of the politer things that they called him), and many of them took an instant dislike to the barbarian girl. It was bad enough having a stupid Sueni and a bloody fishy-boy in the group; now they had a wild horsey-girl too.

But what was Mara's status, exactly? The magistrate had ruled that, until her claim of illegal abduction had been proved, she was the property of Faustus Atticus the Younger (strictly speaking, of the elder Atticus, but his father had waived his rights by accepting the will of the murdered freedman and dispatching the two slaves to his son).

Her claim could perhaps be confirmed by a fire-beacon message to Cascantum, Tryphaenatus had said, if Senator Necro agreed to take the responsibility for sending such a trivial enquiry? And if he was prepared to stay in Cestae for a week or more, until there was a reply? It was a personal matter of very low priority, and Lord Commander Rhaetius might not be willing or able to deal with it promptly.

Aulus and Florianus knew in advance of course that the Senator wouldn't be prepared to do any such thing. All he would want would be to get away from Cestae as quickly as he could, and without meeting Olympiodora, Tryphaenatus, or anyone else from that dreadful family.

Aulus was accordingly instructed by the magistrate to treat the girl with kindness, "as you would a hostage, not a slave", and solemnly enjoined to clarify the matter of her status as soon as he could. He gave his word of honor that we would do so.

"Because," the magistrate continued, quoting some portentous, Terebinthian-style legal commentary, "it is deemed unworthy to hold in servitude any person who is not by reason of their birth or by law a slave." And while it might not have been the unnamed jurist's intention to have his commentary stretched to encompass barbarians as well as Citizens, "we live in difficult times, and in a changing world", Tryphaenatus said.

Aulus promised that he would try to organize a fire-beacon message at the first opportunity. Perhaps Necro could send one from Gladium, if they traveled so far north? The Senator had mentioned that he had a relative who was the senior Staff Officer of one of the divisions stationed there.

Later, they took great pleasure in annoying Necro by telling him how competently, how *subtly* the magistrate had handled the whole complex matter. His personal appearance might be ridiculous, but in the courtroom he had been impressive.

Tryphaenatus hadn't accepted any of the assertions made by the two cavalrymen; yet neither had the assertions been disproved: perhaps there *had* been a big, black horse; perhaps the Sueni *had* intended to deliver Phrygillus to the magistrate; perhaps they *were* under instructions to bring Mara back to Cascantum.

That last point was sensitive. Cestae was not under military jurisdiction, and the two Sueni had broken several laws. On the other hand, who would choose to have a Lord Commander as an enemy? The cavalrymen had therefore been punished, but had got off very lightly: they would remain in detention for a further two days, though under less harsh conditions, and their injuries would be treated.

The three gold pieces, items of disputed ownership and uncertain origin, would be confiscated. The money would be used as follows.

One gold piece would be divided between the several innocent bystanders who had been injured in the course of the affray at the inn, and would also go to cover the costs of the doctor who had been summoned to treat them, and who would now patch up the two cavalrymen.

One gold piece would go to the innkeeper, as compensation for the considerable damage that had been caused and as payment for the stabling of the men's horses during their absence.

And one gold piece would be retained by the court to cover its expenses.

Aulus permitted himself to comment, "Citizen justice at its very best!"

"Humph!" said the Senator, and changed the subject.

With the two days' start that the magistrate had allowed them, it was unlikely that they would be followed by the cavalrymen, especially as the Sueni wouldn't be sure which route they would be following and would be worried about getting back to Cascantum before they were branded as deserters.

Which route *were* they following, though?

They left the main road and gave Laurinum, "gateway to the Riverlands", a broad miss, because Necro was terrified of all the Green assassins who would be lurking in wait for him there. After all, his enemies would be expecting them to travel through Laurinum, with its markets and many excellent hostelries, wouldn't they? So—no Laurinum!

Not going to Laurinum, and *not* crossing the river known as the Northern Twin, would mean leaving the broad road to Trebenna and the East and taking a secondary road that ran alongside the river (and which had fewer and less comfortable inns).

Unless they were they now aiming for the more northerly route, so that they would cross the Great River at Gladium? No, that would involve up to a week of having to camp out on the Plain, with no villages or inns whatsoever. In addition, it would take them too close to the Tower of the Sky, that notorious haunt of wizards and evil-doers, Necro said.

"Which is where Gaius Placidus has gone! And if he hears that I shall be passing nearby, and without a proper armed guard..."

He shuddered.

Actually, Aulus thought, the Cestaeaner had done them proud with an escort of armed riders, who would accompany them as far as the next substantial settlement. This would now have to be one of the smaller towns downriver from Laurinum, but on this side of the river.

Since Necro also strongly wished to avoid going anywhere near Trebenna, that "hot-bed of Green support", as Aulus had once heard the Senator describe it, they would eventually need to leave the riverside road, and the modest comfort of its inns, to cross the Plain until they reached the main coastal road.

Therefore they wouldn't pass through Gladium or get to meet the Senator's cousin, though Necro had in any case reacted scornfully to the suggestion regarding the fire-beacon message that could be sent from there to Cascantum.

"Do you seriously imagine that I would demean myself with such a request? If you are so keen to get rid of the useless girl," he sneered, "buy her a cheap horse, slap it on the rump and let her ride back to her filthy tribe!"

After paying for the mules, Aulus had no money to spare for a horse, even a cheap one. Besides, Mara had no wish to leave Phrygillus. She had apparently sworn to look after him, and she would do so until she was certain that he was safe, happy, and among friends.

That hardly described the situation he was presently in.

There was no-one in their traveling party whom she clearly liked and trusted, except possibly old Minnermus, who would plainly never harm anyone, unless his master's life was in danger. Did she trust Aulus, her own "master"? He couldn't tell.

For his part, he didn't know what to do with her. He couldn't afford to keep an establishment of his own, and while he could (admittedly with some difficulty) imagine little Phrygillus finding a place in the household of his uncle, what role could Mara possibly play? Stable-girl? His uncle's stableman wouldn't be pleased to have a strong-willed barbarian girl foisted on him, however good she was with horses.

Was he tempted to take her to his bed? No, for the moment Aulus had no interest in women. And when he looked at Mara, what was it that he saw? A coltish girl with strong limbs, clear skin, and pleasant features. She had adequate breasts (though much smaller than Fannia's), and he liked the way she walked, which was unlike the way Citizen women did. In fact, there was nothing (apart from her strangely plaited hair) that in isolation wasn't appealing—yet the parts somehow failed to add up to a whole that was attractive to him.

He was used to admiring a different kind of femininity, he told himself, something that was more voluptuous, more sophisticated. (Well, the old Aulus had admired such women!) Mara was simple, and straightforward. There was no feminine mystery to her.

And he wasn't at all surprised when Phrygillus confided in him that she had taught the boy to do her hair in that funny way *to show that she was a virgin.* Aulus could easily believe that she was still intact.

Let her remain so! He wouldn't force himself on her, he had never done that with women anyway, and he would try to protect her from the other men in their party.

But before there was any assault on her virtue, an assault was made on that of Phrygillus. The news came from Beltran, of course, who had heard it from one of Necro's servants.

Forgetting his sulkiness, Beltran told his master the whole story. It had happened on the first night that Phrygillus, Mara and Gorth had had to share a room together, in the dismal little inn that was the only accommodation available in the townlet that they reached after carefully bypassing Laurinum.

Gorth came in and, finding Phrygillus alone, made advances to him. Through the open door the servant, who was minding his own business outside in the corridor, distinctly heard the fishy-boy say that Phrygillus was a "cutie", and that they "could do something nice" that Philotas had shown him. It wouldn't hurt, and Phrygillus might even enjoy it.

The servant was just about to intervene (or so he claimed) when the horsey-girl pushed past him, rushed into the room, and threw Gorth off the bed. Then she jumped on top of him and—can you believe it?—reached down into his tunic and twisted his nipples until he squealed.

"An evil girl, that one," Beltran opined. "But have no fear, master: I shall watch her carefully whenever she comes near you. You will be in no danger! My master the Lord Senator would never forgive me if I let any harm come to you."

Was Mara evil, Aulus thought, or was she just a girl who had grown up with lots of brothers and male cousins?

But it was good to know that Beltran had his best interests at heart and would defend him so stoutly, at least if he was ever attacked by nipple-twisting slave-girls.

After that, Mara reportedly slept between the two boys. And Philotas, who had been told what had happened, was angry with Gorth and snubbed him in favor of the youngest of the litter-bearers, who was muscular but baby-faced and went by the nickname "Flora".

The scribe's nickname was now "Forlex". (Why ever that?)

Sol, what a gold-mine of useless information his personal servant was! Aulus wondered whether his uncle was also familiar with Beltran as an unstoppable source of gossip…

Florianus, too, was taking an interest in the boy. Ever since Cestae, he had been particularly friendly and considerate, even going so far as to offer to help Aulus with his expenses, now that the young Senator-in-waiting was obliged to pay for the bed and keep of two extra attendants (Necro had insisted on that). Aulus was understandably grateful.

Now he suggested taking Phrygillus under his wing, to train him so that the wretch would make a presentable page-boy, able to charm even that grim, humorless old legislator Lucius Atticus. He would also instruct him in personal cleanliness, wash him, and do his hair, which was constantly flopping about and hiding his pretty eyes. (Pretty eyes? Aulus hadn't noticed such details.)

The former High Chamberlain had trained so many footmen and page-boys for Palace service—it would be no great burden for him, and would even give him something with which to keep himself busy!

It was a pity that he couldn't do the same with Mara, who was not promising material as far as any kind of household service was concerned.

Thanks to Necro, no fire-beacon message could be sent in the foreseeable future to confirm her identity as a free woman. She refused to leave the boy, but she had asked him whether he would come with her to the Horse People. She would make him a great warrior!

"Wouldn't that be wonderful?"

He had answered "no", to both questions.

Unless a party of friendly horseys came galloping across the Great Plain to take her back with them by force, leaving little Phrygillus behind, it looked as though she would remain part of their expedition at least until it reached Neopolis.

A more ruthless man than Aulus might have sold her in the slave-market there, or even sooner in Maritima—there were huge slave-markets in both cities that were open all year round. She wouldn't fetch much, but it would be easier to find a buyer there than in the West: as a blonde northerner she might have a certain exotic appeal.

It wouldn't be *right*, though, and Aulus had been brought up to do what was right. Not by his parents—though Lady Pomponia had preached the tiresome Slave cult morality at him endlessly, even as she herself failed to live up to those same moral standards—but by Decimus, and then by his uncle. Which was probably why Aulus had sometimes had twinges of bad conscience over his aimless way of living in recent years.

The magistrate Tryphaenatus had extracted a promise from him. And old Castor had meant well by the girl, and had entrusted her to Aulus. Was he a man of his word?

If a barbarian girl could honor an oath that she had sworn, even though it separated her from her family and her homeland, and forced her to remain in slavery, Faustus Pomponius Atticus the Younger, Citizen of noble birth and future Senator, could hardly aim to do less.

XXIV

DECIMUS FAILS TO KEEP
HIS LIFE SIMPLE

✠ *In the City.*

Julia Placida!

Struggling to prevent the shocking discovery from disturbing his concentration (which might cause him to make a fatal mistake), Decimus stepped down off the wooden beam and maneuvered his way gingerly back to the door. He listened again, and heard the men's voices, and Julia's. Since they were still talking, he would have a few moments to get out of the ruined building safely before Vulpeculus left, with or without his two hirelings.

He succeeded in doing that, and walked briskly back round to the Palace, where he announced his return at one of the side entrances. The gatekeeper there knew him from earlier visits. He surrendered his new weapon to the man, asking him to keep it safe for him until he needed it.

"These days, *all* of us need weapons," the gatekeeper replied, with a sigh. But swords were forbidden inside the Palace, unless you were a Guardsman.

Back inside his quarters, which amounted to no more than a tiny sleeping cubicle, with shared use of a grubby bath-house, he sat on the bed and finally gave way to the flood of thoughts that were oppressing him.

What was happening? What in Sol's name was Vulpeculus up to?

He was definitely holding Julia Placida against her will—those manacles, the chain securing her to the wall—but not, it seemed, to abuse her, though she was prettier than the most expensive painted doll or temple image that Decimus had ever seen.

Why hadn't he already given her up to Naevius? It would have earned him his Blue colleague's trust and gratitude, and Julia would be a massive bargaining counter in negotiations with the Placidi. Gnaeus might even be persuaded to withdraw his forces, away from the City, if doing that would guarantee his niece's life.

Or was Vulpeculus unwilling to hand her over, because he knew what Naevia and the Emperor were likely to do to her? No! Decimus was certain that the Senator wouldn't be squeamish about that. He had seen—no, he had *heard*, unforgettably—how Vulpeculus himself treated young women.

Julia was obviously valuable to him. But what did he intend to do with her? Sell her to the highest bidder?

What game was he playing?

Another idea was growing in his mind, an explanation so monstrous, so unspeakably treacherous, that Decimus refused to believe it. He finally banished it from his thoughts in order to get at least a few hours of sleep.

His first duty the next day would be to pay his respects to Senator Lucius Atticus. To his disgust, he overslept, and it was already late morning by the time that he left the Palace.

The City was quiet, but there was a lowering atmosphere of threat in the streets, made more intense by the leaden sky and an unexpectedly chill wind. Passers-by looked frightened and unhappy. When he had arrived in the City, he had felt no such mood, even with Blood-Drinkers on the march. But they had been an exotic danger beyond the horizon; now it was the Placidi who were on their way, hated, familiar, and bent on revenge.

Decimus wore his new cloak, with the sword tucked under it. It was better to be prepared.

He had the feeling that he was being followed—though by whom?

Vulpeculus? The Senator believed him to be his ally.

Quintus Naevius? He had been trapped into committing himself to Quintus, in a way that permitted no going back, but until Naevia showed signs of being with child his life would not be in danger. Maybe Quintus was concerned to keep him out of harm's way, in case he was needed for a second tryst with his daughter?

Naevius himself? The intentions of his enemy the General (and of Ogilo's liegeman Decimus) were now of far less interest to him than those of the Blood-Drinkers, a brooding presence thankfully still far to the north, or of the vengeful Gnaeus Placidus, whose divisions were rapidly approaching from the south. For the moment, Decimus would be an irrelevance to him.

Or could there be someone else in the City with a malevolent interest in his activities?

Servo greeted him as an old friend, while peering out into the street behind Decimus to see what riffraff might be skulking out there. The habit of half a lifetime (or however long he had been a gatekeeper for). He was not exactly a great conversationalist—what gatekeeper ever was?—yet his pleasure in seeing Decimus again was obviously genuine.

Decimus noted that he was wearing a new tunic. The first person that you met when you visited a wealthy household was always the doorman. That was the first impression that you gained. Lucius Atticus attached great importance to those in his house looking smart and clean (hence his frequent irritation with Aulus on that subject). Just as he would have no truck with the brandings or mutilations sometimes carried out on slaves, his own servants were always well-washed and well-dressed. And well-treated, too.

In return he expected (and usually received) their loyalty. They knew that almost anywhere else they would be much worse off.

The Senator was not available. He was paying a routine social visit to another Green Senator, attended by Sonorus.

Who was Sonorus?

The new footman.

And not with Davus?

That was correct.

Decimus guessed that it was out of consideration that the Senator had not taken Davus, who hated chit-chat. Or maybe Davus had his back problems again.

So Decimus wouldn't be able to see the Senator?

No.

Might it be possible for Decimus to see the secretary instead?

Yes, why not? (Sol, he was slow!)

In the meantime Sinica had come to the house-door to see who the visitor was. Another friendly, smiling face! Servo asked her to escort Decimus through to the library, where the secretary could likely be found.

He was indeed there, poring over a new acquisition to the Senator's modest collection of texts.

Decimus asked whether the maid could stay, since what he would be saying might possibly affect her too, and then, after an exchange of pleasantries and harmless news—Decimus was careful not to give any details of his work for the General—he spelled out what he was hoping Senator Atticus could do to help him.

Davus assured him that his master would be delighted to cooperate. Though Decimus was not the Senator's freedman, this was the house in which Aulus, whom he had served for many years, normally lived. There was no other household in the City to which he had such a close connection. Besides, Senator Atticus was a colleague of the General's in the Green faction. It would therefore be normal for Decimus to visit the house occasionally to pay his respects, and to spend a few hours in the Senator's library. Everyone knew what a bookworm he was!

Decimus laughed. That might well be true, he said, but all those who *weren't* lovers of literature would find the explanation wholly unconvincing. What he needed was a story that those more vulgar people would be willing to believe, something involving sex or money, and the easiest story would be that he paid so many visits to the house because he had a mistress there.

Davus nodded and turned to Sinica. He understood what was wanted. No other female slave under the Senator's roof would be remotely plausible as Decimus's secret lover.

And Sinica stepped forward with a broad, beaming smile.

Oh dear, he had no need for yet more complications in his life!

"All that is required is the *appearance* of a relationship," he said, quickly adding, as he saw the smile on her face begin to fade, that that didn't mean that he wasn't aware of her attractiveness. "Far from it! But I am playing a dangerous game, in the service of my master the General, whose interests are also those of my Lord the Senator. My life must be kept as simple as possible."

She bowed her head demurely.

"Whatever my Lord Decimus desires. Whatever his wishes might be…"

The way that she said it was perfect: false humility tinged faintly with irony, just the way a slave-girl who was your secret mistress *would* talk to you in the presence of others. She was showing him that she already knew how to act the part!

Davus asked whether Decimus might care to use the bath-house? The water had been heated up nicely for the Senator to bathe before he left to visit his colleague.

Although he knew the way, Sinica came with him. They heard female voices, and Sinica told him that they belonged to Lady Cornelia and Lady Fannia. The Senator had given them shelter, and saved their lives, but they were unable to leave the house, and no-one except Sinica was allowed to speak to them.

When they reached the bath-house, she helped him to remove his clothes. He sincerely hoped that she wouldn't strip off too and join him in the water! To his relief she left him and went to continue her other duties in the household. She was a clever woman, and she had understood the situation.

He relaxed in the warm water. His thoughts drifted lazily to Naevia, and although he still couldn't picture her clearly he found himself stiffening at the memory of how she had ridden him, and how he had thrust into her, filling her up with his seed.

He didn't like Naevia. Or trust her. He was even a little frightened of her—the first time a woman had produced this feeling in him. (Most of the slaves in the household of Senator Faustus Atticus had been frightened of Lady Pomponia, who for all her noisy piety ordered far more whippings than her husband did, but Decimus had only ever felt contempt for her.)

Nevertheless, how he would relish a second encounter with her! This time, he would be the one who would be in command. And the longer that it took him to get her pregnant, the longer he would feel safe from her vicious father.

Sinica returned. Fortunately, his erection had begun to subside—he didn't want *her* to see it!

Someone, she said, had come to speak to him. Someone who wasn't welcome in the house. Since Decimus was bathing, Servo had asked Sinica to come to the door, and the man had spoken to her instead.

Would Decimus speak to him? He was someone that they both knew, though she refused to give the man's name. He was unarmed, and meant Decimus no harm. He would be waiting in the old shed on the patch of waste ground behind the house.

Who was he?

No, she wouldn't say—she could get herself into terrible trouble over this.

Could she vouch for him at least?

Yes, she could: she knew him, and he was an honorable man.

Very well, Decimus would see him. He dressed, with Sinica's expert help, and retrieved his sword and cloak from the gatekeeper.

"You should get yourself another cloak, Decimus. Look at it, it's disgusting," Servo told him—a remarkable piece of advice to be offered by a Sueni!

Decimus found his way round to the back of the house, where there was a waste area of scrub and weeds and dog-excrement that was obviously used as a rubbish tip by members of the Atticus household and by slaves from the neighboring houses.

On this waste ground stood a dilapidated shack. It had probably only survived being dismantled one night for firewood because of the vivid curse painted on its side. This was a favored abode (it threatened) of the Horned One, who would render most horribly impotent anyone who disturbed him! (Presumably women never went looking for free firewood.)

Decimus wondered whether it would survive a cold winter, especially now that gangs of ruffians were roaming the streets almost unchallenged.

The shack had no door, just a piece of rough cloth, even cheaper and dirtier than Decimus's cloak, that had been nailed up to cover its doorway. He coughed ostentatiously, and a voice whispered to him to enter—if he was not being followed.

It was the voice of Sextus Placidus.

It wasn't dark at all inside the shack, because of the many cracks between the planks that let in daylight. Decimus saw that, although the man was dirty, and haggard-looking, he was unmistakably Sextus Placidus, with the same oval face and pretty features that his sister had.

He had been living on the streets, like countless other Red fugitives, except that you didn't actually live *on* the streets—you lived in cellars, under aqueducts, behind rubbish tips, and you never slept anywhere where there was no escape route. The Mob was hunting for Reds! He had learnt that they weren't truly dangerous, because they were so loud, and you could hear them coming, but some of Quintus's thugs hunted silently, in small packs.

Sextus had been lucky—so far—and all this time he had been searching for his sister. There was a network of people who could be trusted: secret Red supporters, kind Citizens who felt sorry for them, and others who merely loathed Quintus Naevius.

"But you never turn to people who owe you a favor—they're always the first to betray you! Better to find people who helped *you* once before. You're the living evidence of their virtue. They have an interest in keeping you alive, because it makes them feel good." He smiled wryly. "Funny thing, human nature, isn't it?"

Decimus was amazed. Was this embittered philosopher the same man as the dandified poet, the playboy, the social butterfly, the seducer, Aulus's wastrel friend and dubious inspiration? His eyes were cold and tired. He barely reacted when Decimus told him that the Lady Fannia was safe, and living like her cousin Cornelia under the protection of Aulus's uncle.

"I know," was all he said. "I took them there."

He hadn't tried to see Fannia, but he had been following Decimus ever since he arrived back in the City. (Decimus was pleased that his instinct that he was being observed had proved to be true, and that it hadn't been the Blues who had been tailing him.)

"But why, Master Sextus?"

Because Decimus had access to the Palace, because he could move about freely in the City—and because Sextus simply had no-one else to turn to.

And he wasn't "master" Sextus to anyone. He was a fugitive, barely clinging to life and with one last, desperate hope: that he would be able to save his sister, the sister he had never known.

"I have…contacts. Certain people who hate Naevius, and who have links with my uncle."

"Gnaeus?"

"The one with an army! Naturally, who else? Certainly not Uncle Gaius. He's disappeared. He's probably gone to meet the other wizards."

"Wizards?"

Sextus ignored his question.

"They don't care about me, they only want Julia. Uncle Gnaeus sent a message for me. Find her, it said: Vulpeculus claims to have her. Find her, do nothing, but send word." He paused. "What would that man Vulpeculus want with my sister? I went to his house yesterday, and I crawled in through a drain, but I couldn't find her. That's why I smell so bad! But I saw you riding with Vulpeculus, at the Gate of the Winds. You must know what he's doing?"

"No, I don't. But he wouldn't keep her at his house. So—your uncle wants you to rescue her?"

"No, the message was to find her, but do nothing. I don't understand that! I want to make her safe. I don't like Vulpeculus, and I don't trust him. How can she be safe if she is with him? I must find out where she is. Can't you help me? I know that you're a decent man. If that's not enough, then do it for Aulus's sake! He wouldn't be much use, perhaps, but at least he would try and help me. Aulus would help."

He was right about that. Silly, confused Aulus probably would offer to help—and then get them both killed. Whereas he, Decimus, knew exactly where the girl was being hidden. Could he ever look Aulus in the eye again if he *didn't* help his friend?

He took a deep breath.

"I know where she is. She's being held prisoner. She's in chains, and she's not safe. I think they may be planning to move her—I heard Vulpeculus tell her guards 'two days'. That was yesterday."

Sextus gazed at him in amazement.

"How do you know this? Are you in league with Vulpeculus?"

Decimus couldn't help smiling.

"He *thinks* I am! If we succeed in rescuing her, though, and he finds out, my life won't be worth a copper coin. We'll have to go tonight, and we'll need to kill her guards. Can you use a sword?"

Sextus was indignant.

"No, of course I can't! I'm a poet, not a bloody mercenary."

"Then let me put it a different way. If I gave you a sword, Sextus, could you kill with it?"

The poet's eyes lit up with warmth for the first time.

"To rescue my sister? Yes!"

The two friends were opposites, Decimus thought to himself. He had taught his former master some quite advanced moves in sword-fighting, but Aulus couldn't have brought himself to kill anything on two or four legs that was capable of looking at him. And he had often thrown his weapon down, when Decimus smacked him with the wooden practice sword, and declared that it was time for refreshments!

Sextus, on the other hand, would even need to be shown how to *hold* a sword, but he would plunge it into his enemy's heart with venom if he got the chance.

What a pity that he couldn't mould the two of them into a single, more effective, fighter, if only for a few hours!

"You must wait here," he told Sextus, "until it's dark. I'll fetch a weapon for you and come back and show you how to use it. If there are two men guarding your sister, all you'll need to do is keep one of them busy while I deal with his friend."

"All? That's rather a lot!"

"If there are three, we'll need to be more creative. If there are four, we won't be able to do it."

"And if I fetch some of my friends to help us?"

"No, they'll make too much noise. We'd be heard before we could get anywhere near the guards. It'll be hard enough for two of us. Trust me—I know what I'm doing!"

But did he? He was about to pursue a dangerous and unpredictable course for emotional reasons that he didn't fully understand. He didn't recognize himself. Did it really matter to him so much, what Aulus thought of him?

Whatever he decided, his actions must be ruled by his intelligence. His intelligence was now whispering that it might be wiser to do this on his own, without Sextus blundering about and getting in his way.

In the past, he had carried out missions of this kind quite success-fully on his own. Ogilo had sent him once to kill the leader of a band of Free People marauders that had been terrorizing peaceful villagers in the Valley. He had killed two bodyguards, and then the man himself, a vicious, hulking specimen who knew how to fight. And he had gotten away without a single scratch.

He had planned that expedition carefully—but he had to admit that he'd also been lucky, and that one day his luck was going to run out.

He would plan this one properly, too. He'd show Sextus what he wanted him to do, and hope that the poet didn't disappoint him. He would need him to calm and reassure his sister if she was hysterical. They looked so similar—Julia would recognize him at once!

He went back to the Palace, and was able to steal another dark cloak and a sword. It took him longer, because the gatekeeper was no longer having to deal with irate visitors and confusing wooden dockets, but the man was genuinely not very good at the job he'd been assigned, and so all Decimus had to do was wait.

He chose a cavalry sword for Sextus. Citizen Army swords were more effective in close fighting; however, you needed to know how to use them, and they were shorter, so your opponent got much closer to you. With a long cavalry sword, however, even if Sextus swung it with a blatant lack of skill, the other man would be held at bay for a few moments, and those few moments might be enough.

Also, the more impressive the sword was, the more confident Sextus would feel.

It took him longer to find the tools that he would need to break Julia's manacles and her chain (though the walls in the ruined building were so rotten that he might be able to pull the chain out of the wall with his bare hands). He had to go into the cellars, where there were workshops as well as storerooms, cells, and torture-chambers. There he found a gross-looking, toad-like man who could have been anything—a storekeeper, a craftsman, or a torturer—and asked him for his help.

What exactly was the young master looking for then? He told the man, quite brazenly, that he wanted tools for cracking open manacles. Quintus's boys had sent in some Reds, he said, all shackled together but with no key. They had to be separated before they could be dealt with individually.

"Dealt with, eh?" the man sniggered. "That's normally *our* job!"

But he provided Decimus with what he needed.

Sextus was delighted with his new sword—as happy as a child at the Feast of Sol when the presents are being handed out. He slashed through the air with it, causing Decimus to jump aside. The sword was brand-new, and fiendishly sharp. Any opponent would think twice about getting close to it, at least until he'd realized that Sextus didn't know what he was doing.

There was unfortunately no time to train him, though Decimus gave him a few basic tips. Actually, in his view most Sueni cavalrymen didn't know how to wield a long-sword either, and he suspected that they more often disabled their enemies by riding into them and knocking them over than by using their weapons.

What mattered was that Sextus didn't cut himself on the sharp edges of the sword, especially as he would need to carry it concealed under his cloak because it was so bright.

And he should try not to drop it—it would make an awful lot of noise if he did.

They would go into the ruined building under cover of dark, and hope that the guards had left a lamp or a torch burning so that there would be that faint glimmer of light to guide them. His greatest concern was that the men might have ignored what were probably Vulpeculus's orders and extinguished their lamp or torch in order to sleep, secure in the knowledge that no-one would ever think of entering the haunted ruins in the night-time.

If that were the case, he would have to feel his way towards them very slowly, and leave Sextus further behind. He couldn't risk Sextus stumbling, blundering into something, dropping his sword, or making any sound that might wake them. And he would have to kill them silently, in the darkness, without any wild sword-swinging.

It went as planned. It went even better than planned, with no surprises. (There *were* surprises, but they came afterwards.)

The guards, only two of them, had indeed left a lamp burning, and they were stretched out half-asleep outside the cell. Decimus placed the metal tools slowly and quietly beside the wall, and then leapt on the guards. They heard their attacker far too late.

And Sextus didn't get to wave his sword, let alone use it.

The first man was still struggling to his feet when Decimus stuck him in the side of the throat. He was out of it before it had started.

The second man made the mistake of holding a speech: "You're *dead*, you cunt!" (or words to that effect).

Decimus had learned that you can speechify, or you can fight, but that you shouldn't try to do both. He bent himself double, slipped in under the man's guard, and poked upwards into the soft part of his chin. Then, as the man began to thrash about, he stabbed deep into his neck.

Sextus was horrified by what he had just seen, but Decimus now needed his help.

"Hurry up, search that one, we have to find the key! One of them has it. Hurry!"

Sextus was most reluctant to touch either of the guards, both of whom were still twitching in their death-throes. Decimus told him to hold the lamp instead *and not to drop it*—the poet's hands were shaking so badly. So much for Sextus the warrior!

Once Decimus had found the key, the door could slowly be swung open, with much squeaking and groaning. He took the lamp and went in first.

Julia Placida was standing with her back to the wall, but she wasn't cowering. She must have heard the fight, and as Decimus held up the lamp what she would have seen was an unfamiliar man spattered in blood.

"If you have any decency," she said, "and any honor, please kill me now. Or take me to Naevius himself, but not to his son!"

"My Lady, we have come to free you and to bring you to your uncle's men."

Decimus had spoken without thinking. Did he really mean that? He had just betrayed Vulpeculus—the promise made to him meant nothing—but if he restored Julia to her uncle wouldn't he be betraying his master the General too?

"No," she said, "you're Blues. I know that."

Sextus stepped out from behind Decimus so that she could see him properly. She gasped as the lamplight caught his face.

"Julia, I'm your brother. He's telling the truth! We don't serve Naevius. We're here to rescue you!"

She started crying.

"No you're not!" she sobbed. "Are you really my brother? You can't be! If you were, you wouldn't be trying to kidnap me. No, I won't go with you!"

Decimus was getting worried. There was no time for all this. Vulpeculus might come, or more of his men. They needed to get out of the ruined building quickly.

"My Lady, do you really want to stay here?" She didn't. "I thought not." He tried again. "Shall we take you to your uncle's men? No?" He was now truly confused. "Where would you like us to take you, then?"

She looked at him with widened eyes.

"Anywhere that is safe. Can I trust you?" And then: "Is he really my brother?"

"I swear to you that he is Sextus Placidus, your brother. I am Decimus, the freedman of Aulus Atticus" (which wasn't exactly true), "who is the best friend of Master Sextus, and I've known him for many years."

"And I've been looking for you ever since the day of the bride-show," Sextus added. "We'll take you somewhere safe."

"But not to our uncle's men!"

"As you wish. Though I don't understand why not."

Sextus had had many hideouts in the City, many of them arranged by Red supporters or enemies of Naevius. But the safest was with neither of those.

It was a leper house.

Decimus took a deep breath. Very well, he would take Julia there. Sextus must find his own way, however—three of them crossing the City by night would attract more attention than two, and if they were stopped Sextus might well be recognized.

"You won't like it, my Lady, but you must dirty your face and hands, make them even dirtier than they are now, and after we've reached the street I'm going to have to carry you."

She was a tiny girl, and a light burden for Decimus, who slung her across his shoulder like a sack. He had wrapped her in his cloak, to hide the soiled but expensive clothes she was wearing. With the tools that he had, removing her chain and the manacles had been easy. Sextus had already disappeared into the shadows.

Gangs of drunken Blue thugs or opportunistic criminals were roaming the streets, molesting the few people who were still, unwisely, not yet safely a-bed.

Most of them saw the blood stains on Decimus's clothes, and the sword tied to his belt, and walked on. Once, however, he had to assert that Julia was his daughter (she was so small that it was believable). She'd been seeing a fucking southerner behind his back—he'd given the man what was coming to him, and when he got this one home, since he only hit men, her mother would take a belt to her!

One larger group challenged him more aggressively. What was he doing out on the streets? And who was the girl?

"Who wants to know, brother?"

They were the Protection League of Blue Citizens of the Fullers' Street.

"And you're in our territory. *Brother*."

He knew that from the smell. Wherever fullers worked, it always stank of urine. As they usually did too.

In situations like this you couldn't back down. Decimus knew that he would have to bluff it out, or kill them.

"Excellent! I'll tell Quintus how well you're guarding your quarter."

"And who might *you* be? And whose blood is that? And who's the girl?"

Decimus laughed, making it sound as brutal as he could.

"So many questions! I'm Tarantinus, bodyguard to Marcus Vulpeculus—you know, *the* Marcus Vulpeculus, the Blue Senator and next City Prefect (but don't tell anyone you heard it from me). I've just been trying out my weapon on some Red friends of ours. And this little Red bitch?" He shook Julia lightly. "I'm taking her back with me to test my *other* weapon. Any objections?" He looked around the circle of faces. "Good! There's plenty of Red pussy out there for everyone. Near the Palace is a good place to look."

He was stopped again—by members of the "Sandal-makers' Defence Society"—just before they reached the leper-house. He told them that the girl was a leper. The fullers had found her roaming about drunk...

"The fullers? Those bastards?"

Good, that gave him something to work with.

Lepers weren't allowed to move around freely. All true followers of the Blessed Slave knew that their disgusting disease was a punishment for sinfulness. It was a kindness to even let them live! But the fullers, instead of doing their duty and taking the girl back to the leper-house, had grabbed him and told *him* to do it. He had a sword, yes, but he wasn't stupid, there were ten or a dozen of them, and they knew where he lived...

"Lazy cunts!"

"Typical fullers. They drink their own piss!"

Yes yes. All he wanted to do now was dump the girl with the lepers and go home to his bed.

They were local boys, so perhaps *they* could take her the rest of the way? It was only a couple of streets.

Er, no, they had more pressing duties.

Would they like to escort them, at least?

No, that wasn't necessary either.

And so Decimus and Julia reached the safety of the leper-house, where Sextus was already waiting for them.

The lepers gave them a room to themselves, and offered them food and water. Decimus declined the offer politely. Julia gazed about her in horror. Had she never seen lepers before?

Decimus pointed to the only piece of furniture in the room, a low wooden bench.

"Sit down, my Lady. You too, Sextus."

They both sat down, and glanced at each other shyly and apprehensively, before looking away.

Before he could go on, Julia asked, in a small but firm voice, "Are you Decimus—or Tarantinus? Are you the bodyguard of Vulpeculus? If you are, why did you kill his men?"

"I am who I told you I am. And your brother asked me to help him save you from Vulpeculus."

Sextus butted in.

"Uncle Gnaeus sent me a message that Vulpeculus had you!"

She looked at her brother. She's so beautiful, Decimus thought, and so fragile! He could understand why Maximillus or Naevia would be tempted to hurt her and break her.

This time when she spoke her voice was tremulous, and bitter.

"That message didn't say anything about rescuing me, did it?"

"Well, no..."

"So how do you think our uncle knew where I was?" Sextus stared at her in bewilderment. "*Because Vulpeculus told him. He and Vulpec-*

ulus are working together! Vulpeculus's men captured me, and killed the friends who were sheltering me. He said he wanted to sell me, and named a price. Uncle has a man in the Palace, someone close to the Emperor—someone who can send coded fire-beacon messages that no-one ever challenges. Uncle said 'yes', but then the situation changed, and Vulpeculus had an even better idea. Uncle agreed to that too. They've made a horrible deal. They have evil plans for me."

The dreadful suspicion that Decimus had banished from his thoughts now struck him, with the force of a charging bull.

"Yes, my Lady," he said, "And I know what their plan is. They are going to make you the Queen of the Blood-Drinkers!"

"What?" Sextus was amazed, and horrified. "*What?* What nonsense is that?"

Julia merely smiled, and nodded.

"No nonsense at all. The Great King has demanded a princess of the Imperial blood, and a million gold pieces. That's what Vulpeculus told me. Uncle Gnaeus will pay them the money, and Vulpeculus will send them the princess—me! Now do you understand why I didn't want to go with you? Uncle Gnaeus didn't *want* me to be rescued; he just wanted to know that Vulpeculus wasn't bluffing. So you could only have come from Naevius. And I'd rather go to the Blood-Drinkers than be a toy for that woman and her husband to play with."

While Decimus was rapidly putting the broken pieces together in his mind, Sextus was still dumb-founded.

"It doesn't make sense! You aren't a princess. And why should our uncle give you up to the Blood-Drinkers, and give them so much money as well? He could have found you, and rescued you, and taken you back to Sybaris! And what does Vulpeculus have to gain from all this? He wouldn't get the money any more. I don't understand—"

No, he didn't understand, Decimus told himself, because this was a plot hatched in the deepest, darkest pit of Esbus. *This* was why Vulpeculus had disappeared from the court for two days, but told Decimus to stay there.

"Your sister will be a princess when the Placidi become an Imperial family. And when will that be? When your uncle rules the West as Co-Emperor with Vulpeculus! One of them in Sybaris, one of them in the City! Sharing the Empire—it's been done before."

"Yes," Julia added, "he always hated the City, and feared for his life here."

"The Blood-Drinkers will destroy Ogilo," Decimus continued, "they'll ravage the far north, and then withdraw. Gnaeus Placidus and his divisions will return to the south, and restore the former glory of Sybaris.

The Cause will have won!"

The glance that brother and sister exchanged told him that they knew only too well what the Cause was.

"Naevius still controls the City, though."

"Yes, Sextus, but only with fear. And when the threat to the City is over, because Vulpeculus has made the Blood-Drinkers and the Placidi go away, when Naevius couldn't, who will the grateful Citizens turn to? Which Blue master will they prefer?"

"Vulpeculus! Even if he was only a puppet of my uncle's."

"Your uncle might be able to capture the City or he might not—the people here would fight to the death to keep out the southern heretics—but he couldn't hold it. He needs a local man, a Blue, to do that for him: Marcus Vulpeculus. *Emperor* Vulpeculus." Then he muttered, "And the hour of the fox will have come," though more to himself than out loud.

Instead of asking him what that meant, Julia said, "And our uncles can help Vulpeculus and destroy Naevius, and his son, and Maximillus too, without coming anywhere near the City. Because there are secret ways—"

"The Sleepless Ones."

All three of them remained silent. Sextus had his head in his hands.

"I thought it would all be so easy, so straightforward: just rescue you! But what do we do now?"

His sister glared at him.

"You mean: what do *I* do now? I'll tell you what I'm *not* going to do! I'm not going back to Vulpeculus, or Uncle Gnaeus, because they'll sell me to the Blood-Drinkers. And I'm not going to Naevius either. There! Does that make it any easier for you, brother?"

Her eyes flashed—and Decimus was smitten.

He'd always treated women with respect, but also believed that they should do what they were told. Which was what the men around them told them to do. Naevia, he'd already learnt, had her own ideas about that. And so did this beautiful creature.

He realized that he was about to make another huge mistake.

"My Lady," he said, "just tell me what it is that you want, and we'll do it."

She looked at him thoughtfully.

"Your master the General is my enemy, I know that. But is he an honorable man?"

Decimus didn't hesitate.

"Yes. He wouldn't hurt you—*either* of you—if you asked for his protection."

"Then we'll go to Ogilo. Is it far? Decimus will take us there! Brother?"

Sextus nodded uncomfortably.

"I suppose so. Is there anywhere else for us to go?"

"Then that's settled," she declared.

Decimus said nothing. What he thought was: you fool, what have you done now? Ogilo would be grateful for these hostages, certainly, and interested to learn of the treachery of Vulpeculus. He might even say "thank you". Or he might not. He wouldn't be as grateful, though, as Naevius would be. Or even Vulpeculus, if he took the two young Placidi back to him.

He couldn't do that, of course. But what now?

"Decimus will take us there." "It's settled." Really? Well, that's alright then! It was so easy to say, but how, in Sol's name, and in the name of every other god on earth, and those in the sky, and in the depths of the ocean, and the burning pits of the underworld, was he ever going to manage it—to smuggle them out of the City, and bring them halfway across the north to safety?

He had no idea. But he still said "yes".

XXV

MARA GOES ON A BOAT

✣ *From Cestae to the East.*

It was good to be riding, though Mara sorely missed the "demon". In fact, any horse would have been better than the elderly, flea-bitten mule that they had given her. Phrygillus's mule was no better, but at least the boy was finally learning how to ride.

She had to tell him not to tease the animal. Mules weren't stupid, and they had memories. It might not tip Phrygillus over a cliff, but he could one day find himself being dragged painfully through thornbushes.

He talked to her, and told her his problems. What he mostly said was that he wasn't getting enough food. And there were all kinds of people he didn't like, starting with the fishy-boy. Unfortunately, the three of them had to share a bed. The two boys ought to be playing together, not fighting. Instead, Mara had already had to intervene several times, and teach Gorth the hard way that he couldn't do what he liked with Phrygillus.

The first time, Gorth had attempted to do something dirty to the boy, and Mara had stepped in and given him a nasty surprise. Phrygillus hadn't realized what was going on, or had he? After that, Gorth had tried to involve him in rough games, in which he usually hurt him in some way.

Again, Mara had given fishy-boy a taste of what it was like to be hurt by someone bigger than you were. How he hated her! She didn't care. What mattered was that he left the smaller boy alone.

Once he had touched her during the night.

If he did it once more, she said, she would cut off his man-part.

He didn't do it again.

Phrygillus told her that Florianus sometimes cuddled him. There was no harm in that, was there? He was a eunuch—the scribe Philotas, a most unpleasant man with little ratty eyes, had told her in great detail about eunuchs, and how they were made—so Florianus presumably wouldn't be able to hurt the boy.

Philotas had a second name, "Forlex", which always made people laugh, for some reason that she didn't understand. He paid a lot of attention to them, asking her strange questions about Phrygillus. He only spoke to them when Gorth wasn't there, she noticed, and she quickly concluded that he was another of those sad "boy-lovers" like Castor, and that he was looking for a new *seflar* after Gorth had refused him.

How pathetic these Citizens were!

The boy did nothing to stop Florianus from cuddling him. He liked being cuddled, as Mara knew. And he actually complained to her that his new master didn't cuddle him, and didn't talk to him much. Aulus wasn't looking for a *seflar*, then?

She called him "Aulus", even to his face, and he didn't mind. The leader of the group, a really horrible man called Necro, who was a Senator like Aulus's father in Fanum, became angry about that, but Aulus said that she was a hostage, not a slave, and that he was looking after her until she could return to her own people, where she was a kind of princess, apparently. Phrygillus should call him "Master" (and he did), but she didn't have to. She liked him for that, even though he didn't seem to want to talk to her, either.

Aulus wasn't what the Horse People would consider a *man*—in the whole party, only the Sueni soldier came anywhere close to that, and he didn't count, because he was a swampie. Aulus couldn't ride any better than Phrygillus could, and what would he do if they were attacked? Mara couldn't imagine him fighting anyone. But when he did speak to her, he was kind, and polite. She saw that he was like that with everyone, even with Necro, who didn't deserve it. And she could tell that his slave Beltran was fond of him.

Beltran had been unfriendly at first; then he had become *too* friendly. He had taken a lot of interest in her plaits, and what they stood for. She was gaining experience with men, and how to deal with them. She wasn't going to cut her plaits for anyone, she told Beltran, except for an honorable warrior of the Horse People who had asked her father to give her to him as a wife, and who had won his approval and the approval of her clan.

He would have to be young, but with good horses. And he should be handsome, too.

For a moment, Mara wondered how the Citizens ever found their wives. What father would give his daughter away to someone like Aulus, who wouldn't be able to defend her, or Necro, who was rich, but mean and disgusting? And how had such men as Necro, who dribbled like a baby, and fussed over money, or Aulus's father, who ran like a frightened rabbit from his own wife, become "important"? Among the Horse

People, they would be scorned and despised, and not because of their age. Most men became weaker as they grew older, everyone knew that, but men of wisdom would always be respected.

In one matter, though, she found that she and Necro were of the same opinion, and against everyone else.

The road they were taking avoided all the large towns and cities. Good! She had had quite enough of them. But the people in their party were disappointed, and muttered against Necro, saying that it was his fault and that he was a coward.

Of course he was a coward. An adult man who wasn't sick, he went everywhere in a litter carried by slaves. Did he have no shame at all? Apparently he didn't.

They therefore missed the place called Lorrinum that Geto and Orogo had talked about. She wondered what the two Sueni would do when the magistrate in Kesta released them. She had no wish to see either of them again.

And they went nowhere near a big city called Trebenna. This had many entertainments to offer, she heard people say, and so there was much resentment towards Necro.

They continued along the river-bank, where there were only unwalled villages and very small inns. Philotas said that these were mainly for couriers and the military, because no travelers in their right mind would keep north of the river instead of taking the main road to Trebenna.

Mara didn't care, and her great moment arrived when they finally left the road and cut overland across the Plain for a day and a night.

This was in order to save time and get them to the coastal road quicker, said Aulus; or to avoid the swamps near the mouths of the Twin Rivers, said Urgo (who ought to know all about swamps); or because Necro was shit-scared of going anywhere near Trebenna, said everyone else.

When the time came to set up camp, she cheekily told Urgo that he'd picked the wrong spot (what could *he* know about living out on the Plain?) and that she'd show them a better place, where there was water. She was bluffing a bit, but she trusted her instincts and, sure enough, she soon found what she was looking for.

Whether or not he felt humiliated, Urgo praised her in front of Florianus and the Senator. Florianus smiled, and nodded, but Necro merely looked away.

She didn't care about that, either. Everyone hated the Senator anyway (his litter-slaves most of all).

As they prepared for the night, she heard Aulus say "Isn't this fun?"

What did he mean by that? The Plain, like the similar lands beyond the Great River from which they came, was like a mother to the Horse

People: strict, and fierce, but loving if you knew her ways and followed her rules. You could live well on the grasslands, as the Horse People had done for many generations; it was also easy to die there.

But "fun"?

Next morning, while the slaves were packing and loading the mules, she showed Phrygillus some of the plants and grasses that were growing near their encampment: the poisonous ones, the ones that the mules loved (and had already discovered), and the wholesome-tasting ones, that could be even eaten uncooked (in small amounts), including a long grass that was sweet to chew. Phrygillus, who liked all sweet things, was very impressed.

They reached the coastal road.

"Look, Mara, that's the ocean!" Aulus called out to her. Someone riding behind her sniggered.

She looked, and saw only a great river without a far bank. But the water was constantly moving, and surging onto the land, with a lot of splashing about, before rushing backwards. That night they stayed in a better inn than the ones Mara had experienced so far. While it was still light, Aulus took her and Phrygillus, and Gorth, on a walk to what he called the "beach" (Florianus came too, huffing and puffing to keep up with them).

The fishy-boy was scornful—he had seen all this before—but Mara and Phrygillus were delighted to walk at the water's edge and even take a few steps into the water. Gorth showed them how to skim flat stones to make them jump. He told them to be sure to be out of the water before the sun set, because when it was dark the water-devils and -witches would rise out of the depths looking for careless children to eat. If you still had a foot in the water…

Aulus said that he didn't believe him, and offered to test it himself by going into the water after sunset, but they couldn't wait so long, not if they wanted there to be any decent supper left for them back at the inn. The two boys were both worried about missing out on food.

Maybe Aulus wasn't a *complete* coward, Mara thought (or perhaps he's just silly). She wouldn't have risked it herself. After all, Gorth lived beside the ocean, so surely what he said about such matters could be trusted?

Gorth didn't come back after supper—he had heard that two of Necro's servants had stolen some food from the kitchen and he thought he could persuade them to share it—so she and Phrygillus had a bed to themselves. She cuddled him, and he told her his thoughts, as he usually did when Gorth wasn't there to listen and laugh at him ("What a baby!").

He didn't mind riding the mule. And from what he'd learned, he could ride a horse now! (Mara doubted it.) A horse like Demon! (No, she really couldn't imagine that happening.) And Florianus had been very kind to him, and had a wonderful new master for him.

Mara started—she had been half-asleep. What had the boy just said?

That Florianus was going to bring him to a new master, who was very rich and would pamper him and cuddle him a lot. Not like Aulus.

She shook him. Who was this man?

Mara was worried. She had sworn to protect little Phrygillus, and she believed that when they all returned from this journey the boy would find a home in the place called "the City", where Aulus lived with his uncle. Beltran had said that Aulus's uncle was an honorable man, who treated his slaves fairly. When she had confirmed that this was true, she could make her way back to her own people, knowing that Phrygillus was safe.

He would never be a warrior! The idea of taking him to her clan and raising him among the Horse People had been crazy.

She shook him again.

"Stop it! I don't know what his name is. He lives in Neopolis. Florianus is a friend of his. Now let me sleep!"

That reassured her a little. If this rich man was a friend of Florianus's, maybe he too would be intelligent and kind-hearted. And if Phrygillus found a new home in Neopolis, her road home to her own people might perhaps be shorter.

Of course, she didn't know where Neopolis was yet, or how far away it was. But she would find out—after all, it was where they were going.

She would get no further information out of Phrygillus that night. He was already snoring.

Next morning, they reached a fork in the road. If they turned left, after several days they would come to the fortress of Gladium, which she imagined would be just like Cascantum. Necro decided that they would go straight on: they would therefore have to cross the Great River on a boat, someone said.

They began to meet soldiers on the road. The Great River was the border between the Western Empire and the East, and there would be soldiers guarding the ferry. Mara knew what a ferry was. She had seen such boats crossing the River near Cascantum, when her father had taken her there when she was very young, but she hadn't been on one, because the Citizens had allowed them to bring their heavy wagon-load of horse-dung over the wooden bridge.

Nor had she been on a boat when her clan crossed the Great River. They had ridden north to a place where the wise women had said that they might ford the River for two whole moons without danger. The Citizens had watched them carefully, but there had been no violence.

She wasn't prepared for what they now saw.

Yes, the boats were much the same as she remembered them—small—but the Great River was enormously wide, and the waters looked bad-tempered and angry.

"How can we cross *that*," Philotas said (pointing to the River), "on *that* little thing?" (and he pointed at one of the boats).

Others shared his feeling. She looked around: only Gorth was happy about having to get on a boat. Even Aulus (who had been telling everyone how he was looking forward to the river crossing) seemed to have changed his mind. He asked the Senator whether they shouldn't go to Gladium after all, and cross by the bridge there?

Necro said "no".

Afterwards Florianus commented that, having made his decision, the Senator hadn't wanted to lose face by going back on it. Although she didn't like Necro, she understood that very well.

They would cross in small groups, and each group (except Necro's, of course) would have to include a couple of mules, so that they wouldn't lose all the mules if they put them in two boats, say, and those boats both sank.

"Good planning," Aulus said.

Philotas, who was the leading voice among those most frightened of the crossing, said, "And if a boat sinks with *people* in it? Do boats sink very often? Will the ferrymen jump in and rescue us?"

No, apparently none of the ferrymen could swim. They were too proud to learn. But not a single boat had sunk since the great storm two years ago, when ferrymen and passengers had drowned together.

"Well, that's good to know," said Philotas. "That makes me feel so much better!"

He was being ironical, wasn't he? Mara had become quite good at spotting irony.

Phrygillus piped up, "Will there be a storm today?", and everyone laughed, though Mara thought the laughter sounded nervous.

"I can swim," Gorth whispered to Mara. "I can swim like a fish. But I'm not going to rescue *you*."

"Shut up," Mara told him. "You smell like a fish too."

There were lots of ferry-boats, and plenty of ferrymen who were eager to earn money. Even so, it would take a long time to transport the whole group over to the other side, what with all the mules and the Senator's litter.

The ferrymen soon showed how experienced they were. Very sensibly, they told the servants to put those mules together who liked each other. The slaves reacted with outrage ("Do you think we spend the whole fucking day staring at fucking donkeys?"), talking to the ferrymen in a way they would never talk to their masters. Now Mara was able to make herself useful. Her second great moment had arrived!

Of course mules; just like horses, had their friends and their enemies—not only among the people, but among the other mules too—and she had had days of opportunity to watch them. Mules that got on with each other were put in pairs, lashed together loosely, and then secured with ropes to metal rings.

In each boat, one passenger was given the task of standing with the mules, talking to them and petting them. That would obviously be her job in one of the boats. She also suggested Beltran, and one of Necro's servants, both of whom she had observed riding comfortably and in good control of their mules; and, to his great delight, Florianus. She had watched him, and seen how, whatever he needed to do, he would approach the task carefully and thoughtfully. He might not be a natural or graceful rider, but he learnt quickly.

When the time came, she was taken aback by the way that the boat moved.

It had a small sail, and the ferrymen pulled lustily on long wooden oars. Since they saw Mara as the organizer of the party, they confided in her that it would be an easy crossing: the weather was good, and the flow of the water that had seemed so terrifying to them from the bank was actually very sluggish, because the Great River was so wide. The only problem would be the one that they always had, of having to tack against the current so that they ended up on the other side opposite to where they had started from, and not a great distance further downriver.

The movement was a new experience to her. The boat bucked slightly in the direction that it was traveling, but also tilted to the side and back again, as it was hit by successive waves of the swell of the water. It wasn't like riding a difficult horse; it was more like being on one of the cattle she had ridden as a small child, which had ambled along with a lazy churning motion.

Phrygillus didn't like it. He started wailing and groaning, his face turned gray (or was it green?), and then he sicked up his food onto the deck.

Mara laughed, although she wasn't feeling so good either. A few minutes later she did the same. She suddenly felt extremely queasy, her insides shuddered, and everything came up in an unstoppable, sick rush—though at least she managed to spew it over the side of the boat.

The ferrymen thought it was very funny.

"First time, eh?"

Mara's only comfort was that everyone else in the party (except

Gorth) would be suffering too. And, judging by the way that they looked when all the travelers had finally disembarked, she was probably right on that score. Philotas had been kicked by a mule, she was happy to hear, but otherwise no-one had come to serious harm.

They were now in the East! And they would be traveling onwards to strange and wonderful places. How dearly she would have liked to tell the members of her clan how far she had come—especially the young men, who doubted whether a girl was good for anything more than admiring young men and giving them sons.

Waiting for the delegation on the far river-bank were more ferrymen, and also some unfriendly-looking people who were certainly not warriors, though they were attended by spearmen.

"Officials!" said Florianus, and stepped forward to greet them.

Why him? Mara looked around for the Senator, but he wasn't there.

Someone whispered, "He's hiding in his litter. He's not feeling very well."

Good, she thought. Let him continue to feel not very well for a while, and stay in his litter.

Although she still knew very little about the ways of the Citizens, she was certain that this was not a party that had been sent to meet them. Indeed, no-one, it seemed, had been expecting them. These were just the normal officials who dealt with traders and everyday travelers, not with Imperial delegations.

They clearly weren't impressed by Florianus. Urgo, the Sueni with the big mustaches, wanted to address them, but Aulus was holding him back. He would only make it worse! Like it or not, the Senator would have to leave his litter and speak to them.

Before anything more could happen, the ferrymen shouted and pointed into the distance, where dust was rising. Horsemen! Had the clan sent warriors to rescue her? If they had, she would tell them not to hurt anyone, not even Gorth, but to throw Senator Necro's litter into the Great River, with him inside it.

The horsemen arrived with a flurry of cloaks and shaking of harness. They weren't warriors from her clan, but they were superb horsemen, and their mounts were magnificent animals, proud and black like the "demon". The horsemen's cloaks were likewise black, and so were the plumes that hung from their silvery helmets. Their leader, who wore golden medallions on his chest, looked down majestically at the officials, who shrank back in fear.

The officer spoke to them in a calm, measured voice. What tongue was he speaking in? Was this the famous Eto of the Easterners? It sounded smoother and more musical than the Citizen's Tongue. Mara wanted to learn it! She was sure that she could soon master it.

The officials trembled, and said nothing.

Then the officer turned to the party of arrivals from the West, and started to speak in their tongue, fluently, and with almost no accent. This was a man of true distinction, Mara thought, and not some clumsy Sueni cavalryman.

"Which of you is the Senator?"

A voice behind them called out "I am" and, swiveling round, they saw Necro staggering towards them, propped up on one side by Aulus. They made space to allow him through. He still looked ill.

"You are Senator Necro?"

With his pale, sweaty face and dribbling mouth, the Senator didn't look much like a great man.

"I am Senator Gaius Ambibulus Necro," he announced with an effort, "envoy of his Imperial Lord and Majesty Maximillus, First Citizen and Imperator in the West, to the court of his Imperial cousin and colleague Theodore, Imperator in the East—"

The officer's horse snorted and plunged its head forward, almost knocking the Senator down before its rider reined it in.

"Greetings, my Lord Necro, and may the Blessed Slave shed His gracious mercy on you! My master Lord Asper has sent me to welcome you and your friends and companions. Please excuse my apologies for the behavior of these yokels"—he indicated the officials, still cowering in front of the riders—"whose rudeness was caused by lack of wit, not by ill will."

Necro nodded in acknowledgement.

"I am grateful for your kind words of welcome."

"And now, my Lord, we must bring you to Maritima, and as quickly as possible. Because unless you have already done so in the last two days, you will want to send a fire-beacon message to the City. Or to General Ogilo, if you so prefer."

"To the City, of course. To the Imperial Guardian, Senator Naevius. But why should that be necessary, officer?"

The officer's horse snorted again, and some of the other horses whinnyed and shifted about uneasily. The riders were nervous, and their horses knew that!

"Because your delegation may now need new instructions."

"But Lord Naevius—"

"—is no longer the Imperial Guardian. Lord Naevius is dead."

www.ingramcontent.com/pod-product-compliance
Lightning Source LLC
Chambersburg PA
CBHW020753250626
47155CB00003B/1054